PUDD'NHEAD

AND

THOSE EXTRAORDINARY TWINS

MARK TWAIN was born Samuel Langhorne Clemens in 1835. When Sam was four, the family moved to Hannibal, Missouri, on the Mississippi river, where he spent an idyllic boyhood. His father died when he was twelve, and he was apprenticed to a printer, which began his career of reporting and writing entertaining, humorous sketches. But in 1857 he yielded to his boyhood ambition and trained with the great Horace Bixby as a river-boat pilot (from which experience he took the name Mark Twain). The Civil War, however, put an end to the river traffic – and an end to Twain's career as well. After a brief, hilarious war experience (chronicled in 'The History of a Campaign that Failed') he turned his hand to silver prospecting, went back to journalism, and finally published his first short story in 1865.

Mark Twain's career was a central, representative one in American letters, making the already established role of humorist into a central post of social observation. His worldwide reputation was based on a gift for mixing the boyish mischief and innocence of a naïve, vernacular vision with a dark, bitter view of man as hypocrite, victim and self-deceiver. His finest works are generally considered to be *The Adventures of Tom Sawyer* (1876); *Life on the Mississippi* (1883), not a novel but a superbly evocative memoir, a brilliant account of pilotage and a criticism of the South; *A Connecticut Yankee at King Arthur's Court* (1889); *The American Claimant* (1892); *Pudd'nhead Wilson* (1894); and his masterpiece, *The Adventures of Huckleberry Finn* (1885), one of the world's great books. Mark Twain died in 1910.

MALCOLM BRADBURY was a novelist, critic, television dramatist and Emeritus Professor of American Studies at the University of East Anglia. He was the author of seven novels, including *The History*

Man (1975), winner of the Royal Society of Literature Heinemann Prize, and *Rates of Exchange* (1983), which was short-listed for the Booker Prize. His other novels include *Doctor Criminale* (1992) and *To the Hermitage* (2000). He wrote short-fiction, satires and parodies. Among his many critical works are *The Modern British Novel* (Penguin, 1994; revised edition, 2000) and *Dangerous Pilgrimages: Trans-Atlantic Mythologies and the Novel* (Penguin, 1996). He also edited *The Penguin Book of Modern Short Stories* (Penguin, 1988), *Modernism* (with Professor James McFarlane; Penguin, 1991), and *The Atlas of Literature* (1997). For television he wrote two television novels about the European Community, *The Gravy Train* and *The Gravy Train Goes East*, and many episodes of *A Touch of Frost*, *Dalziel and Pascoe*, *Kavanagh Q.C.* and *Inspector Morse*. He also wrote the screenplays of Tom Sharpe's *Porterhouse Blue*, Kingsley Amis's *The Green Man*, and Stella Gibbons's *Cold Comfort Farm*, now a feature film. In 1991 he was awarded the CBE and was knighted for services to Literature in 1999.

Malcolm Bradbury died on 27 November 2000. Among the many tributes paid to him, the *Guardian* described him as 'one of the most prolific and influential novelists, critics and academics of his generation ... His death marks the close of half a century of academic and literary history, of which he was par excellence the chronicler'. David Lodge said of him in *The Times*: 'He was remarkable for the breadth of his writing. He was not only an important novelist, but a man of letters of a kind that is now rare. He covered the whole range of literary endeavour'.

RICHARD MAXWELL took a doctorate in English literature from the University of Chicago. The author of *The Mysteries of Paris and London* (1992), and editor of *The Victorian Illustrated Book* (2002), he has also written extensively on the historical novels of John Cowper Powys. He is now working on a study of historical fiction between the seventeenth century and the present. He teaches in the Comparative Literature and English departments at Yale University.

MARK TWAIN

Pudd'nhead Wilson

and

Those Extraordinary Twins

Edited with an Introduction and Notes by
MALCOLM BRADBURY

PENGUIN BOOKS

PENGUIN BOOKS

Published by the Penguin Group

Penguin Books Ltd, 80 Strand, London WC2R ORL, England
Penguin Group (USA) Inc., 375 Hudson Street, New York, New York 10014, USA
Penguin Books Australia Ltd, 250 Camberwell Road, Camberwell, Victoria 3124, Australia
Penguin Books Canada Ltd, 10 Alcorn Avenue, Toronto, Ontario, Canada M4V 3B2
Penguin Books India (P) Ltd, 11 Community Centre, Panchsheel Park, New Delhi – 110 017, India
Penguin Books (NZ) Ltd, Cnr Rosedale and Airborne Roads, Albany, Auckland, New Zealand
Penguin Books (South Africa) (Pty) Ltd, 24 Sturdee Avenue, Rosebank 2196, South Africa

Penguin Books Ltd, Registered Offices: 80 Strand, London WC2R ORL, England

www.penguin.com

First published 1894
Published in the Penguin English Library 1969
Reprinted in Penguin Classics 1986
Reprinted with a new Chronology and Further Reading 2004

047

Introduction and Notes copyright © Malcolm Bradbury, 1969
Chronology and Further Reading copyright © Richard Maxwell, 2004
All rights reserved

Set in Granjon Linotype
Printed in England by Clays Ltd, St Ives plc

www.greenpenguin.co.uk

Contents

INTRODUCTION

I

PUDD'NHEAD WILSON derives from Mark Twain's later, darker period, and is much the best work to come out of it. He wrote most of it in the unhappiest decade of his life, the 1890s, when he was in his late fifties, had suffered various financial collapses, and had withdrawn to Europe for seven years in an attempt to economize on his household expenses. Like all the most interesting of his works, it is a bad book with a good book inside it struggling to get out, and in the end remarkably managing to do so. It shows, as does all his later work, deep, dividing forces of moral strain, which express themselves alternatingly in the modes and moods of comedy and tragedy; and it is written with a complexity of tone which gives the book an air both of artistic confusion and incompleteness, and of profound moral depth. The result is in many ways ambiguity – but ambiguity that comes not only from identifiable weakness in the writing (themes not fully assimilated, stories not fully worked out, sudden veerings of tone) but also from the most exacting kind of literary control, from the exercise of an irony so persistent, sharp, and farsighted that it can scarcely leave its objects alone until every possible turn of the screw has been tried. Hence, not surprisingly, the novel has acquired an ambiguous reputation; critics have seemed bewildered both by its surface confusion and its singular force. It is in fact a most remarkable book, a 'problem comedy' (in almost the Shakespearean sense) of the greatest interest. It is also one of the best late-nineteenth-century American novels – a book about the tensions of the difficult decade of transformation in which it was written, the period of the collapse of the age which Twain himself named as the Gilded Age; a book, too, which leads us inescapably into many of the modernist ironies that have been so important for twentieth-century fiction. It is a little less than Twain's greatest novel, but perhaps his most interesting; it is certainly a novel one can't avoid if one wishes to understand Twain, or Twain's importance in the American tradition, or how that tradition confronted new possibilities as it moved into the present century.

For most general readers, and for many critics as well, Mark Twain is the author of one acknowledged masterpiece – *The Adventures of Huckleberry Finn*. It is this book that survived to secure his literary immortality after the enormous universal popularity that Twain enjoyed at a general and a critical level began to subside after his death. We would normally expect that a writer who had produced one masterpiece would show something of the same powers in his other works. In fact there is such a remarkable range of quality in Twain's writing – take, for instance, the qualitative difference between *Huckleberry Finn* and *Tom Sawyer* and then again between that and *Tom Sawyer, Detective* – that it is easy to suppose that Twain's success was almost a happy chance, the strength of this one novel deriving from its essential simplicity or from virtues beyond the author's conscious control. This is very much the sort of view of *Huckleberry Finn* that has prevailed among literary critics. Ever since Van Wyck Brooks's study of Twain, *The Ordeal of Mark Twain*, appeared in 1920, ten years after its subject's death, his assessment that Twain was in some way a disabled or incomplete writer has been general. And *Huckleberry Finn* is usually seen as the triumph over incompleteness, the one book where he overcame the burden of conventional and 'genteel' impulses that 'damaged' his other books. 'If the beauty and greatness of that book spring from the joyous freedom of the author,' said Brooks, 'is it

8

not because, in throwing off the bonds of the bourgeois society whose mould he had been obliged to take, he was reverting not only to a frame of mind he had essentially never outgrown, but to a native idiom as well?' Subsequent critics have gone even further in isolating this book from the others, tending to identify Twain's strength in it with an escape from the things that bound him, arguing that its vernacular language is the language of an unerring vision of truth, urging that its comic liberation from limited social and moral obsessions is a mythic articulation of that pleasure principle which lies at the root of humour. Even Henry Nash Smith, who has in many ways shown how self-conscious a writer Twain was, also makes *Huckleberry Finn* a special case – 'the nearest approach to the full embodiment of vernacular values in fiction' – and so the high point of Twain's art. The books that follow it, Smith says, are obsessed by the realization that the good life represented by Huck and Jim's ride on the raft was 'too special, too vulnerable' and hence turn to treating social experience as a tragic burden – as a result of which the purity of 'vernacular affirmation' is lost. The trouble with such views is that they tend to inhibit appreciation of Twain's other remarkable talents – talents deeply evident in *Pudd'nhead Wilson*.

Pudd'nhead Wilson clearly takes us into a very different kind of imaginative and artistic experience from that of *Huckleberry Finn*. But seen in its own terms it is a very remarkable novel indeed, and a genuine extension of Twain's comic vision into fascinating new possibilities. In setting, time and cultural atmosphere the book bears certain surface resemblances to *Huckleberry Finn*, but no reader moving from the one to the other can miss the striking differences in tone and flavour; clearly it comes from a different spirit in Twain and has a very different development. The earlier book has about it a joyous and idyllic air; it is a

boy's book which extended itself into being a national piece
of folklore and mythology, and we read it easily – with
engaged sympathies, and a kind of enjoyment that comes
from the application of an humane comedy to a situation
that, while morally complex, never ceases to be genially so.
It is a novel of radical ironies, of course; it touches upon the
confusions of man's moral sense as a force in civilization
and substitutes for them a kind of comic resignation to impulse, an abdication of conscience to pleasure, which is outside civilization. *Pudd'nhead Wilson* does, certainly, have
its lyrical elements and its comic euphoria; but it is expressed much more complicatedly, with greater moral dis-
turbance. It is the work of a writer imaginatively very much
further away from his material and its origins in his own
boyhood, separated from his nostalgia, and reaching at far
greater distance for his materials (the book was mostly written in Italy), and it is told by a detached narrator at a clear
historical distance. And finally this distance is realized in the
literary instrument of irony, with ironies that are much more
deeply rooted and more pervasive than anything in *Huckleberry Finn*. Indeed irony dominates *Pudd'nhead Wilson* as
it dominates few other novels; perhaps Conrad's *The Secret
Agent* and Henry James's *Washington Square* are the only
obvious comparisons. It dominates both the working out
of the action, and the tone in which it is presented; and
it creates a singular and somewhat difficult mood, an
extreme reversal of, rather than a counterpart to, *Huckleberry Finn*.

In this respect, *Pudd'nhead Wilson* involves a more
sophisticated collision between those essential materials of
'boy life out on the Mississippi', with which Twain was so
deeply involved, and the imaginative and intellectual pres-
sures of the age in which the book was written – the American 1890s, an era of moral and social turbulence when, in

many ways, American literature was itself being remade. It appeared in 1894, only ten years after the publication of *Huckleberry Finn*, but in that time Twain had changed both in his attitudes toward the material he returned to so often – the Mississippi valley world of his childhood – and in his basic views of man and society. We normally regard Twain not only as an American novelist, but as a regional novelist, the speaking voice of a particular part of American geography and culture – his region being of course the Mississippi Valley area in that hinterland where southern and northern, eastern and western, cultures meet; and his culture being that world as it was fifty years before he wrote about it, in the period when the Mississippi was the central artery of America and the main crossing-point en route for the west. But Twain was also deeply formed by another world, the world of eastern America in the Gilded Age in which he became a writer, a world divided from his other by geography, time and a crucial historical event: the Civil War. Twain's essential intellectual and artistic experience comes from the latter world, a world of national expansion, capitalism, and technical change. Twain was himself a literary capitalist, exploiting the taste of the age, entering on publishing venture, developing even the associated technology – in particular the famous (and for Twain disastrous) Paige typesetting machine. He was part of the literary and intellectual culture of this world; as much made by Hartford, Conn., where he lived much of his literary life, as Hannibal, Mo., where he spent his boyhood from the age of four. He both espoused and distrusted the age, and like many of his contemporaries he came to see it from the standpoint of a pessimistic determinism. But it was out of all this experience that he came to perceive the significance of his Mississippi River material. By the time he became a professional writer, it was material belonging irretrievably to the past; the area's values and economy had been transformed by the Civil War and those rapid technological advances of post-Bellum America in which Twain himself had readily participated. Though it was for him God-given material – simply to treat it evoked a deep nostalgia for a 'half-forgotten Paradise' – he saw the dangers of committing himself too deeply to it, the dangers of, as he said in a letter, 'mental and moral masturbation'. His attitude toward it was typically a distanced one. *Huckleberry Finn* is hardly a nostalgic reaction of his boyhood home. The civilization of St Petersburg is what Huck has to escape, and throughout the book, on the river-journey, Twain touches on the changing and technological aspects of the river; the river world is, as one critic has observed, 'violent, populous and mechanized'. And already the sense of the deterministic and hence selfish base of morality, which obsessed Twain ever since he read and reacted against Lecky's *History of European Morals from Augustus to Charlemagne* (1869) in 1874, is clearly present. But *Huckleberry Finn* does, to a point, associate the river with freedom, from civilization, from conscience, while *Pudd'nhead Wilson* associates it with its opposite, slavery – slavery not just to white masters but to personality, environment, genetic inheritance: slavery for all men. The town of the novel is now not St Petersburg but Dawson's Landing, 'half a day's journey, per steamboat, below St Louis' – *below* now, instead of above, and hence deeper into the South, for it is of utter importance that 'Dawson's Landing was a slaveholding town'. All the critics who have written on the book seem to have overlooked the change of geographical location – though Leslie Fiedler points out that St Petersburg is in spirit a western town, leading to the frontier and 'freedom'; while Dawson's Landing is a southern town, leading 'down river' and into slavery. Imaginatively it is of course true that Twain identifies Dawson's

Landing with Hannibal, higher up the river. But the shift indicates a crucial feature of the whole book – it is the work of a writer concerned with a different kind of recreation, imagining his material in a new way. The distance is implicit in *Huckleberry Finn*, but here Twain finds a new tone and language for dealing with it.

By virtue of this, *Pudd'nhead Wilson* is a more sophisticated novel than most of his others, marked by qualities deriving as much from the movements of late-nineteenth-century American thought as from regional sources. Very much a novel of the 1890s, it contains some of the period's dominant themes, as we find them in writers of Populist slant not only in America – Stephen Crane, Hamlin Garland, Theodore Dreiser – but in England too – Thomas Hardy, Samuel Butler, Bernard Shaw. There is the sense of moral despair created by the emergence of environmentalist and determinist views of man and society; the simultaneous fascination with new forms of scientism, new views of heredity and environment, and new species of technology, that had emerged with these; and the sense of social division, of the gap between genteel values and the brute and urgent forces that demand new accounting. Twain's later pessimism is often attributed to personal causes – a succession of financial collapses associated with the failure of his publishing company and the Paige machine was coupled with family misfortune – but the pessimism is neither new in his work (he had been touching on it for at least twenty years) nor novel in his age. It was therefore very much part of his intellectual development – indeed of his development toward *being* an intellectual. Though never quite that (he remains in a sense a philosophic autodidact) he did feel a growing pressure away from lyric comedy toward a greater satirical or ironic acerbity that reaches its culmination in the unrestrained pessimism of *The Mysterious Stranger*. He did not cease to be a comic writer; in fact *Pudd'nhead Wilson* is among the most remarkable comic novels we have, bringing into the genre new intimations and a tonal range certainly rare in his work. It is very much a socio-moral comedy, a novel about the implications of man's existence as a social animal, and its theme – the ironic treatment of the fate of man confronted with an unaccommodating universe – links it markedly with the vein of speculative pessimistic comedy that comes to us from Melville through into much modern comic fiction. What makes it so ambiguous, so 'problematic', is Twain's remote and detached view of the moral life. It differs from more familiar versions of this form because of its apparent lack of moral clarity; the moral enforcement of the story yields to fascination with the ambiguity of the moral life. Twain was remarkably of his age in feeling that the Moral Sense is not an absolute power but a social acquisition, and as such as vulnerable to change as any other acquisition. He was to say, in a famous late letter: 'We have no *real* morals, but only artificial ones, morals created and preserved by the forced suppression of natural and healthy instincts.' We can read this as a claim on behalf of an instinctive and self-taught morality, but Twain meant, surely, something more depressing – he meant that there was no absolute morality we could espouse, that man was as much the victim of his moral instincts as of any other instinct. And when, as he does in these late novels, he takes society as his subject-matter – society as a social organization, an economy, a body of customs, institutions and classes – he conveys this social density with a curious moral remoteness which makes him seem a different writer. It is this that creates the problematic world of *Pudd'nhead Wilson*, and the singular note of its comedy. The important point is that the book deserves serious attention in these terms, more attention than, often, is suggested by those critics who deplore Twain's loss of lyricism and vernacular insight. There are, indeed, good and positive grounds for Leslie Fiedler's high claim for *Pudd'n-head Wilson*, which is, he says, 'morally ... one of the most honest books in our literature, superior in this one respect to *Huckleberry Finn*'.

2

The novel we now have as *Pudd'nhead Wilson* is a synthesis from several ideas and themes which had obsessed Twain for the larger part of his writing life. What they have in common – and hence, presumably, what brought them to-gether in Twain's mind – is that they are in different ways about moral division, moral schizophrenia, the confusion of moral identity. We have a remarkably clear knowledge of what went into the story, because Twain left an account of it (it occurs in the story 'Those Extraordinary Twins' – re-printed in this volume – which consists largely of material excised from *Pudd'nhead Wilson*) which has been effectively supplemented by scholars. One of these themes Twain had been working on as early as 1896, the year before he married; in a magazine sketch called 'Personal Habits of the Siamese Twins' he undertook a comic commentary on the famous Siamese pair Chang and Eng, who had come out of retire-ment and were exhibiting again. The basis of Twain's comedy was the coexistence of two morally different persons in a shared body; and Twain clearly exploits the situation with a strong sense of his own divided nature, his own inter-nalized Civil War, split between gentility and 'gay immor-ality', between the technological American north and the agrarian American south. The twins had been slave-owners and were known to quarrel violently. Twain has the twins fight on opposite sides in the Civil War (they capture each other, then are exchanged for each other) and quarrel over moral matters (Chang is for temperance; Eng drinks). The comedy culminates in a scene where one is fed with hot water and sugar, the other on whiskey, and both get drunk 'and on hot whiskey punches'. In early 1892, Twain came back to this idea as the basis for a story – the story to which he refers in the opening pages of 'Those Extraordinary Twins', where he talks about the chaotic origins of *Pudd'nhead Wilson*:·

Originally the story was called 'Those Extraordinary Twins'. I meant to make it very short. I had seen a picture of a youthful Italian 'freak' – or 'freaks' – which was – or which were – on exhibition in our cities – a combination consisting of two heads and four arms joined to a single body and a single pair of legs – and I thought I would write an extravagantly fantastic little story with this freak of nature for hero – or heroes – a silly young miss for heroine, and two old ladies and two boys for the minor parts.

This freak (or freaks) obviously interested Twain as material that could be exploited for its *grotesquerie*, in a Dickensian vein, and for the comedy of identity. By making the pair into two different characters and temperaments who have separate heads and arms but have alternate possession by the week of the rest of the anatomy, Twain saw all sorts of possible jokes, and moral ironies, in the situation. One could be a tippler and the other a teetotaller; one could read moral works (*The Whole Duty of Man*) while the other reads libertarian ones (*The Age of Reason*); one could be Democrat and the other a Whig. Twain immersed himself in a plot which exploited most of the available comedy, and we have it now in the form of 'Those Extraordinary Twins'. One of the basic ideas in the book was to be a farcical court-room scene in which the enterprise of a clever lawyer makes it impossible for the court to attribute blame to one or the other; the brilliant sophist was Pudd'nhead Wilson, and this was quite clearly his original function in Twain's mind. It is Pudd'nhead's comic view of identity — already present in the scene at the beginning of the novel when he wants half the dog — that represents Twain's main obsession with the story. In the version we have he follows it up through a duel (hence the need to establish a chivalric code) and a political campaign. And when finally Luigi is elected to the board of aldermen, which is tied, and can't take his seat because Angelo must come too, local government ceases and summary justice is necessary: 'So they hanged Luigi. And so ends the history of "Those Extraordinary Twins".'

The other main idea that became linked with this in Twain's earliest notes for the story was of rather a different kind, though it was also on dualism and a confusion of identity. It was a story about two babies exchanged in the cradle, one a slave and one free. Originally Twain's idea was that the one born a slave — the one who prefigures Tom Driscoll in *Pudd'nhead Wilson* — was to grow up and revenge himself by parricide on the white man who had fathered him. But the story developed not as a tale of revenge but as another tale of dichotomy — that in Tom himself, who passes for white and must, when he discovers the truth about himself, lead a dual existence. And once again an extra character is implied — the ironic, commenting stranger who can unravel the plot. This is the figure of the technical redeemer, the man who comes in from outside with new, advanced knowledge that transforms a socially and morally static society. Twain had already used a version of this figure in *Connecticut Yankee in King Arthur's Court* in the person of Hank Morgan, the Hartford Machine Shop superintendent who is transported back to the feudal world of the sixth century. To begin with, Pudd'nhead was presumably intended to represent little more than a certain kind of cracker-barrel philosopher whose wit exposed the paradox of Siamese twinship. But his role in the novel undoubtedly expanded after Sir Francis Galton's *Finger Prints* appeared in 1892 and gave Twain reason for making much more of Wilson and the whole story of Tom Driscoll. In a letter of 1894 Twain makes it clear that 'I have never thought of Pudd'nhead as a *character*, but only as a piece of machinery – a button or a crank or a lever, with a useful function to perform in a machine, but with no dignity above that.' On the other hand, he did emphasize in a letter to his agent Redpath another important point: '... the finger-prints in this one is virgin ground – absolutely *fresh*, and mighty curious and interesting to anybody.' So while it would be a mistaken emphasis to regard Twain's main fable in the book as being about the intellectual seeking social recognition (which is what some critics have done), Pudd'n-head is important to Twain both as an ironic aphorist who can act, within the story, as a substitute for Twain himself (so his aphorisms at the heads of the chapters are largely drawn from Twain's own notebooks), and a comic blunderer with detective powers of analysis and a strain of scientism. Pudd'nhead's success is itself half-ironic; on the other hand, he alone can provide the means by which objective, factual truth can be established in this world of duplicity and dis-guise. And he provides, therefore, the third comic idea in the developing novel.

Clearly both of these stories were capable of very varied treatments, and it is fascinating to see how, out of the vari-ables, Twain made his way to the version we have. It would seem that he conceived the Tom Driscoll tale originally as subsidiary to the one about the twins:

... the tale kept spreading along, and spreading along, and other people got to intruding themselves and taking up more and more room with their talk and their affairs. Among them came a stranger named Pudd'nhead Wilson, and a woman named Roxana; and presently the doings of these two pushed up into prominence a young fellow named Tom Driscoll, whose proper place was away in the obscure background. Before the book was half finished these three were taking things almost entirely into their own hands and working the whole tale as a private venture of their own – a tale which they had nothing at all to do with, by rights.

Twain whimsically describes how he followed the consequences of these developments. The tale 'changed itself from a farce to a tragedy while I was going along with it,' he said, and so 'I pulled one of the stories out by the roots, and left the other one – a kind of literary Caesarean operation.' But by now the 'mother-story' was the Tom-Roxana one; Twain 'pulled out the farce and left the tragedy. This left the original team in, but only as mere names, not as characters.' One way round his problems now seemed to be to eliminate some of the original cast farcically, by drowning them; but 'they were not even worth drowning; so I removed that detail. Also I took those twins apart and made two separate men of them. They had no occasion to have foreign names now, but it was too much trouble to remove them all through, so I left them christened as they were and made no explanation.

Twain is whimsically frank – though by no means necessarily truthful – about his odd method of composition : 'The reader already knew how the expert works; he knows now how the other kind do it.' Certainly in some ways the results are strange. For instance, two separate items emerged from this process of writing – *Pudd'nhead Wilson*, and 'Those Extraordinary Twins'. Moreover, many of the elements in the finished novel are brought in according to disparate necessities (for instance, the chivalric code, so much emphasized in *Pudd'nhead Wilson*, seems first to have got there to enable the Siamese twins to have their comic duel, while the courtroom scenes were initially intended to provide sophistical comedy for Pudd'nhead). But out of all this Twain did produce something very remarkable. What so clearly marks the finished version is the kind of comic control that Twain decided at some point to exercise; he began to work his myth or myths ironically, and with a remarkable range of tones – so that it is quite in keeping for him to speak of the generic character of the book as both farce and tragedy. This indeed suggests the book's singular quality : the complex tone of the writing, which mixes comic exuberance and extravagance with a deep, detached irony and a capacity for real moral seriousness. It is this treatment, as it fills out through the details of the book, taking shape in its relationships and its images, which enters into material that clearly originates as simple farce – like the Rum Party meeting, where Tom is passed through the crowd after being kicked off the stage, an event really designed to serve the plot of 'Those Extraordinary Twins' – and ties it into a fuller intention. Because of this, the book achieves a grotesqueness, a strangeness of tone and vision, which reminds us of Dickens or even modern comic surrealism. And, as often with Dickens, it manages to pull materials unpromisingly conceived and often roughly executed into a vivid, surreal relationship.

Both the two basic plots that Twain drew upon derive from the stock of traditional literary comedy, and in many respects reach right back into the Greek 'new' comedy of Menander. The old prince and pauper story about two infants, one of high and one of low birth, who are exchanged in the cradle, is a staple of the European comic tradition. The comedy derives from the confusion caused to a stable, hierarchical social system by the change of roles and the consequent imposture, whether known or unknown to the two children *as* imposture. The comic restitution is to end the period of misrule with a restoration of rightful rank to the children. The second basic theme is that of twins who have exchanged identities or are confused with one another; again the opportunities for imposture are taken and each is usually held responsible for the other's actions. This time the theme produces moral rather than social confusion, though again the comic resolution is that of the recognition of rightful identity and the restitution of order. In both stories there are involved paradoxes about identities – personal, moral and social. So Dromio cries in Shakespeare's *Comedy of Errors*: 'Am I Dromio? Am I your man? Am I myself?'; the identity of those involved in the imposture is in question. Moral principles, the relationship of deeds to doers, are thrown into doubt. And so too does the very concept of social organization become confused, the concept of class a moral difficulty – as it does in *Tom Jones* or with Harriet Smith in *Emma*. In addition to such general confusions, the action commonly involves a scoundrel imposter who takes advantage of the situation until he is detached and dismissed – this is Tom Driscoll – and, to counter-balance him, a wisely ducal figure who is concerned with restoring moral or social order – this is, in his final guise, Pudd'nhead Wilson himself. As Twain acknowledges in his story, these fables are essentially European; what is so striking is that Twain reworks them radically to form them as American myths. For instance, he exploits to enormous extent the radical and complete distinction that exists in making the line between his exchanged children the line not between classes but races, and between freedom and slavery; and he exploits its obverse, the absence of personal identity that can exist amid the confusions of American social order, where a man can be made or unmade, as Pudd'nhead is, by a single phrase. Through his work runs, in fact, a deep sense that in

America imposture *is* identity; that values are not beliefs but the product of occasions; and that social identity is virtually an arbitrary matter, depending not on character nor on appearance but on the chance definition of one's nature or colour. Twain's prevailing obsessions in his story with doubleness, duplicity, dressing up, all play on these ambiguities of identity, to the point of suggesting the moral unreality of the individual and the essential strangeness of society. He creates a paradox of a world in which no one can be sure, literally or figuratively, of his own whiteness or blackness, though totally different lives are laid down for those who are socially recognized to be one or the other. So at the end of the novel there is no moral order to restore, simply a group of facts to be established by rational means at a legalistic level; the end of the novel brings good fortune to no one except to Pudd'nhead Wilson, the technological redeemer by whom order in a minimal sense *can* be restored.

It is in these shadings, and what Twain makes of them, that the accent of tragedy comes into the book. When Twain speaks of the book as a 'tragedy' (he titled the first American edition *The Tragedy of Pudd'nhead Wilson*, though Pudd'nhead is the one person for whom the action clearly *isn't* a tragedy) he surely meant to suggest that the story was treated not as a farce but with an inexorable sense of misfortune. It is, in effect, a novel without a hero, an action with an ironically lowering outcome, and in this sense about a world which cannot really be redeemed. Twain's treatment is, in fact, best described as tragi-comic. He chooses to start the novel with its basic determining event – the exchange of the babies in their cradles – and to regard it as the source of all the consequent action. It could have been presented as a happening prior to the main action, or as a mystery to be revealed at the end by Pudd'nhead, but Twain in fact represents it in close detail. In so doing, he humanizes and dramatizes Roxana's emotions at this time, describing her unhappiness, which takes her nearly to suicide, and her self-justification ('T'ain't no sin – *white* folks has done it! ... *Dey's* done it – yes, en dey was de biggest quality in de whole bilin', too – kings!') in such a way as to create a kind of comic exoneration for her. This has the effect of making the main action of the story not the mystery itself, but the question of how truth might be established and restitution made; the imbroglios it will produce in a society which does not know what has happened; and, most significantly, the kind of evolution that can come from this transformation of identity, in this sort of society. Twain could have developed the story from either or both of his exchanged children – the story of the 'Negro' boy who finds out that he is white, or of the 'white' boy who finds he is really Negro. By choosing entirely to emphasize the latter, Twain necessarily chooses a 'tragic' theme, since it involves an almost inevitable final decline from fortune to misfortune, freedom to servitude, rather than the upward movement that might have come from the reverse plot. He tells the story, that is, from the point of view of the one person who, once he knows the truth, must be its victim. It is necessarily a plot about *dis*possession, a fact that Twain emphasizes the more by having Tom find out about his up till then unconscious imposture quite near the beginning of the story, and well before the society does. What is more, Twain chooses not to humanize the person to whom these events happen; Tom is 'a bad baby, from the beginning of his usurpation', and he retains a 'native viciousness'. But Tom's tragedy does not in fact lie in his crimes, which finally go unpunished, but in his race. It is true that we are not humanly disturbed by the action which turns Tom into a victim, since it has a moral logic deriving from his misdeeds, but the important thing is that Twain explores not specific moral detail but the general sources of the irony. 'To all intents and purposes Roxy was as white as anybody, but the one sixteenth of her which was black outvoted the other fifteen parts and made her a negro. She was a slave, and saleable as such. Her child was thirty-one parts white, and he, too, was a slave, and by a fiction of law and custom a negro.' This fiction of law and custom, which decrees radically different destinies for the two children, makes for the significance of the imposture – and the radical difference of fortune that comes to a man when it is discovered. It is out of the paradox of the two environments available for the same man that Twain builds his story.

It is not, then, in the conventional sense a moral story. If a moral novelist is one who explores the significance of single actions, then Twain is not a moral novelist. On such matters he is typically ambiguous; his comedy and the rapid movement of the plot is often an escape from precisely that kind of moral exactness (as in the scene where he forebears from blaming Roxy, made bland by comedy; or the scene where Tom wrongs Roxy by selling her down the river, made less than morally significant by a quick return to the plotting). There is no detailed righting of wrongs, nor even the detailed scrutiny of them. It is significant that Tom is never exposed to others by his own unpleasantness and by the general moral conduct of his life; he is not even suspected of the murder until, by blaming others, he forces the discovery on himself. He is the obvious suspect, in moral terms, who is never suspected because the moral rigour of the book (and the moral concern of the inhabitants of Dawson's Landing) never works with the details of conduct. Morality in this world rather comes to seem, like colour itself, a fiction of law and custom. Twain deals instead in the larger ironies, and works with an action that makes broad restitutions and punishments of an inexorable kind. When

Tom is sold down the river at the end, what happens to him is what probably would have happened even if he had not committed the murder; he is simply socially awarded his right identity, irrespective of the moral implications. To a large extent, Negro slave life, being a social fiction, is exempted from conventional moral judgement, because the punishment is prior to the crime. And in a general sense this is true of the entire world of the novel: in its world, the one virtue is not honesty but honour, just as the one moral instrument is not truth but legal proof. So the final 'putting right' solves nothing morally; it gives each of the twins an unplumbed 'curious fate' into which the telling cannot reach. Leslie Fiedler makes the point that the book avoids the fake 'happy ending' of *Huckleberry Finn* and enforces the logic of its premises; F. R. Leavis stresses likewise that it confronts the worst in human nature with due astringency but without animus. This is true; but the poetic justice that is awarded is virtually independent of the characters. It is the working out of the logic of an ironical universe, and not for any single person in the novel a revelation, an insight, a process of self-discovery. The ending restores the situation violated by Roxy at the beginning without in any way changing the world; it is a comedy which abounds in problems and yet in a sense solves none of them. What it does instead is to leave them ironically exposed. It is this that makes Leslie Fiedler describe the book as an *anti*-detective story – it has a plot that turns on detection, but the denouement of the mystery leaves us not with the usual sense of communal innocence, but rather with a feeling of universal exposure. What we are exposed *to* is an experience of the world in which the fatalities of life totally overshadow our character and our claims to personal identity, moral independence, and social meaning. For beyond such 'freedoms' are the *facts* from which the basic truths about ourselves are derived – the facts of our genetic signature, our subjection to environment, our exposure to what Thomas Hardy called 'life's little ironies', which compound all misfortunes to the point of leaving us in misery.

The plot of *Pudd'nhead Wilson* is a plot founded on this inexorable life in events, rather than on what is more normal in fiction: a plot of social or psychological choices and changes. We would usually associate such a sense of fatality in a writer with the tragic emotion; yet Twain creates a very different tone – a tone of irony which is, in the last analysis, comic. And the comedy comes from a final turn of the screw; if men were only the victim of events in this world, we would sympathize with them, but we are invited to *judge* them too. Tom is not just a victim, wronged by society and fate; he is 'degenerate' as well. Twain's vision is not therefore *utterly* deterministic; and it is out of this fact that the novel's complexity and ambiguity derive. One striking feature of the book is, I have said, that it has no hero – a hero who might serve as the centre of its values, or else as the sympathetic victim of its events. Twain rather lets the action speak for itself – which means that he must speak for it. We must take our sense of its significance entirely from his way of controlling events; and yet in this, too, he is somewhat protean, evasive, oblique. We have difficulty in making, out of his curious tonal variations, his rapid changes of pace, his movements between involvement and detachment, his shifts from comic euphoria to ironic enforcement of the plot, a coherent pattern: a vision. In many respects, clearly, this shifting and comic tone helps Twain avoid levels of explanation that we would find most useful. It enables him to escape us. For instance, Tom's motivation toward stealing and murder are never given us in significant substance; these things are just events. And the level of imposture at which he performs them, in disguise as a girl and an old woman, takes the edge off the reality of these actions; they are almost burlesque performances. Twain constantly strains at the probabilities he has created, the rules of narration he has laid down, to develop his plot. Yet the elliptical quality of the telling does have the effect of making the ironies much more final. When Roxy reveals the facts of his true ancestry to Tom, Twain carefully analyses Tom's response – there is a 'gigantic irruption' which changes his 'moral landscape'. But Twain cannot afford to have us too long concerned with him at that inward level; so Tom gradually drops back 'into his old frivolous and easy-going ways'. Twain must protect his right to distance and irony. And he does this by self-evidently neglecting an artistic opportunity; the imbroglios must develop, the farces of human behaviour continue to operate, the characters must keep coming back for more.

Critics have often tried to provide *Pudd'nhead Wilson* with a simpler plot than it has, or else have accused Twain of evading the significance of his 'slavery' theme. The very variety of their interpretations suggests the ambiguous quality of the book. It has been read, for instance, as a novel which explores the complexities of human nature and civilization in a lively, admirable community in such a way as to create a mature sense of honour, value and human majesty (F. R. Leavis); and as a novel which ironically exposes the dark moral flaw in the same community, by creating in Tom a 'secret agent who carries back across the colour line the repressed guilt that has gathered at the heart of slavery' (James M. Cox). It has been described as a book which shows a world of corrupted identity and common guilt, in which only the honest stranger, Pudd'nhead, can emerge as a true leader (Robert Regan); and as a novel that reveals, behind Pudd'nhead's apparent success, his darker, aphoristic, unpublic knowledge that men are universally slaves

INTRODUCTION

(Leslie Fiedler). These marked differences in interpretative emphasis reveal, above all, the shifting and elusive nature of Twain's presentation. Twain deals with all these matters, but not as final themes; he raises them as possibilities, only to let them go, to subject them to new turns of burlesque and irony. He creates the most significant ideas that belong to his subject, but he does not finally make them his only theme. He touches, for instance, on the proposition that Tom is the revenger; Roxy in one part of her mind sees that as his significance (he is her 'nigger son, lording it among the whites and securely avenging their crimes against her race') but she also sees its opposite ('You has disgraced yo' birth. What would yo' pa think o' you? It's enough to make him turn in his grave'). Twain manages persistently to go beyond all such meanings, and in doing so creates an ultimate mood in ironic comedy – a mood of sublime and final unconcern.

3

To come to an accurate account of the novel, we have to see exactly the way in which Mark Twain presents the book. His method is to create for us, in detail and with some affection, a particular social and moral world that belongs to a given place at a given time; to develop an action that logically comes out of it; and to present it through an independent narration which allows him the extremest freedom to exploit the material exactly as he chooses. The place is Dawson's Landing, Missouri, the time the twenty-three years between 1830 and 1853. The action begins when two babies, one white, one Negro, are exchanged in their cradles, and a cranky newcomer comes to the town; and it covers the period it takes for the children, having completely assimilated their new identities, to be ironically restored to their

former social places, and for the newcomer to win accept-
ance by discovering that he had the answer to this mystery
in his hands all the time. But the development of both
stories comes over a few months in the summer of 1853,
when three things happen to complicate them, bring chaos
to the community, and speed them toward their inevitable
end. Tom Driscoll, the Negro child who has 'passed' as
white, is now grown up and badly in debt, so he begins to
steal; he discovers the terrible secret of his real parentage,
and the way it threatens his entire social existence; and the
two European twins, 'marvellous musical prodigies', come
to the town and bring out its respect for courtliness, grace,
and honour, for all of which Tom has a secret contempt. A
public battle for social survival therefore develops in front
of the entire town. Tom, hostile to the twins, publicly insults them, and is publicly kicked by Luigi. Seeking
revenge, Tom publicly violates the town's code of honour,
but manages to reverse the roles, suggesting that it is the
twins who are dishonourable. Tom's dishonour and his
concealments come to a head when he murders his step-
father, also the town's leading citizen, for money. He
attributes the murder to the twins; but is finally defeated
publicly by Pudd'nhead, who identifies Tom through his
finger-printing as both a murderer and a Negro slave. The
town passes final judgement by accepting Wilson and
selling Tom down the river into the severest form of
slavery.

Throughout this action Dawson's Landing serves as the
public forum and the main source of judgement and arbitra-
tion, while at the same time it creates the situation in which
Tom's subversion arises. Twain therefore must provide a
dense recreation of the life of the place. He starts his story
by describing it vividly to us, stressing its contentment,
peace, and settled traditionalism, and showing the general

basis of its social order and its assumptions. A town with its own parochial vanities, it has a sense of connexion with the world outside and beyond. It fronts onto the Mississippi River – along which ply the transient steamboats bringing 'every imaginable comfort or necessity which the Mississippi communities could want' – and is therefore not a closed community. It links with the east, where Tom goes to college; with the north, where he goes to gamble; with, above all, the south, where he is at last sold into slavery. A well-endowed community, slowly growing, it has a fair sense of elegance and cultivation, and its own, final, standards of society and conduct, for it accepts and rejects what it chooses. Its capacities range from duels of honour to lynch-law. It is a town with two different views of man; there are free men, who are expected to behave with honour, to be 'fine', 'majestic' and 'noble', and there are slaves, who are chattels and property and are expected to behave with subservience and humility.

Carefully and fully, Twain gives us the social meaning of this community, in all its ties of family and kinship, its social groupings, its cohesiveness. There are three main classes, and Twain makes it clear that there is not in the normal sense any social tension between them. At the top there are the leading citizens, 'respected, esteemed, and beloved', most of them either lawyers or speculators in landed estate. Wealthy and feudal in style, they are devoted to the traditional values of gentlemanliness and honour which they have brought with them from their origins among the Virginian 'aristocracy'. Then there are the general populace, a crowd rather than a class, the main public forum. 'Villagers', 'simple folk', they nonetheless share much the same values and enforce the same code. Though tolerant and honest, they are unsophisticated, changeable, and gullible. The main religion is Presbyterian, though other denominations are represented; their political principles are democratic and legalistic (Pudd'nhead finally becomes Democrat mayor); they are politically 'free' and proud of their freedom. The third group is the slaves. 'Dawson's Landing was a slaveholding town,' Twain tells us, simply at first to explain its economics – behind it is its supporting hinterland, 'a rich and slave-worked grain and pork country back of it.' Slavery in Dawson's Landing is friendly and familial, but it is nonetheless an absolute distinction. A slave can be freed, as Roxy is, but the unfreed slave is a chattel and saleable as such. Twain attends carefully to the slaves' customs and manners. They are Methodist, largely, and mildly immoral. They had 'an unfair show in the battle of life, and they held it no sin to take military advantage of the enemy – in a small way; in a small way, but not in a large one.' But they too largely accept the dominant code; particularly Roxy, who has her own strong family feeling and emphasizes her descent from the 'Smith Pocahontases'.

The limits of the town define the main limits of the novel's action (even though Tom goes to St Louis for 'more freedom, in some particulars, than he could have at home', and Roxy finds noble employment on the river-boats). The essential world beyond is the darker slaveholding regime to the south, which exerts a moral sanction on the slaves and suggests a world beyond honour. But the town itself provides the primary norms of the novel; even the three important figures in the action who come from outside it – Pudd'nhead and the twins – adjust to its standards, however much they also expose its provinciality. Though they have seen thousands of such places, the twins settle and take out town citizenship; Pudd'nhead, though elected a fool, remains, accepts the code and castigates Tom in its terms ('You degenerate remnant of an honourable line! I'm thoroughly ashamed of you, Tom!'). The town's social organization thus provides the world of values and morals within which the characters live, with the exception of Tom Driscoll, the one real stranger. And of all its values honour stands supreme – honour with its implication of traditional rank and ancestry, its implication of permanent identity, and its confident suggestion of the potential nobility of man. It is represented above all in the F.F.V.s, the descendents of the First Families of Virginia, the Driscolls and the Howards:

The F.F.V. was born a gentleman; his highest duty in life was to watch over that great inheritance and keep it unsmirched. He must keep his honour spotless. ... These laws required certain things of him which his religion might forbid: then his religion must yield – the laws could not be relaxed to accommodate religions or anything else. Honour stood first; and the laws defined what it was and wherein it differed in certain details from honour as defined by church creeds and by the social laws and customs of some of the minor divisions of the globe that had got crowded out when the sacred boundaries of Virginia were staked out.

But the town assents ('The people took more pride in the duel than in all the other events put together, perhaps. ... In their eyes the principals [in the duel] had reached the summit of human honour'). And beyond the code Twain establishes a general spirit of magnanimity and tolerance; if eccentricity is mocked, gentleness is generally in order. If Percy Northumberland Driscoll is just a fairly humane man towards 'slaves and other animals', he is 'an exceedingly humane man toward the erring of his own race.' And when his estate is sold after his death, Judge Driscoll buys Chambers to prevent Tom selling Chambers down river, 'for public sentiment did not approve of that way of treating the family servants for light cause or no cause.'

As long as identity can remain assured in this society, there seems no likely source of tension. But miscegenation, the mixture of the races, has blurred the lines. Not only is the appearance of honour and virtue available to 'imitation whites', but in Roxy's case it is present as a fact. She, like the Driscolls and Howards, is 'majestic', 'imposing', 'statuesque'; and since Twain uses the vocabulary of honour and nobility to suggest virtue, her 'queenly' role in the latter part of the novel is a quality of real distinction. The situation creates an area of moral paradox and the possibility of imposture both moral and social; and this is Twain's theme. It should here be said that Twain's treatment of the world of honour and nobility is tolerably genial. Not only does he finally permit it to survive and defeat its questioners, but he draws on its values and assumptions sufficiently for us to feel that he has for Dawson's Landing a qualified admiration. Leavis can thus point out that Twain regards many of its values – its sense of honour and civilization – as something worthy of approval, 'the signs of an inward grace'. So indeed he does, though from a position of final independence; the moral world of the characters and the society is certainly not the moral world of the storyteller. The point is that if, as several critics have argued, Tom's ironical situation in between the races reveals a flaw and a crime at the centre of this society, Twain does not make the citizens suffer for it, or expose the falsity of its values, or even confront it with its own paradoxes.

James M. Cox has argued that Tom becomes 'the organic means of dramatizing the last phase of a society trapped by its secret history'. He represents, says Cox, the dark stain of miscegenation, 'an indelible stain disfiguring not only the Driscoll heraldic pattern but that of every white man who upholds the power structure'. So the book portrays a world in which the power of those who rule has shifted to those who serve – to Tom and, above all, to Roxana. He must then argue that Twain suppresses the real significance of his story by the ending. But though Twain treats Roxana with great imaginative force, he does not make her the critic of this society, nor even the final repository of approved virtues. The essential crime she revenges is the crime perpetrated upon her by Tom – and Tom is the darkest figure in the slavery system, representing mastership without compassion and power without honour. In all respects it is he, in his white persona, who invokes the absolute horror of slavery. In relation to him Roxy sinks from 'the sublime height of motherhood to the sombre deeps of unmodified slavery', a slavery that derives not only from the institution as such but from Tom's 'capricious temper and vicious nature'. It is Tom who sells Roxy, casually, down the river, into that darker slavery which itself softens the force of its horror in Dawson's Landing. If, as Leslie Fiedler says, the flow of the river in *Pudd'nhead Wilson* represents 'a nightmare of the passage into captivity', it also sets Dawson's Landing half-free from the extremes of slave-experience and so points to darker ironies. The planter's wife and the overseer who mistreat Roxy are not southern gentry but northerners, 'Yanks', and 'Dey knows how to work a nigger to death, en dey knows how to whale 'em, too. ...' Twain does not directly create a sense of the crime and guilt of Dawson's Landing. What he does is to create a deep sense of the irony of its social life, of virtue irretrievably mingled with wrong – a very different thing.

It is on the mixture of authorial involvement and independence that the sense of implacable irony in the novel depends. Twain draws upon the virtues of the town to establish a sense of virtue and an awareness of the depth of Tom's crimes, while at the same time giving us a strong causal basis both for the virtue and the crimes. One way to see how he establishes this as an irony is to compare him with Jane Austen, in whose novels the social life at its best *is* approved, and provides the basis for her own exacting moral values. In her work social values are not moral values as such; but her irony works to show how they can be, how a certain kind of full and tested social awareness is also, finally, a realized moral awareness. Her viewpoint is independent from the story only in the sense that she views from the position of an absolute, experienced sense of the coexistence of social and moral virtue. Twain however does not suggest that the virtues in his society are in any sense absolute. In *Pudd'nhead Wilson* the fact that the social life conditions the moral life is – however much Twain may respect in his narrative some of the values involved – finally a matter of observation. His irony therefore works from the standpoint of social relativism, and speaks not for moral virtue but out of moral detachment. He does this by making the world of Dawson's Landing one of many possible versions of man, and by showing that there are other forces, genetic and environmental, which make men what they are, without benefit of morals. This is the world as Pudd'nhead sees it in his secret life of ironical reflection, free thought, fascination with 'every new thing that is born into the universe of ideas' (from the sciences of palmistry to fingermarks) and, of course, his Calendar. It is also the world of genetic fact that Twain creates as the reality behind that 'fiction of law and custom' which makes Roxy and Tom, who are mostly white, into Negroes. From this viewpoint, the achieved and positive sense of identity and value on which Dawson's Landing society is built can be treated as a matter of historical event; this training, this community, produced these norms. Society is essentially strange.

So it is out of the ironical relationship between the socially absolute, the confident gullible world of Dawson's Landing, and the historically changeable world in which indentity is finally a fingerprint, that Twain creates his story and establishes his viewpoint and his tone. The contrast is established clearly in the second chapter by Pudd'nhead himself. He sees the white and Negro babies in their baby-wagon and asks Roxy a question which plants in her head an idea which opens up all the comedy, imposture and crime on which the rest of the novel turns: 'How do you tell them apart, Roxy, when they haven't any clothes on?' he asks. Behind the world of assured, traditional communal identity (out of which the code, and the sense of honour and civilization, springs) lies a much more exposed world in which identity is much less certain – but which proves no less cruel than the other. Roxy opens it up further when, about to kill herself and her baby to escape the dangers of slavery, she dresses her baby up in the white child's clothes for the angels to admire – and sees the consequence: 'I *never* knowed you was so lovely. Marse Tommy ain't a bit puttier – not a single bit.' If there is really nothing to choose between a white and a Negro child when their clothes are altered, the social life can be an invention – a 'fiction created by herself'. She makes her baby a 'usurper' to protect him from misfortune. But – this is where Twain's harsher ironies begin – the 'fiction' becomes a reality. Roxy's 'deceptions intended solely for others gradually grow practically into self-deceptions as well'. She loses her son to what she has made him, the master's child, and he becomes 'her darling, her master, and her deity all in one, and in her worship of him she forgot who she was and what he had been'. If the social life is in one sense a fiction and an imposture, it is in another sense an absolute and binding commitment – the only reality beyond ourselves that we have. She does not therefore make Tom into a free agent, but into the victim of his particular circumstances. He is *made*, by Roxy's fiction, into a socially divided man; his Negro inheritance eats into his white status, as Chambers's white inheritance cuts into his Negro status. And his new environment makes him so completely, that he can never be free of what *is* made of him. Tom, like Chambers, can only exist within one of the two identities which Dawson's Landing confers, for neither society nor nature grants total independence.

Twain's refusal to provide an escape-route for Tom, either by creating change in his society or letting the action move significantly beyond Dawson's Landing, prescribes that this must be a novel of ironies. And in order to establish his double vision, his perception of two forms of social being, Twain has to create for himself, within the book, a position of commanding narrative independence, a total mastery over the story. Since Twain often is regarded as less than a conscious artist, it is worth emphasizing with what overall skill and success he accomplishes this task. He makes his narrative voice in the novel that of the comic inventor whose universe belongs to and may be elaborated by him. He does this, not by questioning whether the world he describes is a fact or a fiction, as Henry Fielding does in *Tom Jones*, but by insisting that he is dealing in a 'chronicle' or a 'history' and then showing that the world itself creates burlesques, disguises and paradox. Not only does he move the story at a rapid pace, disposing of old characters and introducing new ones freely to serve his ends, but he keeps us continually aware of the cohesive, paradoxical logic in these events – so that notes established apparently casually at the beginning, like the introduction of Wilson's hobby-horses of palmistry and fingerprinting, and his desire for success in law, typically come to take on further meanings. And by establishing a recurrent pattern of contrasts and doubles, he gives his plotting a dialectical structure, a sense of the concealed behind the revealed, which itself asserts his literary command. If he often works melodramatically (not fully motivating Tom's villainies, for example) and takes obvious chances with his tone in order to introduce marginal episodes, he does singularly create a capacity for a total systematic control of his story, a control that comes from his sense of the fatality of the human condition. Life, like fiction, is a coherent plot.

What gradually emerges from his tone, therefore, is an air of moral remoteness and detachment, coupled with a speculative, almost metaphysical comic mood. This emerges only gradually – so gradually that we can easily miss its presence. The opening scenes indeed work toward a warm evocation of Dawson's Landing, a feeling that it is valuable and complete. The touches that suggest independence – the independence of a narrator who speaks a language and expresses a knowledge beyond that immediately available to any of his characters, historically, socially and geographically – only gradually emerge, as Twain creates mild contrasts, touches of distance ('The candy-striped pole which indicates nobility proud and ancient along the palace-bordered canals of Venice indicated merely the humble barber-shop along the main street of Dawson's Landing'). Yet the note of moral abstraction is already there ('The women were good and commonplace people, and did their duty, and had their reward in clear consciences and the community's approbation') and so is the air of manipulating his world for the purposes of a carefully disposed plot in which men must take their places (so he introduces and at once dismisses Colonel Cecil Burleigh Essex, with whom, he says, 'we have no concern' – but he will prove to be Tom's father). Then too there are the touches of comic burlesque, later to become much more important in the novel:

[Pembroke Howard] was a fine, brave, majestic creature, a gentleman according to the nicest requirements of the Virginian rule, a devoted Presbyterian, an authority on the 'code', and a man always courteously ready to stand up before you in the field if any act or word of his had seemed doubtful or suspicious to you, and explain it with any weapon you might prefer from brad-awls to artillery.

With chapter two, we see the contentment of Dawson's Landing from the viewpoint of the excluded, and Mark Twain can end the chapter with an irony which is not so much tonal as structural:

The culprits flung themselves prone, in an ecstasy of gratitude, and kissed [Percy Driscoll's] feet. ... They were sincere, for like a god he had stretched forth his mighty hand and closed the gates of hell against them. He knew, himself, that he had done a noble and gracious thing, and was privately well pleased with his magnanimity; and that night he set the incident down in his diary, so that his son might read it in after years, and be thereby moved to deeds of gentleness and humanity himself.

The passage seems half-straight, half-mocking, part of that odd middle tone that lets Twain walk between his two worlds. But what is clear is that this very act of magnanimity leads straight to Roxy's exchanging the babies. Thus the son for whom Driscoll sets down the incident is, through it, to become a slave; while the child he comes to think his son is to grow far beyond deeds of gentleness and humanity. From now on such fatalities will overshadow all such acts, and already Twain's tone asserts that commanding view of the story, forwards and backwards. Henceforth the world of solid contentment loses its solidity; men become imposters or dupes, usurpers or slaves, victims of their virtue as well as of their vice.

Twain goes on to control this new, estranged world with the remorseless long logic that constitutes his vision. The events started by Pudd'nhead's question, developed by Percy Driscoll's 'magnanimity' and set in train by Roxy's motherly fears for her child now begin to take on their own independent meanings, remote from any intent on the part of the characters. For Tom grows into the duplicity that he represents, both socially – as a white Negro – and emotionally – as the lost son. He is ironically placed between forces that at first seem to conspire to protect him to excess; spoiled by his mother as her son, he is spoiled too by his other 'parents' (while Chambers is beaten into submission by both parties). He grows into a malevolent personality, who assimilates into himself the weakness of both races – he has the cruelty of the bad master and the profligacy of the bad aristocrat, coupled with the cowardice and amorality of the bad slave. So aligned, he stands in ironical relationship to both sides, the universal polar opposite. He is an aristocrat without honour and a master without humanity, a mocking double of the real thing. If Roxy is both slave and queen, then he is master and coward; if Percy Driscoll is the over-fond step-father and the honourable man, he is the unfeeling son and the dishonourable 'imitation white'. Finally rejecting both inheritances, he kills the man who thinks himself his step-father and sells his mother down the river.

Twain develops this on the one hand in the form of a comedy of moral chaos. Tom's burlesques, concealments and duplicites show up the gullibility of the town and the touches of absurdity in the leading citizens. Their whole confident view of appearance and experience is questioned. The aristrocrat is assumed to do no wrong; so, looking at Tom, they cannot see. Much of the subsequent comedy and farce comes out of this, and Twain rehearses its implications blandly, enjoying the strategems and successes on both sides.

The town, as a citizen observes at the end, becomes the
'pudd'nhead'. But if Twain is remorseless in dealing with
Tom's victims and morally not very concerned with Tom's
villainies, this is because he is also establishing *another*
species of irony. This is the irony of fatalistic tragedy, by
which Tom becomes himself a victim of his situation. For
he is not a free agent; rather he is committed and divided
by all that has happened to him. He is committed as Negro
by his birth and the claim of his mother upon him; he is
committed as white by his upbringing and the various
'fathers' he is given. So he is irretrievably connected with
others in a pattern which can leave him with no meaningful
centre. Twain establishes all the ironies of these connections
– for instance, his life is led at the expense of Chambers's,
and Twain stresses this in a characteristic neat touch;
Chambers 'unfortunately' saves Tom from drowning and is
christened by the other boys Tom's 'niggerpappy' because
he is 'the author of his new being' (for, of course, the *second*
time) – as a persistent basis for the development of his story.
The paradox in him is ingrained and inescapable, he is
trapped by the attempt to set him free. He is the product of
his environment, his divided patronage, possibly even by
genetic throwback, as Roxy suggests: 'It's de nigger in you,
dat's what it is. Thirty-one parts o' you is white, en on'y one
part nigger, en dat po' little one part is yo' *soul*.' So as
Twain comically exposes the paradoxes in the town, he also
fatalistically exposes the paradox in man. The basic logic
in the story, the essential direction of its progress, is towards
the remorseless tragic irony that Roxy, who has changed
Tom with Chambers in order to save him from being sold
down the river, ensures that, fatality working as it does in
this world, that is exactly what must happen to him.
    For Twain to show this, his irony must be an under-
standing, a vision, and so, we finally realize, it is. It comes

from his absolute command of his story, his sense of an irony in the human condition so great that none of the characters can be fully aware of it. Fate overshadows character, and itself works by paradox. Roxy loses her banked money; the property Tom stole is stolen from him by a 'brother-thief'; the twins enter the judge's house just a moment after Tom has killed him; Pudd'nhead only makes his discovery because Tom comes, at the last minute, to taunt him with his failure. Twain of course commands such fates, sometimes with glaring obviousness; but it is in his very persistence that his power finally lies. The 'free grace' that the Lord gives, according to the Negro preacher who illustrates his doctrine with the story of the exchanged royal babies, is not to be had. It is an infallible, post-Darwinian determinism that finally locates Tom, a species of knowledge that comes not out of the world of the book but from the late-nineteenth-century fatalism of vision that Twain develops in the course of telling his story. It is environment that makes man, and because of this he has a final identity – the one that Puddn'head makes public and meaningful in the courtroom scene at the end:

Every human being carries with him from his cradle to his grave certain physical marks which do not change their character, and by which he can always be identified – and that without shade of doubt or question. These marks are his signature, his physiological autograph, so to speak, and this autograph cannot be counterfeited, nor can he disguise it or hide it away, nor can it become illegible by the wear and the mutations of time. ... You have often heard of twins who were so exactly alike that when dressed alike their own parents could not tell them apart. Yet there was never a twin born into this world that did not carry from birth to death a sure identifier in this mysterious and marvellous natal autograph. That once known to you, his fellow-twin could never personate him and deceive you.

4

Pudd'nhead Wilson is not of course a perfect novel. It has
many lacunae, and a good deal of material explicable only in
terms of previous versions of the story. At times, Mark
Twain is obvious or gauche. Often his humour releases the
pressure of the book in just those places where it most
needs it; the playful episodes about the twins and about
Tom's elaborate disguises clearly get somewhat out of hand
in a japing, Tom Sawyerish way. He is evidently careless
about specific motivations – why does Tom commit his
crimes in Dawson's Landing; why does Judge Driscoll,
without checking at all, accept that the twins are dishonourable assassins; why doesn't Pudd'nhead conclude at the
end that he has simply mixed up his slides; why, before this,
does he not check the prints on the knife with his collection?
Structurally more confusing is the unresolved question of
whether Tom is bad because of the treatment he receives or
because 'bad' Negro blood comes out in him; the confusion,
though it has advantages for the novel, clearly raises the
possibility that Twain regards the two races as morally dis-
tinct. There are other unmistakeable flaws; the fact remains
that they are the flaws of a most remarkable novel – so
wide-ranging in tone that strain is inevitable, so remorse-
lessly plotted the bare bones must show from time to time,
so deeply soaked in irony that it cannot in the normal sense
be contained. The elusive quality of the narrative style
finally becomes the source of a comic-ironic distance, a
rigorous moral realism; it touches the book with a surrealis-
tic tragi-comic perception, an instinct for genial and malevolent anarchy, that we associate with much twentieth-century
black-humour writing. The remorseless, problematic prob-
ing continues right to the end of the book – making even the
traditional comic resolution into yet another inexorable

disaster. Man, once made, is not to be unmade; and Chambers cannot become the Tom Driscoll he once was:

The real heir suddenly found himself rich and free, but in a most embarrassing situation. He could neither read nor write, and his speech was the basest dialect of the negro quarter. His gait, his attitudes, his gestures, his bearing, his laugh – all were vulgar and uncouth; his manners were the manners of a slave. Money and fine clothes could not mend these defects or cover them up, they only made them the more glaring and the more pathetic. The poor fellow could not endure the terrors of the white man's parlour, and felt at home and at peace nowhere but in the kitchen. The family pew was a misery to him, yet he could nevermore enter into the solacing refuge of the 'nigger gallery' – that was closed to him for good and all.

As for Tom, he too must revert to what he was. His fate, the logical culmination of all the ironies of the book, is itself so complete an irony that its intimations can hardly be grasped: they reach back again into the meaning of slavery, and guilt, and the vision of man as property. The last sentence *is* a sentence, echoing the supreme horror of the novel:

Everybody granted that if 'Tom' were white and free it would be unquestionably right to punish him – it would be no loss to anybody; but to shut up a valuable slave for life – that was quite another matter.

As soon as the Governor understood the case, he pardoned Tom at once, and the creditors sold him down the river.

MALCOLM BRADBURY

FURTHER READING

Anderson, Frederick and Kenneth M. Sanderson, *Mark Twain: The Critical Heritage* (London: Routledge & Kegan Paul, 1971). Includes three contemporary reviews of *Pudd'nhead Wilson*. The *Critic* is sceptical: 'What *is* this? Is it literature? Is Mr. Clemens a "writer" at all?' (Perhaps no more so than Dickens is literature.) The *Atheneum*, more respectfully, praises the portrait of Roxana.

Berger, Sidney, *'Pudd'nhead Wilson' and 'Those Extraordinary Twins'* (New York: W. W. Norton, 1980). Berger, after a sustained textual examination of *Pudd'nhead*, provides an illuminating 'textual introduction' along with tables of variants. He notes interestingly that the Morgan manuscript is titled *Pudd'nhead Wilson, A Tale* rather than *The Tragedy of Pudd'nhead Wilson*. Berger reproduces the illustrations from the first American edition by C. H. Warren and F. M. Senior; these are often trivializing images, but they do provide significant clues to contemporary understandings of *Pudd'nhead* (particularly in their bizarre glosses on the racial dimensions).

Brewton, Vince, '"An honour as well as a pleasure": Dueling, Violence, and Race in *Pudd'nhead Wilson*', *Southern Quarterly* 38 (Summer 2000), pp. 101–18. Working against an argument of Sundquist (in Gillman and Robinson), Brewton suggests that *Pudd'nhead Wilson* is 'a significant representation of the old South' rather than mainly or only an allegory of Reconstruction. He draws on a close study of duelling to imagine a 'dialogue within the text between narrative of Old South and New'.

Brodwin, Stanley, 'Blackness and the Adamic Myth in Mark Twain's *Pudd'nhead Wilson*', *Texas Studies in Language and Literature* 15 (Spring 1973), pp. 167–76. 'Temptation, pride, banishment, and damnation, dramatized in biblical terms, provide the key to the novel's meaning.'

Cox, James, *Mark Twain: The Fate of Humor* (Princeton: Princeton University Press, 1966). Wilson both precipitates the crisis of the novel 'by his own idle remark to Roxy' and concludes it in his unmasking of Driscoll. This is a particularly intense and thorough discussion of the novel's form in connection with its 'erotic' motives.

Crews, Frederick, 'The Parting of the Twains', review of Gillman, *Dark Twins* and of Sherwood Cummings, *Mark Twain and Science*, in *New York Review of Books* 36 (20 July 1989), pp. 39–44. Both apoplectic and shrewd, Crews offers a stimulating, often unfair, critique of Gillman and of a larger tendency in academic works to treat Twain as a symptom of political and social confusions rather than as a novelist in conscious control of his material. Crews is at his most interesting in disputing Gillman on fingerprinting. He is less convincing on the evils of 'social constructivism' – especially since the novel itself seems like the ultimate social constructivist text, suggesting that what it means to be black is to think that you are (and to have other people think so too), regardless of details like skin colour and genetic makeup.

Fiedler, Leslie, 'As Free as Any Cretur', *New Republic* 133 (15 and 22 August 1955), pp. 17–19, 16–18. Fiedler pursues a phantom masterwork: 'What a book the original might have been, before *Those Extraordinary Twins* was detached and Pudd'nhead's *Calendar* expurgated – a rollicking atrocious melange of bad taste and half understood intentions and nearly intolerable insights into evil, translated into a nightmare worthy of America.' He

anticipates a fascination with contradiction developed by
New Historicist criticism.

Gillman, Susan, *Dark Twins: Imposture and Identity in
Mark Twain's America* (Chicago: University of Chicago
Press, 1989). Chapter 3 argues *Pudd'nhead* should be read
as intertangled with its 'twin' novel on the farcical
adventures of Siamese twins; this illuminates Twain's
preoccupation with miscegenation, race, individual
responsibility, freakishness and bonds that are also forms
of bondage.

Gillman, Susan and Forrest G. Robinson (eds.), *Mark
Twain's 'Pudd'nhead Wilson': Race, Conflict, and Culture*
(Durham, NC: Duke University Press, 1990). A stimulating collection on the announced theme, taking (by and
large) a New Historicist approach.

Griffith, Clark, *Achilles and the Tortoise: Mark Twain's
Fictions* (Tuscaloosa: University of Alabama Press, 1998).
Offering an adventurous if uneven reading, Griffith puts
special emphasis on the role of the Italian aristocrats –
especially on Luigi's 'well-aimed swift kick', read as the
generative physical shock at the centre of the novel.

Howe, Lawrence, *Mark Twain and the Novel: The Double-
Cross of Authority* (Cambridge: Cambridge University
Press, 1998). Chapter 4 argues that 'Twain's shifting
identification from Roxana to Wilson ... suggests that
the tragedy extends beyond the text, that Twain's liberal
consciousness was tragically flawed as well.'

Jehlens, Myra, 'The Ties That Bind: Race and Sex in
Pudd'nhead Wilson', *American Literary History* 2 (Spring
1990), pp. 39–55. '*Pudd'nhead Wilson* exemplifies the
tragedy of the imagination, a literary kind that, ironically, only a historical criticism can fully appreciate.' An
unusually deft New Historicist reading.

Kaplan, Justin, *Mr. Clemens and Mark Twain: A Biography*

(New York: Simon and Schuster, 1991). A classic (and very readable) life of Clemens.

Leavis, F. R., 'Mark Twain's Neglected Classic', Introduction to Zodiac Press edn (1955). Leavis is in an appreciative mood. In balancing the demands of aristocratic and democratic values, Dawson's Landing shows 'the outward signs of an inward grace'. It uses 'the sensational and the melodramatic ... for the purpose of significant art'. Twain treats racial themes with 'poised humanity'. This is all so different from most critical evaluations at the present that it gains value for striking its own tone, even if Leavis's judgements are not always plausible.

Parker, Hershel, *'Pudd'nhead Wilson*: Jack-Leg Author, Unreadable Text and Sense-Making Critics', in *Flawed Texts and Verbal Icons: Literary Authority in American Fiction* (Evanston: Northwestern University Press, 1984), pp. 147–80. Parker argues that the text was put together in a somewhat random and contingent way; he suggests many of the 'sense-making' activities of critics actually make no sense. The premise is crucially important; the conclusion does not necessarily follow from it.

Railton, Stephen, 'The Tragedy of Mark Twain, by Pudd'nhead Wilson', *Nineteenth-Century Literature* 56 (2002), pp. 518–44. This salvo in the Pudd'nhead wars asks why the novel is a tragedy, and why, most particularly, the tragedy of Wilson. Taking the (now familiar) line that *Pudd'nhead* is caught up in some of the least enlightened Reconstruction ideologies, Railton suggests that Wilson produces 'a communally self-serving narrative' that traps him within the corrupt confines of public success, perhaps like Twain himself. Railton makes illuminating links between Twain's performance anxieties and those of his hero; he also comments on an 1895 dramatization, suggesting what it might show about the public understanding of the book.

Smith, Henry Nash, *Mark Twain: The Development of a Writer* (Cambridge: Harvard University Press, 1962). Smith reads *Pudd'nhead* as a critique of antebellum Southern culture, activated largely through the figure of Wilson, a 'transcendent' character basically unattached to his milieu. Wilson and Driscoll are really no more than bundles of themes; *Pudd'nhead's* only fully realized character, in a realistic sense, is Roxana.

Sundquist, Eric, 'Mark Twain and Homer Plessy', *Representations* 24 (Autumn 1989), pp. 102–27. Sundquist compares the cultural and formal logic of *Pudd'nhead Wilson* and that of the 1896 Supreme Court decision 'Plessy v. Ferguson' which articulated the 'separate but equal' doctrine.

Wigger, Anne, 'The Composition of Mark Twain's *Pudd'nhead Wilson* and *Those Extraordinary Twins*: Chronology and Development', *Modern Philology* 55 (1957), pp. 93–102. The fundamental early essay on the morass of manuscripts from which Twain worked. With Berger's edition, it is an essential starting-point for textual studies.

Wonham, Henry, 'Getting to the Bottom of Pudd'nhead Wilson; Or, a Critical Vision Focused (Too Well?) for Irony', *Arizona Quarterly* 50 (Autumn 1994), pp. 111–26. Wonham comes to grips with forty years of *Pudd'nhead Wilson* criticism, from Fiedler, through New Critical readings focused on questions of textual unity, to recent New Historicist efforts. 'Whether one faults *Pudd'nhead Wilson* ... for failing to achieve "transcendent unity", or praises the novel ... for laying bare "rifts" in nineteenth-century ideology, the gesture toward an unwritten foundational, potentially authorizing master-text is the same.' He also argues that 'the novel itself parodies the "drive to cultural stability"'. Richard Maxwell

A NOTE ON THE TEXT

THE text of *Pudd'nhead Wilson* used in this edition is taken from that of the first edition, published by Chatto and Windus in London in 1894 under the title *Pudd'nhead Wilson, A Tale*. The American edition, which appeared shortly after the London edition, also in 1894, was published by the American Publishing Company and titled *The Tragedy of Pudd'nhead Wilson and the Comedy of Those Extraordinary Twins*. Previously that year, the story had been serialized in the *Century Magazine* (December 1893 – June 1894). An advertising item, *Pudd'nhead Wilson's Calendar for 1894*, drawn up to draw attention to this serial publication, has been used here as illustration. The text of 'Those Extraordinary Twins' is taken from the Author's National Edition of Mark Twain's works, published by Harper and Brothers, New York and London, in 1899–1900.

Facsimile of the title page of the first edition of
Pudd'nhead Wilson, a Tale, *1894*

PUDD'NHEAD WILSON

A TALE

BY

MARK TWAIN

(SAMUEL L. CLEMENS)

WITH A PORTRAIT OF THE AUTHOR BY JAMES MAPES DODGE
AND SIX ILLUSTRATIONS BY LOUIS LOEB

London
CHATTO & WINDUS, PICCADILLY
1894

A Whisper to the Reader

A PERSON who is ignorant of legal matters is always liable to make mistakes when he tries to photograph a court scene with his pen; and so I was not willing to let the law chapters in this book go to press without first subjecting them to rigid and exhausting revision and correction by a trained barrister – if that is what they are called. These chapters are right, now, in every detail, for they were rewritten under the immediate eye of William Hicks, who studied law part of a while in south-west Missouri thirty-five years ago and then came over here to Florence for his health and is still helping for exercise and board in Macaroni Vermicelli's horse-feed shed which is up the back alley as you turn around the corner out of the Piazza del Duomo just beyond the house where that stone that Dante used to sit on six hundred years ago is let into the wall when he let on to be watching them build Giotto's campanile and yet always got tired looking as soon as Beatrice passed along on her way to get a chunk of chestnut cake to defend herself with in case of a Ghibelline outbreak before she got to school, at the same old stand where they sell the same old cake to this day and it is just as light and good as it was then, too, and this is not flattery, far from it. He was a little rusty on his law, but he rubbed up for this book, and those two or three legal chapters are right and straight, now. He told me so himself.

Given under my hand this second day of January, 1893, at the Villa Viviani, village of Settignano, three miles back of Florence, on the hills – the same certainly affording the most charming view to be found on this planet, and with it the most dream-like and enchanting sunsets to be found in any planet or even in any solar system – and given, too, in the swell room of the house, with the busts of Cerretani senators and other grandees of this line looking approvingly down upon me as they used to look down upon Dante, and mutely asking me to adopt them into my family, which I do with pleasure, for my remotest ancestors are but spring chickens compared with these robed and stately antiques, and it will be a great and satisfying lift for me, that six hundred years will.

MARK TWAIN

CHAPTER I

There is no character, howsoever good and fine, but it
can be destroyed by ridicule, howsoever poor and witless.
Observe the ass, for instance: his character is about
perfect, he is the choicest spirit among all the humbler
animals, yet see what ridicule has brought him to.
Instead of feeling complimented when we are called an
ass, we are left in doubt. – *Pudd'nhead Wilson's Calendar*

Tell the truth or trump – but get the trick. – *Pudd'nhead
Wilson's Calendar*

THE scene of this chronicle is the town of Dawson's Landing, on the Missouri side of the Mississippi, half a day's
journey, per steamboat, below St Louis.[1]

In 1830 it was a snug little collection of modest one- and
two-storey frame dwellings whose white-washed exteriors
were almost concealed from sight by climbing tangles of
rose-vines, honeysuckles, and morning-glories. Each of these
pretty homes had a garden in front, fenced with white pal-
ings and opulently stocked with hollyhocks, marigolds,
touch-me-nots, prince's-feathers and other old-fashioned
flowers; while on the window-sills of the houses stood
wooden boxes containing moss-rose plants and terra-cotta
pots in which grew a breed of geranium whose spread of
intensely red blossoms accented the prevailing pink tint of
the rose-clad house-front like an explosion of flame. When
there was room on the ledge outside of the pots and boxes
for a cat, the cat was there – in sunny weather – stretched
at full length, asleep and blissful, with her furry belly to
the sun and a paw curved over her nose. Then that house
was complete, and its contentment and peace were made

manifest to the world by this symbol, whose testimony is infallible. A home without a cat – and a well-fed, well-petted, and properly revered cat – may be a perfect home, perhaps, but how can it prove title?

All along the streets, on both sides, at the outer edge of the brick sidewalks, stood locust-trees with trunks protected by wooden boxing, and these furnished shade for summer and a sweet fragrance in spring, when the clusters of buds came forth. The main street, one block back from the river and running parallel with it, was the sole business street. It was six blocks long, and in each block two or three brick stores three stories high towered above interjected bunches of little frame shops. Swinging signs creaked in the wind, the street's whole length. The candy-striped pole which indicates nobility proud and ancient along the palace-bordered canals of Venice indicated merely the humble barber-shop along the main street of Dawson's Landing. On a chief corner stood a lofty unpainted pole wreathed from top to bottom with tin pots and pans and cups, the chief tin-monger's noisy notice to the world (when the wind blew) that his shop was on hand for business at that corner.

The hamlet's front was washed by the clear waters of the great river; its body stretched itself rearward up a gentle incline; its most rearward border fringed itself out and scattered its houses about the base-line of the hills; the hills rose high, inclosing the town in a half-moon curve, clothed with forests from foot to summit.

Steamboats passed up and down every hour or so. Those belonging to the little Cairo line and the little Memphis line always stopped; the big Orleans liners stopped for hails only, or to land passengers or freight; and this was the case also with the great flotilla of 'transients'. These latter came out of a dozen rivers – the Illinois, the Missouri, the Upper Mississippi, the Ohio, the Monongahela, the Tennessee, the

Red River, the White River, and so on; and were bound every whither and stocked with every imaginable comfort or necessity which the Mississippi's communities could want, from the frosty Falls of St Anthony down through nine climates to torrid New Orleans.

Dawson's Landing was a slaveholding town,[2] with a rich, slave-worked grain and pork country back of it. The town was sleepy and comfortable and contented. It was fifty years old,[3] and was growing slowly – very slowly, in fact, but still it was growing.

The chief citizen was York Leicester Driscoll, about forty years old, judge of the county court. He was very proud of his old Virginian ancestry,[4] and in his hospitalities and his rather formal and stately manners he kept up its traditions. He was fine and just and generous. To be a gentleman – a gentleman without stain or blemish – was his only religion, and to it he was always faithful. He was respected, esteemed, and beloved by all the community. He was well off, and was gradually adding to his store. He and his wife were very nearly happy, but not quite, for they had no children. The longing for the treasure of a child had grown stronger and stronger as the years slipped away, but the blessing never came – and was never to come.

With this pair lived the Judge's widowed sister, Mrs Rachel Pratt, and she also was childless – childless, and sorrowful for that reason, and not to be comforted. The women were good and commonplace people, and did their duty, and had their reward in clear consciences and the community's approbation. They were Presbyterians, the Judge was a free-thinker.

Pembroke Howard, lawyer and bachelor, aged about forty, was another old Virginian grandee with proved descent from the First Families. He was a fine, brave, majestic creature, a gentleman according to the nicest requirements of the Virginian rule, a devoted Presbyterian, an authority on the 'code', and a man always courteously ready to stand up before you in the field if any act or word of his had seemed doubtful or suspicious to you, and explain it with any weapon you might prefer from brad-awls to artillery. He was very popular with the people, and was the Judge's dearest friend.

Then there was Colonel Cecil Burleigh Essex, another F.F.V.[5] of formidable calibre; however, with him we have no concern.

Percy Northumberland Driscoll, brother to the Judge, and younger than he by five years, was a married man, and had had children around his hearthstone; but they were attacked in detail by measles, croup, and scarlet fever, and this had given the doctor a chance with his effective ante-diluvian methods; so the cradles were empty. He was a prosperous man, with a good head for speculations, and his fortune was growing. On the 1st of February, 1830, two boy babes were born in his house: one to him, the other to one of his slave girls, Roxana by name. Roxana was twenty years old. She was up and around the same day, with her hands full, for she was tending both babies.

Mrs Percy Driscoll died within the week. Roxy remained in charge of the children. She had her own way, for Mr Driscoll soon absorbed himself in his speculations and left her to her own devices.

In that same month of February Dawson's Landing gained a new citizen. This was Mr David Wilson, a young fellow of Scotch parentage. He had wandered to this remote region from his birthplace in the interior of the State of New York to seek his fortune. He was twenty-five years old, college-bred, and had finished a post-college course in an Eastern law school a couple of years before.

He was a homely, freckled, sandy-haired young fellow,

PUDD'NHEAD WILSON

with an intelligent blue eye that had frankness and comradeship in it and a covert twinkle of a pleasant sort. But for an
unfortunate remark of his, he would no doubt have entered at once upon a successful career at Dawson's Landing.
But he made his fatal remark the first day he spent in the
village, and it 'gaged' him. He had just made the acquaintance of a group of citizens when an invisible dog began to
yelp and snarl and howl and make himself very comprehensively disagreeable, whereupon young Wilson said, much
as one who is thinking aloud —
'I wish I owned half of that dog.'
'Why?' somebody asked.
'Because I would kill my half.'
The group searched his face with curiosity, with anxiety
even, but found no light there, no expression that they
could read. They fell away from him as from something
uncanny, and went into privacy to discuss him. One said:
' 'Pears to be a fool.'
' 'Pears?' said another. '*Is*, I reckon you better say.'
'Said he wished he owned *half* of the dog, the idiot,' said
a third. 'What did he reckon would become of the other half
if he killed his half? Do you reckon he thought it would
live?'
'Why, he must have thought it, unless he *is* the downrightest fool in the world; because if he hadn't thought it,
he would have wanted to own the whole dog, knowing that
if he killed his half and the other half died, he would be
responsible for that half just the same as if he had killed
that half instead of his own. Don't it look that way to you,
gents?'
'Yes, it does. If he owned one half of the general dog, it
would be so; if he owned one end of the dog and another
person owned the other end, it would be so, just the same;
particularly in the first case, because if you kill one half of

59

a general dog there ain't any man that can tell whose half it was, but if he owned one end of the dog, maybe he could kill his end of it and –'

'No, he couldn't either; he couldn't and not be responsible if the other end died, which it would. In my opinion the man ain't in his right mind.'

'In my opinion he hain't *got* any mind.'

No. 3 said: 'Well, he's a lummox, any way.'

'That's what he is,' said No. 4. 'he's a labrick – just a Simon-pure labrick, if ever there was one.'

'Yes, sir, he's a dam fool, that's the way I put him up,' said No. 5. 'Anybody can think different that wants to, but those are my sentiments.'

'I'm with you, gentlemen,' said No. 6. 'Perfect jackass – yes, and it ain't going too far to say he is a pudd'nhead. If he ain't a pudd'nhead, I ain't no judge, that's all.'

Mr Wilson stood elected. The incident was told all over the town, and gravely discussed by everybody. Within a week he had lost his first name; Pudd'nhead took its place. In time he came to be liked, and well liked, too; but by that time the nickname had got well stuck on, and it stayed. That first day's verdict made him a fool, and he was not able to get it set aside, or even modified. The nickname soon ceased to carry any harsh or unfriendly feeling with it, but it held its place, and was to continue to hold its place for twenty long years.

CHAPTER 2

Adam was but human – this explains it all. He did not want the apple for the apple's sake; he wanted it only because it was forbidden. The mistake was in not forbidding the serpent; then he would have eaten the serpent. – *Pudd'nhead Wilson's Calendar*

PUDD'NHEAD WILSON had a trifle of money when he arrived, and he bought a small house on the extreme western verge of the town. Between it and Judge Driscoll's house there was only a grassy yard, with a paling fence dividing the properties in the middle. He hired a small office down in the town, and hung out a tin sign with these words on it:

DAVID WILSON

ATTORNEY AND COUNSELLOR-AT-LAW

SURVEYING, CONVEYANCING, ETC.

But his deadly remark had ruined his chance – at least in the law. No clients came. He took down his sign after a while, and put it up on his own house with the law features knocked out of it. It offered his services now in the humble capacities of land-surveyor and expert accountant. Now and then he got a job of surveying to do, and now and then a merchant got him to straighten out his books. With Scotch patience and pluck he resolved to live down his reputation and work his way into the legal field yet. Poor fellow, he could not foresee that it was going to take him such a weary long time to do it.

He had a rich abundance of idle time, but it never hung heavy on his hands, for he interested himself in every new thing that was born into the universe of ideas, and studied it and experimented upon it at his house. One of his pet fads was palmistry. To another one he gave no name, neither would he explain to anybody what its purpose was, but merely said it was an amusement. In fact, he had found that his fads added to his reputation as a pudd'nhead; therefore, he was growing chary of being too communicative about them. The fad without a name was one which dealt with people's finger-marks.[1] He carried in his coat pocket a shallow box with grooves in it, and in the grooves strips of glass five inches long and three inches wide. Along the lower edge of each strip was pasted a slip of white paper. He asked people to pass their hands through their hair (thus collecting upon them a thin coating of the natural oil), and then make a thumbmark on a glass strip, following it with the mark of the ball of each finger in succession. Under this row of faint grease-prints he would write a record on the strip of white paper, thus:

JOHN SMITH, *right hand* --

and add the day of the month and the year, and then take Smith's left hand on another glass strip, and add name and date and the words 'left hand'. The strips were now returned to the grooved box, and took their place among what Wilson called his 'records'.

He often studied his records, examining and poring over them with absorbing interest until far into the night; but what he found there, if he found anything, he revealed to no one. Sometimes he copied on paper the involved and delicate pattern left by the ball of a finger, and then vastly enlarged it with a pantograph, so that he could examine its web of curving lines with ease and convenience.

One sweltering afternoon -- it was the first day of July, 1830 -- he was at work over a set of tangled account-books in his workroom, which looked westward over a stretch of vacant lots, when a conversation outside disturbed him. It was carried on in yells, which showed that the people engaged in it were not close together.

'Say, Roxy, how does yo' baby come on?' This from the distant voice.

'Fust-rate; how does *you* come on, Jasper?' This yell was from close by.

'Oh, I's middlin'; hain't got noth'n' to complain of. I's gwine to come a-court'n' you bimeby, Roxy.'

'*You* is, you black mud-cat! Yah – yah – yah! I got somep'n' better to do den 'sociat'n' wid niggers as black as you is. Is ole Miss Cooper's Nancy done give you de mitten?' Roxy followed this sally with another discharge of care-free laughter.

'You's jealous, Roxy; dat's what's de matter wid *you*, you hussy – yah – yah – yah! Dat's de time I got you!'

'Oh, yes, *you* got me, hain't you? 'Clah to goodness if dat conceit o' yo'n strikes in, Jasper, it gwine to kill you sho'. If you b'longed to me I'd sell you down de river [2] 'fo' you git too fur gone. Fust time I runs acrost yo' marster, I's gwine to tell him so.'

This idle and aimless jabber went on and on, both parties enjoying the friendly duel, and each well satisfied with his own share of the wit exchanged – for wit they considered it.

Wilson stepped to the window to observe the combatants; he could not work while their chatter continued. Over in the vacant lots was Jasper, young, coal-black, and of magnificent build, sitting on a wheelbarrow in the pelting sun – at work, supposably, whereas he was in fact only preparing for it by taking an hour's rest before beginning. In front of Wilson's porch stood Roxy, with a local handmade baby-wagon, in which sat her two charges – one at each end, and facing each other. From Roxy's manner of speech a stranger would have expected her to be black, but she was not. Only one sixteenth of her was black, and that sixteenth did not show.

She was of majestic form and stature; her attitudes were imposing and statuesque, and her gestures and movements distinguished by a noble and stately grace. Her complexion was very fair, with the rosy glow of vigorous health in the cheeks, her face was full of character and expression, her eyes were brown and liquid, and she had a heavy suit of fine soft hair which was also brown, but the fact was not apparent because her head was bound about with a checkered handkerchief and the hair was concealed under it. Her face was shapely, intelligent, and comely – even beautiful. She had an easy, independent carriage – when she was among her own caste – and a high and 'sassy' way withal; but, of course, she was meek and humble enough where white people were.

To all intents and purposes Roxy was as white as anybody,[3] but the one sixteenth of her which was black outvoted the other fifteen parts and made her a negro. She was a slave, and saleable as such. Her child was thirty-one parts white, and he, too, was a slave and, by a fiction of law and custom, a negro. He had blue eyes and flaxen curls like his white comrade; but even the father of the white child was able to tell the children apart – little as he had commerce with them – by their clothes: for the white babe wore ruffled soft muslin and a coral necklace, while the other wore merely a coarse tow-linen shirt which barely reached to its knees, and no jewellery.

The white child's name was Thomas à Becket Driscoll; the other's name was Valet de Chambre: no surname – slaves hadn't the privilege. Roxana had heard that phrase somewhere; the fine sound of it had pleased her ear, and, as she had supposed it was a name, she loaded it on to her darling. It soon got shortened to 'Chambers', of course.

Wilson knew Roxy by sight, and when the duel of wit began to play out, he stepped outside to gather in a record or two. Jasper went to work energetically, at once, perceiving that his leisure was observed. Wilson inspected the children and asked –

'How old are they, Roxy?'

'Bofe de same age, sir – five months. Bawn de fust o' Feb'uary.'

'They're handsome little chaps. One's just as handsome as the other, too.'

A delighted smile exposed the girl's white teeth and she said:

'Bles yo' soul, Misto Wilson, it's pow'ful nice o' you to say dat, 'ca'se one of 'em ain't on'y a nigger. Mighty prime little nigger, *I* al'ays says, but dat's 'ca'se it's mine, o' course.'

'How do you tell them apart, Roxy, when they haven't any clothes on?'

Roxy laughed a laugh proportioned to her size, and said:

'Oh, *I* kin tell 'em 'part, Misto Wilson, but I bet Marse Percy couldn't, not to save his life.'

Wilson chatted along for awhile, and presently got Roxy's finger-prints for his collection – right hand and left – on a couple of his glass strips; then labelled and dated them, and took the 'records' of both children, and labelled and dated them also.

Two months later, on the 3rd of September, he took this trio of finger-marks again. He liked to have a 'series', two or three 'takings' at intervals during the period of childhood, these to be followed by others at intervals of several years.

The next day – that is to say, on the 4th of September – something occurred which profoundly impressed Roxana. Mr Driscoll missed another small sum of money – which is a way of saying that this was not a new thing, but had happened before. In truth it had happened three times before.

Driscoll's patience was exhausted. He was a fairly humane man toward slaves and other animals; he was an exceedingly humane man toward the erring of his own race. Theft he could not abide, and plainly there was a thief in his house. Necessarily the thief must be one of his negroes. Sharp measures must be taken. He called his servants before him. There were three of these, besides Roxy: a man, a woman, and a boy twelve years old. They were not related. Mr Driscoll said:

'You have all been warned before. It has done no good. This time I will teach you a lesson. I will sell the thief. Which of you is the guilty one?'

They all shuddered at the threat, for here they had a good home, and a new one was likely to be a change for the worse. The denial was general. None had stolen anything – not money, anyway – a little sugar, or cake, or honey, or something like that, that 'Marse Percy wouldn't mind or miss', but not money – never a cent of money. They were eloquent in their protestations, but Mr Driscoll was not moved by them. He answered each in turn with a stern 'Name the thief!'

The truth was, all were guilty but Roxana; she suspected that the others were guilty, but she did not know them to be so. She was horrified to think how near she had come to being guilty herself; she had been saved in the nick of time by a revival in the coloured Methodist Church, a fortnight before, at which time and place she 'got religion'. The very next day after that gracious experience, while her change of style was fresh upon her and she was vain of her purified condition, her master left a couple of dollars lying unprotected on his desk, and she happened upon that temptation when she was polishing around with a dust-rag. She looked at the money awhile with a steadily rising resentment, then she burst out with –

'Dad blame dat revival, I wisht it had 'a' be'n put off till to-morrow!'

Then she covered the tempter with a book, and another member of the kitchen cabinet got it. She made this sacrifice as a matter of religious etiquette; as a thing necessary just now, but by no means to be wrested into a precedent; no, a week or two would limber up her piety, then she would be rational again, and the next two dollars that got left out in the cold would find a comforter – and she could name the comforter.

Was she bad? Was she worse than the general run of her race? No. They had an unfair show in the battle of life, and they held it no sin to take military advantage of the enemy – in a small way; in a small way, but not in a large one. They would smouch provisions from the pantry whenever they got a chance; or a brass thimble, or a cake of wax, or an emery-bag, or a paper of needles, or a silver spoon, or a dollar bill, or small articles of clothing, or any other property of light value; and so far were they from considering such reprisals sinful, that they would go to church and shout and pray their loudest and sincerest with their plunder in their pockets. A farm smoke-house had to be heavily padlocked, for even the coloured deacon himself could not resist a ham when Providence showed him in a dream, or otherwise, where such a thing hung lonesome and longed for some-one to love. But with a hundred hanging before him the deacon would not take two – that is, on the same night. On frosty nights the humane negro prowler would warm the end of a plank and put it up under the cold claws of chickens roosting in a tree; a drowsy hen would step on to the comfortable board, softly clucking her gratitude, and the prowler would dump her into his bag, and later into his stomach, perfectly sure that in taking this trifle from the man who daily robbed him of an inestimable treasure – his liberty – he was not committing any sin that God would remember against him in the Last Great Day.

'Name the thief!'

For the fourth time Mr Driscoll had said it, and always in the same hard tone. And now he added these words of awful import:

'I give you one minute' – he took out his watch. 'If at the end of that time you have not confessed, I will not only sell all four of you, *but* – I will sell you DOWN THE RIVER!'

It was equivalent to condemning them to hell! No Missouri negro doubted this. Roxy reeled in her tracks and the colour vanished out of her face; the others dropped to their knees as if they had been shot; tears gushed from their eyes, their supplicating hands went up, and three answers came in the one instant:

'I done it!'

'I done it!'

'I done it! – have mercy, marster – Lord have mercy on us po' niggers!'

'Very good,' said the master, putting up his watch, 'I will sell you *here*, though you don't deserve it. You ought to be sold down the river.'

The culprits flung themselves prone, in an ecstasy of gratitude, and kissed his feet, declaring that they would never forget his goodness and never cease to pray for him as long as they lived. They were sincere, for like a god he had stretched forth his mighty hand and closed the gates of hell against them. He knew, himself, that he had done a noble and gracious thing, and was privately well pleased with his magnanimity; and that night he set the incident down in his diary, so that his son might read it in after years, and be thereby moved to deeds of gentleness and humanity himself.

CHAPTER 3

Whoever has lived long enough to find out what life is, knows how deep a dept of gratitude we owe to Adam, the first great benefactor of our race. He brought death into the world. – *Pudd'nhead Wilson's Calendar*

PERCY DRISCOLL slept well the night he saved his house-minions from going down the river, but no wink of sleep visited Roxy's eyes. A profound terror had taken possession of her. Her child could grow up and be sold down the river! The thought crazed her with horror. If she dozed and lost herself for a moment, the next moment she was on her feet, and flying to her child's cradle to see if it was still there. Then she would gather it to her heart and pour out her love upon it in a frenzy of kisses, moaning, crying, and saying 'Dey sha'n't, oh, dey *sha'n't!* yo' po' mammy will kill you fust!'

Once, when she was tucking it back in its cradle again, the other child nestled in its sleep and attracted her attention. She went and stood over it a long time, communing with herself:

'What has my po' baby done, dat he couldn't have yo' luck? He hain't done noth'n'. God was good to you; why warn't he good to him? Dey can't sell *you* down de river. I hates yo' pappy; he ain't got no heart – for niggers he ain't, anyways. I hates him, en I could kill him!' She paused awhile, thinking; then she burst into wild sobbings again, and turned away, saying, 'Oh, I got to kill my chile, dey ain't no yuther way, – killin' *him* wouldn't save de chile fum goin' down de river. Oh, I got to do it, yo' po' mammy's

69

got to kill you to save you, honey' – she gathered her baby to her bosom, now, and began to smother it with caresses – 'Mammy's got to kill you – how *kin* I do it? But yo' mammy ain't gwine to desert you, – no, no; *dah*, don't cry – she gwine *wid* you, she gwine to kill herself too. Come along, honey, come along wid mammy; we gwine to jump in de river, den de troubles o' dis worl' is all over – dey don't sell po' niggers down the river over *yonder*.'

She started toward the door, crooning to the child and hushing it; midway she stopped, suddenly. She had caught sight of her new Sunday gown – a cheap curtain calico thing, a conflagration of gaudy colours and fantastic figures. She surveyed it wistfully, longingly.

'Hain't ever wore it yet,' she said, 'en it's jist lovely.' Then she nodded her head in response to a pleasant idea, and added, 'No, I ain't gwine to be fished out, wid everybody lookin' at me, in dis mis'able ole linsey-woolsey.'

She put down the child and made the change. She looked in the glass and was astonished at her beauty. She resolved to make her death-toilet perfect. She took off her handkerchief-turban and dressed her glossy wealth of hair 'like white folks'; she added some odds and ends of rather lurid ribbon and a spray of atrocious artificial flowers; finally she threw over her shoulders a fluffy thing called a 'cloud' in that day, which was of a blazing red complexion. Then she was ready for the tomb.

She gathered up her baby once more; but when her eye fell upon its miserably short little gray tow-linen shirt and noted the contrast between its pauper shabbiness and her own volcanic irruption of infernal splendours her mother-heart was touched, and she was ashamed.

'No, dolling, mammy ain't gwine to treat you so. De angels is gwine to 'mire you jist as much as dey does yo' mammy. Ain't gwine to have 'em putt'n' dey han's up 'fo' dey eyes en sayin' to David en Goliah en dem yuther prophets, "Dat chile is dress' too indelicate fo' dis place."'

By this time she had stripped off the shirt. Now she clothed the naked little creature in one of Thomas à Becket's snowy long baby-gowns, with its bright blue bows and dainty flummery of ruffles.

'Dah – now you's fixed.' She propped the child in a chair and stood off to inspect it. Straightway her eyes began to widen with astonishment and admiration, and she clapped her hands and cried out, 'Why, it do beat all! I *never* knowed you was so lovely. Marse Tommy ain't a bit puttier – not a single bit.'

She stepped over and glanced at the other infant; she flung a glance back at her own; then one more at the heir of the house. Now a strange light dawned in her eyes, and in a moment she was lost in thought. She seemed in a trance; when she came out of it she muttered, 'When I 'uz a-washin' 'em in de tub, yistiddy, his own pappy asked me which of 'em was his'n.'

She began to move about like one in a dream. She undressed Thomas à Becket, stripping him of everything, and put the tow-linen shirt on him. She put his coral necklace on her own child's neck. Then she placed the children side by side, and after earnest inspection she muttered –

'Now who would b'lieve clo'es could do de like o' dat? Dog my cats if it ain't all *I* kin do to tell t' other fum which, let alone his pappy.'

She put her cub in Tommy's elegant cradle and said: 'You's young Marse *Tom* fum dis out, en I got to practise and git used to 'memberin' to call you dat, honey, or I's gwine to make a mistake sometime en git us bofe into trouble. Dah – now you lay still en don't fret no mo', Marse Tom – oh, thank de good Lord in heaven, you's saved, you's saved! – dey ain't no man kin ever sell mammy's po' little honey down de river now!'

She put the heir of the house in her own child's unpainted pine cradle, and said, contemplating its slumbering form uneasily:

'I's sorry for you, honey; I's sorry, God knows I is – but what *kin* I do, what could I do? Yo' pappy would sell him to somebody, some time, en den he'd go down de river, sho', en I couldn't, couldn't *couldn't* stan' it.'

She flung herself on her bed and began to think and toss, toss and think. By-and-by she sat suddenly upright, for a comforting thought had flown through her worried mind:

' 'Tain't no sin – *white* folks has done it! It ain't no sin, glory to goodness it ain't no sin! *Dey's* done it – yes, en dey was de biggest quality in de whole bilin', too – kings!'

She began to muse; she was trying to gather out of her memory the dim particulars of some tale she had heard some time or other. At last she said:

'Now I's got it; now I 'member. It was dat ole nigger preacher dat tole it, de time he come over here fum Illinois en preached in de nigger church. He said dey ain't nobody kin save his own self – can't do it by faith, can't do it by works, can't do it no way at all. Free grace is de *on'y* way, en dat don't come fum nobody but jis' de Lord; en *he* kin give it to anybody he please, saint or sinner – *he* don't kyer. He do jis' as He's a mineter. He s'lect out anybody dat suit him, en put another one in his place, en make de fust one happy for ever en leave t' other one to burn wid Satan. De preacher said it was jist like dey done in Englan' one time, long time ago. De queen she lef' her baby layin' aroun' one day, en went out callin'; en one o' de niggers roun' 'bout de place dat was 'mos' white, she come in en see de chile layin' aroun', en tuck en put her own chile's clo'es on de queen's chile, en den lef' her own chile layin' aroun' en tuck and

toted de queen's chile home to de nigger-quarter, en nobody
ever foun' it out, en her chile was de king bimeby, en sole de
queen's chile down de river one time when dey had to settle
up de estate. Dah, now – de preacher said it his own self, en
it ain't no sin, 'ca'se white folks done it. *Dey* done it – yes,
dey done it; en not on'y jis' common white folks nuther, but
de biggest quality dey is in de whole bilin'. Oh, I's *so* glad I
'member 'bout dat!'

She got up light-hearted and happy, and went to the
cradles and spent what was left of the night 'practising'.
She would give her own child a light pat and say humbly,
'Lay still, Marse Tom,' then give the real Tom a pat and say
with severity, 'Lay *still*, Chambers! – does you want me to
take somep'n' *to* you?'

As she progressed with her practice, she was surprised to
see how steadily and surely the awe which had kept her
tongue reverent and her manner humble toward her young
master was transferring itself to her speech and manner
toward the usurper, and how similarly handy she was becoming in transferring her motherly curtness of speech and
peremptoriness of manner to the unlucky heir of the ancient
house of Driscoll.

She took occasional rests from practising, and absorbed
herself in calculating her chances.

'Dey'll sell dese niggers to-day fo' stealin' de money, den
dey'll buy some mo' dat don't know de chillen – so *dat's* all
right. When I takes de chillen out to git de air, de minute
I'se roun' de corner I'se gwine to gaum dey mouths all
roun' wid jam, den dey can't *nobody* notice dey's changed.
Yes, I gwineter do dat till I's safe, if it's a year.

'Dey ain't but one man dat I's afeared of, en dat's dat
Pudd'nhead Wilson. Dey calls him a pudd'nhead, en says
he's a fool. My lan', dat man ain't no mo' fool den I is! He's
de smartes' man in dis town, less'n it's Jedge Driscoll or

maybe Pem Howard. Blame dat man, he worries me wid dem ornery glasses o' hisn; *I* b'lieve he's a witch. But nemmine, I's gwine to happen aroun' dah one o' dese days en let on dat I reckon he wants to print de chillen's fingers ag'in; en if *he* don't notice dey's changed, I bound dey ain't nobody gwine to notice it, en den I's safe, sho'. But I reckon I'll tote along a hoss-shoe to keep off de witch-work.'

The new negroes gave Roxy no trouble, of course. The master gave her none, for one of his speculations was in jeopardy, and his mind was so occupied that he hardly saw the children when he looked at them, and all Roxy had to do was to get them both into a gale of laughter when he came about; then their faces were mainly cavities exposing gums, and he was gone again before the spasm passed and the little creatures resumed a human aspect.

Within a few days the fate of the speculation became so dubious that Mr Percy went away with his brother the Judge, to see what could be done with it. It was a land speculation as usual, and it had gotten complicated with a lawsuit. The men were gone seven weeks. Before they got back, Roxy had paid her visit to Wilson, and was satisfied. Wilson took the finger-prints, labelled them with the names and with the date – October the first – put them carefully away and continued his chat with Roxy, who seemed very anxious that he should admire the great advance in flesh and beauty which the babies had made since he took their finger-prints a month before. He complimented their improvement to her contentment; and as they were without any disguise of jam or other stain, she trembled all the while and was miserably frightened lest at any moment he –

But he didn't. He discovered nothing; and she went home jubilant, and dropped all concern about the matter permanently out of her mind.

CHAPTER 4

Adam and Eve had many advantages, but the principal one was that they escaped teething. – *Pudd'nhead Wilson's Calendar*

There is this trouble about special providences – namely, there is so often a doubt as to which party was intended to be the beneficiary. In the case of the children, the bears, and the prophet, the bears got more real satisfaction out of the episode than the prophet did, because they got the children. – *Pudd'nhead Wilson's Calendar*

THIS history must henceforth accommodate itself to the change which Roxana has consummated, and call the real heir 'Chambers' and the usurping little slave 'Thomas à Becket' – shortening this latter name to 'Tom', for daily use, as the people about him did.

'Tom' was a bad baby, from the very beginning of his usurpation. He would cry for nothing; he would burst into storms of devilish temper without notice, and let go scream after scream and squall after squall, then climax the thing with 'holding his breath' – that frightful speciality of the teething nursling, in the throes of which the creature exhausts its lungs, then is convulsed with noiseless squirmings and twistings and kickings in the effort to get its breath, while the lips turn blue and the mouth stands wide and rigid, offering for inspection one wee tooth set in the lower rim of a hoop of red gums; and when the appalling stillness has endured until one is sure the lost breath will never return, a nurse comes flying, and dashes water in the child's face, and – presto! the lungs fill, and instantly discharge a shriek, or a yell, or a howl which bursts the listening ear and surprises the owner of it into saying words which would not go well with a halo if he had one. The baby Tom would claw anybody who came within reach of his nails, and pound anybody he could reach with his rattle. He would scream for water until he got it, and then throw cup and all on the floor and scream for more. He was indulged in all his caprices, howsoever troublesome and exasperating they might be; he was allowed to eat anything he wanted, particularly things that would give him the stomachache.

When he got to be old enough to begin to toddle about and say broken words and get an idea of what his hands were for, he was a more consummate pest than ever. Roxy got no rest while he was awake. He would call for anything and everything he saw, simply saying, 'Awnt it!' (want it), which was a command. When it was brought, he said in a frenzy, and motioning it away with his hands, 'Don't awnt it! don't awnt it!' and the moment it was gone he set up frantic yells of 'Awnt it! awnt it! awnt it!' and Roxy had to give wings to her heels to get that thing back to him again before he could get time to carry out his intention of going into convulsions about it.

What he preferred above all other things was the tongs. This was because his 'father' had forbidden him to have them lest he break windows and furniture with them. The moment Roxy's back was turned he would toddle to the presence of the tongs and say, 'Like it!' and cock his eye to one side to see if Roxy was observing; then, 'Awnt it!' and cock his eye again; then, 'Hab it!' with another furtive glance; and finally, 'Take it!' – and the prize was his. The next moment the heavy implement was raised aloft; the next, there was a crash and a squall, and the cat was off on three legs to meet an engagement; Roxy would arrive just as the lamp or a window went to irremediable smash.

Tom got all the petting, Chambers got none. Tom got all the delicacies, Chambers got mush and milk, and clabber[2] without sugar. In consequence Tom was a sickly child and Chambers wasn't. Tom was 'fractious', as Roxy called it, and overbearing; Chambers was meek and docile.

With all her splendid common sense and practical everyday ability, Roxy was a doting fool of a mother. She was this toward her child – and she was also more than this: by the fiction created by herself, he was become her master; the necessity of recognising this relation outwardly and of perfecting herself in the forms required to express the recognition, had moved her to such diligence and faithfulness in practising these forms that this exercise soon concreted itself into habit; it became automatic and unconscious; then a natural result followed: deceptions intended solely for others gradually grew practically into self-deceptions as well; the mock reverence became real reverence, the mock obsequiousness real obsequiousness, the mock homage real homage; the little counterfeit rift of separation between imitation-slave and imitation-master widened and widened, and became an abyss, and a very real one – and on one side of it stood Roxy, the dupe of her own deceptions, and on the other stood her child, no longer a usurper to her, but her accepted and recognized master. He was her darling, her master, and her deity all in one, and in her worship of him she forgot who she was and what he had been.

In babyhood Tom cuffed and banged and scratched Chambers unrebuked, and Chambers early learned that between meekly bearing it and resenting it, the advantage all lay with the former policy. The few times that his persecutions had moved him beyond control and made him fight back had cost him very dear at head-quarters; not at the hands of Roxy, for if she ever went beyond scolding him sharply for 'forgitt'n' who his young marster was', she at least never extended her punishment beyond a box on the ear. No, Percy Driscoll was the person. He told Chambers that under no provocation whatever was he privileged to lift his hand against his little master. Chambers overstepped the line three times, and got three such convincing canings from the man who was his father and didn't know it, that he took Tom's cruelties in all humility after that, and made no more experiments.

Outside of the house the two boys were together all through their boyhood. Chambers was strong beyond his years, and a good fighter; strong because he was coarsely fed and hard worked about the house, and a good fighter because Tom furnished him plenty of practice – on white boys whom he hated and was afraid of. Chambers was his constant bodyguard, to and from school; he was present on the playground at recess to protect his charge. He fought himself into such a formidable reputation, by-and-by, that Tom could have changed clothes with him, and 'ridden in peace', like Sir Kay in Launcelot's armour.

He was good at games of skill, too. Tom staked him with marbles to play 'keeps' with, and then took all the winnings away from him. In the winter season Chambers was on hand, in Tom's worn-out clothes, with 'holy' red mittens, and 'holy' shoes, and pants 'holy' at the knees and seat, to drag a sled up the hill for Tom, warmly clad, to ride down on; but he never got a ride himself. He built snowmen and snow fortifications under Tom's directions. He was Tom's patient target when Tom wanted to do some snowballing, but the target couldn't fire back. Chambers carried Tom's skates to the river and strapped them on him, then trotted around after him on the ice, so as to be on hand when wanted; but he wasn't ever asked to try the skates himself.

In summer the pet pastime of the boys of Dawson's Landing was to steal apples, peaches, and melons from the farmers' fruit-waggons – mainly on account of the risk they ran of getting their heads laid open with the butt of the farmer's whip. Tom was a distinguished adept at these thefts – by proxy. Chambers did his stealing, and got the peach-stones, apple-cores, and melon-rinds for his share.

Tom always made Chambers go in swimming with him, and stay by him as a protection. When Tom had had enough, he would slip out and tie knots in Chambers's shirt, dip the knots in the water to make them hard to undo, then dress himself and sit by and laugh while the naked shiverer tugged at the stubborn knots with his teeth.

Tom did his humble comrade these various ill turns partly out of native viciousness, and partly because he hated him for his superiorities of physique and pluck, and for his manifold cleverness. Tom couldn't dive, for it gave him splitting headaches. Chambers could dive without inconvenience, and was fond of doing it. He excited so much admiration, one day, among a crowd of white boys, by throwing back somersaults from the stern of a canoe, that it wearied Tom's spirit, and at last he shoved the canoe underneath Chambers while he was in the air – so he came down on his head in the canoe-bottom; and while he lay unconscious, several of Tom's ancient adversaries saw that their long-desired opportunity was come, and they gave the false heir such a drubbing that with Chambers's best help he was hardly able to drag himself home afterward.

When the boys were fifteen and upward, Tom was 'showing off' in the river one day, when he was taken with a cramp, and shouted for help. It was a common trick with the boys – particularly if a stranger was present – to pretend a cramp and howl for help; then when the stranger came tearing hand over hand to the rescue, the howler would go on struggling and howling till he was close at hand, then replace the howl with a sarcastic smile and swim blandly away, while the town boys assailed the dupe with a volley of jeers and laughter. Tom had never tried this joke as yet, but was supposed to be trying it now, so the boys held warily back; but Chambers believed his master was in earnest, therefore he swam out, and arrived in time, unfortunately, and saved his life.

This was the last feather. Tom had managed to endure everything else, but to have to remain publicly and permanently under such an obligation as this to a nigger, and to this nigger of all niggers – this was too much. He heaped insults upon Chambers for 'pretending' to think he was in earnest in calling for help, and said that anybody but a blockheaded nigger would have known he was funning and left him alone.

Tom's enemies were in strong force here, so they came out with their opinions quite freely. They laughed at him, and called him coward, liar, sneak, and other sorts of pet names, and told him they meant to call Chambers by a new name after this, and make it common in the town – 'Tom Driscoll's niggerpappy,' – to signify that he had had a second birth into this life, and that Chambers was the author of his new being. Tom grew frantic under these taunts, and shouted:

'Knock their heads off, Chambers! knock their heads off! What do you stand there with your hands in your pockets for?'

Chambers expostulated, and said: 'But, Marse Tom, dey's too many of 'em – dey's –'

'Do you hear me?'

'Please, Marse Tom, don't make me! Dey's so many of 'em dat –'

Tom sprang at him and drove his pocket-knife into him two or three times before the boys could snatch him away and give the wounded lad a chance to escape. He was considerably hurt, but not seriously. If the blade had been a little longer his career would have ended there.

Tom had long ago taught Roxy 'her place'. It had been many a day now since she had ventured a caress or a fondling epithet in his quarter. Such things, from a 'nigger', were repulsive to him, and she had been warned to keep her distance and remember who she was. She saw her darling gradually cease from being her son, she saw *that* detail perish utterly; all that was left was master – master, pure and simple, and it was not a gentle mastership either. She saw herself sink from the sublime height of motherhood to the sombre deeps of unmodified slavery. The abyss of separation between her and her boy was complete. She was merely his chattel, now, his convenience, his dog, his cringing and helpless slave, the humble and unresisting victim of his capricious temper and vicious nature.

Sometimes she could not go to sleep, even when worn out with fatigue, because her rage boiled so high over the day's experiences with her boy. She would mumble and mutter to herself:

'He struck me, en I warn't no way to blame – struck me in de face, right before folks. En he's al'ays callin' me nigger-wench, en hussy, en all dem mean names, when I's doin' de very bes' I kin. Oh, Lord, I done so much for him – I lift' him away up to what he is – en dis is what I git for it.'

Sometimes when some outrage of peculiar offensiveness stung her to the heart, she would plan schemes of vengeance and revel in the fancied spectacle of his exposure to the world as an impostor and a slave; but in the midst of these joys fear would strike her: she had made him too strong; she could prove nothing, and – heavens, she might get sold down the river for her pains! So her schemes always went for nothing, and she laid them aside in impotent rage against the fates, and against herself for playing the fool on that fatal September day in not providing herself with a witness for use in the day when such a thing might be needed for the appeasing of her vengeance-hungry heart.

And yet the moment Tom happened to be good to her, and kind — and this occurred every now and then — all her sore places were healed, and she was happy; happy and proud, for this was her son, her nigger son, lording it among the whites and securely avenging their crimes against her race.

There were two grand funerals in Dawson's Landing that fall — the fall of 1845. One was that of Colonel Cecil Burleigh Essex, the other that of Percy Driscoll.

On his death-bed Driscoll set Roxy free [2] and delivered his idolised ostensible son solemnly into the keeping of his brother the Judge and his wife. Those childless people were glad to get him. Childless people are not difficult to please.

Judge Driscoll had gone privately to his brother, a month before, and bought Chambers. He had heard that Tom had been trying to get his father to sell the boy down the river, and he wanted to prevent the scandal — for public sentiment did not approve of that way of treating family servants for light cause or for no cause.

Percy Driscoll had worn himself out in trying to save his great speculative landed estate, and had died without succeeding. He was hardly in his grave before the boom collapsed and left his hitherto envied young devil of an heir a pauper. But that was nothing; his uncle told him he should be his heir and have all his fortune when he died; so Tom was comforted.

Roxy had no home now; so she resolved to go around and say good-bye to her friends and then clear out and see the world — that is to say, she would go chambermaiding on a steamboat, the darling ambition of her race and sex.

Her last call was on the black giant, Jasper. She found him chopping Pudd'nhead Wilson's winter provision of wood.

Wilson was chatting with him when Roxy arrived. He asked her how she could bear to go off chambermaiding and leave her boys; and chaffingly offered to copy off a series of their finger-prints, reaching up to their twelfth year, for her to remember them by; but she sobered in a moment, wondering if he suspected anything; then she said she believed she didn't want them. Wilson said to himself, 'The drop of black blood in her is superstitious; she thinks there's some devilry, some witch-business about my glass mystery somewhere; she used to come here with an old horseshoe in her hand; it could have been an accident, but I doubt it.'

CHAPTER 5

Training is everything. The peach was once a bitter almond; cauliflower is nothing but cabbage with a college education. – Pudd'nhead Wilson's Calendar

Remark of Dr Baldwin's, concerning upstarts: We don't care to eat toadstools that think they are truffles. – Pudd'nhead Wilson's Calendar

MRS YORK DRISCOLL enjoyed two years of bliss with that prize, Tom – bliss that was troubled a little at times, it is true, but bliss nevertheless; then she died, and her husband and his childless sister, Mrs Pratt, continued the bliss-business at the old stand. Tom was petted and indulged and spoiled to his entire content – or nearly that. This went on till he was nineteen, then he was sent to Yale. He went handsomely equipped with 'conditions',[1] but otherwise he was not an object of distinction there. He remained at Yale two years, and then threw up the struggle. He came home with his manners a good deal improved; he had lost his surliness and brusqueness, and was rather pleasantly soft and smooth now; he was furtively, and sometimes openly, ironical of speech, and given to gently touching people on the raw, but he did it with a good-natured semiconscious air that carried it off safely, and kept him from getting into trouble. He was as indolent as ever and showed no very strenuous desire to hunt up an occupation. People argued from this that he preferred to be supported by his uncle until his uncle's shoes should become vacant. He brought back one or two new habits with him, one of which he rather openly practised – tippling – but concealed another, which was gambling. It would not do to gamble where his uncle could hear of it; he knew that quite well.

Tom's Eastern polish was not popular among the young people. They could have endured it, perhaps, if Tom had stopped there; but he wore gloves, and that they couldn't stand, and wouldn't; so he was mainly without society. He brought home with him a suit of clothes of such exquisite style and cut and fashion – Eastern fashion, city fashion – that it filled everybody with anguish and was regarded as a peculiarly wanton affront. He enjoyed the feeling which he was exciting, and paraded the town serene and happy all day; but the young fellows set a tailor to work that night, and when Tom started out on his parade next morning he found the old deformed negro bell-ringer straddling along in his wake tricked out in a flamboyant curtain-calico exaggeration of his finery, and imitating his fancy Eastern graces as well as he could.

Tom surrendered, and after that clothed himself in the local fashion. But the dull country town was tiresome to him, since his acquaintanceship with livelier regions, and it grew daily more and more so. He began to make little trips to St Louis for refreshment. There he found companionship to suit him, and pleasures to his taste, along with more freedom, in some particulars, than he could have at home. So during the next two years his visits to the city grew in frequency and his tarryings there grew steadily longer in duration.

He was getting into deep waters. He was taking chances, privately, which might get him into trouble some day – in fact, *did*.

Judge Driscoll had retired from the bench and from all business activities in 1850, and had now been comfortably idle three years. He was President of the Freethinkers' Society, and Pudd'nhead Wilson was the other member.

The society's weekly discussions were now the old lawyer's main interest in life. Pudd'nhead was still toiling in obscurity at the bottom of the ladder, under the blight of that unlucky remark which he had let fall twenty-three years before about the dog.

Judge Driscoll was his friend, and claimed that he had a mind above the average, but that was regarded as one of the Judge's whims, and it failed to modify the public opinion. Or rather, that was one of the reasons why it failed, but there was another and better one. If the Judge had stopped with bare assertion, it would have had a good deal of effect; but he made the mistake of trying to prove his position. For some years Wilson had been privately at work on a whimsical almanac, for his amusement – a calendar, with a little dab of ostensible philosophy, usually in ironical form, appended to each date; and the Judge thought that these quips and fancies of Wilson's were neatly turned and cute; so he carried a handful of them around, one day, and read them to some of the chief citizens. But irony was not for those people; their mental vision was not focused for it. They read those playful trifles in the solidest earnest, and decided without hesitancy that if there had ever been any doubt that Dave Wilson was a pudd'nhead – which there hadn't – this revelation removed that doubt for good and all. That is just the way in this world; an enemy can partly ruin a man, but it takes a good-natured injudicious friend to complete the thing and make it perfect. After this the Judge felt tenderer than ever toward Wilson, and surer than ever that his calendar had merit.

Judge Driscoll could be a freethinker and still hold his place in society because he was the person of most consequence in the community, and therefore could venture to go his own way and follow out his own notions. The other member of his pet organization was allowed the like liberty because he was a cipher in the estimation of the public, and nobody attached any importance to what he thought or did. He was liked, he was welcome enough all around, but he simply didn't count for anything.

The widow Cooper – affectionately called 'aunt Patsy' by everybody – lived in a snug and comely cottage with her daughter Rowena, who was nineteen, romantic, amiable, and very pretty, but otherwise of no consequence. Rowena had a couple of young brothers – also of no consequence.

The widow had a large spare room which she let to a lodger, with board, when she could find one, but this room had been empty for a year now, to her sorrow. Her income was only sufficient for the family support, and she needed the lodging-money for trifling luxuries. But now, at last, on a flaming June day, she found herself happy; her tedious wait was ended; her year-worn advertisement had been answered; and not by a village applicant, oh, no! – this letter was from away off yonder in the dim great world to the North : it was from St Louis. She sat on her porch gazing out with unseeing eyes upon the shining reaches of the mighty Mississippi, her thoughts steeped in her good fortune. Indeed it was specially good fortune, for she was to have two lodgers instead of one.

She had read the letter to the family, and Rowena had danced away to see to the cleaning and airing of the room by the slave woman Nancy, and the boys had rushed abroad in the town to spread the great news, for it was a matter of public interest, and the public would wonder and not be pleased if not informed. Presently Rowena returned, all ablush with joyous excitement, and begged for a re-reading of the letter. It was framed thus :

HONOURED MADAM, – My brother and I have seen your advertisement, by chance, and beg leave to take the room you offer.

We are twenty-four years of age and twins. We are Italians by birth, but have lived long in the various countries of Europe, and several years in the United States. Our names are Luigi and Angelo Capello. You desire but one guest; but, dear madam, if you will allow us to pay for two, we will not incommode you. We shall be down Thursday.

'Italians! How romantic! Just think, ma – there's never been one in this town, and everybody will be dying to see them, and they're all *ours*! Think of that!'

'Yes, I reckon they'll make a grand stir.'

'Oh, indeed they will! The whole town will be on its head! Think – they've been in Europe and everywhere! There's never been a traveller in this town before. Ma, I shouldn't wonder if they've seen kings!'

'Well, a body can't tell; but they'll make stir enough, without that.'

'Yes, that's of course. Luigi – Angelo. They're lovely names; and so grand and foreign – not like Jones and Robinson and such. Thursday they are coming, and this is only Tuesday; it's a cruel long time to wait. Here comes Judge Driscoll in at the gate. He's heard about it. I'll go and open the door.'

The Judge was full of congratulations and curiosity. The letter was read and discussed. Soon Justice Robinson arrived with more congratulations, and there was a new reading and a new discussion. This was the beginning. Neighbour after neighbour, of both sexes, followed, and the procession drifted in and out all day and evening and all Wednesday and Thursday. The letter was read and re-read until it was nearly worn out; everybody admired its courtly and gracious tone, and smooth and practised style, everybody was sympathetic and excited, and the Coopers were steeped in happiness all the while.

The boats were very uncertain in low water, in these

primitive times. This time the Thursday boat had not arrived at ten at night – so the people had waited at the landing all day for nothing; they were driven to their homes by a heavy storm without having had a view of the illustrious foreigners.

Eleven o'clock came; and the Cooper house was the only one in the town that still had lights burning. The rain and thunder were booming yet, and the anxious family were still waiting, still hoping. At last there was a knock at the door and the family jumped to open it. Two negro men entered, each carrying a trunk, and proceeded upstairs toward the guest-room. Then entered the twins – the handsomest, the best dressed, the most distinguised-looking pair of young fellows the West had ever seen. One was a little fairer than the other, but otherwise they were exact duplicates.[2]

CHAPTER 6

Let us endeavour so to live that when we come to die
even the undertaker will be sorry. – *Pudd'nhead Wilson's Calendar*

Habit is habit, and not to be flung out of the window
by any man, but coaxed downstairs a step at a time. –
Pudd'nhead Wilson's Calendar

AT breakfast in the morning, the twins' charm of manner
and easy and polished bearing made speedy conquest of the
family's good graces. All constraint and formality quickly
disappeared, and the friendliest feeling succeeded. Aunt
Patsy called them by their Christian names almost from the
beginning. She was full of the keenest curiosity about them,
and showed it; they responded by talking about themselves,
which pleased her greatly. It presently appeared that in their
early youth they had known poverty and hardship. As the
talk wandered along the old lady watched for the right
place to drop in a question or two concerning that matter,
and when she found it she said to the blonde twin, who was
now doing the biographies in his turn while the brunette
one rested:

'If it ain't asking what I ought not to ask, Mr Angelo,
how did you come to be so friendless and in such trouble
when you were little? Do you mind telling? But don't, if
you do.'

'Oh, we don't mind it at all, madam; in our case it was
merely misfortune, and nobody's fault. Our parents were
well to do, there in Italy, and we were their only child. We
were of the old Florentine nobility' – Rowena's heart gave
a great bound, her nostrils expanded, and a fine light played

90

in her eyes – 'and when the war broke out my father was on the losing side and had to fly for his life. His estates were confiscated, his personal property seized, and there we were, in Germany, strangers, friendless, and in fact paupers. My brother and I were ten years old, and well educated for that age, very studious, very fond of our books, and well grounded in the German, French, Spanish, and English languages. Also, we were marvellous musical prodigies – if you will allow me to say it, it being only the truth.

'Our father survived his misfortunes only a month, our mother soon followed him, and we were alone in the world. Our parents could have made themselves comfortable by exhibiting us as a show, and they had many and large offers; but the thought revolted their pride, and they said they would starve and die first. But what they wouldn't consent to do we had to do without the formality of consent. We were seized for the debts occasioned by their illness and their funerals, and placed among the attractions of a cheap museum in Berlin to earn the liquidation money. It took us two years to get out of that slavery. We travelled all about Germany, receiving no wages, and not even our keep. We had to be exhibited for nothing, and beg our bread.

'Well, madam, the rest is not of much consequence. When we escaped from that slavery at twelve years of age, we were in some respects men. Experience had taught us some valuable things; among others, how to take care of ourselves, how to avoid and defeat sharks and sharpers, and how to conduct our own business for our own profit and without other people's help. We travelled everywhere – years and years – picking up smatterings of strange tongues, familiarising ourselves with strange sights and strange customs, accumulating an education of a wide and varied and curious sort. It was a pleasant life. We went to Venice – to London, Paris, Russia, India, China, Japan –'

At this point Nancy the slave woman thrust her head in at the door and exclaimed:

'Ole Missus, de house is plum' jam full o' people, en dey's jes a-spi'lin' to see de gen'lmen!' She indicated the twins with a nod of her head, and tucked it back out of sight again.

It was a proud occasion for the widow, and she promised herself high satisfaction in showing off her fine foreign birds before her neighbours and friends – simple folk who had hardly ever seen a foreigner of any kind, and never one of any distinction or style. Yet her feeling was moderate indeed when contrasted with Rowena's. Rowena was in the clouds, she walked on air; this was to be the greatest day, the most romantic episode, in the colourless history of that dull country town. She was to be familiarly near the source of its glory and feel the full flood of it pour over her and about her; the other girls could only gaze and envy, not partake.

The widow was ready, Rowena was ready, so also were the foreigners.

The party moved along the hall, the twins in advance, and entered the open parlour door, whence issued a low hum of conversation. The twins took a position near the door, the widow stood at Luigi's side, Rowena stood beside Angelo, and the march-past and the introductions began. The widow was all smiles and contentment. She received the procession and passed it on to Rowena.

'Good mornin', Sister Cooper' – hand-shake.

'Good morning, Brother Higgins – Count Luigi Capello, Mr Higgins' – hand-shake, followed by a devouring stare and 'I'm glad to seé ye,' on the part of Higgins, and a courteous inclination of the head and a pleasant 'Most happy!' on the part of Count Luigi.

'Good mornin', Roweny' – hand-shake.

'Good morning, Mr Higgins – present you to Count Angelo Capello.' Hand-shake, admiring stare, 'Glad to see ye,' – courteous nod, smily 'Most happy!' and Higgins passes on.

None of these visitors was at ease, but, being honest people, they didn't pretend to be. None of them had ever seen a person bearing a title of nobility before, and none had been expecting to see one now, consequently the title came upon them as a kind of pile-driving surprise, and caught them unprepared. A few tried to rise to the emergency, and got out an awkward 'My lord', or 'Your lordship', or something of that sort, but the great majority were overwhelmed by the unaccustomed word and its dim and awful associations with gilded courts and stately ceremony and anointed kingship, so they only fumbled through the hand-shake and passed on, speechless. Now and then, as happens at all receptions everywhere, a more than ordinarily friendly soul blocked the procession and kept it waiting while he inquired how the brothers liked the village, and how long they were going to stay, and if their families were well, and dragged in the weather, and hoped it would get cooler soon, and all that sort of thing, so as to be able to say, when they got home, 'I had quite a long talk with them;' but nobody did or said anything of a regrettable kind, and so the great affair went through to the end in a creditable and satisfactory fashion.

General conversation followed, and the twins drifted about from group to group, talking easily and fluently and winning approval, compelling admiration and achieving favour from all. The widow followed their conquering march with a proud eye, and every now and then Rowena said to herself with deep satisfaction, 'And to think they are ours – all ours!'

There were no idle moments for mother or daughter.

Eager inquiries concerning the twins were pouring into their enchanted ears all the time; each was the constant centre of a group of breathless listeners; each recognized that she knew now for the first time the real meaning of that great word Glory, and perceived the stupendous value of it, and understood why men in all ages had been willing to throw away meaner happinesses, treasure, life itself, to get a taste of its sublime and supreme joy. Napoleon and all his kind stood accounted for – and justified.

When Rowena had at last done all her duty by the people in the parlour, she went upstairs to satisfy the longings of an over-flow meeting there, for the parlour was not big enough to hold all the comers. Again she was besieged by eager questioners, and again she swam in sunset seas of glory. When the forenoon was nearly gone, she recognized with a pang that this most splendid episode of her life was almost over, that nothing could prolong it, that nothing quite its equal could ever fall to her fortune again. But never mind, it was sufficient unto itself; the grand occasion had moved on an ascending scale from the start, and was a noble and memorable success. If the twins could but do some crowning act, now, to climax it, something unusual, something startling, something to concentrate upon themselves the company's loftiest admiration, something in the nature of an electric surprise –

Here a prodigious slam-banging broke out below, and everybody rushed down to see. It was the twins knocking out a classic four-handed piece on the piano in great style. Rowena was satisfied – satisfied down to the bottom of her heart.

The young strangers were kept long at the piano. The villagers were astonished and enchanted with the magnificence of their performance, and could not bear to have them stop. All the music that they had ever heard before

seemed spiritless prentice-work and barren of grace or charm
when compared with these intoxicating floods of melodious
sound. They realised that for once in their lives they were
hearing masters.

CHAPTER 7

One of the most striking differences between a cat and
a lie is that a cat has only nine lives. — *Pudd'nhead
Wilson's Calendar*

THE company broke up reluctantly, and drifted toward
their several homes, chatting with vivacity, and all agreeing
that it would be many a long day before Dawson's Landing
would see the equal of this one again. The twins had
accepted several invitations while the reception was in progress, and had also volunteered to play some duets at an
amateur entertainment for the benefit of a local charity.
Society was eager to receive them to its bosom. Judge Driscoll had the good fortune to secure them for an immediate
drive, and to be the first to display them in public. They
entered his buggy with him, and were paraded down the
main street, everybody flocking to the windows and sidewalks to see.

The Judge showed the strangers the new graveyard, and
the gaol, and where the richest man lived, and the Free-
masons' Hall, and the Methodist Church, and the Presbyterian Church, and where the Baptist Church was going
to be when they got some money to build it with, and
showed them the town hall and the slaughter-house, and
got out the independent fire company in uniform and had
them put out an imaginary fire; then he let them inspect the
muskets of the militia company, and poured out an exhaust-
less stream of enthusiasm over all these splendours, and
seemed very well satisfied with the responses he got, for the
twins admired his admiration, and paid him back the best
they could, though they could have done better if some fif-

teen or sixteen hundred thousand previous experiences of this sort in various countries had not already rubbed off a considerable part of the novelty of it.

The Judge laid himself out hospitably to make them have a good time, and if there was a defect anywhere it was not his fault. He told them a good many humorous anecdotes, and always forgot the nub, but they were always able to furnish it, for these yarns were of a pretty early vintage, and they had had many a rejuvenating pull at them before. And he told them all about his several dignities, and how he had held this and that and the other place of honour or profit, and had once been to the legislature, and was now president of the Society of Freethinkers. He said the society had been in existence four years, and already had two members, and was firmly established. He would call for the brothers in the evening if they would like to attend a meeting of it.

Accordingly he called for them, and on the way he told them all about Pudd'nhead Wilson, in order that they might get a favourable impression of him in advance, and be prepared to like him. This scheme succeeded – the favourable impression was achieved. Later it was confirmed and solidified when Wilson proposed that out of courtesy to the strangers the usual topics be put aside and the hour be devoted to conversation upon ordinary subjects and the cultivation of friendly relations and good-fellowship – a proposition which was put to vote and carried.

The hour passed quickly away in lively talk, and when it was ended the lonesome and neglected Wilson was richer by two friends than he had been when it began. He invited the twins to look in at his lodgings, presently, after disposing of an intervening engagement, and they accepted with pleasure.

Toward the middle of the evening they found themselves on the road to his house. Pudd'nhead was at home waiting for them, and putting in his time puzzling over a thing which had come under his notice that morning. The matter was this: He happened to be up very early – at dawn in fact; and he crossed the hall, which divided his cottage through the centre, and entered a room to get something there. The window of the room had no curtains, for that side of the house had long been unoccupied, and through this window he caught sight of something which surprised and interested him. It was a young woman – a young woman where properly no young woman belonged; for she was in Judge Driscoll's house, and in the bedroom over the Judge's private study or sitting-room. This was young Tom Driscoll's bedroom. He and the Judge, the Judge's widowed sister Mrs Pratt, and three negro servants were the only people who belonged in the house. Who, then, might this young lady be? The two houses were separated by an ordinary yard, with a low fence running back through its middle from the street in front to the lane in the rear. The distance was not great, and Wilson was able to see the girl very well, the window-shades of the room she was in being up, and the window also. The girl had on a neat and trim summer dress, patterned in broad stripes of pink and white, and her bonnet was equipped with a pink veil. She was practising steps, gaits, and attitudes, apparently; she was doing the thing gracefully, and was very much absorbed in her work. Who could she be, and how came she to be in young Tom Driscoll's room?

Wilson had quickly chosen a position from which he could watch the girl without running much risk of being seen by her, and he remained there hoping she would raise her veil and betray her face. But she disappointed him. After a matter of twenty minutes she disappeared, and although he stayed at his post half an hour longer, she came no more.

Toward noon he dropped in at the Judge's, and talked with Mrs Pratt about the great event of the day, the levee of the distinguished foreigners at Aunt Patsy Cooper's. He asked after her nephew Tom, and she said he was on his way home, and that she was expecting him to arrive a little before night; and added that she and the Judge were gratified to gather from his letters that he was conducting himself very nicely and creditably – at which Wilson winked to himself privately. Wilson did not ask if there was a newcomer in the house, but he asked questions that would have brought light-throwing answers as to that matter if Mrs Pratt had had any light to throw; so he went away satisfied that he knew of things that were going on in her house of which she herself was not aware.

He was now waiting for the twins, and still puzzling over the problem of who that girl might be, and how she happened to be in that young fellow's room at daybreak in the morning.

CHAPTER 8

The holy passion of Friendship is of so sweet and steady
and loyal and enduring a nature that it will last through
a whole lifetime, if not asked to lend money. –
Pudd'nhead Wilson's Calendar

Consider well the proportions of things. It is better to
be a young June-bug than an old bird of paradise. –
Pudd'nhead Wilson's Calendar

I T is necessary now to hunt up Roxy.

At the time she was set free and went away chamber-maiding, she was thirty-five. She got a berth as second chambermaid on a Cincinnati boat in the New Orleans trade, the *Grand Mogul*. A couple of trips made her wonted and easy-going at the work, and infatuated her with the stir and adventure and independence of steamboat life. Then she was promoted and become head chambermaid. She was a favourite with the officers, and exceedingly proud of their joking and friendly ways with her.

During eight years she served three parts of the year on that boat, and the winters on a Vicksburg packet. But now for two months she had had rheumatism in her arms, and was obliged to let the wash-tub alone. So she resigned. But she was well fixed – rich, as she would have described it; for she had lived a steady life, and had banked four dollars every month in New Orleans as a provision for her old age. She said in the start that she had 'put shoes on one bar'footed nigger to tromple on her with', and that one mistake like that was enough; she would be independent of the human race thenceforth for evermore if hard work and economy could accomplish it. When the boat touched the levee at New Orleans she bade good-bye to her comrades on the *Grand Mogul* and moved her kit ashore.

But she was back in an hour. The bank had gone to smash and carried her four hundred dollars with it. She was a pauper, and homeless. Also disabled bodily, at least for the present. The officers were full of sympathy for her in her trouble, and made up a little purse for her. She resolved to go to her birthplace; she had friends there among the negroes, and the unfortunate always help the unfortunate, she was well aware of that; those lowly comrades of her youth would not let her starve.

She took the little local packet at Cairo, and now she was on the home-stretch. Time had worn away her bitterness against her son, and she was able to think of him with seren-ity. She put the vile side of him out of her mind, and dwelt only on recollections of his occasional acts of kindness to her. She gilded and otherwise decorated these, and made them very pleasant to contemplate. She began to long to see him. She would go and fawn upon him, slave-like[1] - for this would have to be her attitude, of course - and maybe she would find that time had modified him, and that he would be glad to see his long-forgotten old nurse and treat her gently. That would be lovely; that would make her forget her woes and her poverty.

Her poverty! That thought inspired her to add another castle to her dream: maybe he would give her a trifle now and then - maybe a dollar, once a month, say; any little thing like that would help, oh, ever so much.

By the time she reached Dawson's Landing she was her old self again; her blues were gone, she was in high feather. She would get along, surely; there were many kitchens where the servants would share their meals with her, and also steal sugar and apples and other dainties for her to carry home - or give her a chance to pilfer them herself, which would

answer just as well. And there was the church. She was a
more rabid and devoted Methodist than ever, and her piety
was no sham, but was strong and sincere. Yes, with plenty
of creature comforts and her old place in the amen corner in
her possession again, she would be perfectly happy and at
peace thenceforward to the end.

She went to Judge Driscoll's kitchen first of all. She was
received there in great form and with vast enthusiasm. Her
wonderful travels, and the strange countries she had seen
and the adventures she had had, made her a marvel, and a
heroine of romance. The negroes hung enchanted upon the
great story of her experiences, interrupting her all along
with eager questions, with laughter, exclamations of delight
and expressions of applause; and she was obliged to confess
to herself that if there was anything better in this world
than steamboating, it was the glory to be got by telling
about it. The audience loaded her stomach with their din-
ners and then stole the pantry bare to load up her basket.

Tom was in St Louis. The servants said he had spent
the best part of his time there during the previous two years.
Roxy came every day, and had many talks about the family
and its affairs. Once she asked why Tom was away so much.
The ostensible 'Chambers' said:

'De fac' is, ole marster kin git along better when young
marster's away den he kin when he's in de town; yes, en
he love him better, too; so he gives him fifty dollahs a
month —'

'No, is dat so? Chambers, you's a-jokin', ain't you?'

' 'Clah to goodness I ain't, mammy; Marse Tom tole me
so his own self. But nemmine, 't ain't enough.'

'My lan', what de reason 't ain't enough?'

'Well, I 's gwine to tell you, if you gimme a chanst,
mammy. De reason it ain't enough is 'ca'se Marse Tom
gambles.'

Roxy threw up her hands in astonishment, and Chambers
went on:

'Ole marster found it out, 'ca'se he had to pay two hundred dollahs for Marse Tom's gamblin' debts, en dat's true,
mammy, jes as dead certain as you's bawn.'

'Two – hund'd – dollahs! Why, what is you talkin' 'bout?
Two – hund'd – dollahs. Sakes alive, it's 'mos' enough
to buy a tol'able good secondhand nigger wid. En you ain't
lyin', honey? – you wouldn't lie to yo' ole mammy?'

'It's God's own truth, jes as I tell you – two hund'd dollahs – I wisht I may never stir outen my tracks if it ain't
so. En, oh, my lan', ole Marse was jes a-hoppin'! he was
b'ilin' mad, I tell you! He tuck 'n' dissenhurrit him.'

He licked his chops with relish after that stately word.
Roxy struggled with it a moment, then gave it up and
said:

'Dissen*whiched* him?'

'Dissenhurrit him.'

'What's dat? What do it mean?'

'Means he bu'sted de will.'

'Bu's—ted de will! He wouldn't *ever* treat him so! Take
it back, you mis'able imitation nigger dat I bore in sorrow
en tribbilation.'

Roxy's pet castle – an occasional dollar from Tom's pocket
– was tumbling to ruin before her eyes. She could not
abide such a disaster as that; she couldn't endure the
thought of it. Her remark amused Chambers:

'Yah-yah-yah! Jes listen to dat! If I's imitation, what is
you? Bofe of us is imitation *white* – dat's what we is – en
pow'ful good imitation too – yah-yah-yah! – we don't
'mount to noth'n' as imitation *niggers*; en as for –'

'Shet up yo' foolin', 'fo' I knock you side de head, en
tell me 'bout de will. Tell me 'tain't bu'sted – do, honey, en
I'll never forget you.'

'Well, *'taint* – 'ca'se dey's a new one made, en Marse Toms' all right ag'in. But what is you in sich a sweat 'bout it for, mammy? 'Tain't none o' your business I don't reckon.'

' 'Tain't none o' my business? Whose business is it den, I'd like to know? Wuz I his mother tell he was fifteen years old, or wusn't I? – you answer me dat. En you speck I could see him turned out po' en ornery on de worl' en never care noth'n' 'bout it? I reckon if you'd ever be'n a mother yo'self, Valet de Chambers, you wouldn't talk sich foolishness as dat.'

'Well, den, ole Marse forgive him en fixed up de will ag'in – do dat satisfy you?'

Yes, she was satisfied now, and quite happy and sentimental over it. She kept coming daily, and at last she was told that Tom had come home. She began to tremble with emotion, and straightway sent to beg him to let his 'po' ole nigger mammy have jes one sight of him en die for joy.'

Tom was stretched at his lazy ease on a sofa when Chambers brought the petition. Time had not modified his ancient detestation of the humble drudge and protector of his boyhood; it was still bitter and uncompromising. He sat up and bent a severe gaze upon the fair face of the young fellow whose name he was unconsciously using and whose family rights he was enjoying. He maintained the gaze until the victim of it had become satisfactorily pallid with terror, then he said:

'What does the old rip want with me?'

The petition was meekly repeated.

'Who gave you permission to come and disturb me with the social attentions of niggers?'

Tom had risen. The other young man was trembling now, visibly. He saw what was coming, and bent his head sideways, and put up his left arm to shield it. Tom rained cuffs upon the head and its shield, saying no word: the victim received each blow with a beseeching, 'Please, Marse Tom! – oh, please, Marse Tom!' Seven blows – then Tom said, 'Face the door – march!' He followed behind with one, two, three solid kicks. The last one helped the pure-white slave over the door sill, and he limped away mopping his eyes with his old ragged sleeve. Tom shouted after him, 'Send her in!'

Then he flung himself panting on the sofa again, and rasped out the remark, 'He arrived just at the right moment; I was full to the brim with bitter thinkings, and nobody to take it out of. How refreshing it was! I feel better.'

Tom's mother entered now, closing the door behind her, and approached her son with all the wheedling and suppli-cating servilities that fear and interest can impart to the words and attitudes of the born slave. She stopped a yard from her boy and made two or three admiring exclamations over his manly stature and general handsomeness, and Tom put an arm under his head and hoisted a leg over the sofa-back in order to look properly indifferent.

'My lan', how you is growed, honey! 'Clah to goodness, I wouldn't a-knowed you, Marse Tom! 'deed I wouldn't! Look at me good; does you 'member old Roxy? – does you know yo' old nigger mammy, honey? Well now, I kin lay down en die in peace, 'ca'se I'se seed –'

'Cut it short, — it, cut it short! What is it you want?'

'You heah dat? Jes de same old Marse Tom, al'ays so gay and funnin' wid de ole mammy. I 'uz jes as shore –'

'Cut it short, I tell you, and get along! What do you want?'

This was a bitter disappointment. Roxy had for so many days nourished and fondled and petted her notion that Tom would be glad to see his old nurse, and would make her proud and happy to the marrow with a cordial word or two, that it took two rebuffs to convince her that he was not funning, and that her beautiful dream was a fond and foolish vanity, a shabby and pitiful mistake. She was hurt to the heart, and so ashamed that for a moment she did not quite know what to do or how to act. Then her breast began to heave, the tears came, and in her forlornness she was moved to try that other dream of hers – an appeal to her boy's charity; and so, upon the impulse, and without reflection, she offered her supplication:

'Oh, Marse Tom, de po' ole mammy is in sich hard luck dese days; en she's kinder crippled in de arms en can't work, en if you could gimme a dollah – on'y jes one little dol –'

Tom was on his feet so suddenly that the supplicant was startled into a jump herself.

'A dollar! – give you a dollar! I've a notion to strangle you! Is *that* your errand here? Clear out! and be quick about it!'

Roxy backed slowly toward the door. When she was half-way she stopped, and said mournfully:

'Marse Tom, I nussed you when you was a little baby, en I raised you all by myself tell you was 'most a young man; en now you is young en rich, en I is po' en gitt'n' ole, en I come heah b'lievin' dat you would he'p de ole mammy 'long down de little road dat's lef' 'twix' her en de grave, en –'

Tom relished this tune less than any that had preceded it, for it began to wake up a sort of echo in his conscience; so he interrupted and said with decision, though without asperity, that he was not in a situation to help her, and wasn't going to do it.

'Ain't you ever gwine to he'p me, Marse Tom?'

'No! Now go away and don't bother me any more.'

Roxy's head was down, in an attitude of humility. But now the fires of her old wrongs flamed up in her breast and began to burn fiercely. She raised her head slowly, till it was well up, and at the same time her great frame unconsciously assumed an erect and masterful attitude, with all the majesty and grace of her vanished youth in it. She raised her finger and punctuated with it.

'You has said de word. You has had yo' chance, en you has trompled it under yo' foot. When you git another one, you'll git down on yo' knees en *beg* for it!'

A cold chill went to Tom's heart, he didn't know why; for he did not reflect that such words, from such an incongruous source, and so solemnly delivered, could not easily fail of that effect. However, he did the natural thing: he replied with bluster and mockery:

'*You'll* give me a chance — *you!* Perhaps I'd better get down on my knees now! But in case I don't — just for argument's sake — what's going to happen, pray?'

'Dis is what is gwine to happen. I's gwine as straight to yo' uncle as I kin walk, en tell him every las' thing I knows 'bout you.'

Tom's cheek blenched, and she saw it. Disturbing thoughts began to chase each other through his head. 'How can she know? And yet she must have found out — she looks it. I've had the will back only three months, and am already deep in debt again, and moving heaven and earth to save myself from exposure and destruction, with a reasonably fair show of getting the thing covered up if I'm let alone, and now this fiend has gone and found me out somehow or other. I wonder how much she knows? Oh, oh, oh, it's enough to break a body's heart! But I've got to humour her — there's no other way.'

Then he worked up a rather sickly sample of a gay laugh and a hollow chipperness of manner, and said:

'Well, well, Roxy dear, old friends like you and me mustn't quarrel. Here's your dollar – now tell me what you know.'

He held out the wild-cat bill; she stood as she was, and made no movement. It was her turn to scorn persuasive foolery now, and she did not waste it. She said, with a grim implacability in voice and manner which made Tom almost realise that even a former slave can remember for ten minutes insults and injuries returned for compliments and flatteries received, and can also enjoy taking revenge for them when the opportunity offers.

'What does I know? I'll tell you what I knows. I knows enough to bu'st dat will to flinders – en more, mind you, *more!*'

Tom was aghast.

'More?' he said. 'What do you call more? Where's there any room for more?'

Roxy laughed a mocking laugh, and said scoffingly, with a toss of her head, and her hands on her hips:

'Yes! – oh, I reckon! *Co'se* you'd like to know – wid yo' po' little ole rag dollah. What you reckon I'se gwine to tell *you* for? – you ain't got no money. I'se gwine to tell yo' uncle – en I'll do it dis minute, too – he'll gimme *five* dollahs for de news, en mighty glad, too.'

She swung herself around disdainfully, and started away. Tom was in a panic. He seized her skirts, and implored her to wait. She turned and said, loftily:

'Look-a-heah, what 'uz it I tole you?'

'You – you – I don't remember anything. What was it you told me?'

'I tole you dat de next time I give you a chance you'd git down on yo' knees en beg for it.'

Tom was stupefied for a moment. He was panting with excitement. Then he said:

'Oh, Roxy, you wouldn't require your young master to do such a horrible thing. You can't mean it.'

'I'll let you know mighty quick whether I means it or not! You call me names, en as good as spit on me when I comes here, po' en ornery en 'umble, to praise you for bein' growed up so fine en handsome, en tell you how I used to nuss you en tend you en watch you when you 'uz sick en hadn't no mother but me in de whole worl', en beg you to give de po' ole nigger a dollah for to git her sum'n' to eat, en you call me names – *names*, dad blame you! Yassir, I gives you jes one chance mo', and dat's *now*, en it las' on'y a half second – you hear?'

Tom slumped to his knees and began to beg, saying:

'You see I'm begging, and it's honest begging, too! Now tell me, Roxy, tell me.'

The heir of two centuries of unatoned insult and outrage looked down on him and seemed to drink in deep draughts of satisfaction. Then she said:

'Fine nice young white gen'l'man kneelin' down to a nigger-wench! I'se wanted to see dat jes once befo' I'se called. Now, Gabr'el, blow de hawn, I'se ready ... Git up!'

Tom did it. He said, humbly:

'Now, Roxy, don't punish me any more. I deserved what I've got, but be good and let me off with that. Don't go to uncle. Tell me – I'll give you the five dollars.'

'Yes, I bet you will; en you won't stop dah, nuther. But I ain't gwine to tell you heah –'

'Good gracious, no!'

'Is you 'feared o' de ha'nted house?'

'N – no.'

'Well, den, you come to de ha'nted house 'bout ten or 'leven to-night, en climb up de ladder, 'ca'se de sta'r-steps is broke down, en you'll fine me. I'se a-roostin' in de ha'nted house 'cas'e I can't 'ford to roos' nowher's else.' She started toward the door, but stopped and said, 'Gimme de dollah bill!' He gave it to her. She examined it and said, 'H'm – like enough de bank's bu'sted.' She started again, but halted again. 'Has you got any whisky?'

'Yes, a little.'

'Fetch it!'

He ran to his room overhead and brought down a bottle which was two-thirds full. She tilted it up and took a drink. Her eyes sparkled with satisfaction, and she tucked the bottle under her shawl, saying, 'It's prime. I'll take it along.'

Tom humbly held the door for her, and she marched out as grim and erect as a grenadier.

CHAPTER 9

Why is it that we rejoice at a birth and grieve at a funeral? It is because we are not the person involved. – *Pudd'nhead Wilson's Calendar*

It is easy to find fault, if one has that disposition. There was once a man who, not being able to find any other fault with coal, complained that there were too many prehistoric toads in it. – *Pudd'nhead Wilson's Calendar*

TOM flung himself on the sofa, and put his throbbing head in his hands, and rested his elbows on his knees. He rocked himself back and forth and moaned.

'I've knelt to a nigger-wench!' he muttered. 'I thought I had struck the deepest depths of degradation before, but oh, dear, it was nothing to this. ... Well, there is one consolation, such as it is – I've struck bottom this time; there's nothing lower.'

But that was a hasty conclusion.

At ten that night he climbed the ladder in the haunted house, pale, weak, and wretched. Roxy was standing in the door of one of the rooms, waiting, for she had heard him.

This was a two-storey log house which had acquired the reputation a few years before of being haunted, and that was the end of its usefulness. Nobody would live in it afterward, or go near it by night, and most people even gave it a wide berth in the daytime. As it had no competition, it was called *the* haunted house. It was getting crazy and ruinous, now, from long neglect. It stood three hundred yards beyond Pudd'nhead Wilson's house, with nothing between but vacancy. It was the last house in the town at that end.

Tom followed Roxy into the room. She had a pile of clean straw in the corner for a bed, some cheap but well-kept clothing was hanging on the wall, there was a tin lantern freckling the floor with little spots of light, and there were various soap- and candle-boxes scattered about, which served for chairs. The two sat down. Roxy said:

'Now den, I'll tell you straight off, en I'll begin to k'leck de money later on; I ain't in no hurry. What does you reckon I'se gwine to tell you?'

'Well, you – you – oh, Roxy, don't make it too hard for me! Come right out and tell me you've found out somehow what a scrape I'm in on account of dissipation and foolishness.'

'Disposition en foolishness! *No*, sir, dat ain't it. Dat jist ain't nothin' at all, 'longside o' what *I* knows.'

Tom stared at her, and said:

'Why, Roxy, what do you mean?'

She rose, and gloomed above him like a Fate.

'I means dis – en its de Lord's truth. You ain't no more kin to ole Marse Driscoll den I is! – *dat's* what I means!' and her eyes flamed with triumph.

'What?'

'Yassir, en *dat* ain't all! You's a *nigger!* – *bawn* a nigger en a *slave!* – en you's a nigger en a slave dis minute; en if I opens my mouf ole Marse Driscoll'll sell you down de river befo' you is two days older den what you is now.'

'It's a thundering lie, you miserable old blatherskite!'

'It ain't no lie, nuther. It's jes de truth, en nothin' *but* de truth, so he'p me. Yassir – you's my *son* –'

'You devil!'

'En dat po' boy dat you's be'n a-kickin' en a'cuffing to-day is Percy Driscoll's son en yo' *marster* –'

'You beast!'

'En *his* name's Tom Driscoll, en *yo'* name's Valet de

Chambers, en you ain't *got* no fambly name, beca'se niggers don't *have* 'em!'

Tom sprang up and seized a billet of wood and raised it; but his mother only laughed at him, and said:

'Set down, you pup! Does you think you kin skyer me? It ain't in you, nor de likes of you. I reckon you'd shoot me in de back, maybe, if you got a chance, for dat's jist yo' style — *I* knows you, thoo en thoo — but I don't mind gitt'n' killed, beca'se all dis is down in writin', en it's in safe hands, too, en de man dat's got it knows whah to look for de right man when I gits killed. Oh, bless yo' soul, if you puts yo' mother up for as big a fool as *you* is, you's pow'ful mistaken, I kin tell you! Now den, you set still en behave yo'self; en don't you git up ag'in till I tell you!'

Tom fretted and chafed awhile in a whirlwind of disorganizing sensations and emotions, and finally said, with something like settled conviction:

'The whole thing is moonshine; now then, go ahead and do your worst; I'm done with you.'

Roxy made no answer. She took the lantern and started toward the door. Tom was in a cold panic in a moment.

'Come back, come back!' he wailed. 'I didn't mean it, Roxy; I take it all back, and I'll never say it again! Please come back, Roxy!'

The woman stood a moment, then she said gravely:

'Dah's one thing you's got to stop, Valet de Chambers. You can't call me *Roxy*, same as if you was my equal. Chillen don't speak to dey mammies like dat. You'll call me ma or mammy, dat's what you'll call me - leastways when dey ain't nobody aroun'. *Say* it!'

It cost Tom a struggle, but he got it out.

'Dat's all right. Don't you ever forget it ag'in, if you knows what's good for you. Now den, you has said you wouldn't ever call it lies en moonshine ag'in. I'll tell you dis, for a warnin': if you ever does say it ag'in, it's de *las'* time you'll ever say it to me; I'll tramp as straight to de Judge as I kin walk, en tell him who you is, en *prove* it. Does you b'lieve me when I says dat?'

'Oh,' groaned Tom, 'I more than believe it; I *know* it.'

Roxy knew her conquest was complete. She could have proved nothing to anybody, and her threat about the writings was a lie; but she knew the person she was dealing with, and had made both statements without any doubt as to the effect they would produce.

She went and sat down on her candle-box, and the pride and pomp of her victorious attitude made it a throne. She said:

'Now den, Chambers, we's gwine to talk business, en dey ain't gwine to be no mo' foolishness. In de fust place, you gits fifty dollahs a month; you's gwine to han' over half of it to yo' ma. Plank it out!'

But Tom had only six dollars in the world. He gave her that, and promised to start fair on next month's pension.

'Chambers, how much is you in debt?'

Tom shuddered, and said:

'Nearly three hundred dollars.'

'How is you gwine to pay it?'

Tom groaned out: 'Oh, I don't know; don't ask me such awful questions.'

But she stuck to her point until she wearied a confession out of him: he had been prowling about in disguise, stealing small valuables from private houses; in fact, had made a good deal of a raid on his fellow-villagers a fortnight before, when he was supposed to be in St Louis; but he doubted if he had sent away enough stuff to realise the required amount, and was afraid to make a further venture in the present excited state of the town. His mother approved of his conduct, and offered to help, but this frightened him. He tremblingly ventured to say that if she would retire from the town he should feel better and safer, and could hold his head higher – and was going on to make an argument, but she interrupted and surprised him pleasantly by saying she was ready; it didn't make any difference to her where she stayed, so that she got her share of the pension regularly. She said she would not go far, and would call at the haunted house once a month for her money. Then she said:

'I don't hate you so much now, but I've hated you a many a year – and anybody would. Didn't I change you off, en give you a good fambly en a good name, en made you a white gen'l'man en rich, wid store clothes on – en what did I git for it? You despised me all de time, en was al'ays sayin' mean hard things to me befo' folks, en wouldn't ever let me forgit I's a nigger – en – en –'

She fell to sobbing, and broke down. Tom said: 'But you know I didn't know you were my mother; and besides –'

'Well, nemmine 'bout dat, now; let it go. I'se gwine to fo'git it.' Then she added fiercely, 'En don't you ever make me remember it ag'in, or you'll be sorry, I tell you.'

When they were parting, Tom said, in the most persuasive way he could command:

'Ma, would you mind telling me who was my father?'

He had supposed he was asking an embarrassing question. He was mistaken. Roxy drew herself up with a proud toss of her head, and said:

'Does I mine tellin' you? No, dat I don't! You ain't got no 'casion to be shame' o' yo' father, I kin tell you. He wuz de highest quality in dis whole town – ole Virginny stock. Fust famblies, he wuz. Jes as good stock as de Driscolls en de Howards, de bes' day dey ever seed.' She put on a little prouder air, if possible, and added impressively: 'Does you 'member Cunnel Cecil Burleigh Essex, dat died de same year yo' young Marse Tom Driscoll's pappy died, en all de Masons en Odd Fellers en Churches turned out en give him de bigges' funeral dis town ever seed? Dat's de man.'

Under the inspiration of her soaring complacency the departed graces of her earlier days returned to her, and her bearing took to itself a dignity and state that might have passed for queenly if her surroundings had been a little more in keeping with it.

'Dey ain't another nigger in dis town dat's as high-bawn as you is. Now den, go 'long! En jes you hold yo' head up as high as you want to — you has de right, en dat I kin swah.'

Chapter 10

All say, 'How hard it is that we have to die' – a strange
complaint to còme from the mouths of people who have
had to live. – *Pudd'nhead Wilson's Calendar*

When angry, count four; when very angry, swear. –
Pudd'nhead Wilson's Calendar

EVERY now and then, after Tom went to bed, he had sudden wakings out of his sleep, and his first thought was, 'Oh, joy, it was all a dream!' Then he laid himself heavily down again, with a groan and the muttered words, 'A nigger! I am a nigger! Oh, I wish I was dead!'

He woke at dawn with one more repetition of this horror, and then he resolved to meddle no more with that treacherous sleep. He began to think. Sufficiently bitter thinkings they were. They wandered along something after this fashion:

'Why were niggers *and* whites made? What crime did the uncreated first nigger commit that the curse of birth was decreed for him? And why is this awful difference made between white and black? ... How hard the nigger's fate seems, this morning! – yet until last night such a thought never entered my head.'

He sighed and groaned an hour or more away. Then 'Chambers' came humbly in to say that breakfast was nearly ready. 'Tom' blushed scarlet to see this aristocratic white youth cringe to him, a nigger, and call him 'Young Marster'. He said roughly:

'Get out of my sight!' and when the youth was gone, he muttered: 'He has done me no harm, poor wretch, but he is

an eyesore to me now, for he is Driscoll the young gentleman, and I am a – oh, I wish I was dead!'

A gigantic irruption, like that of Krakatoa a few years ago,
with the accompanying earthquakes, tidal waves, and
clouds of volcanic dust, changes the face of the surrounding
landscape beyond recognition, bringing down the high
lands, elevating the low, making fair lakes where deserts
had been, and deserts where green prairies had smiled
before. The tremendous catastrophe which had befallen
Tom had changed his moral landscape in much the same
way. Some of his low places he found lifted to ideals, some
of his ideals had sunk to the valleys, and lay there with the
sackcloth and ashes of pumice-stone and sulphur on their
ruined heads.

For days he wandered in lonely places, thinking, thinking,
thinking – trying to get his bearings. It was new work. If
he met a friend, he found that the habit of a lifetime had in
some mysterious way vanished – his arm hung limp, instead
of involuntarily extending the hand for a shake. It was the
'nigger' in him asserting its humility, and he blushed and
was abashed. And the 'nigger' in him was surprised when
the white friend put out his hand for a shake with him. He
found the 'nigger' in him involuntarily giving the road, on
the sidewalk, to the white rowdy and loafer. When Rowena,
the dearest thing his heart knew, the idol of his secret worship, invited him in, the 'nigger' in him made an embarrassed excuse and was afraid to enter and sit with the dread
white folks on equal terms. The 'nigger' in him went
shrinking and skulking here and there and yonder, and
fancying it saw suspicion and maybe detection in all faces,
tones, and gestures. So strange and uncharacteristic was
Tom's conduct that people noticed it, and turned to look
after him when he passed on; and when he glanced back –
as he could not help doing, in spite of his best resistance –

and caught that puzzled expression in a person's face, it gave him a sick feeling, and he took himself out of view as quickly as he could. He presently came to have a hunted sense and a hunted look, and then he fled away to the hill-tops and the solitudes. He said to himself that the curse of Ham was upon him.

He dreaded his meals; the 'nigger' in him was ashamed to sit at the white folks' table, and feared discovery all the time; and once when Judge Driscoll said, 'What's the matter with you? You look as meek as a nigger,' he felt as secret murderers are said to feel when the accuser says, 'Thou art the man!' Tom said he was not well, and left the table.

His ostensible 'aunt's' solicitudes and endearments were become a terror to him, and he avoided them.

And all the time hatred of his ostensible 'uncle' was steadily growing in his heart; for he said to himself, 'He is white; and I am his chattel, his property, his goods, and he can sell me, just as he could his dog.'

For as much as a week after this Tom imagined that his character had undergone a pretty radical change. But that was because he did not know himself.

In several ways his opinions were totally changed, and would never go back to what they were before, but the main structure of his character was not changed and could not be changed. One or two very important features of it were altered, and in time effects would result from this if opportunity offered – effects of a quite serious nature too. Under the influence of a great mental and moral upheaval his character and habits had taken on the appearance of complete change, but after a while, with the subsidence of the storm both began to settle toward their former places. He dropped gradually back into his old frivolous and easy-going ways and conditions of feeling and manner of speech, and no familiar of his could have detected anything in him that differentiated him from the weak and careless Tom of other days.

The theft-raid which he had made upon the village turned out better than he had ventured to hope. It produced the sum necessary to pay his gaming-debts, and saved him from exposure to his uncle and another smashing of the will. He and his mother learned to like each other fairly well. She couldn't love him as yet, because there 'warn't nothing *to* him', as she expressed it, but her nature needed something or somebody to rule over, and he was better than nothing. Her strong character and aggressive and commanding ways compelled Tom's admiration in spite of the fact that he got more illustrations of them than he needed for his comfort. However, as a rule, her conversation was made up of racy tattle about the privacies of the chief families of the town (for she went harvesting among their kitchens every time she came to the village), and Tom enjoyed this. It was just in his line. She always collected her half of his pension punctually, and he was always at the haunted house to have a chat with her on these occasions. Every now and then she paid him a visit there on between-days also.

Occasionally he would run up to St Louis for a few weeks, and at last temptation caught him again. He won a lot of money, but lost it, and with it a deal more besides, which he promised to raise as soon as possible.

For this purpose he projected a new raid on his town. He never meddled with any other town, for he was afraid to venture into houses whose ins and outs he did not know and the habits of whose households he was not acquainted with. He arrived at the haunted house in disguise on the Wednesday before the advent of the twins – after writing his Aunt Pratt that he would not arrive until two days after – and lay in hiding there with his mother until toward daylight Friday morning, when he went to his uncle's house and entered by the back way with his own key, and slipped up to his room, where he could have the use of mirror and toilet articles. He had a suit of girl's clothes with him in a bundle as a disguise for his raid, and was wearing a suit of his mother's clothing, with black gloves and veil. By dawn he was tricked out for his raid, but he caught a glimpse of Pudd'nhead Wilson through the window over the way, and knew that Pudd'nhead had caught a glimpse of him. So he entertained Wilson with some airs and graces and attitudes for a while, then stepped out of sight and resumed the other disguise, and by-and-by went down and out the back way and started down town to reconnoitre the scene of his intended labours.

But he was ill at ease. He had changed back to Roxy's dress, with the stoop of age added to the disguise, so that Wilson would not bother himself about a humble old woman leaving a neighbour's house by the back way in the early morning, in case he was still spying. But supposing Wilson had seen him leave, and had thought it suspicious, and had also followed him? The thought made Tom cold. He gave up the raid for the day, and hurried back to the haunted house by the obscurest route he knew. His mother was gone; but she came back by-and-by, with the news of the grand reception at Patsy Cooper's, and soon persuaded him that the opportunity was like a special providence, it was so inviting and perfect. So he went raiding after all, and made a nice success of it while everybody was gone to Patsy Cooper's. Success gave him nerve and even actual intrepidity; insomuch, indeed, that after he had conveyed his harvest to his mother in a back alley he went to the reception himself, and added several of the valuables of that house to his takings.

After this long digression we have now arrived once more

at the point where Pudd'nhead Wilson, while waiting for the arrival of the twins on that same Friday evening, sat puzzling over the strange apparition of that morning – a girl in young Tom Driscoll's bedroom; fretting, and guessing, and puzzling over it, and wondering who the shameless creature might be.

CHAPTER II

There are three infallible ways of pleasing an author,
the three form a rising scale of compliment: 1, to tell
him you have read one of his books; 2, to tell him you
have read all of his books; 3, to ask him to let you read
the manuscript of his forthcoming book. No. 1 admits
you to his respect; No. 2 admits you to his admiration;
No. 3 carries you clear into his heart. – *Pudd'nhead
Wilson's Calendar*

As to the Adjective: when in doubt, strike it out. –
Pudd'nhead Wilson's Calendar

THE twins arrived presently, and talk began. It flowed
along chattily and sociably, and under its influence the new
friendship gathered ease and strength. Wilson got out his
Calendar, by request, and read a passage or two from it,
which the twins praised quite cordially. This pleased the
author so much that he complied gladly when they asked
him to lend them a batch of the work to read at home. In
the course of their wide travels they had found out that
there are three sure ways of pleasing an author; they were
now working the best of the three.

There was an interruption now. Young Tom Driscoll
appeared and joined the party. He pretended to be seeing
the distinguished strangers for the first time when they rose
to shake hands; but this was only a blind, as he had already
had a glimpse of them at the reception, while robbing the
house. The twins made mental note that he was smooth-
faced and rather handsome, and smooth and undulatory in
his movements – graceful, in fact. Angelo thought he had a
good eye; Luigi thought there was something veiled and

sly about it. Angelo thought he had a pleasant free-and-easy way of talking; Luigi thought it was more so than was agreeable. Angelo thought he was a sufficiently nice young man; Luigi reserved his decision. Tom's first contribution to the conversation was a question which he had put to Wilson a hundred times before. It was always cheerily and good-naturedly put, and always inflicted a little pang, for it touched a secret sore; but this time the pang was sharp, since strangers were present.

'Well, how does the law come on? Had a case yet?'

Wilson bit his lip, but answered, 'No – not yet,' with as much indifference as he could assume. Judge Driscoll had generously left the law feature out of the Wilson biography which he had furnished to the twins. Young Tom laughed pleasantly, and said:

'Wilson's a lawyer, gentlemen, but he doesn't practise now.'

The sarcasm bit, but Wilson kept himself under control, and said without passion:

'I don't practise, it is true. It is true that I have never had a case, and have had to earn a poor living for twenty years as an expert accountant in a town where I can't get hold of a set of books to untangle as often as I should like. But it is also true that I did fit myself well for the practice of the law. By the time I was your age, Tom, I had chosen a profession, and was soon competent to enter upon it.' Tom winced. 'I never got a chance to try my hand at it, and I may never get a chance; and yet if I ever do get it, I shall be found ready, for I have kept up my law-studies all these years.'

'That's it; that's good grit! I like to see it. I've a notion to throw all my business your way. My business and your law-practice ought to make a pretty gay team, Dave,' and the young fellow laughed again.

'If you will throw –' Wilson had thought of the girl in Tom's bedroom, and was going to say, 'If you will throw the surreptitious and disreputable part of your business my way, it may amount to something,' but thought better of it, and said: 'However, this matter doesn't fit well in a general conversation.'

'All right, we'll change the subject; I guess you were about to give me another dig, anyway, so I'm willing to change. How's the Awful Mystery flourishing these days? Wilson's got a scheme for driving plain window-glass out of the market by decorating it with greasy finger-marks, and getting rich by selling it at famine prices to the crowned heads over in Europe to outfit their palaces with. Fetch it out, Dave.'

Wilson brought three of his glass strips, and said,

'I get the subject to pass the fingers of his right hand through his hair, so as to get a little coating of the natural oil on them, and then press the balls of them on the glass. A fine and delicate print of the lines in the skin results, and is permanent if it doesn't come in contact with something able to rub it off. You begin, Tom.'

'Why, I think you took my finger-marks once or twice before.'

'Yes; but you were a little boy the last time, only about twelve years old.'

'That's so. Of course, I've changed entirely since then, and variety is what the crowned heads want, I guess.'

He passed his fingers through his crop of short hair, and pressed them one at a time on the glass. Angelo made a print of his fingers on another glass, and Luigi followed with a third. Wilson marked the glasses with names and date, and put them away. Tom gave one of his little laughs, and said:

'I thought I wouldn't say anything, but if variety is what

you are after, you have wasted a piece of glass. The hand-print of one twin is the same as the hand-print of the fellow-twin.'

'Well, it's done now, and I like to have them both, any-way,' said Wilson, returning to his place.

'But look here, Dave,' said Tom, 'you used to tell people's fortunes, too, when you took their finger-marks. Dave's just an all-round genius — a genius of the first water, gentlemen; a great scientist running to seed here in this village, a prophet with the kind of honour that prophets generally get at home — for here they don't give shucks for his scien-tifics, and they call his skull a notion factory — hey, Dave, ain't it so? But never mind; he'll make his mark some day — finger-mark, you know — he-he! But really, you want to let him take a shy at your palms once; it's worth twice the price of admission, or your money's returned at the door. Why, he'll read your wrinkles as easy as a book, and not only tell you fifty or sixty things that's going to happen to you but fifty or sixty thousand that ain't. Come, Dave, show the gentlemen what an inspired Jack-at-all-science we've got in this town, and don't know it.'

Wilson winced under this nagging and not very cour-teous chaff, and the twins suffered with him and for him. They rightly judged now that the best way to relieve him would be to take the thing in earnest and treat it with respect, ignoring Tom's rather overdone raillery; so Luigi said:

'We have seen something of palmistry in our wanderings, and know very well what astonishing things it can do. If it isn't a science, and one of the greatest of them, too, I don't know what its other name ought to be. In the Orient —'

Tom looked surprised and incredulous. He said:

'That juggling a science? But, really, you ain't serious, are you?'

'Yes, entirely so. Four years ago we had our hands read out to us as if our palms had been covered with print.'

'Well, do you mean to say there was actually anything in it?' asked Tom, his incredulity beginning to weaken a little.

'There was this much in it,' said Angelo: 'what was told us of our characters was minutely exact – we could not have bettered it ourselves. Next, two or three memorable things that had happened to us were laid bare – things which no one present but ourselves could have known about.'

'Why, it's rank sorcery!' exclaimed Tom, who was now becoming very much interested. 'And how did they make out with what was going to happen to you in the future?'

'On the whole, quite fairly,' said Luigi. 'Two or three of the most striking things foretold have happened since; much the most striking one of all happened within that same year. Some of the minor prophecies have come true; some of the minor and some of the major ones have not been fulfilled yet, and, of course, may never be: still, I should be more surprised it they failed to arrive than if they didn't.'

Tom was entirely sobered and profoundly impressed. He said, apologetically:

'Dave, I wasn't meaning to belittle that science; I was only chaffing – chattering, I reckon I'd better say. I wish you would look at their palms. Come, won't you?'

'Why, certainly, if you want me to; but you know I've had no chance to become an expert, and don't claim to be one. When a past event is somewhat prominently recorded in the palm I can generally detect that, but minor ones often escape me – not always, of course, but often – but I haven't much confidence in myself when it comes to reading the future. I am talking as if palmistry was a daily study with me, but that is not so. I haven't examined half a dozen hands in the last half-dozen years; you see, the people got to

PUDD'NHEAD WILSON

joking about it, and I stopped to let the talk die down. I'll
tell you what we'll do, Count Luigi: I'll make a try at your
past, and if I have any success there – no, on the whole, I'll
let the future alone; that's really the affair of an expert.'

He took Luigi's hand. Tom said:

'Wait – don't look yet, Dave! Count Luigi, here's paper
and pencil. Set down that thing that you said was the most
striking one that was foretold to you, and happened less
than a year afterward, and give it to me so I can see if Dave
finds it in your hand.'

Luigi wrote a line privately, and folded up the piece of
paper and handed it to Tom, saying,

'I'll tell you when to look at it, if he finds it.'

Wilson began to study Luigi's palm, tracing life-lines,
heart-lines, head-lines, and so on, and noting carefully their
relations with the cobweb of finer and more delicate marks
and lines that enmeshed them on all sides; he felt of the
fleshy cushion at the base of the thumb, and noted its shape;
he felt of the fleshy side of the hand between the wrist and
the base of the little finger, and noted its shape also; he
painstakingly examined the fingers, observing their form,
proportions, and natural manner of disposing themselves
when in repose. All this process was watched by the three
spectators with absorbing interest, their heads bent together
over Luigi's palm, and nobody disturbing the stillness with
a word. Wilson now entered upon a close survey of the
palm again, and his revelations began.

He mapped out Luigi's character and disposition, his
tastes, aversions, proclivities, ambitions, and eccentricities
in a way which sometimes made Luigi wince and the others
laugh, but both twins declared that the chart was artistically
drawn and was correct.

Next, Wilson took up Luigi's history. He proceeded
cautiously and with hesitation now, moving his fingers

slowly along the great lines of the palm, and now and then halting it at a 'star' or some such landmark, and examining that neighbourhood minutely. He proclaimed one or two past events; Luigi confirmed his correctness, and the search went on. Presently Wilson glanced up suddenly with a surprised expression.

'Here is a record of an incident which you would perhaps not wish me to—'

'Bring it out,' said Luigi, good-naturedly; 'I promise you it sha'n't embarrass me.'

But Wilson still hesitated, and did not seem quite to know what to do. Then he said:

'I think it is too delicate a matter to – to – I believe I would rather write it or whisper it to you and let you decide for yourself whether you want it talked out or not.'

'That will answer,' said Luigi; 'write it.'

Wilson wrote something on a slip of paper and handed it to Luigi, who read it to himself and said to Tom:

'Unfold your slip and read it, Mr Driscoll.'

Tom read:

' "*It was prophesied that I would kill a man. It came true before the year was out.*' "

Tom added, 'Great Scott!'

Luigi handed Wilson's paper to Tom, and said:

'Now read this one.'

Tom read:

' "*You have killed some one, but whether man, woman, or child, I do not make out.*" '

'Caesar's ghost!' commented Tom, with astonishment. 'It beats anything that was ever heard of! Why, a man's own hand is his deadliest enemy! Just think of that – a man's own hand keeps a record of the deepest and fatalest secrets of his life, and is treacherously ready to expose him to any black-magic stranger that comes along. But what do you let a person look at your hand for, with that awful thing printed in it?'

'Oh,' said Luigi, reposefully, 'I don't mind it. I killed the man for good reasons, and I don't regret it.'

'What were the reasons?'

'Well, he needed killing.'

'I'll tell you why he did it, since he won't say himself,' said Angelo, warmly. 'He did it to save my life, that's what he did it for. So it was a noble act, and not a thing to be hid in the dark.'

'So it was, so it was,' said Wilson; 'to do such a thing to save a brother's life is a great and fine action.'

'Now come,' said Luigi, 'it is very pleasant to hear you say these things, but for unselfishness, or heroism, or magnanimity, the circumstances won't stand scrutiny. You overlook one detail: suppose I hadn't saved Angelo's life, what would have become of mine? If I had let the man kill him, wouldn't he have killed me too? I saved my own life, you see.'

'Yes; that is your way of talking,' said Angelo; 'but I know you – I don't believe you thought of yourself at all. I keep that weapon yet that Luigi killed the man with, and I'll show it to you some time. That incident makes it interesting, and it had a history before it came into Luigi's hands which adds to its interest. It was given to Luigi by a great Indian prince, the Gaikowar of Baroda, and it had been in his family two or three centuries. It killed a good many disagreeable people who troubled that hearthstone at one time and another. It isn't much to look at, except that it isn't shaped like other knives, or dirks, or whatever it may be called. Here, I'll draw it for you.' He took a sheet of paper and made a rapid sketch. 'There it is – a broad and murderous blade, with edges like a razor for sharpness. The devices engraved on it are the ciphers or names of its long line of possessors. I had Luigi's name added in Roman letters myself with our coat of arms, as you see. You notice what a curious handle the thing has. It is solid ivory, polished like a mirror, and is four or five inches long – round, and as thick as a large man's wrist, with the end squared off flat, for your thumb to rest on; for you grasp it, with your thumb resting on the blunt end – so – and lift it aloft and strike downward. The Gaikowar showed us how the thing was done when he gave it to Luigi, and before that night was ended Luigi had used the knife, and the Gaikowar was a man short by reason of it. The sheath is magnificently ornamented with gems of great value. You will find the sheath more worth looking at than the knife itself, of course.'

Tom said to himself:

'It's lucky I came here. I would have sold that knife for a song; I supposed the jewels were glass.'

'But go on; don't stop,' said Wilson. 'Our curiosity is up now, to hear about the homicide. Tell us about that.'

'Well, briefly, the knife was to blame for that, all round. A native servant slipped into our room in the palace in the night, to kill us and steal the knife on account of the fortune incrusted on its sheath, without a doubt. Luigi had it under his pillow; we were in bed together. There was a dim night-light burning. I was asleep; but Luigi was awake, and he thought he detected a vague form nearing the bed. He slipped the knife out of the sheath and was ready and un-embarrassed by hampering bed-clothes, for the weather was hot and we hadn't any. Suddenly that native rose at the bedside, and bent over me with his right hand lifted and a dirk in it aimed at my throat; but Luigi grabbed his wrist, pulled him downward, and drove his own knife into the man's neck. That is the whole story.'

Wilson and Tom drew deep breaths, and after some

general chat about the tragedy, Pudd'nhead said, taking Tom's hand:

'Now, Tom, I've never had a look at your palms, as it happens; perhaps you've got some little questionable privacies that need – hel-lo!'

Tom had snatched away his hand, and was looking a good deal confused.

'Why, he's blushing!' said Luigi.

Tom darted an ugly look at him, and said sharply:

'Well, if I am, it ain't because I'm a murderer!' Luigi's dark face flushed, but before he could speak or move, Tom added with anxious haste: 'Oh, I beg a thousand pardons. I didn't mean that; it was out before I thought, and I'm very, very sorry – you must forgive me!'

Wilson came to the rescue, and smoothed things down as well as he could; and in fact was entirely successful as far as the twins were concerned, for they felt sorrier for the affront put upon him by his guest's outburst of ill manners than for the insult offered to Luigi. But the success was not so pronounced with the offender. Tom tried to seem at his ease, and he went through the motions fairly well, but at bottom he felt resentful toward all the three witnesses of his exhibition; in fact, he felt so annoyed at them for having witnessed it and noticed it, that he almost forgot to feel annoyed at himself for placing it before them. However, something presently happened which made him almost comfortable, and brought him nearly back to a state of charity and friendliness. This was a little spat between the twins; not much of a spat, but still a spat; and before they got far with it they were in a decided condition of irritation with each other. Tom was charmed; so pleased, indeed, that he cautiously did what he could to increase the irritation while pretending to be actuated by more respectable motives. By his help the fire got warmed up to the blazing-point,

and he might have had the happiness of seeing the flames
show up in another moment, but for the interruption
of a knock on the door — an interruption which fretted
him as much as it gratified Wilson. Wilson opened the
door.

The visitor was a good-natured, ignorant, energetic,
middle-aged Irishman named John Buckstone, who was a
great politician in a small way, and always took a large
share in public matters of every sort. One of the town's
chief excitements, just now, was over the matter of rum.
There was a strong rum party and a strong anti-rum party.[1]
Buckstone was training with the rum party, and he had
been sent to hunt up the twins and invite them to attend a
mass-meeting of that faction. He delivered his errand, and
said the clans were already gathering in the big hall over the
market-house. Luigi accepted the invitation cordially,
Angelo less cordially, since he disliked crowds, and did not
drink the powerful intoxicants of America. In fact, he was
even a teetotaler sometimes — when it was judicious to be
one.

The twins left with Buckstone, and Tom Driscoll joined
company with them uninvited.

In the distance one could see a long wavering line of
torches drifting down the main street, and could hear the
throbbing of the bass drum, the clash of cymbals, the
squeaking of a fife or two, and the faint roar of remote
hurrahs. The tail-end of this procession was climbing the
market-house stairs when the twins arrived in its neighbourhood; when they reached the hall it was full of people,
torches, smoke, noise, and enthusiasm. They were con-
ducted to the platform by Buckstone — Tom Driscoll still
following — and were delivered to the chairman in the midst
of a prodigious explosion of welcome. When the noise had
moderated a little, the chair proposed that 'our illustrious

guests be at once elected, by complimentary acclamation, to membership in our ever-glorious organization, the paradise of the free, and the perdition of the slave.'

This eloquent discharge opened the floodgates of enthusiasm again, and the election was carried with thundering unanimity. Then arose a storm of cries:

'Wet them down! Wet them down! Give them a drink!'

Glasses of whisky were handed to the twins. Luigi waved his aloft, then brought it to his lips; but Angelo set his down. There was another storm of cries:

'What's the matter with the other one?' 'What is the blonde one going back on us for?' 'Explain! Explain!'

The chairman inquired, and then reported:

'We have made an unfortunate mistake, gentlemen. I find that the Count Angelo Capello is opposed to our creed – is a teetotaler, in fact, and was not intending to apply for membership with us. He desires that we reconsider the vote by which he was elected. What is the pleasure of the house?'

There was a general burst of laughter, plentifully accented with whistlings and cat-calls, but the energetic use of the gavel presently restored something like order. Then a man spoke from the crowd, and said that while he was very sorry that the mistake had been made, it would not be possible to rectify it at the present meeting. According to the bylaws, it must go over to the next regular meeting for action. He would not offer a motion, as none was required. He desired to apologize to the gentleman in the name of the house, and begged to assure him that, as far as it might lie in the power of the Sons of Liberty,[2] his temporary membership in the order would be made pleasant to him.

This speech was received with great applause, mixed with cries of—

'That's the talk!' 'He's a good fellow, anyway, if he *is* a teetotaler!' 'Drink his health!' 'Give him a rouser, and no heel-taps!'

Glasses were handed round, and everybody on the platform drank Angelo's health, while the house bellowed forth in song:

> For he's a jolly good fel-low,
> For he's a jolly good fel-low,
> For he's a jolly good fe-el-low,
> Which nobody can deny.

Tom Driscoll drank. It was his second glass, for he had drunk Angelo's the moment that Angelo had set it down. The two drinks made him very merry — almost idiotically so — and he began to take a most lively and prominent part in the proceedings, particularly in the music and cat-calls and side-remarks.

The chairman was still standing at the front, the twins at his side. The extraordinarily close resemblance of the brothers to each other suggested a witticism to Tom Driscoll, and just as the chairman began a speech he skipped forward and said with an air of tipsy confidence to the audience:

'Boys, I move that he keeps still and lets this human philopena [3] snip you out a speech.'

The descriptive aptness of the phrase caught the house, and a mighty burst of laughter followed.

Luigi's southern blood leaped to the boiling-point in a moment under the sharp humiliation of this insult delivered in the presence of four hundred strangers. It was not in the young man's nature to let the matter pass, or to delay the squaring of the account. He took a couple of strides and halted behind the unsuspecting joker. Then he drew back and delivered a kick of such titanic vigour that it lifted Tom clear over the footlights and landed him on the heads of the front row of the Sons of Liberty.

Even a sober person does not like to have a human being emptied on him when he is not doing any harm; a person who is not sober cannot endure such an attention at all. The nest of Sons of Liberty that Driscoll landed in had not a sober bird in it: in fact, there was probably not an entirely sober one in the auditorium. Driscoll was promptly and indignantly flung on to the heads of Sons in the next row, and these Sons passed him on toward the rear, and then immediately began to pummel the front-row Sons who had passed him to them. This course was strictly followed by bench after bench as Driscoll travelled in his tumultuous and airy flight toward the door; so he left behind him an ever lengthening wake of raging and plunging and fighting and swearing humanity. Down went group after group of torches, and presently above the deafening clatter of the gavel, roar of angry voices, and crash of succumbing benches, rose the paralysing cry of 'Fire!'

The fighting ceased instantly; the cursing ceased; for one distinctly defined moment there was a dead hush, a motionless calm, where the tempest had been; then with one impulse the multitude awoke to life and energy again, and went surging and struggling and swaying, this way and that, its outer edges melting away through windows and doors, and gradually lessening the pressure and relieving the mass.

The fire-boys were never on hand so suddenly before; for there was no distance to go, this time, their quarters being in the rear end of the market-house. There was an engine company and a hook-and-ladder company. Half of each was composed of rummies and the other half of anti-rummies, after the moral and political share-and-share-alike fashion of the frontier town of the period. Enough anti-rummies were loafing in quarters to man the engine and the ladders. In two minutes they had their red shirts and helmets on – they never stirred officially in unofficial costume – and as the mass meeting overhead smashed through the long row of windows and poured out upon the roof of the arcade, the deliverers were ready for them with a powerful stream of water, which washed some of them off the roof and nearly drowned the rest. But water was preferable to fire, and still the stampede from the windows continued, and still the pitiless drenchings assailed it until the building was empty; then the fireboys mounted to the hall and flooded it with water enough to annihilate forty times as much fire as there was there; for a village fire-company does not often get a chance to show off, and so when it does get a chance it makes the most of it. Such citizens of that village as were of a thoughtful and judicious temperament did not insure against fire; they insured against the fire company.

CHAPTER 12

Courage is resistance to fear, mastery of fear – not absence of fear. Except a creature be part coward it is not a compliment to say it is brave; it is merely a loose misapplication of the word. Consider the flea! – incomparably the bravest of all the creatures of God, if ignorance of fear were courage. Whether you are asleep or awake he will attack you, caring nothing for the fact that in bulk and strength you are to him as are the massed armies of the earth to a sucking child; he lives both day and night and all days and nights in the very lap of peril and the immediate presence of death, and yet is no more afraid than is the man who walks the streets of a city that was threatened by an earthquake ten centuries before. When we speak of Clive, Nelson, and Putnam as men who 'didn't know what fear was', we ought always to add the flea – and put him at the head of the procession. – *Pudd'nhead Wilson's Calendar*

JUDGE DRISCOLL was in bed and asleep by ten o'clock on Friday night, and he was up and gone a-fishing before daylight in the morning with his friend Pembroke Howard. These two had been boys together in Virginia when that State still ranked as the chief and most imposing member of the Union, and they still coupled the proud and affectionate adjective 'Old' with her name when they spoke of her. In Missouri a recognised superiority attached to any person who hailed from Old Virginia; and this superiority was exalted to supremacy when a person of such nativity could also prove descent from the First Families of that great commonwealth. The Howards and Driscolls were of this aristocracy. In their eyes it was a nobility. It had its unwritten laws, and they were as clearly defined and as strict

as any that could be found among the printed statutes of the
land. The F.F.V. was born a gentleman; his highest duty
in life was to watch over that great inheritance and keep it
unsmirched. He must keep his honour spotless. Those laws
were his chart; his course was marked out on it; if he
swerved from it by so much as half a point of the compass
it meant shipwreck to his honour; that is to say, degradation
from his rank as a gentleman. These laws required certain
things of him which his religion might forbid: then his
religion must yield – the laws could not be relaxed to accommodate religions or anything else. Honour stood first; and
the laws defined what it was and wherein it differed in certain details from honour as defined by church creeds and
by the social laws and customs of some of the minor divisions
of the globe that had got crowded out when the sacred
boundaries of Virginia were staked out.

If Judge Driscoll was the recognised first citizen of
Dawson's Landing, Pembroke Howard was easily its recognised second citizen. He was called 'the great lawyer' – an
earned title. He and Driscoll were of the same age – a year
or two past sixty.

Although Driscoll was a Freethinker and Howard a
strong and determined Presbyterian, their warm intimacy
suffered no impairment in consequence. They were men
whose opinions were their own property and not subject to
revision and amendment, suggestion or criticism, by anybody, even their friends.

The day's fishing finished, they came floating down-
stream in their skiff, talking national politics and other
high matters, and presently met a skiff coming up from
town, with a man in it, who said:

'I reckon you know one of the new twins gave your
nephew a kicking last night, Judge?'

'Did *what*?'

'Gave him a kicking.'

The old Judge's lips paled, and his eyes began to flame. He choked with anger for a moment, then he got out what he was trying to say.

'Well – well – go on! Give me the details.'

The man did it. At the finish the Judge was silent a minute, turning over in his mind the shameful picture of Tom's flight over the footlights; then he said, as if musing aloud: 'H'm – I don't understand it. I was asleep at home. He didn't wake me. Thought he was competent to manage his affair without my help, I reckon.' His face lit up with pride and pleasure at that thought, and he said with a cheery complacency, 'I like that – it's the true old blood – hey, Pembroke?'

Howard smiled an iron smile, and nodded his head approvingly. Then the news-bringer spoke again.

'But Tom beat the twin on the trial.'

The Judge looked at the man wonderingly, and said:

'The trial? What trial?'

'Why, Tom had him up before Judge Robinson for assault and battery.'

The old man shrank suddenly together like one who has received a death-stroke. Howard sprang for him as he sank forward in a swoon, and took him in his arms, and bedded him on his back in the boat. He sprinkled water in his face, and said to the startled visitor:

'Go, now – don't let him come to and find you here. You see what an effect your heedless speech has had; you ought to have been more considerate than to blurt out such a cruel piece of slander as that.'

'I'm right down sorry I did it now, Mr Howard, and I wouldn't have done it if I had thought: but it ain't a slander; it's perfectly true, just as I told him.'

He rowed away. Presently the old Judge came out of his

faint and looked up piteously into the sympathetic face that was bent over him.

'Say it ain't true, Pembroke; tell me it ain't true!' he said in a weak voice.

There was nothing weak in the deep organ-tones that responded:

'You know it's a lie as well as I do, old friend. He is of the best blood of the Old Dominion.'

'God bless you for saying it!' said the old gentleman, feverently. 'Ah, Pembroke, it was such a blow!'

Howard stayed by his friend, and saw him home, and entered the house with him. It was dark, and past supper-time, but the Judge was not thinking of supper; he was eager to hear the slander refuted from head-quarters, and as eager to have Howard hear it too. Tom was sent for, and he came immediately. He was bruised and lame, and was not a happy-looking object. His uncle made him sit down, and said:

'We have been hearing about your adventure, Tom, with a handsome lie added to it for embellishment. Now pulverise that lie to dust! What measures have you taken? How does the thing stand?'

Tom answered guilelessly: 'It don't stand at all; it's all over. I had him up in court and beat him. Pudd'nhead Wilson defended him – first case he ever had, and lost it. The Judge fined the miserable hound five dollars for the assault.'

Howard and the Judge sprang to their feet with the opening sentence – why, neither knew; then they stood gazing vacantly at each other. Howard stood a moment, then sat mournfully down without saying anything. The Judge's wrath began to kindle, and he burst out:

'You cur! You scum! You vermin! Do you mean to tell me that blood of my race has suffered a blow and crawled to a court of law about it? Answer me!'

Tom's head drooped, and he answered with an eloquent silence. His uncle stared at him with a mixed expression of amazement and shame and incredulity that was sorrowful to see. At last he said:

'Which of the twins was it?'

'Count Luigi.'

'You have challenged him?'

'N – no,' hesitated Tom, turning pale.

'You will challenge him to-night. Howard will carry it.'

Tom began to turn sick, and to show it. He turned his hat round and round in his hand, his uncle glowering blacker and blacker upon him as the heavy seconds drifted by; then at last he began to stammer, and said piteously:

'Oh, please don't ask me to do it, uncle! He is a murderous devil – I never could – I – I'm afraid of him!'

Old Driscoll's mouth opened and closed three times before he could get it to perform its office; then he stormed out:

'A coward in my family! A Driscoll a coward! Oh, what have I done to deserve this infamy!' He tottered to his secretary in the corner repeating that lament again and again in heartbreaking tones, and got out of a drawer a paper, which he slowly tore to bits, scattering the bits absently in his track as he walked up and down the room, still grieving and lamenting. At last he said:

'There it is, shreds and fragments once more – my will. Once more you have forced me to disinherit you, you base son of a most noble father! Leave my sight! Go – before I spit on you!'

The young man did not tarry. Then the Judge turned to Howard:

'You will be my second, old friend?'

'Of course.'

'There is pen and paper. Draft the cartel, and lose no time.'

'The Count shall have it in his hands in fifteen minutes,' said Howard.

Tom was very heavy-hearted. His appetite was gone with his property and his self-respect. He went out the back way and wandered down the obscure lane grieving, and wondering if any course of future conduct, however discreet and carefully perfected and watched over, could win back his uncle's favour and persuade him to reconstruct once more that generous will which had just gone to ruin before his eyes. He finally concluded that it could. He said to himself that he had accomplished this sort of triumph once already, and that what had been done once could be done again. He would set about it. He would bend every energy to the task, and he would score that triumph once more, cost what it might to his convenience, limit as it might his frivolous and liberty-loving life.

'To begin,' he said to himself, 'I'll square up with the proceeds of my raid, and then gambling has got to be stopped – and stopped short off. It's the worst vice I've got – from my standpoint, anyway, because it's the one he can most easily find out, through the impatience of my creditors. He thought it expensive to have to pay two hundred dollars to them for me once. Expensive – *that*! Why, it cost me the whole of his fortune – but of course he never thought of that; some people can't think of any but their own side of a case. If he had known how deep I am in, now, the will would have gone to pot without waiting for a duel to help. Three hundred dollars! It's a pile! But he'll never hear of it, I'm thankful to say. The minute I've cleared it off, I'm safe; and I'll never touch a card again. Anyway, I won't while he lives, I make oath to that. I'm entering on my last reform – I know it – yes, and I'll win; but after that, if I ever slip again I'm gone.'

CHAPTER 13

When I reflect upon the number of disagreeable people who I know have gone to a better world, I am moved to lead a different life. – Pudd'nhead Wilson's Calendar

October. This is one of the peculiarly dangerous months to speculate in stocks in. The others are July, January, September, April, November, May, March, June, December, August, and February. – Pudd'nhead Wilson's Calendar

THUS mournfully communing with himself Tom moped along the lane past Pudd'nhead Wilson's house, and still on and on between fences inclosing vacant country on each hand till he neared the haunted house, then he came moping back again, with many sighs and heavy with trouble. He sorely wanted cheerful company. Rowena! His heart gave a bound at the thought, but the next thought quieted it – the detested twins would be there.

He was on the inhabited side of Wilson's house, and now as he approached it he noticed that the sitting-room was lighted. This would do; others made him feel unwelcome sometimes, but Wilson never failed in courtesy toward him, and a kindly courtesy does at least save one's feelings, even if it is not professing to stand for a welcome. Wilson heard footsteps at his threshold, then the clearing of a throat.

'It's that fickle-tempered, dissipated young goose – poor devil, he finds friends pretty scarce to-day, likely, after the disgrace of carrying a personal-assault case into a law-court.'

A dejected knock. 'Come in!'

Tom entered, and drooped into a chair, without saying anything. Wilson said kindly:

'Why, my boy, you look desolate. Don't take it so hard. Try and forget you have been kicked.'

'Oh, dear,' said Tom, wretchedly, 'it's not that, Pudd'nhead – it's not that. It's a thousand times worse than that – oh, yes, a million times worse.'

'Why, Tom, what do you mean? Has Rowena –'

'Flung me? No, but the old man has.'

Wilson said to himself, 'Aha!' and thought of the mysterious girl in the bedroom. 'The Driscolls have been making discoveries!' Then he said aloud, gravely:

'Tom, there are some kinds of dissipation which –'

'Oh, shucks, this hasn't got anything to do with dissipation. He wanted me to challenge that derned Italian savage, and I wouldn't do it.'

'Yes, of course he would do that,' said Wilson in a meditative matter-of-course way; 'but the thing that puzzled me was, why he didn't look to that last night, for one thing, and why he let you carry such a matter into a court of law at all, either before the duel or after it. It's no place for it. It was not like him. I couldn't understand it. How did it happen?'

'It happened because he didn't know anything about it. He was asleep when I got home last night.'

'And you didn't wake him? Tom, is that possible?'

Tom was not getting much comfort here. He fidgeted a moment, then said:

'I didn't choose to tell him – that's all. He was going a-fishing before dawn, with Pembroke Howard, and if I got the twins into the common calaboose [1] – and I thought sure I could – I never dreamed of their slipping out on a paltry fine for such an outrageous offence – well, once in the calaboose they would be disgraced, and uncle wouldn't want any duels with that sort of characters, and wouldn't allow any.'

'Tom, I am ashamed of you! I don't see how you could treat your good uncle so. I am a better friend of his than you are; for if I had known the circumstances, I would have kept that case out of court until I got word to him and let him have a gentleman's chance.'

'You would?' exclaimed Tom, with lively surprise. 'And it your first case! And you know perfectly well there never would have *been* any case if he had got that chance, don't you? And you'd have finished your days a pauper nobody, instead of being an actually launched and recognized lawyer today. And you would really have done that, would you?'

'Certainly.'

Tom looked at him a moment or two, then shook his head sorrowfully and said:

'I believe you – upon my word I do. I don't know why I do, but I do. Pudd'nhead Wilson, I think you're the biggest fool I ever saw.'

'Thank you.'

'Don't mention it.'

'Well, he has been requiring you to fight the Italian and you have refused. You degenerate remnant of an honourable line! I'm thoroughly ashamed of you, Tom!'

'Oh, that's nothing! I don't care for anything, now that the will's torn up again.'

'Tom, tell me squarely – didn't he find any fault with you for anything but those two things – carrying the case into court and refusing to fight?'

He watched the young fellow's face narrowly, but it was entirely reposeful, and so also was the voice that answered:

'No, he didn't find any other fault with me. If he had had any to find, he would have begun yesterday, for he was just in the humour for it. He drove that jack-pair around town and showed them the sights, and when he came home he couldn't find his father's old silver watch that don't keep time and he thinks so much of, and couldn't remember what he did with it three or four days ago when he saw it last; and so when I arrived he was all in a sweat about it, and when I suggested that it probably wasn't lost but stolen, it put him in a regular passion and he said I was a fool – which convinced me, without any trouble, that that was just what he was afraid *had* happened, himself, but did not want to believe it, because lost things stand a better chance of being found again than stolen ones.'

'Whe-ew!' whistled Wilson; 'score another on the list.'

'Another what?'

'Another theft!'

'Theft?'

'Yes, theft. That watch isn't lost, it's stolen. There's been another raid on the town – and just the same old mysterious sort of thing that has happened once before, as you remember.'

'You don't mean it!'

'It's as sure as you are born! Have you missed anything yourself?'

'No. That is, I did miss a silver pencil-case that Aunt Mary Pratt gave me last birthday –'

'You'll find it's stolen – that's what you'll find out.'

'No, I shan't; for when I suggested theft about the watch and got such a rap, I went and examined my room, and the pencil-case was missing, but it was only mislaid, and I found it again.'

'You are sure you missed nothing else?'

'Well, nothing of consequence. I missed a small plain gold ring worth two or three dollars, but that will turn up. I'll look again.'

'In my opinion you'll not find it. There's been a raid, I tell you. Come *in!*'

Mr Justice Robinson entered, followed by Buckstone and the town-constable, Jim Blake. They sat down, and after some wandering and aimless weather-conversation Wilson said:

'By the way, we've just added another to the list of thefts, maybe two. Judge Driscoll's old silver watch is gone, and Tom here has missed a gold ring.'

'Well, it is a bad business,' said the Justice, 'and gets worse the further it goes. The Hankses, the Dobsons, the Pilligrews, the Ortons, the Grangers, the Hales, the Fullers, the Holcombs, in fact everybody that lives around about Patsy Cooper's has been robbed of little things like trinkets and teaspoons and suchlike small valuables that are easily carried off. It's perfectly plain that the thief took advantage of the reception at Patsy Cooper's, when all the neighbours were in her house and all their niggers hanging around her fence for a look at the show, to raid the vacant houses undisturbed. Patsy is miserable about it; miserable on account of the neighbours, and particularly miserable on account of her foreigners, of course; so miserable on their account that she hasn't any room to worry about her own little losses.'

'It's the same old raider,' said Wilson. 'I suppose there isn't any doubt about that.'

'Constable Blake doesn't think so.'

'No, you're wrong there,' said Blake; 'the other times it was a man; there was plenty of signs of that, as we know, in the profession, though we never got hands on him; but this time it's a woman.'

Wilson thought of the mysterious girl straight off. She was always in his mind now. But she failed him again. Blake continued:

'She's a stoop-shouldered old woman with a covered bas-ket on her arm, in a black veil, dressed in mourning. I saw her going aboard the ferry-boat yesterday. Lives in Illinois, I reckon; but I don't care where she lives, I'm going to get her – she can make herself sure of that.'

'What makes you think she's the thief?'

'Well, there ain't any other, for one thing; and for an-other, some of the nigger draymen that happened to be driving along saw her coming out of or going into houses, and told me so – and it just happens that they was *robbed* houses, every time.'

It was granted that this was plenty good enough circum-stantial evidence. A pensive silence followed, which lasted some moments, then Wilson said:

'There's one good thing, anyway. She can't either pawn or sell Count Luigi's costly Indian dagger.'

'My!' said Tom, 'Is *that* gone?'

'Yes.'

'Well, that was a haul! But why can't she pawn it or sell it?'

'Because when the twins went home from the Sons of Liberty meeting last night, news of the raid was sifting in from everywhere, and Aunt Patsy was in distress to know if they had lost anything. They found that the dagger was gone, and they notified the police and pawnbrokers every-where. It was a great haul, yes, but the old woman won't get anything out of it, because she'll get caught.'

'Did they offer a reward?' asked Buckstone.

'Yes; five hundred dollars for the knife, and five hundred more for the thief.'

'What a leather-headed idea!' exclaimed the constable. 'The thief da'sn't go near them, nor send anybody. Who-ever goes is going to get himself nabbed, for there ain't any pawnbroker that's going to lose the chance to –'

If anybody had noticed Tom's face at that time, the grey-green colour of it might have provoked curiosity; but nobody did. He said to himself: 'I'm gone! I never can square up; the rest of the plunder won't pawn or sell for half of the bill. Oh, I know it – I'm gone, I'm gone – and this time it's for good. Oh, this is awful – I don't know what to do, nor which way to turn!'

'Softly, softly,' said Wilson to Blake. 'I planned their scheme for them at midnight last night, and it was all finished up shipshape by two this morning. They'll get their dagger back, and then I'll explain to you how the thing was done.'

There were strong signs of a general curiosity, and Buckstone said:

'Well, you have whetted us up pretty sharp, Wilson, and I'm free to say that if you don't mind telling us in confidence –'

'Oh, I'd as soon tell as not, Buckstone, but as long as the twins and I agreed to say nothing about it, we must let it stand so. But you can take my word for it you won't be kept waiting three days. Somebody will apply for that reward pretty promptly, and I'll show you the thief and the dagger both very soon afterward.'

The constable was disappointed, and also perplexed. He said:

'It may all be – yes, and I hope it will, but I'm blamed if I can see my way through it. It's too many for yours truly.'

The subject seemed about talked out. Nobody seemed to have anything further to offer. After a silence the justice of the peace informed Wilson that he and Buckstone and the constable had come as a committee, on the part of the Democratic party, to ask him to run for mayor – for the little town was about to become a city and the first charter election was approaching. It was the first attention which Wilson had ever received at the hands of any party; it was a sufficiently humble one, but it was a recognition of his *début* into the town's life and activities at last; it was a step upward, and he was deeply gratified. He accepted, and the committee departed, followed by young Tom.

CHAPTER 14

The true Southern watermelon is a boon apart, and not
to be mentioned with commoner things. It is chief of
this world's luxuries, king by the grace of God over all
the fruits of the earth. When one has tasted it, he knows
what the angels eat. It was not a Southern watermelon
that Eve took; we know it because she repented. –
Pudd'nhead Wilson's Calendar

ABOUT the time that Wilson was bowing the committee
out, Pembroke Howard was entering the next house to report. He found the old Judge sitting grim and straight in his
chair, waiting.

'Well, Howard – the news?'

'The best in the world.'

'Accepts, does he?' and the light of battle gleamed
joyously in the Judge's eye.

'Accepts? Why, he jumped at it.'

'Did, did he? Now that's fine – that's very fine. I like that.
When is it to be?'

'Now! Straight off! To-night! An admirable fellow –
admirable!'

'Admirable? He's a darling! Why, it's an honour as well
as a pleasure to stand up before such a man. Come – off with
you! Go and arrange everything – and give him my
heartiest compliments. A rare fellow, indeed; an admirable
fellow, as you have said!'

Howard hurried away, saying:

'I'll have him in the vacant stretch between Wilson's and
the haunted house within the hour, and I'll bring my own
pistols.'

Judge Driscoll began to walk the floor in a state of pleased

excitement; but presently he stopped, and began to think –
began to think of Tom. Twice he moved toward the secretary, and twice he turned away again; but finally he said:

'This may be my last night in the world – I must not take
the chance. He is worthless and unworthy, but it is largely
my fault. He was entrusted to me by my brother on his dying bed, and I have indulged him to his hurt, instead of
training him up severely, and making a man of him. I have
violated my trust, and I must not add the sin of desertion to
that. I have forgiven him once already, and would subject
him to a long and hard trial before forgiving him again, if I
could live; but I must not run that risk. No, I must restore
the will. But if I survive the duel, I will hide it away, and he
will not know, and I will not tell him until he reforms and I
see that his reformation is going to be permanent.'

He redrew the will, and his ostensible nephew was heir
to a fortune again. As he was finishing his task, Tom,
wearied with another brooding tramp, entered the house
and went tiptoeing past the sitting-room door. He glanced
in, and hurried on, for the sight of his uncle had nothing but
terrors for him to-night. But his uncle was writing! That
was unusual at this late hour. What could he be writing? A
chill of anxiety settled down upon Tom's heart. Did that
writing concern him? He was afraid so. He reflected that
when ill luck begins, it does not come in sprinkles, but in
showers. He said he would get a glimpse of that document
or know the reason why. He heard some one coming, and
stepped out of sight and hearing. It was Pembroke Howard.
What could be hatching?

Howard said, with great satisfaction:

'Everything's right and ready. He's gone to the battle-
ground with his second and the surgeon – also with his
brother. I've arranged it all with Wilson – Wilson's his
second. We are to have three shots apiece.'

'Good! How is the moon?'

'Bright as day, nearly. Perfect, for the distance – fifteen yards. No wind – not a breath; hot and still.'

'All good; all first-rate. Here, Pembroke, read this, and witness it.'

Pembroke read and witnessed the will, then gave the old man's hand a hearty shake and said:

'Now that's right, York – but I knew you would do it. You couldn't leave that poor chap to fight along without means or profession, with certain defeat before him, and I knew you wouldn't, for his father's sake if not for his own.'

'For his dead father's sake I couldn't, I know; for poor Percy – but you know what Percy was to me. But mind – Tom is not to know of this unless I fall to-night.'

'I understand. I'll keep the secret.'

The Judge put the will away, and the two started for the battle-ground. In another minute the will was in Tom's hands. His misery vanished, his feelings underwent a tremendous revulsion. He put the will carefully back in its place, and spread his mouth and swung his hat once, twice, three times around his head, in imitation of three rousing huzzas, no sound issuing from his lips. He fell to communing with himself excitedly and joyously, but every now and then he let off another volley of dumb hurrahs.

He said to himself: 'I've got the fortune again, but I'll not let on that I know about it. And this time I'm going to hang on to it. I take no more risks. I'll gamble no more, I'll drink no more, because – well, because I'll not go where there is any of that sort of thing going on, again. It's the sure way, and the only sure way; I might have thought of that sooner – well, yes, if I had wanted to. But now – dear me, I've had a bad scare this time, and I'll take no more chances. Not a single chance more. Land! I persuaded myself this evening that I could fetch him around without any great amount of effort, but I've been getting more and more heavy-hearted and doubtful straight along, ever since. If he tells me about this thing, all right; but if he doesn't, I sha'n't let on. I – well, I'd like to tell Pudd'nhead Wilson, but – no, I'll think about that; perhaps I won't.' He whirled off another dead huzza, and said: 'I'm reformed, and this time I'll stay so, sure!'

He was about to close with a final grand silent demonstration, when he suddenly recollected that Wilson had put it out of his power to pawn or sell the Indian knife, and that he was once more in awful peril of exposure by his creditors for that reason. His joy collapsed utterly, and he turned away and moped toward the door, moaning and lamenting over the bitterness of his luck. He dragged himself upstairs, and brooded in his room a long time, disconsolate and forlorn, with Luigi's Indian knife for a text. At last he sighed and said:

'When I supposed these stones were glass and this ivory bone, the thing hadn't any interest for me because it hadn't any value, and couldn't help me out of my trouble. But now – why, now it is full of interest; yes, and of a sort to break a body's heart. It's a bag of gold that has turned to dirt and ashes in my hands. It could save me, and save me so easily, and yet I've got to go to ruin. It's like drowning with a life-preserver in my reach. All the hard luck comes to me, and all the good luck goes to other people – Pudd'nhead Wilson, for instance; even his career has got a sort of a little start at last, and what has he done to deserve it, I should like to know? Yes, he has opened his own road, but he isn't content with that, but must block mine. It's a sordid, selfish world, and I wish I was out of it.' He allowed the light of the candle to play upon the jewels of the sheath, but the flashings and sparklings had no charm for his eye; they were only just so many pangs to his heart. 'I must not say anything to Roxy about this thing,' he said, 'she is too daring. She would be for digging these stones out and selling them, and then – why, she would be arrested and the stones traced, and then –' The thought made him quake, and he hid the knife away, trembling all over and glancing furtively about, like a criminal who fancies that the accuser is already at hand.

Should he try to sleep? Oh, no, sleep was not for him; his trouble was too haunting, too afflicting for that. He must have somebody to mourn with. He would carry his despair to Roxy.

He had heard several distant gunshots, but that sort of thing was not uncommon, and they had made no impression upon him. He went out at the back door, and turned westward. He passed Wilson's house and proceeded along the lane, and presently saw several figures approaching Wilson's place through the vacant lots. These were the duellists returning from the fight; he thought he recognised them, but as he had no desire for white people's company, he stooped down behind the fence until they were out of his way.

Roxy was feeling fine. She said:

'Whah was you, child? Warn't you in it?'

'In what?'

'In de duel.'

'Duel? Has there been a duel?'

' 'Co'se dey has. De ole Jedge has be'n havin' a duel wid one o' dem twins.'

'Great Scott!' Then he added to himself: 'That's what made him re-make the will; he thought he might get killed, and it softened him toward me. And that's what he and Howard were so busy about. . . . Oh dear, if the twin had only killed him, I should be out of my –'

'What is you mumblin' 'bout, Chambers? Whah was you? Didn't you know dey was gwyne to be a duel?'

'No, I didn't. The old man tried to get me to fight one with Count Luigi, but he didn't succeed, so I reckon he concluded to patch up the family honour himself.'

He laughed at the idea, and went rambling on with a detailed account of his talk with the Judge, and how shocked and ashamed the Judge was to find that he had a coward in his family. He glanced up at last, and got a shock himself. Roxana's bosom was heaving with suppressed passion, and she was glowering down upon him with measureless contempt written in her face.

'En you refuse' to fight a man dat kicked you, 'stid o' jumpin' at de chance! En you ain't got no mo' feelin' den to come en tell me, dat fetched sich a po' low-down ornery rabbit into de worl'! Pah! it make me sick! It's de nigger in you, dat's what it is. Thirty-one parts o' you is white, en on'y one part nigger, en dat po' little one part is yo' *soul*. 'Tain't wuth savin'; tain't wuth totin' out on a shovel en throwin' in de gutter. You has disgraced yo' birth. What would yo' pa think o' you? It's enough to make him turn in his grave.'

The last three sentences stung Tom into a fury, and he said to himself that if his father were only alive and in reach of assassination his mother would soon find that he had a very clear notion of the size of his indebtedness to that man, and was willing to pay it up in full, and would do it too, even at risk of his life; but he kept his thought to himself; that was safest in his mother's present state.

'Whatever has come o' yo' Essex blood? Dat's what I can't understan'. En it ain't on'y jist Essex blood dat's in you, not by a long sight — 'deed it ain't! My great-great-great-gran'-father en yo great-great-great-great-gran'father was ole Cap'n John Smith,[1] de highest blood dat Ole Vir-

ginny ever turned out, en *his* great-great-gran'mother, or
somers along back dah, was Pocahontas de Injun queen, en
her husbun' was a nigger king outen Africa – en yit here
you is, a slinkin' outen a duel en disgracin' our whole line
like a ornery low-down hound! Yes, it's de nigger in you!'

She sat down on her candle-box and fell into a reverie.
Tom did not disturb her; he sometimes lacked prudence,
but it was not in circumstances of this kind. Roxana's storm
went gradually down, but it died hard, and even when it
seemed to be quite gone, it would now and then break out
in a distant rumble, so to speak, in the form of muttered
ejaculations. One of these was, 'Ain't nigger enough in him
to show in his finger-nails, en dat takes mighty little – yit
dey's enough to paint his soul.'

Presently she muttered, 'Yassir, enough to paint a whole
thimbleful of 'em.' At last her ramblings ceased altogether,
and her countenance began to clear – a welcome sign to
Tom, who had learned her moods, and knew she was on the
threshold of good-humour, now. He noticed that from time
to time she unconsciously carried her finger to the end of her
nose. He looked closer and said:

'Why, mammy, the end of your nose is skinned. How did
that come?'

She sent out the sort of whole-hearted peal of laughter
which God has vouchsafed in its perfection to none but the
happy angels in heaven and the bruised and broken black
slave on the earth, and said:

'Dad fetch dat duel, I be'n in it myself.'

'Gracious! did a bullet do that?'

'Yassir, you bet it did!'

'Well, I declare! Why, how did that happen?'

'Happen dis-away. I 'uz a-sett'n' here kinder dozin' in
de dark, en *che-bang!* goes a gun, right out dah. I skips
along out towards t'other end o' de house to see what's

gwyne on, en stops by de ole winder on de side towards
Pudd'nhead Wilson's house dat ain't got no sash in it — but
dey ain't none of 'em got any sashes, fur as dat's concerned
— en I stood dah in de dark en look out, en dar in de moonlight, right down under me 'uz one o' de twins a-cussin' —
not much, but jist a-cussin' soft — it 'uz de brown one dat
'uz cussin', 'ca'se he 'uz hit in de shoulder. En Doctor Claypool he 'uz a-workin' at him, en Pudd'nhead Wilson he 'uz
a-he'pin', en ole Jedge Driscoll en Pem Howard 'uz a-
standin' out yonder a little piece waitin' for 'em to git
ready agin. En treckly dey squared off en give de word, en
bang-bang went de pistols, en de twin he say, 'Ouch!' — hit
him on de han' dis time — en I hear dat same bullet go *spat!*
ag'in' de logs under de winder; en de nex' time dey shoot,
de twin say, 'Ouch!' ag'in, en I done it too, 'ca'se de bullet
glance on his cheek-bone en skip up here en glance on de
side o' de winder en whiz right acrost my face en tuck de
hide off'n my nose — why, if I'd 'a' be'n jist a inch or a inch
en a half furder 'twould 'a' tuck de whole nose en disfig-
ger me. Here's de bullet; I hunted her up.'

'Did you stand there all the time?'

'Dat's a question to ask, ain't it! What else would I do?
Does I git a chance to see a duel every day?'

'Why, you were right in range! Weren't you afraid?'

The woman gave a sniff of scorn.

' 'Fraid! De Smith-Pocahontases ain't 'fraid o' nothin', let
alone bullets.'

'They've got pluck enough, I suppose; what they lack is
judgment. *I* wouldn't have stood there.'

'Nobody's accusin' you!'

'Did anybody else get hurt?'

'Yes, we all got hit 'cep' de blon' twin en de doctor en de
seconds. De Jedge didn't git hurt, but I hear Pudd'nhead say
de bullet snip some o' his ha'r off.'

''George!' said Tom to himself, 'to come so near being out of my trouble, and miss it by an inch. Oh dear, dear, he will live to find me out and sell me to some nigger-trader yet – yes, and he would do it in a minute.' Then he said aloud, in a grave tone:

'Mother, we are in an awful fix.'

Roxana caught her breath with a spasm, and said:

'Chile! What you hit a body so sudden for, like dat? What's be'n en gone en happen'?'

'Well, there's one thing I didn't tell you. When I wouldn't fight, he tore up the will again, and –'

Roxana's face turned a dead white, and she said:

'Now you's *done!* – done for ever! Dat's de end. Bofe un us is gwyne to starve to –'

'Wait and hear me through, can't you? I reckon that when he resolved to fight, himself, he thought he might get killed and not have a chance to forgive me any more in this life, so he made the will again, and I've seen it, and it's all right. But –'

'Oh, thank goodness, den we's safe ag'in! – safe! en so what did you want to come here en talk sich dreadful –'

'Hold *on*, I tell you, and let me finish. The swag I gathered won't half square me up, and the first thing we know, my creditors – well, you know what'll happen.'

Roxana dropped her chin, and told her son to leave her alone – she must think this matter out. Presently she said impressively:

'You got to go mighty keerful now, I tell you! En here's what you got to do. He didn't git killed, en if you gives him de least reason, he'll bust de will ag'in, en dat's de *las'* time, now you hear me! So – you's got to show him what you kin do in de nex' few days. You's got to be pison good, en let him see it; you got to do everything dat'll make him b'lieve in you, en you got to sweeten aroun' ole Aunt Pratt, too –

she's pow'ful strong wid de Jedge, en de bes' frien' you got. Nex', you'll go 'long away to Sent Louis, en dat'll *keep* him in yo' favour. Den you go en make a bargain wid dem people. You tell 'em he ain't gwyne to live long – en dat's de fac', too – en tell 'em you'll pay 'em intrust, en big intrust, too – ten per – what you call it?'

'Ten per cent. a month?'

'Dat's it. Den you take and sell yo' truck aroun', a little at a time, en pay de intrust. How long will it las'?'

'I think there's enough to pay the interest five or six months.'

'Den you's all right. If he don't die in six months, dat don't make no diff'rence – Providence'll provide. You's gwyne to be safe – if you behaves.' She bent an austere eye on him and added, 'En you *is* gwyne to behave – does you know dat?'

He laughed and said he was going to try, anyway. She did not unbend. She said gravely:

'Tryin' ain't de thing. You's gwyne to *do* it. You ain't gwyne to steal a pin – 'ca'se it ain't safe no mo'; en you ain't gwyne into no bad comp'ny – not even once, you under-stand; en you ain't gwyne to drink a drop – nary single drop; en you ain't gwyne to gamble one single gamble – not one! Dis ain't what you's gwyne to *try* to do, it's what you's gwyne to *do*. En I'll tell you how I knows it. Dis is how. I's gwyne to foller along to Sent Louis my own self; en you's gwyne to come to me every day o' yo' life, en I'll look you over; en if you fails in one single one o' dem things – jist *one* – I take my oath I'll come straight down to dis town en tell de Jedge you's a nigger en a slave – en *prove* it!' She paused to let her words sink home. Then she added: 'Chambers, does you b'lieve me when I says dat?'

Tom was sober enough now. There was no levity in his voice when he answered:

'Yes, mother. I know, now, that I am reformed – and permanently. Permanently – and beyond the reach of any human temptation.'

'Den g' long home en begin!'

CHAPTER 15

Nothing so needs reforming as other people's habits. – *Pudd'nhead Wilson's Calendar*

Behold, the fool saith, 'Put not all thine eggs in the one basket' – which is but a manner of saying, 'Scatter your money and your attention;' but the wise man saith, 'Put all your eggs in the one basket and – WATCH THAT BASKET.' – *Pudd'nhead Wilson's Calendar*

WHAT a time of it Dawson's Landing was having! All its life it had been asleep, but now it hardly got a chance for a nod, so swiftly did big events and crashing surprises come along in one another's wake: Friday morning, first glimpse of Real Nobility, also grand reception at Aunt Patsy Cooper's, also great robber-raid; Friday evening, dramatic kicking of the heir of the chief citizen in presence of four hundred people; Saturday morning, emergence as practising lawyer of the long-submerged Pudd'nhead Wilson; Saturday night, duel between chief citizen and titled stranger.

The people took more pride in the duel than in all the other events put together, perhaps. It was a glory to their town to have such a thing happen there. In their eyes the principals had reached the summit of human honour. Everybody paid homage to their names; their praises were in all mouths. Even the duellists' subordinates came in for a handsome share of the public approbation: wherefore Pudd'nhead Wilson was suddenly become a man of consequence. When asked to run for the mayoralty Saturday night he was risking defeat, but Sunday morning found him a made man and his success assured.

The twins were prodigiously great now; the town took them to its bosom with enthusiasm. Day after day, and night after night, they went dining and visiting from house to house, making friends, enlarging and solidifying their popularity, and charming and surprising all with their musical prodigies, and now and then heightening the effects with samples of what they could do in other directions, out of their stock of rare and curious accomplishments. They were so pleased that they gave the regulation thirty days' notice, the required preparation for citizenship, and resolved to finish their days in this pleasant place. That was the climax. The delighted community rose as one man and applauded; and when the twins were asked to stand for seats in the forthcoming aldermanic board, and consented, the public contentment was rounded and complete.

Tom Driscoll was not happy over these things; they sunk deep, and hurt all the way down. He hated the one twin for kicking him, and the other one for being the kicker's brother.

Now and then the people wondered why nothing was heard of the raider, or of the stolen knife or the other plunder, but nobody was able to throw any light on that matter. Nearly a week had drifted by, and still the thing remained a vexed mystery.

On Saturday Constable Blake and Pudd'nhead Wilson met on the street, and Tom Driscoll joined them in time to open their conversation for them. He said to Blake: 'You are not looking well, Blake; you seem to be annoyed about something. Has anything gone wrong in the detective business? I believe you fairly and justifiably claim to have a pretty good reputation in that line, isn't it so?' – which made Blake feel good, and look it; but Tom added, 'for a

country detective' – which made Blake feel the other way,
and not only look it, but betray it in his voice.

'Yes, sir, I *have* got a reputation; and it's as good as anybody's in the profession, too, country or no country.'

'Oh, I beg pardon; I didn't mean any offence. What I
started out to ask was only about the old woman that raided
the town – the stoop-shouldered old woman, you know, that
you said you were going to catch; and I knew you would,
too, because you have the reputation of never boasting, and
– well, you – you've caught the old woman?'

'D— the old woman!'

'Why, sho! you don't mean to say you haven't caught
her?'

'No; I haven't caught her. If anybody could have caught
her, I could; but nobody couldn't. I don't care who he is.'

'I am sorry, real sorry – for your sake; because when it
gets around that a detective has expressed himself so con-
fidently, and then –'

'Don't you worry, that's all – don't you worry; and as for
the town, the town needn't worry either. She's my meat –
make yourself easy about that. I'm on her track; I've got
clues that –'

'That's good! Now if you could get an old veteran detective down from St Louis to help you find out what the
clues mean, and where they lead to, and then –'

'I'm plenty veteran enough myself, and I don't need anybody's help. I'll have her inside of a we – inside of a month.
That I'll swear to!'

Tom said carelessly:

'I suppose that will answer – yes, that will answer. But I
reckon she is pretty old, and old people don't often outlive
the cautious pace of the professional detective when he has
got his clues together and is out on his still-hunt.'

Blake's dull face flushed under this gibe, but before he

could set his retort in order Tom had turned to Wilson, and was saying, with placid indifference of manner and voice:

'Who got the reward, Pudd'nhead?'

Wilson winced slightly, and saw that his own turn was come.

'What reward?'

'Why, the reward for the thief, and the other one for the knife.'

Wilson answered – and rather uncomfortably, to judge by his hesitating fashion of delivering himself:

'Well, the – well, in fact, nobody has claimed it yet.'

Tom seemed surprised.

'Why, is that so?'

Wilson showed a trifle of irritation when he replied:

'Yes, it's so. And what of it?'

'Oh, nothing. Only I thought you had struck out a new idea, and invented a scheme that was going to revolutionise the time-worn and ineffectual methods of the –' He stopped, and turned to Blake, who was happy now that another had taken his place on the gridiron: 'Blake, didn't you understand him to intimate that it wouldn't be necessary for you to hunt the old woman down?'

'B'George, he said he'd have thief and swag both inside of three days – he did, by hokey! and that's just about a week ago. Why, I said at the time that no thief and no thief's pal was going to try to pawn or sell a thing where he knowed the pawnbroker could get both rewards by taking *him* into camp *with* the swag. It was the blessedest idea that ever I struck!'

'You'd change your mind,' said Wilson, with irritated bluntness, 'if you knew the entire scheme instead of only part of it.'

'Well,' said the constable, pensively, 'I had the idea that it wouldn't work, and up to now I'm right, anyway.'

'Very well, then, let it stand at that, and give it a further show. It has worked at least as well as your own methods, you perceive.'

The constable hadn't anything handy to hit back with, so he discharged a discontented sniff, and said nothing.

After the night that Wilson had partly revealed his scheme at his house, Tom had tried for several days to guess out the secret of the rest of it, but had failed. Then it occurred to him to give Roxana's smarter head a chance at it. He made a supposititious case, and laid it before her. She thought it over, and delivered her verdict upon it. Tom said to himself, 'She's hit it, sure!' He thought he would test that verdict, now, and watch Wilson's face; so he said reflectively:

'Wilson, you're not a fool — a fact of recent discovery. Whatever your scheme was, it had sense in it, Blake's opinion to the contrary notwithstanding. I don't ask you to reveal it, but I will suppose a case — a case which will answer as a starting-point for the real thing I am going to come at, and that's all I want. You offered five hundred dollars for the knife, and five hundred for the thief. We will suppose, for argument's sake, that the first reward is *advertised*, and the second offered by *private letter* to pawnbrokers and —'

Blake slapped his thigh, and cried out:

'By Jackson, he's got you, Pudd'nhead! Now why couldn't I or *any* fool have thought of that?'

Wilson said to himself, 'Anybody with a reasonably good head would have thought of it. I am not surprised that Blake didn't detect it; I am only surprised that Tom did. There is more to him than I supposed.' He said nothing aloud, and Tom went on:

'Very well. The thief would not suspect that there was a trap, and he would bring or send the knife, and say he

bought it for a song, or found it in the road, or something
like that, and try to collect the reward, and be arrested —
wouldn't he?'

'Yes,' said Wilson.

'I think so,' said Tom. 'There can't be any doubt of it.
Have you ever seen that knife?'

'No.'

'Has any friend of yours?'

'Not that I know of.'

'Well, I begin to think I understand why your scheme
failed.'

'What do you mean, Tom? What are you driving at?'
asked Wilson, with a dawning sense of discomfort.

'Why, that there *isn't* any such knife.'

'Look here, Wilson,' said Blake, 'Tom Driscoll's right,
for a thousand dollars — if I had it.'

Wilson's blood warmed a little, and he wondered if he
had been played upon by those strangers; it certainly had
something of that look. But what could they gain by it? He
threw out that suggestion. Tom replied:

'Gain? Oh, nothing that you would value, maybe. But
they are strangers making their way in a new community.
Is it nothing to them to appear as pets of an Oriental prince
— at no expense? Is it nothing to them to be able to dazzle
this poor little town with thousand-dollar rewards — at no
expense? Wilson, there isn't any such knife, or your scheme
would have fetched it to light. Or if there is any such knife,
they've got it yet. I believe, myself, that they've seen such a
knife, for Angelo pictured it out with his pencil too swiftly
and handily for him to have been inventing it, and of course
I can't swear that they've never had it; but this I'll go bail
for — if they had it when they came to this town, they've got
it yet.'

Blake said:

168

'It looks mighty reasonable, the way Tom puts it; it most certainly does.'

Tom responded, turning to leave:

'You find the old woman, Blake, and if she can't furnish the knife, go and search the twins!'

Tom sauntered away. Wilson felt a good deal depressed. He hardly knew what to think. He was loth to withdraw his faith from the twins, and was resolved not to do it on the present indecisive evidence; but – well, he would think, and then decide how to act.

'Blake, what do you think of this matter?'

'Well, Pudd'nhead, I'm bound to say I put it up the way Tom does. They hadn't the knife; or if they had it, they've got it yet.'

The men parted. Wilson said to himself:

'I believe they had it; if it had been stolen, the scheme would have restored it, that is certain. And so I believe they've got it yet.'

Tom had no purpose in his mind when he encountered those two men. When he began his talk he hoped to be able to gall them a little and get a trifle of malicious entertainment out of it. But when he left, he left in great spirits, for he perceived that just by pure luck and no troublesome labour he had accomplished several delightful things: he had touched both men on a raw spot and seen them squirm; he had modified Wilson's sweetness for the twins with one small bitter taste that he wouldn't be able to get out of his mouth right away; and, best of all, he had taken the hated twins down a peg with the community; for Blake would gossip around freely, after the manner of detectives, and within a week the town would be laughing at them in its sleeve for offering a gaudy reward for a bauble which they either never possessed or hadn't lost. Tom was very well satisfied with himself.

Tom's behaviour at home had been perfect during the entire week. His uncle and aunt had seen nothing like it before. They could find no fault with him anywhere.

Saturday evening he said to the Judge:

'I've had something preying on my mind, uncle, and as I am going away, and might never see you again, I can't bear it any longer. I made you believe I was afraid to fight that Italian adventurer. I had to get out of it on some pretext or other, and maybe I chose badly, being taken unawares, but no honourable person could consent to meet him in the field, knowing what I knew about him.'

'Indeed. What was that?'

'Count Luigi is a confessed assassin.'

'Incredible!'

'It is perfectly true. Wilson detected it in his hand, by palmistry, and charged him with it, and cornered him up so close that he had to confess; but both twins begged us on their knees to keep the secret, and swore they would lead straight lives here; and it was all so pitiful that we gave our word of honour never to expose them while they kept that promise. You would have done it yourself, uncle.'

'You are right, my boy, I would. A man's secret is still his own property, and sacred, when it has been surprised out of him like that. You did well, and I am proud of you.' Then he added mournfully: 'But I wish I could have been saved the shame of meeting an assassin on the field of honour.'

'It couldn't be helped, uncle. If I had known you were going to challenge him I should have felt obliged to sacrifice my pledged word in order to stop it, but Wilson couldn't be expected to do otherwise than keep silent.'

'Oh no; Wilson did right, and is in no way to blame. Tom, Tom, you have lifted a heavy load from my heart; I was stung to the very soul when I seemed to have discovered that I had a coward in my family.'

'You may imagine what it cost *me* to assume such a part, uncle.'

'Oh, I know it, poor boy, I know it. And I can understand how much it has cost you to remain under that unjust stigma to this time. But it is all right now, and no harm is done. You have restored my comfort of mind, and with it your own; and both of us had suffered enough.'

The old man sat awhile plunged in thought; then he looked up with a satisfied light in his eye, and said: 'That this assassin should have put the affront upon me of letting me meet him on the field of honour as if he were a gentleman is a matter which I will presently settle — but not now. I will not shoot him until after election. I see a way to ruin them both before; I will attend to that first. Neither of them shall be elected, that I promise. You are sure that the fact that he is an assassin has not got abroad?'

'Perfectly certain of it, sir.'

'It will be a good card. I will fling a hint at it from the stump on the polling-day. It will sweep the ground from under both of them.'

'There's not a doubt of it. It will finish them.'

'That and outside work among the voters will, to a certainty. I want you to come down here by-and-by and work privately among the rag-tag and bob-tail. You shall spend money among them; I will furnish it.'

Another point scored against the detested twins! Really it was a great day for Tom. He was encouraged to chance a parting shot, now, at the same target, and did it.

'You know that wonderful Indian knife that the twins have been making such a to-do about? Well, there's no track or trace of it yet; so the town is beginning to sneer and gossip and laugh. Half the people believe they never had any such knife, the other half believe they had it and have got it still. I've heard twenty people talking like that to-day.'

Yes, Tom's blemishless week had restored him to the favour of his aunt and uncle.

His mother was satisfied with him, too. Privately, she believed she was coming to love him, but she did not say so. She told him to go along to St Louis, now, and she would get ready and follow. Then she smashed her whisky bottle and said:

'Dah now! I's a-gwyne to make you walk as straight as a string, Chambers, en so I's bown' you ain't gwyne to git no bad example out o' yo' mammy. I tole you you couldn't go into no bad comp'ny. Well, you's gwyne into my comp'ny, en I's gwyne to fill de bill. Now, den, trot along, trot along!'

Tom went aboard one of the big transient boats that night with his heavy satchel of miscellaneous plunder, and slept the sleep of the unjust, which is serener and sounder than the other kind, as we know by the hanging-eve history of a million rascals. But when he got up in the morning, luck was against him again: a brother-thief had robbed him while he slept, and gone ashore at some intermediate landing.

CHAPTER 16

If you pick up a starving dog and make him prosperous,
he will not bite you. This is the principal difference
between a dog and a man. – *Pudd'nhead Wilson's
Calendar*

We know all about the habits of the ant, we know all
about the habits of the bee, but we know nothing at all
about the habits of the oyster. It seems almost certain
that we have been choosing the wrong time for studying
the oyster. – *Pudd'nhead Wilson's Calendar*

WHEN Roxana arrived, she found her son in such despair
and misery that her heart was touched and her motherhood
rose up strong in her. He was ruined past hope now; his
destruction would be immediate and sure, and he would be
an outcast and friendless. That was reason enough for a
mother to love a child; so she loved him, and told him so. It
made him wince, secretly – for she was a 'nigger'. That he
was one himself was far from reconciling him to that despised race.

Roxana poured out endearments upon him, to which he
responded uncomfortably, but as well as he could. And she
tried to comfort him, but that was not possible. These in-
timacies quickly became horrible to him, and within the
hour he began to try to get up courage enough to tell her so,
and require that they be discontinued or very considerably
modified. But he was afraid of her; and besides, there came
a lull, now, for she had begun to think. She was trying to invent a saving plan. Finally she started up, and said she
had found a way out. Tom was almost suffocated by the joy
of this sudden good news. Roxana said:

173

'Here is de plan, en she'll win, sure. I's a nigger, en no-body ain't gwyne to doubt it dat hears me talk. I's wuth six hund'd dollahs. Take en sell me, en pay off dese gamblers.'

Tom was dazed. He was not sure he had heard aright. He was dumb for a moment; then he said:

'Do you mean that you would be sold into slavery to save me?'

'Ain't you my chile? En does you know anything dat a mother won't do for her chile? Dey ain't nothin' a white mother won't do for her chile. Who made 'em so? De Lord done it. En who made de niggers? De Lord made 'em. In de inside, mothers is all de same. De good Lord he made 'em so. I's gwyne to be sole into slavery, en in a year you's gwyne to buy yo' ole mammy free ag'in. I'll show you how. Dat's de plan.'

Tom's hopes began to rise, and his spirits along with them. He said:

'It's lovely of you, mammy — it's just —'

'Say it ag'in! En keep on sayin' it! It's all de pay a body kin want in dis worl', en it's mo den enough. Laws bless you, honey, when I's slavin' aroun', en dey 'buses me, if I knows you's a-sayin' dat, 'way off yonder somers, it'll heal up all de sore places, en I kin stan' 'em.'

'I *do* say it again, mammy, and I'll keep on saying it, too. But how am I going to sell you? You're free, you know.'

'Much diff'rence dat make! White folks ain't partic'lar. De law kin sell me now if dey tell me to leave de State in six months en I don't go. You draw up a paper — bill o' sale — en put it 'way off yonder, down in de middle o' Kaintuck somers, en sign some names to it, en say you'll sell me cheap 'ca'se you's hard up; you'll fine you ain't gwyne to have no trouble. You take me up de country a piece, en sell me on a farm; dem people ain't gwyne to ask no questions if I's a bargain.'

Tom forged a bill of sale and sold his mother to an Arkansas cotton-planter for a trifle over six hundred dollars. He did not want to commit this treachery,[1] but luck threw the man in his way, and this saved him the necessity of going up country to hunt up a purchaser, with the added risk of having to answer a lot of questions, whereas this planter was so pleased with Roxy that he asked next to none at all. Besides, the planter insisted that Roxy wouldn't know where she was at first, and that by the time she found out she would already have become contented. And Tom argued with himself that it was an immense advantage for Roxy to have a master who was so pleased with her, as this planter manifestly was. In almost no time his flowing reasonings carried him to the point of even half believing he was doing Roxy a splendid surreptitious service in selling her 'down the river'. And then he kept diligently saying to himself all the time: 'It's for only a year. In a year I buy her free again; she'll keep that in mind, and it'll reconcile her.' Yes; the little deception could do no harm, and everything would come out right and pleasant in the end, anyway. By agreement, the conversation in Roxy's presence was all about the man's 'up-country' farm, and how pleasant a place it was, and how happy the slaves were there; so poor Roxy was entirely deceived, and easily, for she was not dreaming that her own son could be guilty of treason to a mother who, by voluntarily going into slavery – slavery of any kind, mild or severe, or of any duration, brief or long – was making a sacrifice for him compared with which death would have been a poor and commonplace one. She lavished tears and loving caresses upon him privately, and then went away with her owner – went away broken-hearted, and yet proud of what she was doing, and glad that it was in her power to do it.

Tom squared his accounts, and resolved to keep to the

very letter of his reform, and never to put that will in jeopardy again. He had three hundred dollars left. According to his mother's plan, he was to put that safely away, and add her half of his pension to it monthly. In one year this fund would buy her free again.

For a whole week he was not able to sleep well, so much the villainy which he had played upon his trusting mother preyed upon his rag of a conscience; but after that he began to get comfortable again, and was presently able to sleep like any other miscreant.

The boat bore Roxy away from St Louis at four in the afternoon, and she stood on the lower guard abaft the paddle-box and watched Tom through a blur of tears until he melted into the throng of people and disappeared; then she looked no more, but sat there on a coil of cable crying till far into the night. When she went to her foul steerage-bunk at last, between the clashing engines, it was not to sleep but only to wait for the morning, and, waiting, grieve.

It had been imagined that she 'would not know', and would think she was travelling up stream. She! Why, she had been steamboating for years. At dawn she got up and went listlessly and sat down on the cable-coil again. She passed many a snag whose 'break' could have told her a thing to break her heart, for it showed a current moving in the same direction that the boat was going; but her thoughts were elsewhere, and she did not notice. But at last the roar of a bigger and nearer break than usual brought her out of her torpor, and she looked up, and her practised eye fell upon that tell-tale rush of water. For one moment her petrified gaze fixed itself there. Then her head dropped upon her breast, and she said:

'Oh, de good Lord God have mercy on po' sinful me – *I's sole down de river!*'

CHAPTER 17

Even popularity can be overdone. In Rome, along at first, you are full of regrets that Michelangelo died; but by-and-by you only regret that you didn't see him do it. – *Pudd'nhead Wilson's Calendar*

July 4. – Statistics show that we lose more fools on this day than in all the other days of the year put together. This proves, by the number left in stock, that one Fourth of July per year is now inadequate, the country has grown so. – *Pudd'nhead Wilson's Calendar*

THE summer weeks dragged by, and then the political campaign opened – opened in pretty warm fashion, and waxed hotter and hotter daily. The twins threw themselves into it with their whole heart, for their self-love was engaged. Their popularity, so general at first, had suffered afterward; mainly because they had been *too* popular, and so a natural reaction had followed. Besides, it had been diligently whispered around that it was curious – indeed, *very* curious – that that wonderful knife of theirs did not turn up – *if* it was so valuable, or *if* it had ever existed. And with the whisperings went chucklings and nudgings and winks, and such things have an effect. The twins considered that success in the election would reinstate them, and that defeat would work them irreparable damage. Therefore they worked hard, but not harder than Judge Driscoll and Tom worked against them in the closing days of the canvas. Tom's conduct had remained so letter-perfect during two whole months now that his uncle not only trusted him with money with which to persuade voters, but trusted him to go and get it himself out of the safe in the private sitting-room.

The closing speech of the campaign was made by Judge Driscoll, and he made it against both of the foreigners. It was disastrously effective. He poured out rivers of ridicule upon them, and forced the big mass-meeting to laugh and applaud. He scoffed at them as adventurers, mountebanks, side-show riff-raff, dime-museum freaks; he assailed their showy titles with measureless derision; he said they were back-alley barbers disguised as nobilities, pea-nut peddlers masquerading as gentlemen, organ-grinders bereft of their brother-monkey. At last he stopped and stood still. He waited until the place had become absolutely silent and expectant, then he delivered his deadliest shot; delivered it with ice-cold seriousness and deliberation, with a significant emphasis upon the closing words: he said he believed that the reward offered for the lost knife was humbug and buncombe, and that its owner would know where to find it whenever he should have occasion *to assassinate somebody*.

Then he stepped from the stand, leaving a startled and impressive hush behind him instead of the customary explosion of cheers and party cries.

The strange remark flew far and wide over the town and made an extraordinary sensation. Everybody was asking, 'What could he mean by that?' And everybody went on asking that question, but in vain; for the Judge only said he knew what he was talking about, and stopped there; Tom said he hadn't any idea what his uncle meant, and Wilson, whenever he was asked what he thought it meant, parried the question by asking the questioner what *he* thought it meant.

Wilson was elected, the twins were defeated – crushed, in fact, and left forlorn and substantially friendless. Tom went back to St Louis happy.

Dawson's Landing had a week of repose now, and it needed it. But it was in an expectant state, for the air was full of rumours of a new duel. Judge Driscoll's election labours had prostrated him, but it was said that as soon as he was well enough to entertain a challenge he would get one from Count Luigi.

The brothers withdrew entirely from society, and nursed their humiliation in privacy. They avoided the people, and went out for exercise only late at night, when the streets were deserted.

CHAPTER 18

Gratitude and treachery are merely the two extremities of the same procession. You have seen all of it that is worth staying for when the band and the gaudy officials have gone by. – *Pudd'nhead Wilson's Calendar*

Thanksgiving Day – Let all give humble, hearty, and sincere thanks, now, but the turkeys. In the island of Fiji they do not use turkeys, they use plumbers. It does not become you and me to sneer at Fiji. – *Pudd'nhead Wilson's Calendar*

THE Friday after the election was a rainy one in St Louis. It rained all day long, and rained hard, apparently trying its best to wash that soot-blackened town white, but of course not succeeding. Toward midnight Tom Driscoll arrived at his lodgings from the theatre in the heavy downpour, and closed his umbrella and let himself in; but when he would have shut the door, he found that there was another person entering – doubtless another lodger; this person closed the door and tramped upstairs behind Tom. Tom found his door in the dark, and entered it and turned up the gas. When he faced about, lightly whistling, he saw the back of a man. The man was closing and locking his door for him. His whistle faded out and he felt uneasy. The man turned round, a wreck of shabby old clothes sodden with rain and all a-drip, and showed a black face under an old slouch hat. Tom was frightened. He tried to order the man out but the words refused to come, and the other man got the start. He said, in a low voice:

'Keep still – I's yo' mother!'

Tom sunk in a heap on a chair, and gasped out:

'It was mean of me, and base – I know it; but I meant it for the best, I did indeed – I can swear it.'

Roxana stood awhile looking mutely down on him while he writhed in shame and went on incoherently babbling self-accusations mixed with pitiful attempts at explanation and palliation of his crime; then she seated herself and took off her hat, and her unkempt masses of long brown hair tumbled down about her shoulders.

'It ain't no fault o' yo'n dat dat ain't grey,' she said sadly, noticing the hair.

'I know it, I know it! I'm a scoundrel. But I swear I meant it for the best. It was a mistake, of course, but I thought it was for the best, I truly did.'

Roxy began to cry softly, and presently words began to find their way out between her sobs. They were uttered lamentingly, rather than angrily –

'Sell a pusson down de river – *down de river!* – for de bes'! I wouldn't treat a dog so! I is all broke down en wore out, now, en so I reckon it ain't in me to storm aroun' no mo', like I used to when I 'uz trompled on en 'bused. I don't know – but maybe it's so. Leastways, I's suffered so much dat mournin' seem to come mo' handy to me now den stormin'.'

These words should have touched Tom Driscoll, but if they did, that effect was obliterated by a stronger one – one which removed the heavy weight of fear which lay upon him, and gave his crushed spirit a most grateful rebound, and filled all his small soul with a deep sense of relief. But he kept prudently still, and ventured no comment. There was a voiceless interval of some duration, now, in which no sounds were heard but the beating of the rain upon the panes, the sighing and complaining of the winds, and now and then a muffled sob from Roxana. The sobs became more and more infrequent, and at last ceased. Then the refugee began to talk again.

'Shet down dat light a little. More. More yit. A pusson dat is hunted don't like de light. Dah – dat'll do. I kin see whah you is, en dat's enough. I's gwyne to tell you de tale, en cut it jes' as short as I kin, en den I'll tell you what you's got to do. Dat man dat bought me ain't a bad man, he's good enough, as planters goes; en if he could a had his way I'd a ben a house servant in his fambly en ben comfortable; but his wife she was a Yank, en not right down good-lookin', en she riz up ag'in me straight off; so den dey sent me out to de quarter 'mongst de common fiel' han's. Dat woman warn't satisfied, even wid dat, but she worked up de overseer ag'in me, she 'uz dat jealous en hateful; so de overseer he had me out befo' day in de mawnins en worked me de whole long day as long as dey'uz any light to see by; en many's de lashins I got 'ca'se I couldn't come up to de work o' de stronges'. Dat overseer wuz a Yank, too, outen New Englan', en anybody down South kin tell you what dat mean. *Dey* knows how to work a nigger to death, en dey knows how to whale 'em, too – whale 'em till dey backs is welted like a washboard. 'Long at fust my marster say de good word for me to de overseer, but dat 'uz bad for me; for de mistis she fine it out, an' arter dat I jes' ketched it at every turn – dey warn't no mercy for me no mo'.'

Tom's heart was fired – with fury against the planter's wife; and he said to himself, 'But for that meddlesome fool, everything would have gone all right.' He added a deep and bitter curse against her.

The expression of this sentiment was fiercely written in his face, and stood thus revealed to Roxana by a white glare of lightning which turned the sombre dusk of the room into dazzling day at that moment. She was pleased – pleased and grateful; for did not that expression show that her child was capable of grieving for his mother's wrongs and of feeling resentment toward her persecutors? – a thing which she had been doubting. But her flash of happiness was but a flash, and went out again and left her spirit dark; for she said to herself, 'He sole me down de river – he can't feel for a body long; dis'll pass en go.' Then she took up her tale again.

' 'Bout ten days ago I 'uz sayin' to myself dat I could not las' many mo' weeks I 'uz so wore out wid de awful work en de lashins, en so down-hearted en misable. En I didn't care no mo', nuther – life warn't wuth noth'n to me if I got to go on like dat. Well, when a body is in a frame o' mine like dat, what do a body care what a body do? Dey was a little sickly nigger wench 'bout ten year ole dat 'uz good to me, en hadn't no mammy, po' thing, en I loved her en she loved me; en she come out whah I 'uz workin' en she had a roasted tater, en tried to slip it to me – robbin' herself, you see, 'ca'se she knowed de overseer didn't gimme enough to eat – en he ketched her at it, en give her a lick acrost de back wid his stick which 'uz as thick as a broom-handle, en she drop' screamin' on de groun', en squirmin' en wallerin' aroun' in de dust like a spider dat's got crippled. I couldn't stan' it. All de hell-fire dat 'uz ever in my heart flame' up, en I snatch de stick outen his han' en laid him flat. He laid dah moanin' en cussin', en all out of his head, you know, en de niggers 'uz plum sk'yerd to death. Dey gathered 'roun' him to he'p him, en I jumped on his hoss en took out for de river as tight as I could go. I knowed what dey would do wid me. Soon as he got well he would start en work me to death if marster let him; en if dey didn't do dat they'd sell me furder down de river, en dat's de same thing. So I 'lowed to drown myself en git out o' my troubles. It 'uz gitt'n toward dark. I 'uz at de river in two minutes. Den I see a canoe, en I says dey ain't no use to drown myself tell I got to; so I ties de hoss in de edge o' de timber en shove out down de river, keepin' in under de shelter o' de bluff bank en prayin' for de dark to shet down quick. I had a pow'ful good start, 'ca'se de big house 'uz three mile back fum de river en on'y de work-mules to ride dah on, en on'y niggers to ride 'em, en *dey* warn't gwyne to hurry – dey'd gimme all de chance dey could. Befo' a body could go to de house en back it would be long pas' dark, en dey couldn't track de hoss en fine out which way I went tell mawnin', en de niggers would tell 'em all de lies dey could 'bout it.

'Well, de dark come, en I went on a-spinnin' down de river. I paddled mo'n two hours, den I warn't worried no mo', so I quite paddlin', en floated down de current, considerin' what I 'uz gwyne to do if I didn't have to drown myself. I made up some plans, en floated along, turnin' 'em over in my mind. Well, when it 'uz a little pas' midnight as I reckoned, en I had come fifteen or twenty mile, I see de lights o' a steamboat layin' at de bank, whah dey warn't no town en no woodyard, en putty soon I ketched de shape o' de chimbly-tops ag'in de stars, en den good gracious me, I most jumped out o' my skin for joy! It 'uz de *Gran' Mogul* – I 'uz chambermaid on her for eight seasons in de Cincinnati en Orleans trade. I slid 'long pas' – don't see nobody stirrin' nowhah – hear 'em a-hammerin' away in de engine-room, den I knowed what de matter was – some o' de machinery's broke. I got asho' below de boat and turn' de canoe loose, den I goes 'long up, en dey 'uz jes' one plank out, en I step' board de boat. It 'uz pow'ful hot, deckhan's en roustabouts 'uz sprawled aroun' asleep on de fo'cas'l'; de second mate, Jim Bangs, he sot dah on the bitts wid his head down, asleep – 'ca'se dat's de way de second mate stan' de cap'n's watch! – en de ole watchman, Billy Hatch, he 'uz a-noddin' on de companion way; – en I knowed

'em all; en, lan', but dey did look good! I says to myself,
I wisht old marster'd come along *now* en try to take me –
bless yo' heart, I's 'mong frien's, I is. So I tromped right
along 'mongst 'em, en went up on de biler deck en 'way
back aft to de ladies' cabin guard, en sot down dah in de
same cheer dat I'd sot in mos' a hund'd million times, I
reckon; en it 'uz jist home agin, I tell you!

'In 'bout an hour I heard de ready-bell jingle, en den de
racket begin. Putty soon I hear de gong strike. 'Set her back
on de outside," I says to myself – "I reckon I knows dat
music!" I hear de gong ag'in. "Come ahead on de inside,"
I says. Gong ag'in. "Stop de outside." Gong ag'in. "Come
ahead on de outside – now we's pinted for Sent Louis, en I's
outer de woods en ain't got to drown myself at all." I
knowed de *Mogul* 'uz in de Sent Louis trade now, you see.
It 'uz jes' fair daylight when we passed our plantation, en I
seed a gang o' niggers en white folks huntin' up en down
de sho', en troublin' deyselves a good deal 'bout me; but I
warn't troublin' myself none 'bout dem.

' 'Bout dat time Sally Jackson, dat used to be my second
chambermaid, en 'uz head chambermaid now, she come out
on de guard, en 'uz pow'ful glad to see me, en so 'uz all
de officers; en I tole 'em I'd got kidnapped en sole down
de river, en dey made me up twenty dollahs en give it to me,
en Sally she rigged me out wid good clo'es, en when I got
here I went straight to whah you used to wuz, en den I
come to dis house en dey say you's away, but 'spected back
every day; so I didn't dast to go down to de river to Dawson's, 'ca'se I might miss you.

'Well, las' Monday I 'uz pass'n by one o' dem places in
Fourth street whah dey sticks up runaway-nigger bills, en
he'ps to ketch 'em, en I seed my marster! I 'most flopped
down on de groun', I felt so gone. He had his back to me, en
'uz talkin' to de man en givin' him some bills – nigger-bills,

I reckon, en I's de nigger. He's offerin' a reward – dat's it. Ain't I right, don't you reckon?'

Tom had been gradually sinking into a state of ghastly terror, and he said to himself, now, 'I'm lost, no matter what turns things take! This man has said to me that he thinks there was something suspicious about that sale. He said he had a letter from a passenger on the *Grand Mogul* saying that Roxy came here on that boat and that everybody on board knew all about the case; so he says that her coming here instead of flying to a free state looks bad for me, and that if I don't find her for him, and that pretty soon, he will make trouble for me. I never believed that story; I couldn't believe she would be so dead to all motherly instincts as to come here, knowing the risk she would run of getting me into irremediable trouble. And after all, here she is! And I stupidly swore I would help him find her, thinking it was a perfectly safe thing to promise. If I venture to deliver her up, she – she – but how can I help myself? I've got to do that or pay the money, and where's the money to come from? I – I – well, I should think that if he would swear to treat her kindly hereafter – and she says, herself, that he is a good man – and if he would swear to never allow her to be overworked, or ill fed, or –'

A flash of lightning exposed Tom's pallid face, drawn and rigid with these worrying thoughts. Roxana spoke up sharply now, and there was apprehension in her voice:

'Turn up dat light! I want to see yo' face better. Dah now – lemme look at you. Chambers, you's as white as yo' shirt! Has you seen dat man? Has he ben to see you?'

'Ye-s.'

'When?'

'Monday noon.'

'Monday noon! Was he on my track?'

'He – well, he thought he was. That is, he hoped he was. This is the bill you saw.' He took it out of his pocket.

'Read it to me!'

She was panting with excitement, and there was a dusky glow in her eyes that Tom could not translate with certainty, but there seemed to be something threatening about it. The handbill had the usual rude woodcut of a turbaned negro woman running, with the customary bundle on a stick over her shoulder, and the heading in bold type, '$100 REWARD.'[1] Tom read the bill aloud – at least the part that described Roxana and named the master and his St Louis address and the address of the Fourth Street agency; but he left out the item that applicants for the reward might also apply to Mr Thomas Driscoll.

'Gimme de bill!'

Tom had folded it and was putting it in his pocket. He felt a chilly streak creeping down his back, but said, as carelessly as he could:

'The bill? Why, it isn't any use to you, you can't read it. What do you want with it?'

'Gimme de bill!' Tom gave it to her, but with a reluctance which he could not entirely disguise. 'Did you read it *all* to me?'

'Certainly I did.'

'Hole up yo' han' en swah to it.'

Tom did it. Roxana put the bill carefully away in her pocket, with her eyes fixed upon Tom's face all the while, then she said:

'Yo's lyin'!'

'What would I want to lie about it for?'

'I don't know – but you is. Dat's my opinion, anyways. But nemmine 'bout dat. When I seed dat man, I 'uz dat sk'yerd dat I could scasely wobble home. Den I give a nigger man a dollar for dese clo'es, en I ain't be'n in a house sence, night ner day, till now. I blacked my face en laid hid in de cellar of a ole house dat's burnt down, daytimes, en robbed de sugar hogsheads en grain sacks on de wharf, nights, to git somethin' to eat, en never dast to try to buy noth'n, en I's 'mos' starved. En I never dast to come near dis place till dis rainy night, when dey ain't no people roun' scasely. But to-night I ben astannin' in de dark alley ever sence night come, waitin' for you to go by. En here I is.'

She fell to thinking. Presently she said:

'You seed dat man at noon, las' Monday?'

'Yes.'

'I seed him de middle o' dat arternoon. He hunted you up, didn't he?'

'Yes.'

'Did he give you de bill dat time?'

'No, he hadn't got it printed yet.'

Roxana darted a suspicious glance at him.

'Did you he'p him fix up de bill?'

Tom cursed himself for making that stupid blunder, and tried to rectify it by saying he remembered, now, that it *was* at noon Monday that the man gave him the bill. Roxana said:

'You's lyin' agin, sho'.' Then she straightened up and raised her finger:

'Now den! I's gwyne to ast you a question, en I wants to know how you's gwyne to git aroun' it. You knowed he 'uz arter me; en if you runs off, 'stid o' stayin' here to he'p him, he'd know dey 'uz somthin' wrong 'bout dis business, en den he would inquire 'bout you, en dat would take him to yo' uncle, en yo' uncle would read de bill en see dat you ben sellin' a free nigger down de river, en you know *him*, I reckon! He'd tar up de will en kick you outen de house. Now, den, you answer me dis question: hain't you tole dat man dat I would be sho' to come here, en den you would fix it so he could set a trap en ketch me?'

Tom recognised that neither lies nor arguments could help him any longer – he was in a vice, with the screw turned on, and out of it there was no budging. His face began to take on an ugly look, and presently he said, with a snarl:

'Well, what could I do? You see, yourself, that I was in his grip and couldn't get out.'

Roxy scorched him with a scornful gaze awhile, then she said:

'What could you do? You could be Judas to yo' own mother to save yo' wuthless hide! Would anybody b'lieve it? No – a dog couldn't! You is de low-downest orneriest hound dat was ever pupp'd into dis worl' – en I's 'sponsible for it!' And she spat on him.

He made no effort to resent this. Roxy reflected a moment, then she said:

'Now I'll tell you what you's gwyne to do. You's gwyne to give dat man de money dat you's got laid up, en make him wait till you kin go to de Jedge en git de res' en buy me free agin.'

'Thunder! What are you thinking of? Go and ask him for three hundred dollars and odd? What would I tell him I want with it, pray?'

Roxy's answer was delivered in a serene and level voice:

'You'll tell him you's sole me to pay yo' gambling debts, en dat you lied to me en was a villain, en dat I 'quires you to git dat money en buy me back ag'in.'

'Why, you've gone stark mad! He would tear the will to shreds in a minute – don't you know that?'

'Yes, I does.'

'Then you don't believe I'm idiot enough to go to him, do you?'

'I don't b'lieve nothin' 'bout it – I *knows* it! I knows it beca'se you knows dat if you don't raise dat money I'll go to him myself, en den he'll sell *you* down the river, en you kin see how you like it!'

Tom rose trembling, and excited, and there was an evil light in his eye. He strode to the door and said he must get out of this suffocating place for a moment and clear his brain in the fresh air so that he could determine what to do. The door wouldn't open. Roxy smiled grimly, and said:

'I's got the key, honey – set down. You needn't cle'r up yo' brain none to fine out what you gwyne to do – *I* knows what you's gwyne to do.' Tom sat down and began to pass his hands through his hair with a helpless and desperate air. Roxy said: 'Is dat man in dis house?'

Tom glanced up with a surprised expression and asked:

'What gave you such an idea?'

'You done it. Gwyne out to cle'r yo' brain! In de fust place you ain't got none to cle'r, en in de second place yo' ornery eye tole on you. You's de low-downest hound dat ever – but I done tole you dat befo'. Now, den, dis is Friday. You kin fix it up wid dat man, en tell him you's gwyne away to git de res' o' de money, en dat you'll be back wid it nex' Tuesday, or maybe Wednesday. You understan'?'

Tom answered sullenly: 'Yes.'

'En when you gits de new bill o' sale dat sells me to my own self, take en send it in de mail to Mr Pudd'nhead Wilson, en write on de back dat he's to keep it till I come. You understan'?'

'Yes.'

'Dat's all, den. Take yo' umbreller, en put on yo' hat.'

'Why?'

'Beca'se you's gwyne to see me home to de wharf. You see dis knife? I's toted it aroun' sence de day I seed dat man en bought dese clo'es en it. If he ketched me, I'uz gwyne to kill myself wid it. Now start along, en go sof', en lead de way; en if you gives a sign in dis house, or if anybody comes up to you in de street, I's gwyne to jam it into you. Chambers, does you b'lieve me when I says dat?'

'It's no use to bother me with that question. I know your word's good.'

'Yes, it's diff'rent from yo'n! Shet de light out en move along – here's de key.'

They were not followed. Tom trembled every time a late straggler brushed by them on the street, and half expected to feel the cold steel in his back. Roxy was right at his heels and always in reach. After tramping a mile they reached a wide vacancy on the deserted wharves, and in this dark and rainy desert they parted.

As Tom trudged home his mind was full of dreary thoughts and wild plans; but at last he said to himself, wearily:

'There is but the one way out. I must follow her plan. But with a variation – I will not ask for the money and ruin myself, I will *rob* the old skinflint.'

CHAPTER 19

Few things are harder to put up with than the annoyance of a good example. – Pudd'nhead Wilson's Calendar

It were not best that we should all think alike; it is difference of opinion that makes horse-races. – Pudd'n-head Wilson's Calendar

DAWSON'S LANDING was comfortably finishing its season of dull repose and waiting patiently for the duel. Count Luigi was waiting, too; but not patiently, rumour said. Sunday came, and Luigi insisted on having his challenge conveyed. Wilson carried it. Judge Driscoll declined to fight with an assassin – 'that is,' he added, significantly, 'in the field of honour.'

Elsewhere, of course, he would be ready. Wilson tried to convince him that if he had been present himself when Angelo told about the homicide committed by Luigi, he would not have considered the act discreditable to Luigi; but the obstinate old man was not to be moved.

Wilson went back to his principal and reported the failure of his mission. Luigi was incensed, and asked how it could be that the old gentleman, who was by no means dull-witted, held his trifling nephew's evidence and inferences to be of more value than Wilson's. But Wilson laughed, and said:

'That is quite simple; that is easily explicable. I am not his doll – his baby – his infatuation: his nephew is. The Judge and his late wife never had any children. The Judge and his wife were past middle age when this treasure fell into their lap. One must make allowances for a parental instinct that has been starving for twenty-five or thirty years. It is famished, it is crazed with hunger by that time, and will be entirely satisfied with anything that comes handy; its taste is atrophied, it can't tell mud-cat from shad. A devil born to a young couple is measurably recognisable by them as a devil before long, but a devil adopted by an old couple is an angel to them, and remains so, through thick and thin. Tom is this old man's angel; he is infatuated with him. Tom can persuade him into things which other people can't − not all things, I don't mean that, but a good many − particularly one class of things: the things that create or abolish personal partialities or prejudices in the old man's mind. The old man liked both of you. Tom conceived a hatred for you. That was enough; it turned the old man around at once. The oldest and strongest friendship must go to the ground when one of these late-adopted darlings throws a brick at it.'

'It's a curious philosophy,' said Luigi.

'It ain't a philosophy at all − it's a fact. And there is something pathetic and beautiful about it, too. I think there is nothing more pathetic than to see one of these poor old childless couples taking a menagerie of yelping little worthless dogs to their hearts; and then adding some cursing and squawking parrots and a jackass-voiced macaw; and next a couple of hundred screeching song-birds, and presently some foetid guinea-pigs and rabbits, and a harem of cats. It is all a groping and ignorant effort to construct out of base metal and brass filings, so to speak, something to take the place of that golden treasure denied them by Nature − a child. But this is a digression. The unwritten law of this region requires you to kill Judge Driscoll on sight, and he and the community will expect that attention at your hands − though of course your own death by his bullet will answer every purpose. Look out for him! Are you heeled – that is, fixed?'

'Yes; he shall have his opportunity. If he attacks me I will respond.'

As Wilson was leaving he said:

'The Judge is still a little used up by his campaign work, and will not get out for a day or so, but when he does get out, you want to be on the alert.'

About eleven at night the twins went out for exercise, and started on a long stroll in the veiled moonlight.

Tom Driscoll had landed at Hackett's Store, two miles below Dawson's, just about half an hour earlier, the only passenger for that lonely spot, and had walked up the shore road and entered Judge Driscoll's house without having encountered any one either on the road or under the roof.

He pulled down his window-blinds and lit his candle. He laid off his coat and hat and began his preparations. He unlocked his trunk and got his suit of girl's clothes out from under the male attire in it and laid it by. Then he blacked his face with burnt cork and put the cork in his pocket. His plan was to slip down to his uncle's private sitting-room below, pass into the bedroom, steal the safe-key from the old gentleman's clothes, and then go back and rob the safe. He took up his candle to start. His courage and confidence were high, up to this point, but both began to waver a little now. Suppose he should make a noise, by some accident, and get caught – say, in the act of opening the safe? Perhaps it would be well to go armed. He took the Indian knife from its hiding-place, and felt a pleasant return of his waning courage. He slipped stealthily down the narrow stair, his hair rising and his pulses halting at the slightest creak. When he was half-way down, he was disturbed to perceive that the landing below was touched by a faint glow of light. What could that mean? Was his uncle still up? No, that

was not likely; he must have left his night-taper there when
he went to bed. Tom crept on down, pausing at every step
to listen. He found the door standing open, and glanced in.
What he saw pleased him beyond measure. His uncle was
asleep on the sofa; on a small table at the head of the sofa a
lamp was burning low, and by it stood the old man's small
tin cash-box, closed. Near the box was a pile of bank-notes
and a piece of paper covered with figures in pencil. The
safe-door was not open. Evidently the sleeper had wearied
himself with work upon his finances, and was taking a rest.

Tom set his candle on the stairs, and began to make his
way toward the pile of notes, stooping low as he went.
When he was passing his uncle, the old man stirred in his
sleep, and Tom stopped instantly – stopped, and softly
drew the knife from its sheath, with his heart thumping
and his eyes fastened upon his benefactor's face. After a
moment or two he ventured forward again – one step –
reached for his prize and seized it, dropping the knife-
sheath. Then he felt the old man's strong grip upon him,
and a wild cry of 'Help! help!' rang in his ear. Without
hesitation he drove the knife home – and was free. Some of
the notes escaped from his left hand and fell in the blood on
the floor. He dropped the knife and snatched them up and
started to fly; transferred them to his left hand and seized
the knife again, in his fright and confusion, but remembered
himself and flung it from him, as being a dangerous witness
to carry away with him.

He jumped for the stair-foot, and closed the door behind
him; and as he snatched his candle and fled upward, the
stillness of the night was broken by the sound of urgent
footsteps approaching the house. In another moment he was
in his room, and the twins were standing aghast over the
body of the murdered man!

Tom put on his coat, buttoned his hat under it, threw on

his suit of girl's clothes, dropped the veil, blew out his light, locked the room door by which he had just entered, taking the key, passed through his other door into the back hall, locked that door and kept the key, then worked his way along in the dark and descended the back-stairs. He was not expecting to meet anybody, for all interest was centred in the other part of the house now. His calculation proved correct. By the time he was passing through the back-yard, Mrs Pratt, her servants, and a dozen half-dressed neighbours had joined the twins and the dead, and accessions were still arriving at the front door.

As Tom, quaking as with a palsy, passed out at the gate, three women came flying from the house on the opposite side of the lane. They rushed by him and in at the gate, asking him what the trouble was there, but not waiting for an answer. Tom said to himself, 'Those old maids waited to dress; they did the same thing the night Stevens's house burned down next door.' In a few minutes he was in the haunted house. He lit a candle and took off his girl-clothes. There was blood on him all down his left side, and his right hand was red with the stains of the blood-soaked notes which he had crushed in it; but otherwise he was free from this sort of evidence. He cleansed his hand on the straw, and cleaned most of the smut from his face. Then he burned his male and female attire to ashes, scattered the ashes, and put on a disguise proper for a tramp. He blew out his light, went below, and was soon loafing down the river road with the intent to borrow and use one of Roxy's devices. He found a canoe and paddled off down stream, setting the canoe adrift as dawn approached, and making his way by land to the next village, where he kept out of sight till a transient steamer came along, and then took deck passage for St Louis. He was ill at ease until Dawson's Landing was behind him; then he said to himself: 'All the detectives on earth couldn't trace me now; there's not a vestige of a clue left in the world; that homicide will take its place with the permanent mysteries, and people won't get done trying to guess out the secret of it for fifty years.'

In St Louis, next morning, he read this brief telegram in the papers – dated at Dawson's Landing:

Judge Driscoll, an old and respected citizen, was assassinated here about midnight by a profligate Italian nobleman or barber, on account of a quarrel growing out of the recent election. The assassin will probably be lynched.

'One of the twins!' soliloquised Tom; 'how lucky! It is the knife that has done him this grace. We never know when fortune is trying to favour us. I actually cursed Pudd'nhead Wilson in my heart for putting it out of my power to sell that knife. I take it back now.'

Tom was now rich and independent. He arranged with the planter, and mailed to Wilson the new bill of sale which sold Roxana to herself; then he telegraphed his Aunt Pratt:

Have seen the awful news in the papers and am almost prostrate with grief. Shall start by packet to-day. Try to bear up till I come.

When Wilson reached the house of mourning, and had gathered such details as Mrs Pratt and the rest of the crowd could tell him, he took command as mayor and gave orders that nothing should be touched, but everything left as it was until Justice Robinson should arrive and take the proper measures as coroner. He cleared everybody out of the room but the twins and himself. The sheriff soon arrived and took the twins away to gaol. Wilson told them to keep heart, and promised to do his best in their defence when the case should come to trial. Justice Robinson came presently, and with him Constable Blake. They examined the room thoroughly. They found the knife and the sheath. Wilson noticed that there were finger-prints on the knife-handle. That pleased him, for the twins had required the earliest comers to make a scrutiny of their hands and clothes, and neither these people nor Wilson himself had found any blood-stains upon them. Could there be a possibility that the twins had spoken the truth when they said they found the man dead when they ran into the house in answer to the cry for help? He thought of that mysterious girl at once. But this was not the sort of work for a girl to be engaged in. No matter, Tom Driscoll's room must be examined.

After the coroner's jury had viewed the body and its surroundings, Wilson suggested a search upstairs, and he went along. The jury forced an entrance to Tom's room, but found nothing, of course.

The coroner's jury found that the homicide was committed by Luigi, and that Angelo was accessory to it.

The town was bitter against the unfortunates, and for the first few days after the murder they were in constant danger of being lynched. The grand jury presently indicted Luigi for murder in the first degree, and Angelo as accessory before the fact. The twins were transferred from the city goal to the country prison to await trial.

Wilson examined the finger-marks on the knife-handle, and said to himself: 'Neither of the twins made those marks.' Then manifestly there was another person concerned, either in his own interest or as hired assassin.

But who could it be? That, he must try to find out. The safe was not open, the cash-box was closed, and had three thousand dollars in it. Then robbery was not the motive, and revenge was. Where had the murdered man an enemy except Luigi? There was but that one person in the world with a deep grudge against him.

The mysterious girl! The girl was a great trial to Wilson.

If the motive had been robbery, the girl might answer, but there wasn't any girl that would want to take this old man's life for revenge. He had no quarrels with girls; he was a gentleman.

Wilson had perfect tracings of the finger-marks of the knife-handle; and among his glass-records he had a great array of the finger-prints of women and girls, collected during the last fifteen or eighteeen years, but he scanned them in vain, they successfully withstood every test; among them were no duplicates of the prints on the knife.

The presence of the knife on the stage of the murder was a worrying circumstance for Wilson. A week previously he had as good as admitted to himself that he believed Luigi had possessed such a knife, and that he still possessed it, notwithstanding his pretence that it had been stolen. And now here was the knife, and with it the twins. Half the town had said the twins were humbugging when they claimed that they had lost their knife, and now these people were joyful, and said, 'I told you so.'

If their finger-prints had been on the handle – but it was useless to bother any further about that; the finger-prints on the handle were *not* theirs – that he knew perfectly.

Wilson refused to suspect Tom; for first, Tom couldn't murder anybody – he hadn't character enough; secondly, if he could murder a person he wouldn't select his doting benefactor and nearest relative; thirdly, self-interest was in the way; for while the uncle lived, Tom was sure of a free support and a chance to get the destroyed will revived again, but with the uncle gone that chance was gone too. It was true the will had really been revived, as was now discovered, but Tom could not have been aware of it, or he would have spoken of it, in his native talky, unsecretive way. Finally, Tom was in St Louis when the murder was done, and got the news out of the morning journals, as was shown by his telegram to his aunt. These speculations were unemphasised sensations rather than articulated thoughts, for Wilson would have laughed at the idea of seriously connecting Tom with the murder.

Wilson regarded the case of the twins as desperate – in fact, about hopeless. For he argued that if a confederate was not found, an enlightened Missouri jury would hang them, sure; if a confederate was found, that would not improve the matter, but simply furnish one more person for the sheriff to hang. Nothing could save the twins but the discovery of a person who did the murder on his sole personal account – an undertaking which had all the aspect of the impossible. Still, the person who made the finger-prints must be sought. The twins might have no case *with* him, but they certainly would have none without him.

So Wilson mooned around, thinking, thinking, guessing, guessing, day and night, and arriving nowhere. Whenever he ran across a girl or a woman he was not acquainted with, he got her finger-prints, on one pretext or another; and they always cost him a sigh when he got home, for they never tallied with the finger-marks on the knife-handle.

As to the mysterious girl, Tom swore he knew no such girl, and did not remember ever seeing a girl wearing a dress like the one described by Wilson. He admitted that he did not always lock his room, and that sometimes the servants forgot to lock the house-doors; still, in his opinion the girl must have made but few visits, or she would have been discovered. When Wilson tried to connect her with the stealing-raid, and thought she might have been the old woman's confederate, if not the very thief herself disguised as an old woman, Tom seemed struck, and also much interested, and said he would keep a sharp eye out for this person or persons, although he was afraid that she or they would be too smart to venture again into a town where everybody would now be on the watch for a good while to come.

Everybody was pitying Tom, he looked so quiet and sorrowful, and seemed to feel his great loss so deeply. He was playing a part, but it was not all a part. The picture of his alleged uncle, as he had last seen him, was before him in the dark pretty frequently, when he was awake, and called again in his dreams, when he was asleep. He wouldn't go into the room where the tragedy had happened. This charmed the doting Mrs Pratt, who 'realised now, as she had never done before', she said, what a sensitive and delicate nature her darling had, and how he adored his poor uncle.

CHAPTER 20

Even the clearest and most perfect circumstantial evidence is likely to be at fault, after all, and therefore ought to be received with great caution. Take the case of any pencil, sharpened by any woman; if you have witnesses, you will find she did it with a knife; but if you take simply the aspect of the pencil, you will say she did it with her teeth. — *Pudd'nhead Wilson's Calendar*

THE weeks dragged along, no friend visiting the gaoled twins but their counsel and Aunt Patsy Cooper, and the day of trial came at last — the heaviest day in Wilson's life; for with all his tireless diligence he had discovered no sign or trace of the missing confederate. 'Confederate' was the term he had long ago privately accepted for that person — not as being unquestionably the right term, but as being at least possibly the right one, though he was never able to understand why the twins didn't vanish and escape, as the confederate had done, instead of remaining by the murdered man and getting caught there.

The court-house was crowded, of course, and would remain so to the finish, for not only in the town itself, but in the country for miles around the trial was the one topic of conversation among the people. Mrs Pratt, in deep mourning, and Tom with a weed on his hat, had seats near Pembroke Howard, the public prosecutor, and back of them sat a great array of friends of the family. The twins had but one friend present to keep their counsel in countenance, their poor old sorrowing landlady. She sat near Wilson, and looked her friendliest. In the 'nigger corner' sat Chambers; also Roxy, with good clothes on, and her bill of sale in her pocket. It was her most precious possession, and she never parted with it, day or night. Tom had allowed her thirty-five dollars a month ever since he came into his property, and had said that he and she ought to be grateful to the twins for making them rich; but had roused such a temper in her by this speech that he did not repeat the argument afterward. She said the old Judge had treated her child a thousand times better than he deserved, and had never done her an unkindness in his life; so she hated these outlandish devils for killing him, and shouldn't ever sleep satisfied till she saw them hanged for it. She was here to watch the trial now, and was going to lift up just one 'hooraw' over it if the County Judge put her in gaol a year for it. She gave her turbaned head a toss and said, 'When dat verdic' comes, I'se gwyne to lif' dat *roof*, now I *tell* you.'

Pembroke Howard briefly sketched the State's case. He said he would show by a chain of circumstantial evidence, without break or fault in it anywhere, that the principal prisoner at the bar committed the murder; that the motive was partly revenge, and partly a desire to take his own life out of jeopardy, and that his brother, by his presence, was a consenting accessory to the crime; a crime which was the basest known to the calendar of human misdeeds – assassination; that it was conceived by the blackest of hearts and consummated by the cowardliest of hands; a crime which had broken a loving sister's heart, blighted the happiness of a young nephew who was as dear as a son, brought inconsolable grief to many friends, and sorrow and loss to the whole community. The utmost penalty of the outraged law would be exacted, and upon the accused, now present at the bar, that penalty would unquestionably be executed. He would reserve further remark until his closing speech.

He was strongly moved, and so also was the whole house; Mrs Pratt and several other women were weeping when he sat down, and many an eye that was full of hate was riveted upon the unhappy prisoners.

Witness after witness was called by the State, and questioned at length; but the cross-questioning was brief. Wilson knew they could furnish nothing valuable for his side. People were sorry for Pudd'nhead; his budding career would get hurt by this trial.

Several witnesses swore they heard Judge Driscoll say in his public speech that the twins would be able to find their lost knife again when they needed it to assassinate somebody with. This was not news, but now it was seen to have been sorrowfully prophetic, and a profound sensation quivered through the hushed court-room when those dismal words were repeated.

The public prosecutor rose and said that it was within his knowledge, through a conversation held with Judge Driscoll on the last day of his life, that counsel for the defence had brought him a challenge from the person charged at this bar with murder; that he had refused to fight with a confessed assassin – 'that is, on the field of honour', but had added significantly, that he would be ready for him elsewhere. Presumably the person here charged with murder was warned that he must kill or be killed the first time he should meet Judge Driscoll. If counsel for the defence chose to let the statement stand so, he would not call him to the witness stand. Mr Wilson said he would offer no denial. (Murmurs in the house – 'It is getting worse and worse for Wilson's case.')

Mrs Pratt testified that she heard no outcry, and did not know what woke her up, unless it was the sound of rapid footsteps approaching the front door. She jumped up and ran out in the hall just as she was, and heard the footsteps flying up the front steps and then following behind her as she ran to the sitting-room. There she found the accused standing over her murdered brother. (Here she broke down and sobbed. Sensation in the court.) Resuming, she said the persons entering behind her were Mr Rogers and Mr Buckstone.

Cross-examined by Wilson, she said the twins proclaimed their innocence; declared that they had been taking a walk, and had hurried to the house in response to a cry for help which was so loud and strong that they had heard it at a considerable distance; that they begged her and the gentlemen just mentioned to examine their hands and clothes — which was done, and no bloodstains found.

Confirmatory evidence followed, from Rogers and Buckstone.

The finding of the knife was verified, the advertisement minutely describing it and offering a reward for it was put in evidence, and its exact correspondence with that description proven. Then followed a few minor details, and the case for the State was closed.

Wilson said that he had three witnesses, the Misses Clarkson, who would testify that they met a veiled young woman leaving Judge Driscoll's premises by the back gate a few minutes after the cries for help were heard, and that their evidence, taken with certain circumstantial evidence which he would call the court's attention to, would in his opinion convince the court that there was still one person concerned in this crime who had not yet been found, and also that a stay of proceedings ought to be granted, in justice to his clients, until that person should be discovered. As it was late, he would ask leave to defer the examination of his three witnesses until the next morning.

The crowd poured out of the place and went flocking away in excited groups and couples, talking the events of the session over with vivacity and consuming interest, and everybody seemed to have had a satisfactory and enjoyable day except the accused, their counsel, and their old-lady friend. There was no cheer among these, and no substantial hope.

In parting with the twins Aunt Patsy did attempt a good-night with a gay pretence of hope and cheer in it, but broke down without finishing.

Absolutely secure as Tom considered himself to be, the opening solemnities of the trial had nevertheless oppressed him with a vague uneasiness, his being a nature sensitive to even the smallest alarms; but from the moment that the poverty and weakness of Wilson's case lay exposed to the court, he was comfortable once more, even jubilant. He left the courtroom sarcastically sorry for Wilson. 'The Clarksons met an unknown woman in the back lane,' he said to himself — '*that* is his case! I'll give him a century to find her in — a couple of them if he likes. A woman who doesn't exist any longer, and the clothes that gave her her sex burnt up, and the ashes thrown away — oh, certainly he'll find *her* easy enough!' This reflection set him to admiring, for the hundredth time, the shrewd ingenuities by which he had insured himself against detection — more, against even suspicion.

'Nearly always in cases like this there is some little detail or other overlooked, some wee little track or trace left behind, and detection follows; but here there's not even the faintest suggestion of a trace left. No more than a bird leaves when it flies through the air — yes, through the night, you may say. The man that can track a bird through the air in the dark and find that bird is the man to track me out and find the Judge's assassin — no other need apply. And that is the job that has been laid out for poor Pudd'nhead Wilson, of all people in the world! Lord, it will be pathetically funny to see him grubbing and groping after that woman that don't exist, and the right person sitting under his very nose all the time!' The more he thought the situation over, the more the humour of it struck him. Finally he said: 'I'll never let him hear the last of that woman. Every time I catch him in company, to his dying day, I'll ask him, in the guileless, affectionate way that used to gravel him so when I inquired how his unborn law-business was coming along, "Got on her track yet – hey, Pudd'nhead"' He wanted to laugh, but that would not have answered; there were people about, and he was mourning for his uncle. He made up his mind that it would be good entertainment to look in on Wilson that night and watch him worry over his barren law-case and goad him with an exasperating word or two of sympathy and commiseration now and then.

Wilson wanted no supper, he had no appetite. He got out all the finger-prints of girls and women in his collection of 'records', and pored gloomily over them an hour or more, trying to convince himself that that troublesome girl's marks were there somewhere and had been overlooked. But it was not so. He drew back his chair, clasped his hands over his head, and gave himself up to dull and arid musings.

Tom Driscoll dropped in, an hour after dark, and said with a pleasant laugh as he took a seat:

'Hello, we've gone back to the amusements of our days of neglect and obscurity for consolation, have we?' and he took up one of the glass strips and held it against the light to inspect it. 'Come, cheer up, old man, there's no use in losing your grip and going back to this child's-play merely because this big sun-spot is drifting across your shiny new disk. It'll pass, and you'll be all right again' – and he laid the glass down. 'Did you think you could win always?'

'Oh, no,' said Wilson, with a sigh, 'I didn't expect that, but I can't believe Luigi killed your uncle, and I feel very sorry for him. It makes me blue. And you would feel as I do, Tom, if you were not prejudiced against those young fellows.'

'I don't know about that,' and Tom's countenance darkened, for his memory reverted to his kicking. 'I owe them no goodwill, considering the brunette one's treatment of me that night. Prejudice or no prejudice, Pudd'nhead, I don't like them, and when they get their deserts you're not going to find me sitting on the mourner's bench.'

He took up another strip of glass, and exclaimed:

'Why, here's old Roxy's label! Are you going to ornament the royal palaces with nigger paw marks, too? By the date here, I was seven months old when this was done, and she was nursing me and her little nigger cub. There's a line straight across her thumb-print. How comes that?' and Tom held out the piece of glass to Wilson.

'That is common,' said the bored man, wearily. 'Scar of a cut or a scratch, usually.' And he took the strip of glass indifferently, and raised it toward the lamp.

All the blood sunk suddenly out of his face, his hand quaked, and he gazed at the polished surface before him with the glassy stare of a corpse.

'Great Heavens! what's the matter with you, Wilson? Are you going to faint?'

Tom sprang for a glass of water and offered it, but Wilson shrank shuddering from him, and said:

'No, no! – take it away!' His breast was rising and falling, and he moved his head about in a dull and wandering way, like a person who has been stunned. Presently he said, 'I shall feel better when I get to bed; I have been overwrought to-day – yes, and overworked for many days.'

'Then I'll leave you and let you to get to your rest. Goodnight, old man.' But as Tom went out he couldn't deny himself a small parting gibe: 'Don't take it so hard; a body can't win every time; you'll hang somebody yet.'

Wilson muttered to himself, 'It is no lie to say I am sorry I have to begin with you, miserable dog though you are!'

He braced himself up with a glass of cold whisky and went to work again. He did not compare the new finger-marks unintentionally left by Tom a few minutes before on Roxy's glass with the tracings of the marks left on the knife-handle, there being no need of that (for his trained eye), but busied himself with another matter, muttering from time to time, 'Idiot that I was! – Nothing but a *girl* would do me – a man in girl's clothes never occurred to me.' First, he hunted out the plate containing the finger-prints made by Tom when he was twelve years old, and laid it by itself; then he brought forth the marks made by Tom's baby fingers when he was a suckling of seven months, and placed these two plates with the one containing this subject's newly (and unconsciously) made record.

'Now the series is complete,' he said with satisfaction, and sat down to inspect these things and enjoy them.

But his enjoyment was brief. He stared a considerable time at the three strips, and seemed stupefied with astonishment. At last he put them down and said: 'I can't make it out at all. Hang it! the baby's don't tally with the others!'

He walked the floor for half an hour, puzzling over his enigma, then he hunted out two other glass plates.

He sat down and puzzled over these things a good while, but kept muttering, 'It's no use – I can't understand it. They don't tally right, and yet I'll swear the names and dates are right, and so of course they *ought* to tally. I never labelled one of these things carelessly in my life. There is a most extraordinary mystery here.'

He was tired out now, and his brains were beginning to clog. He said he would sleep himself fresh, and then see what he could do with this riddle. He slept through a troubled and unrestful hour, then unconsciousness began to shred away, and presently he rose drowsily to a sitting posture. 'Now what was that dream?' he said, trying to recall it. 'What was that dream? It seemed to unravel that puz—'

He landed in the middle of the floor at a bound, without finishing the sentence, and ran and turned up his light and seized his 'records.' He took a single swift glance at them and cried out—

'It's so! Heavens, what a revelation! And for twenty-three years no man has ever suspected it!'

CHAPTER 21

He is useless on top of the ground; he ought to be under
it, inspiring the cabbages. - *Pudd'nhead Wilson's*
Calendar

April 1. - This is the day upon which we are reminded
of what we are on the other three hundred and sixty-
four. - *Pudd'nhead Wilson's Calendar*

WILSON put on enough clothes for business purposes and
went to work under a high pressure of steam. He was awake
all over. All sense of weariness had been swept away by the
invigorating refreshment of the great and hopeful discovery
which he had made. He made fine and accurate reproduc-
tions of a number of his 'records', and then enlarged them
on a scale of ten to one with his pantagraph. He did these
pantagraph enlargements on sheets of white cardboard, and
made each individual line of the bewildering maze of whorls
or curves or loops which constituted the 'pattern' of a
'record' stand out bold and black by reinforcing it with ink.
To the untrained eye the collection of delicate originals
made by the human finger on the glass plates looked about
alike; but when enlarged ten times they resembled the
markings of a block of wood that has been sawed across the
grain, and the dullest eye could detect at a glance, and at a
distance of many feet, that no two of the patterns were alike.
When Wilson had at last finished his tedious and difficult
work, he arranged its results according to a plan in which a
progressive order and sequence was a principal feature, then
he added to the batch several pantagraph enlargements
which he had made from time to time in bygone years.

The night was spent and the day well advanced now. By the time he had snatched a trifle of breakfast it was nine o'clock, and the court ready to begin its sitting. He was in his place twelve minutes later with his 'records'.

Tom Driscoll caught a slight glimpse of the 'records', and nudged his nearest friend and said, with a wink, 'Pudd'n-head's got a rare eye to business – thinks that as long as he can't win his case it's at least a noble good chance to advertise his palace-window decorations without any expense.' Wilson was informed that his witnesses had been delayed, but would arrive presently; but he rose and said he should probably not have occasion to make use of their testimony. (An amused murmur ran through the room – 'It's a clean back-down! he gives up without hitting a lick!') Wilson continued – 'I have other testimony – and better.' (This compelled interest, and evoked murmurs of surprise that had a detectable ingredient of disappointment in them.) 'If I seem to be springing this evidence upon the court, I offer as my justification for this, that I did not discover its existence until late last night, and have been engaged in examining and classifying it ever since, until half an hour ago. I shall offer it presently; but first I wish to say a few preliminary words.

'May it please the court, the claim given the front place, the claim most persistently urged, the claim most strenu-ously and I may even say aggressively and defiantly insisted upon by the prosecution, is this – that the person whose hand left the blood-stained finger-prints upon the handle of the Indian knife is the person who committed the murder.' Wilson paused, during several moments, to give impressiveness to what he was about to say, and then added, tranquilly, '*We grant that claim.*'

It was an electrical surprise. No one was prepared for such an admission. A buzz of astonishment rose on all sides, and people were heard to intimate that the overworked lawyer had lost his mind. Even the veteran Judge, accustomed as he was to legal ambushes and masked batteries in criminal procedure, was not sure that his ears were not deceiving him, and asked counsel what it was he had said. Howard's impassive face betrayed no sign, but his attitude and bearing lost something of their careless confidence for a moment. Wilson resumed:

'We not only grant that claim, but we welcome it and strongly endorse it. Leaving that matter for the present, we will now proceed to consider other points in the case which we propose to establish by evidence, and shall include that one in the chain in its proper place.'

He had made up his mind to try a few hardy guesses, in mapping out his theory of the origin and motive of the murder – guesses designed to fill up gaps in it – guesses which could help if they hit, and would probably do no harm if they didn't.

'To my mind, certain circumstances of the case before the court seem to suggest a motive for the homicide quite different from the one insisted on by the State. It is my conviction that the motive was not revenge, but robbery. It has been urged that the presence of the accused brothers in that fatal room, just after notification that one of them must take the life of Judge Driscoll or lose his own the moment the parties should meet, clearly signifies that the natural instinct of self-preservation moved my clients to go there secretly and save Count Luigi by destroying his adversary.

'Then why did they stay there, after the deed was done? Mrs Pratt had time, although she did not hear the cry for help, but woke up some moments later, to run to that room – and there she found these men standing, and making no effort to escape. If they were guilty, they ought to have been running out of the house at the same time that she was running to that room. If they had had such a strong instinct toward self-preservation as to move them to kill that unarmed man, what had become of it now, when it should have been more alert than ever? Would any of us have remained there? Let us slander not our intelligence to that degree.

'Much stress has been laid upon the fact that the accused offered a very large reward for the knife with which this murder was done; that no thief came forward to claim that extraordinary reward; that the latter fact was good circumstantial evidence that the claim that the knife had been stolen was a vanity and a fraud; that these details, taken in connection with the memorable and apparently prophetic speech of the deceased concerning that knife, and the final discovery of that very knife in the fatal room where no living person was found present with the slaughtered man but the owner of the knife and his brother, form an indestructible chain of evidence which fixes the crime upon those unfortunate strangers.

'But I shall presently ask to be sworn, and shall testify that there was a large reward offered for the *thief*, also; that it was offered secretly and not advertised; that this fact was indiscreetly mentioned – or at least tacitly admitted – in what was supposed to be safe circumstances, but may *not* have been. The thief may have been present himself.' (Tom Driscoll had been looking at the speaker, but dropped his eyes at this point.) 'In that case he would retain the knife in his possession, not daring to offer it for sale, or for pledge in a pawnshop.' (There was a nodding of heads among the audience by way of admission that this was not a bad stroke.) 'I shall prove to the satisfaction of the jury that there *was* a person in Judge Driscoll's room several minutes before the accused entered it.' (This produced a strong sensation; the last drowsy-head in the court-room roused up, now, and made preparation to listen.) 'If it shall seem necessary, I will prove by the Misses Clarkson that they met a veiled person – ostensibly a woman – coming out of the back gate a few minutes after the cry for help was heard. This person was not a woman, but a man dressed in woman's clothes.' (Another sensation. Wilson had his eye on Tom when he hazarded this guess, to see what effect it would produce. He was satisfied with the result, and said to himself, 'It was a success – he's hit!')

'The object of that person in that house was robbery, not murder. It is true that the safe was not open, but there was an ordinary tin cash-box on the table, with three thousand dollars in it. It is easily supposable that the thief was concealed in the house; that he knew of this box, and of its owner's habit of counting its contents and arranging his accounts at night – if he had that habit, which I do not assert, of course; that he tried to take the box while its owner slept, but made a noise and was seized, and had to use the knife to save himself from capture; and that he fled without his booty because he heard help coming.

'I have now done with my theory, and will proceed to the evidences by which I propose to try to prove its soundness.' Wilson took up several of his strips of glass. When the audience recognized these familiar mementoes of Pudd'n-head's old-time childish 'puttering' and folly, the tense and funereal interest vanished out of their faces, and the house burst into volleys of relieving and refreshing laughter, and Tom chirked up and joined in the fun himself; but Wilson was apparently not disturbed. He arranged his 'records' on the table before him, and said:

'I beg the indulgence of the court while I make a few remarks in explanation of some evidence which I am about to introduce, and which I shall presently ask to be allowed to verify under oath on the witness stand. Every human being carries with him from his cradle to his grave certain physical marks which do not change their character, and by which he can always be identified – and that without shade of doubt or question. These marks are his signature, his physiological autograph, so to speak, and this autograph cannot be counterfeited, nor can he disguise it or hide it away, nor can it become illegible by the wear and the mutations of time. This signature is not his face – age can change that beyond recognition; it is not his hair, for that can fall out; it is not his height, for duplicates of that exist, it is not his form, for duplicates of that exist also, whereas this signature is each man's very own – there is no duplicate of it among the swarming populations of the globe!' (The audience were interested once more.)

'This autograph consists of the delicate lines or corrugations with which Nature marks the insides of the hands and the soles of the feet. If you will look at the balls of your fingers – you that have very sharp eyesight – you will observe that these dainty curving lines lie close together, like those that indicate the borders of oceans in maps, and that they form various clearly defined patterns, such as arches, circles, long curves, whorls, etc., and that these patterns differ on the different fingers.' (Every man in the room had his hand up to the light, now, and his head canted to one side, and was minutely scrutinising the balls of his fingers; there were whispered ejaculations of 'Why, it's so – I never noticed that before!') 'The patterns on the right hand are not the same as those on the left.' (Ejaculations of 'Why, that's so, too!') 'Taken finger for finger, your patterns differ from your neighbour's.' (Comparisons were made all over the house – even the Judge and jury were absorbed in this curious work.) 'The patterns of a twin's right hand are not the same as those on his left. One twin's patterns are never the same as his fellow-twin's patterns – the jury will find

that the patterns upon the finger-balls of the accused follow
this rule.' (An examination of the twins' hands was begun
at once.) 'You have often heard of twins who were so exactly
alike that when dressed alike their own parents could not
tell them apart. Yet there was never a twin born into this
world that did not carry from birth to death a sure identifier
in this mysterious and marvellous natal autograph. That
once known to you, his fellow-twin could never personate
him and deceive you.'

Wilson stopped and stood silent. Inattention dies a quick
and sure death when a speaker does that. The stillness gives
warning that something is coming. All palms and finger-
balls went down, now, all slouching forms straightened, all
heads came up, all eyes were fastened upon Wilson's face.
He waited yet one, two, three moments, to let his pause
complete and perfect its spell upon the house; then, when
through the profound hush he could hear the ticking of the
clock on the wall, he put out his hand and took the Indian
knife by the blade and held it aloft where all could see the
sinister spots upon its ivory handle; then he said, in a level,
passionless voice:

'Upon this haft stands the assassin's natal autograph,
written in the blood of that helpless and unoffending old
man who loved you and whom you all loved. There is but
one man in the whole earth whose hand can duplicate that
crimson sign' – he paused and raised his eyes to the pendu-
lum swinging back and forth – 'and please God we will
produce that man in this room before the clock strikes
noon!'

Stunned, distraught, unconscious of its own movement,
the house half rose, as if expecting to see the murderer
appear at the door, and a breeze of muttered ejaculations
swept the place. 'Order in the court! – sit down!' This from
the sheriff. He was obeyed, and quiet reigned again. Wilson

stole a glance at Tom, and said to himself: 'He is flying signals of distress, now; even people who despise him are pitying him; they think this is a hard ordeal for a young fellow who has lost his benefactor by so cruel a stroke – and they are right.' He resumed his speech:

'For more than twenty years I have amused my compulsory leisure with collecting these curious physical signatures in this town. At my house I have hundreds upon hundreds of them. Each and every one is labelled with name and date; not labelled the next day, or even the next hour, but in the very minute that the impression was taken. When I go upon the witness stand I will repeat under oath the things which I am now saying. I have the finger-prints of the court, the sheriff, and every member of the jury. There is hardly a person in this room, white or black, whose natal signature I cannot produce, and not one of them can so disguise himself that I cannot pick him out from a multitude of his fellow-creatures and unerringly identify him by his hands. And if he and I should live to be a hundred I could still do it!' (The interest of the audience was steadily deepening now.)

'I have studied some of these signatures so much that I know them as well as the bank cashier knows the autograph of his oldest customer. While I turn my back now, I beg that several persons will be so good as to pass their fingers through their hair, and then press them upon one of the panes of the window near the jury, and that among them the accused may set *their* finger-marks. Also, I beg that these experimenters, or others, will set their finger-marks upon another pane, and add again the marks of the accused, but not placing them in the same order or relation to the other signatures as before – for, by one chance in a million a person might happen upon the right marks by pure guesswork *once*, therefore I wish to be tested twice.'

He turned his back, and the two panes were quickly covered with delicately-lined oval spots, but visible only to such persons as could get a dark background for them – the foliage of a tree outside, for instance. Then, upon call, Wilson went to the window, made his examination, and said:

'This is Count Luigi's right hand; this one, three signatures below, is his left. Here is Count Angelo's right; down here is his left. Now for the other pane: here and here are Count Luigi's, here and here are his brother's.' He faced about. 'Am I right?'

A deafening explosion of applause was the answer. The Bench said:

'This certainly approaches the miraculous!'

Wilson turned to the window again and remarked, pointing with his finger:

'This is the signature of Mr Justice Robinson.' (Applause.) 'This, of Constable Blake.' (Applause.) 'This, of John Mason, juryman.' (Applause.) 'This, of the sheriff.' (Applause.) 'I cannot name the others, but I have them all at home, named and dated, and could identify them all by my finger-print records.'

He moved to his place through a storm of applause – which the sheriff stopped, and also made the people sit down, for they were all standing and struggling to see, of course. Court, jury, sheriff, and everybody had been too absorbed in observing Wilson's performance to attend to the audience earlier.

'Now then,' said Wilson, 'I have here the natal autographs of two children, thrown up to ten times the natural size by the pantagraph, so that anyone who can see at all can tell the markings apart at a glance. We will call the children *A* and *B*. Here are *A's* finger-marks taken at the age of five months. Here they are again, taken at seven months.' (Tom started.) 'They are alike, you see. Here are

B's at five months, and also at seven months. They, too, exactly copy each other, but the patterns are quite different from *A's*, you observe. I shall refer to these again presently, but we will turn them face down now.

'Here, thrown up ten sizes, are the natal autographs of the two persons who are here before you accused of murdering Judge Driscoll. I made these pantagraph copies last night, and will so swear when I go upon the witness stand. I ask the jury to compare them with the finger-marks of the accused upon the window-panes, and tell the court if they are the same.'

He passed a powerful magnifying-glass to the foreman.

One juryman after another took the cardboard and the glass and made the comparison. Then the foreman said to the Judge:

'Your honour, we are all agreed that they are identical.'

Wilson said to the foreman:

'Please turn that cardboard face down, and take this one, and compare it searchingly, by the magnifier, with the fatal signature upon the knife-handle, and report your finding to the court.'

Again the jury made minute examination, and again reported:

'We find them to be exactly identical, your honour.'

Wilson turned toward the counsel for the prosecution, and there was a clearly recognisable note of warning in his voice when he said:

'May it please the court, the State has claimed, strenuously and persistently, that the blood-stained finger-prints upon that knife-handle were left there by the assassin of Judge Driscoll. You have heard us grant that claim, and welcome it.' He turned to the jury. 'Compare the finger-prints of the accused with the finger-prints left by the assassin – and report.'

The comparison began. As it proceeded all movement and all sound ceased, and the deep silence of an absorbed and waiting suspense settled upon the house; and when at last the words came, *'They do not even resemble,'* a thunder-crash of applause followed and the house sprang to its feet, but was quickly repressed by official force and brought to order again. Tom was altering his position every few minutes, now, but none of his changes brought repose nor any small trifle of comfort. When the house's attention was becoming fixed once more, Wilson said gravely, indicating the twins with a gesture:

'These men are innocent. I have no further concern with them.' (Another outbreak of applause began, but was promptly checked.) 'We will now proceed to find the guilty.' (Tom's eyes were starting from their sockets. Yes, it was a cruel day for the bereaved youth, everybody thought.) 'We will return to the infant autographs of *A* and *B*. I will ask the jury to take these large pantagraph facsimilies of *A's* marked five months and seven months. Do they tally?'

The foreman responded, 'Perfectly.'

'Now examine this pantagraph, taken at eight months, and also marked *A*. Does it tally with the other two?'

The surprised response was,

'No – *they differ widely.'*

'You are quite right. Now take these two pantagraphs of *B's* autograph, marked five months and seven months. Do they tally with each other?'

'Yes – perfectly.'

'Take this third pantagraph marked *B*, eight months. Does it tally with *B's* other two?'

'By no means!'

'Do you know how to account for those strange discrepancies? I will tell you. For a purpose unknown to us, but probably a selfish one, somebody changed those children in the cradle.'

This produced a vast sensation, naturally. Roxana was astonised at this admirable guess, but not disturbed by it. To guess the exchange was one thing, to guess who did it quite another. Pudd'nhead Wilson could do wonderful things, no doubt, but he couldn't do impossible ones. Safe? She was perfectly safe. She smiled privately.

'Between the ages of seven months and eight months those children were changed in the cradle' – he made one of his effect-collecting pauses, and added – 'and the person who did it is in this house!'

Roxy's pulses stood still! The house was thrilled as with an electric shock, and the people half rose as if to seek a glimpse of the person who had made that exchange. Tom was growing limp; the life seemed oozing out of him. Wilson resumed:

'*A* was put into *B's* cradle in the nursery; *B* was transferred to the kitchen and became a negro and a slave' – (Sensation – confusion of angry ejaculations) – 'but within a quarter of an hour he will stand before you white and free!' (Burst of applause, checked by the officers.) 'From seven months onward until now, *A* has still been a usurper, and in my finger-records he bears *B's* name. Here is his pantagraph at the age of twelve. Compare it with the assassin's signature upon the knife-handle. Do they tally?'

The foreman answered,

'*To the minutest detail!*'

Wilson said solemnly, 'The murderer of your friend and mine – York Driscoll of the generous hand and the kindly spirit – sits in your midst. Valet de Chambre, negro and slave – falsely called Thomas à Becket Driscoll – make upon the window the finger-prints that will hang you!'

Tom turned his ashen face imploringly towards the

speaker, made some impotent movements with his white lips, then slid limp and lifeless to the floor.

Wilson broke the awed silence with the words:

'There is no need. He has confessed.'

Roxy flung herself upon her knees, covered her face with her hands, and out through her sobs the words struggled:

'De Lord have mercy on me, po' misable sinner dat I is!'

The clock struck twelve.

The court rose; the new prisoner, handcuffed, was removed.

Conclusion

It is often the case that the man who can't tell a lie thinks he is the best judge of one. – *Pudd'nhead Wilson's Calendar*

October 12. – The Discovery. – It was wonderful to find America, but it would have been more wonderful to miss it. – *Pudd'nhead Wilson's Calendar*

THE town sat up all night to discuss the amazing events of the day, and swop guesses as to when Tom's trial would begin. Troop after troop of citizens came to serenade Wilson, and require a speech, and shout themselves hoarse over every sentence that fell from his lips – for all his sentences were golden now, all were marvellous. His long fight against hard luck and prejudice was ended; he was a made man for good.

And as each of these roaring gangs of enthusiasts marched away, some remorseful member of it was quite sure to raise his voice and say:

'And this is the man the likes of us has called a pudd'nhead for more than twenty years. He has resigned from that position, friends.'

'Yes, but it isn't vacant – we're elected.'

The twins were heroes of romance now, and with rehabilitated reputations. But they were weary of Western adventure, and straightway retired to Europe.

Roxy's heart was broken. The young fellow upon whom she had inflicted twenty-three years of slavery continued the false heir's pension of thirty-five dollars a month to her, but her hurts were too deep for money to heal; the spirit in her eye was quenched, her martial bearing departed with it, and the voice of her laughter ceased in the land. In her church and its affairs she found her only solace.

The real heir suddenly found himself rich and free, but in a most embarrassing situation. He could neither read nor write, and his speech was the basest dialect of the negro quarter. His gait, his attitudes, his gestures, his bearing, his laugh – all were vulgar and uncouth; his manners were the manners of a slave. Money and fine clothes could not mend these defects or cover them up, they only made them the more glaring and the more pathetic. The poor fellow could not endure the terrors of the white man's parlour, and felt at home and at peace nowhere but in the kitchen. The family pew was a misery to him, yet he could nevermore enter into the solacing refuge of the 'nigger gallery' – that was closed to him for good and all. But we cannot follow his curious fate further – that would be a long story.

The false heir made a full confession and was sentenced to imprisonment for life. But now a complication came up. The Percy Driscoll estate was in such a crippled shape when its owner died that it could pay only sixty per cent. of its great indebtedness, and was settled at that rate. But the creditors came forward now, and complained that inasmuch as through an error for which *they* were in no way to blame the false heir was not inventoried at that time with the rest of the property, great wrong and loss had thereby been inflicted upon them. They rightly claimed that 'Tom' was lawfully their property and had been so for eight years; that they had already lost sufficiently in being deprived of his services during that long period, and ought not to be required to add anything to that loss; that if he had been delivered up to them in the first place, they would have sold him and he could not have murdered Judge Driscoll, therefore it was not he that had really committed the mur-

der, the guilt lay with the erroneous inventory. Everybody
saw that there was reason in this. Everybody granted that if
'Tom' were white and free it would be unquestionably right
to punish him – it would be no loss to anybody; but to shut
up a valuable slave for life – that was quite another matter.

As soon as the Governor understood the case, he pardoned
Tom at once, and the creditors sold him down the river.

THOSE
EXTRAORDINARY
TWINS

A MAN who is not born with the novel-writing gift has a troublesome time of it when he tries to build a novel. I know this from experience. He has no clear idea of his story; in fact he has no story. He merely has some people in his mind, and an incident or two, also a locality. He knows these people, he knows the selected locality, and he trusts that he can plunge those people into those incidents with interesting results. So he goes to work. To write a novel? No – that is a thought which comes later; in the beginning he is only proposing to tell a little tale; a very little tale; a six-page tale. But as it is a tale which he is not acquainted with, and can only find out what it is by listening as it goes along telling itself, it is more than apt to go on and on and on till it spreads itself into a book. I know about this, because it has happened to me so many times.

And I have noticed another thing: that as the short tale grows into the long tale, the original intention (or motif) is apt to get abolished and find itself superseded by a quite different one. It was so in the case of a magazine sketch which I once started to write – a funny and fantastic sketch about a prince and a pauper; it presently assumed a grave cast of its own accord, and in that new shape spread itself out into a book. Much the same thing happened with 'Pudd'nhead Wilson'. I had a sufficiently hard time with that tale, because it changed itself from a farce to a tragedy while I was going along with it – a most embarrassing circumstance. But what was a great deal worse was, that it was not one story, but two stories tangled together; and they obstructed and interrupted each other at every turn and created no end of confusion and annoyance. I could not offer the book for publication, for I was afraid it would unseat the

229

reader's reason. I did not know what was the matter with it, for I had not noticed, as yet, that it was two stories in one. It took me months to make that discovery. I carried the manuscript back and forth across the Atlantic two or three times, and read it and studied over it on shipboard; and at last I saw where the difficulty lay. I had no further trouble. I pulled one of the stories out by the roots, and left the other one – a kind of literary Cæsarean operation.

Would the reader care to know something about the story which I pulled out? He has been told many a time how the born-and-trained novelist works. Won't he let me round and complete his knowledge by telling him how the jack-leg does it?

Originally the story was called 'Those Extraordinary Twins'. I meant to make it very short. I had seen a picture of a youthful Italian 'freak' – or 'freaks' – which was – or which were – on exhibition in our cities – a combination consisting of two heads and four arms joined to a single body and a single pair of legs – and I thought I would write an extravagantly fantastic little story with this freak of nature for hero – or heroes – a silly young miss for heroine, and two old ladies and two boys for the minor parts. I lavishly elaborated these people and their doings, of course. But the tale kept spreading along, and spreading along, and other people got to intruding themselves and taking up more and more room with their talk and their affairs. Among them came a stranger named Pudd'nhead Wilson, and a woman named Roxana; and presently the doings of these two pushed up into prominence a young fellow named Tom Driscoll, whose proper place was away in the obscure background. Before the book was half finished those three were taking things almost entirely into their own hands and working the whole tale as a private venture of their own – a tale which they had nothing at all to do with, by rights.

When the book was finished and I came to look around to see what had become of the team I had originally started out with – Aunt Patsy Cooper, Aunt Betsy Hale, the two boys, and Rowena the light-weight heroine – they were nowhere to be seen; they had disappeared from the story some time or other. I hunted about and found them – found them stranded, idle, forgotten, and permanently useless. It was very awkward. It was awkward all around; but more particularly in the case of Rowena, because there was a love-match on, between her and one of the twins that constituted the freak, and I had worked it up to a blistering heat and thrown in a quite dramatic love-quarrel, wherein Rowena scathingly denounced her betrothed for getting drunk, and scoffed at his explanation of how it had happened, and wouldn't listen to it, and had driven him from her in the usual 'forever' way; and now here she sat crying and broken-hearted; for she had found that he had spoken only the truth; that it was not he, but the other half of the freak, that had drunk the liquor that made him drunk; that her half was a prohibitionist and had never drunk a drop in his life, and, although tight as a brick three days in the week, was wholly innocent of blame; and indeed, when sober, was constantly doing all he could to reform his brother, the other half, who never got any satisfaction out of drinking, anyway, because liquor never affected him. Yes, here she was, stranded with that deep injustice of hers torturing her poor torn heart.

I didn't know what to do with her. I was as sorry for her as anybody could be, but the campaign was over, the book was finished, she was side-tracked, and there was no possible way of crowding her in, anywhere. I could not leave her there, of course; it would not do. After spreading her out so, and making such a to-do over her affairs, it would be absolutely necessary to account to the reader for her. I thought and thought and studied and studied; but I arrived at nothing. I finally saw plainly that there was really no way but one – I must simply give her the grand bounce. It grieved me to do it, for after associating with her so much I had come to kind of like her after a fashion, notwithstanding she was such an ass and said such stupid, irritating things and was so nauseatingly sentimental. Still it had to be done. So, at the top of Chapter XVII, I put a 'Calendar' remark concerning July the Fourth, and began the chapter with this statistic:

'Rowena went out in the back yard after supper to see the fireworks and fell down the well and got drowned.'

It seemed abrupt, but I thought maybe the reader wouldn't notice it, because I changed the subject right away to something else. Anyway it loosened up Rowena from where she was stuck and got her out of the way, and that was the main thing. It seemed a prompt good way of weeding out people that had got stalled, and a plenty good enough way for those others; so I hunted up the two boys and said 'they went out back one night to stone the cat and fell down the well and got drowned'. Next I searched around and found old Aunt Patsy Cooper and Aunt Betsy Hale where they were aground, and said 'they went out back one night to visit the sick and fell down the well and got drowned.' I was going to drown some of the others, but I gave up the idea, partly because I believed that if I kept that up it would arouse attention, and perhaps sympathy with those people, and partly because it was not a large well and would not hold any more anyway.

Still the story was unsatisfactory. Here was a set of new characters who were become inordinately prominent and who persisted in remaining so to the end; and back yonder was an older set who made a large noise and a great to-do for a little while and then suddenly played out utterly and fell down the well. There was a radical defect somewhere, and I must search it out and cure it.

The defect turned out to be the one already spoken of — two stories in one, a farce and a tragedy. So I pulled out the farce and left the tragedy. This left the original team in, but only as mere names, not as characters. Their prominence was wholly gone; they were not even worth drowning; so I removed that detail. Also I took those twins apart and made two separate men of them. They had no occasion to have foreign names now, but it was too much trouble to remove them all through, so I left them christened as they were and made no explanation.

CHAPTER I

THE conglomerate twins were brought on the stage in Chapter I of the original extravaganza. Aunt Patsy Cooper has received their letter applying for board and lodging, and Rowena, her daughter, insane with joy, is begging for a hearing of it:

'Well, set down then, and be quiet a minute and don't fly around so; it fairly makes me tired to see you. It starts off so: "HONORED MADAM —"'

'I like that, ma, don't you? It shows they're high-bred.'

'Yes, I noticed that when I first read it. "My brother and I have seen your advertisement, by chance, in a copy of your local journal —"'

'It's so beautiful and smooth, ma — don't you think so?'

'Yes, seems so to me — "and beg leave to take the room you offer. We are twenty-four years of age, and twins —"'

'Twins! How sweet! I do hope they are handsome, and I just know they are! Don't you hope they are, ma?'

'Land, I ain't particular. "We are Italians by birth —"'

'It's so romantic! Just think — there's never been one in this town, and everybody will want to see them, and they're all *ours!* Think of that!'

'— "but have lived long in the various countries of Europe, and several years in the United States."'

'Oh, just think what wonders they've seen, ma! Won't it be good to hear them talk?'

'I reckon so; yes, I reckon so. "Our names are Luigi and Angelo Capello —"'

'Beautiful, perfectly beautiful! Not like Jones and Robinson and those horrible names.'

234

' "You desire but one guest, but dear madam, if you will allow us to pay for two we will not discommode you. We will sleep together in the same bed. We have always been used to this, and prefer it." And then he goes on to say they will be down Thursday.'

'And this is Tuesday – I don't know how I'm ever going to wait, ma! The time does drag along so, and I'm so dying to see them! Which of them do you reckon is the tallest, ma?'

'How do you s'pose I can tell, child? Mostly they are the same size – twins are.'

'Well then, which do you reckon is the best looking?'

'Goodness knows – I don't.'

'I think Angelo is; it's the prettiest name, anyway. Don't you think it's a sweet name, ma?'

'Yes, it's well enough. I'd like both of them better if I knew the way to pronounce them – the Eyetalian way, I mean. The Missouri way and the Eyetalian way is different, I judge.'

'Maybe – yes. It's Luigi that writes the letter. What do you reckon is the reason Angelo didn't write it?'

'Why, how can I tell? What's the difference who writes it, so long as it's done?'

'Oh, I hope it wasn't because he is sick! You don't think he is sick, do you, ma?'

'Sick your granny; what's to make him sick?'

'Oh, there's never any telling. These foreigners with that kind of names are so delicate, and of course that kind of names are not suited to our climate – you wouldn't expect it.'

[And so-on and so-on, no end. The time drags along; Thursday comes: the boat arrives in a pouring storm toward midnight.]

At last there was a knock at the door and the anxious

family jumped to open it. Two negro men entered, each carrying a trunk, and proceeded upstairs toward the guest-room. Then followed a stupefying apparition – a double-headed human creature with four arms, one body, and a single pair of legs! It – or they, as you please – bowed with elaborate foreign formality, but the Coopers could not respond immediately; they were paralysed. At this moment there came from the rear of the group a fervent ejaculation – 'My lan'!' – followed by a crash of crockery, and the slave-wench Nancy stood petrified and staring, with a tray of wrecked tea-things at her feet. The incident broke the spell, and brought the family to consciousness. The beautiful heads of the new-comer bowed again, and one of them said with easy grace and dignity:

'I crave the honor, madam and miss, to introduce to you my brother, Count Luigi Capello,' (the other head bowed) 'and myself – Count Angelo; and at the same time offer sincere apologies for the lateness of our coming, which was unavoidable,' and both heads bowed again.

The poor old lady was in a whirl of amazement and confusion, but she managed to stammer out:

'I'm sure I'm glad to make your acquaintance, sir – I mean, gentlemen. As for the delay, it is nothing, don't mention it. This is my daughter Rowena, sir – gentlemen. Please step into the parlor and sit down and have a bite and sup; you are dreadful wet and must be uncomfortable – both of you, I mean.'

But to the old lady's relief they courteously excused themselves, saying it would be wrong to keep the family out of their beds longer; then each head bowed in turn and uttered a friendly good-night, and the singular figure moved away in the wake of Rowena's small brothers, who bore candles, and disappeared up the stairs.

The widow tottered into the parlor and sank into a chair

with a gasp, and Rowena followed, tongue-tied and dazed. The two sat silent in the throbbing summer heat unconscious of the million-voiced music of the mosquitoes, unconscious of the roaring gale, the lashing and thrashing of the rain along the windows and the roof, the white glare of the lightning, the tumultuous booming and bellowing of the thunder; conscious of nothing but that prodigy, that uncanny apparition that had come and gone so suddenly – that weird strange thing that was so soft-spoken and so gentle of manner and yet had shaken them up like an earthquake with the shock of its gruesome aspect. At last a cold little shudder quivered along down the widow's meager frame and she said in a weak voice:

'Ugh, it was awful – just the mere look of that phillipene!'

Rowena did not answer. Her faculties were still caked, she had not yet found her voice. Presently the widow said, a little resentfully:

'Always been *used* to sleeping together – in fact, *prefer* it. And I was thinking it was to accommodate me. I thought it was very good of them, whereas a person situated as that young man is –'

'Ma, you oughtn't to begin by getting up a prejudice against him. I'm sure he is good-hearted and means well. Both of his faces show it.'

'I'm not so certain about that. The one on the left – I mean the one on *its* left – hasn't near as good a face, in my opinion, as its brother.'

'That's Luigi.'

'Yes, Luigi; anyway it's the dark-skinned one; the one that was west of his brother when they stood in the door. Up to all kinds of mischief and disobedience when he was a boy, I'll be bound. I lay his mother had trouble to lay her hand on him when she wanted him. But the one on the right is as good as gold, I can see that.'

'That's Angelo.'

'Yes, Angelo, I reckon, though I can't tell t' other from which by their names, yet awhile. But it's the right-hand one – the blonde one. He has such kind blue eyes, and curly copper hair and fresh complexion –'

'And such a noble face! – oh, it *is* a noble face, ma, just royal, you may say! And beautiful – deary me, how beautiful! But both are that; the dark one's as beautiful as a picture. There's no such wonderful faces and handsome heads in this town – none that even begin. And such hands – especially Angelo's – so shapely and –'

'Stuff, how could you tell which they belonged to? – they had gloves on.'

'Why, didn't I see them take off their hats?'

'That don't signify. They might have taken off each other's hats. Nobody could tell. There was just a wormy squirming of arms in the air – seemed to be a couple of dozen of them, all writhing at once, and it just made me dizzy to see them go.'

'Why, ma, I hadn't any difficulty. There's two arms on each shoulder –'

'There, now. One arm on each shoulder belongs to each of the creatures, don't it? For a person to have two arms on one shoulder wouldn't do him any good, would it? Of course not. Each has an arm on each shoulder. Now then, you tell me which of them belongs to which, if you can. *They* don't know, themselves – they just work whichever arm comes handy. Of course they do; especially if they are in a hurry and can't stop to think which belongs to which.'

The mother seemed to have the rights of the argument, so the daughter abandoned the struggle. Presently the widow rose with a yawn and said:

'Poor thing, I hope it won't catch cold; it was powerful wet, just drenched, you may say. I hope it has left its boots outside, so they can be dried.' Then she gave a little start, and looked perplexed. 'Now I remember I heard one of them ask Joe to call him at half after seven – I think it was the one on the left – no, it was the one to the east of the other one – but I didn't hear the other one say anything. I wonder if he wants to be called too. Do you reckon it's too late to ask?'

'Why, ma, it's not necessary. Calling one is calling both. If one gets up, the other's *got* to.'

'Sho, of course; I never thought of that. Well, come along, maybe we can get some sleep, but I don't know, I'm so shook up with what we've been through.'

The stranger had made an impression on the boys, too. They had a word of talk as they were getting to bed. Henry, the gentle, the humane, said:

'I feel ever so sorry for it, don't you, Joe?'

But Joe was a boy of this world, active, enterprising, and had a theatrical side to him:

'Sorry? Why, how you talk! It can't stir a step without attracting attention. It's just grand!'

Henry said, reproachfully:

'Instead of pitying it, Joe, you talk as if –'

'Talk as if *what*? I know one thing mighty certain: if you can fix me so I can eat for two and only have to stub toes for one, I ain't going to fool away no such chance just for sentiment.'

The twins were wet and tired, and they proceeded to undress without any preliminary remarks. The abundance of sleeve made the partnership-coat hard to get off, for it was like skinning a tarantula; but it came at last, after much tugging and perspiring. The mutual vest followed. Then the brothers stood up before the glass, and each took off his own cravat and collar. The collars were of the standing kind, and came high up under the ears, like the sides of a wheelbarrow, as required by the fashion of the day. The cravats were as broad as a bank bill, with fringed ends which stood far out to right and left like the wings of a dragon-fly, and this also was strictly in accordance with the fashion of the time. Each cravat, as to color, was in perfect taste, so far as its owner's complexion was concerned – a delicate pink, in the case of the blonde brother, a violent scarlet in the case of the brunette – but as a combination they broke all the laws of taste known to civilization. Nothing more fiendish and irreconcilable than those shrieking and blaspheming colors could have been contrived. The wet boots gave no end of trouble – to Luigi. When they were off at last, Angelo said, with bitterness:

'I wish you wouldn't wear such tight boots, they hurt my feet.'

Luigi answered with indifference:

'My friend, when I am in command of our body, I choose my apparel according to my own convenience, as I have remarked more than several times already. When you are in command, I beg you will do as you please.'

Angelo was hurt, and the tears came into his eyes. There was gentle reproach in his voice, but not anger, when he replied:

'Luigi, I often consult your wishes, but you never consult mine. When I am in command I treat you as a guest; I try to make you feel at home; when you are in command you treat me as an intruder, you make me feel unwelcome. It embarrasses me cruelly in company, for I can see that people notice it and comment on it.'

'Oh, damn the people,' responded the brother languidly, and with the air of one who is tired of the subject.

A slight shudder shook the frame of Angelo, but he said nothing and the conversation ceased. Each buttoned his own share of the night-shirt in silence; then Luigi, with Paine's

'Age of Reason' in his hand, sat down in one chair and put his feet in another and lit his pipe, while Angelo took his 'Whole Duty of Man', and both began to read. Angelo presently began to cough; his coughing increased and became mixed with gaspings for breath, and he was finally obliged to make an appeal to his brother's humanity:

'Luigi, if you would only smoke a little milder tobacco, I am sure I could learn not to mind it in time, but this is so strong, and the pipe is so rank that –'

'Angelo, I wouldn't be such a baby! I have learned to smoke in a week, and the trouble is already over with me; if you would try, you could learn too, and then you would stop spoiling my comfort with your everlasting complaints.'

'Ah, brother, that is a strong word – everlasting – and isn't quite fair. I only complain when I suffocate; you know I don't complain when we are in the open air.'

'Well, anyway, you could learn to smoke yourself.'

'But my *principles*, Luigi, you forget my principles. You would not have me do a thing which I regard as a sin?'

'Oh, bosh!'

The conversation ceased again, for Angelo was sick and discouraged and strangling; but after some time he closed his book and asked Luigi to sing 'From Greenland's Icy Mountains' with him, but he would not, and when he tried to sing by himself Luigi did his best to drown his plaintive tenor with a rude and rollicking song delivered in a thundering bass.

After the singing there was silence, and neither brother was happy. Before blowing the light out Luigi swallowed half a tumbler of whisky, and Angelo, whose sensitive organization could not endure intoxicants of any kind, took a pill to keep it from giving him the headache.

CHAPTER 2

THE family sat in the breakfast-room waiting for the twins to come down. The widow was quiet, the daughter was alive with happy excitement. She said:

'Ah, they're a boon, ma, just a boon! don't you think so?'

'Laws, I hope so, I don't know.'

'Why, ma, yes you do. They're so fine and handsome, and high-bred and polite, so every way superior to our gawks here in this village; why, they'll make life different from what it was – so humdrum and commonplace, you know – oh, you may be sure they're full of accomplishments, and knowledge of the world, and all that, that will be an immense advantage to society here. Don't you think so, ma?'

'Mercy on me, how should I know, and I've hardly set eyes on them yet.' After a pause she added, 'They made considerable noise after they went up.'

'Noise? Why, ma, they were singing! And it was beautiful, too.'

'Oh, it was well enough, but too mixed-up, seemed to me.'

'Now, ma, honor bright, did you ever hear "Greenland's Icy Mountains" sung sweeter – now did you?'

'If it had been sung by itself, it would have been uncommon sweet, I don't deny it; but what they wanted to mix it up with "Old Bob Ridley" for, I can't make out. Why, they don't go together, at all. They are not of the same nature. "Bob Ridley" is a common rackety slam-bang secular song, one of the rippingest and rantingest and noisest there is. I am no judge of music, and I don't claim it, but in my opinion nobody can make those two songs go together right.'

'Why, ma, I thought –'

'It don't make any difference what you thought, it can't be done. They tried it, and to my mind it was a failure. I never heard such a crazy uproar; seemed to me, sometimes, the roof would come off; and as for the cats – well, I've lived a many a year, and seen cats aggravated in more ways than one, but I've never seen cats take on the way they took on last night.'

'Well, I don't think that that goes for anything, ma, because it is the nature of cats that any sound that is unusual –'

'Unusual! You may well call it so. Now if they are going to sing duets every night, I do hope they will both sing the same tune at the same time, for in my opinion a duet that is made up of two different tunes is a mistake; especially when the tunes ain't any kin to one another, that way.'

'But, ma, I think it must be a foreign custom; and it must be right too, and the best way, because they have had every opportunity to know what is right, and it don't stand to reason that with their education they would do anything but what the highest musical authorities have sanctioned. You can't help but admit that, ma.'

The argument was formidably strong; the old lady could not find any way around it; so, after thinking it over a while she gave in with a sigh of discontent, and admitted that the daughter's position was probably correct. Being vanquished, she had no mind to continue the topic at that disadvantage, and was about to seek a change when a change came of itself. A footstep was heard on the stairs, and she said:

'There – he's coming!'

'*They*, ma – you ought to say *they* – it's nearer right.'

The new lodger, rather shoutingly dressed but looking

superbly handsome, stepped with courtly carriage into the trim little breakfast-room and put out all his cordial arms at once, like one of those pocket-knifes with a multiplicity of blades, and shook hands with the whole family simultaneously. He was so easy and pleasant and hearty that all embarrassment presently thawed away and disappeared, and a cheery feeling of friendliness and comradeship took its place. He – or preferably they – were asked to occupy the seat of honor at the foot of the table. They consented with thanks, and carved the beefsteak with one set of their hands while they distributed it at the same time with the other set.

'Will you have coffee, gentlemen, or tea?'

'Coffee for Luigi, if you please, madam, tea for me.'

'Cream and sugar?'

'For me, yes, madam; Luigi takes his coffee black. Our natures differ a good deal from each other, and our tastes also.'

The first time the negro girl Nancy appeared in the door and saw the two heads turned in opposite directions and both talking at once, then saw the commingling arms feed potatoes into one mouth and coffee into the other at the same time, she had to pause and pull herself out of a faintness that came over her; but after that she held her grip and was able to wait on the table with fair courage.

Conversation fell naturally into the customary grooves. It was a little jerky, at first, because none of the family could get smoothly through a sentence without a wobble in it here and a break there, caused by some new surprise in the way of attitude or gesture on the part of the twins. The weather suffered the most. The weather was all finished up and disposed of, as a subject, before the simple Missourians had gotten sufficiently wonted to the spectacle of one body feeding two heads to feel composed and reconciled in the presence of so bizarre a miracle. And even after everybody's mind became tranquilized there was still one slight distraction left: the hand that picked up a biscuit carried it to the wrong head, as often as any other way, and the wrong mouth devoured it. This was a puzzling thing, and marred the talk a little. It bothered the widow to such a degree that she presently dropped out of the conversation without knowing it, and fell to watching and guessing and talking to herself.

'Now that hand is going to take that coffee to – no, it's gone to the other mouth; I can't understand it; and now, here is the dark complected hand with a potato on its fork, I'll see what goes with it – there, the light complected head's got it, as sure as I live!' Finally Rowena said:

'Ma, what is the matter with you? Are you dreaming about something?'

The old lady came to herself and blushed; then she explained with the first random thing that came into her mind: 'I saw Mr Angelo take up Mr Luigi's coffee, and I thought maybe he – sha'n't I give *you* a cup, Mr Angelo?'

'Oh no, madam, I am very much obliged, but I never drink coffee, much as I would like to. You did see me take up Luigi's cup, it is true, but if you noticed, I didn't carry it to my mouth, but to his.'

'Y – es, I thought you did. Did you mean to?'

'How?'

The widow was a little embarrassed again. She said:

'I don't know but what I'm foolish, and you mustn't mind; but you see, he got the coffee I was expecting to see you drink, and you got a potato that I thought he was going to get. So I thought it might be a mistake all around, and everybody getting what wasn't intended for him.'

Both twins laughed and Luigi said:

'Dear madam, there wasn't any mistake. We are always

helping each other that way. It is a great economy for us both; it saves time and labor. We have a system of signs which nobody can notice or understand but ourselves. If I am using both my hands and want some coffee, I make the sign and Angelo furnishes it to me; and you saw that when he needed a potato I delivered it.'

'How convenient!'

'Yes, and often of the extremest value. Take the Mississippi boats, for instance. They are always over-crowded. There is table-room for only half of the passengers, therefore they have to get a second table for the second half. The stewards rush both parties, they give them no time to eat a satisfying meal, both divisions leave the table hungry. It isn't so with us. Angelo books himself for the one table, I book myself for the other. Neither of us eats anything at the other's table, but just simply works – works. Thus, you see there are four hands to feed Angelo, and the same four to feed me. Each of us eats two meals.'

The old lady was dazed with admiration, and kept saying, 'It is *per*fectly wonderful, perfectly wonderful!' and the boy Joe licked his chops enviously, but said nothing – at least aloud.

'Yes,' continued Luigi, 'our construction may have its disadvantages – in fact, *has* – but it also has its compensations of one sort and another. Take travel, for instance. Travel is enormously expensive, in all countries; we have been obliged to do a vast deal of it – come, Angelo, don't put any more sugar in your tea, I'm just over one indigestion and don't want another right away – been obliged to do a deal of it, as I was saying. Well, we always travel as one person, since we occupy but one seat; so we save half the fare.'

'How romantic!' interjected Rowena, with effusion.

'Yes, my dear young lady, and how practical too, and economical. In Europe, beds in the hotels are not charged with the board, but separately – another saving, for we stood to our rights and paid for the one bed only. The landlords often insisted that as both of us occupied the bed we ought –'

'No, they didn't,' said Angelo. 'They did it only twice, and in both cases it was a double bed – a rare thing in Europe – and the double bed gave them some excuse. Be fair to the landlords; twice doesn't constitute "often".'

'Well, that depends – that depends. I knew a man who fell down a well twice. He said he didn't mind the first time, but he thought the second time was once too often. Have I misused that word, Mrs Cooper?'

'To tell the truth, I was afraid you had, but it seems to look, now, like you hadn't.' She stopped, and was evidently struggling with the difficult problem a moment, then she added in the tone of one who is convinced without being converted, 'It seems so, but I can't somehow tell why.'

Rowena thought Luigi's retort was wonderfully quick and bright, and she remarked to herself with satisfaction that there wasn't any young native of Dawson's Landing that could have risen to the occasion like that. Luigi detected the applause in her face, and expressed his pleasure and his thanks with his eyes; and so eloquently withal, that the girl was proud and pleased, and hung out the delicate sign of it on her cheeks.

Luigi went on, with animation:

'Both of us get a bath for one ticket, theater seat for one ticket, pew-rent is on the same basis, but at peep-shows we pay double.'

'We have much to be thankful for,' said Angelo, impressively, with a reverent light in his eye and a reminiscent tone in his voice, 'we have been greatly blessed. As a rule, what one of us has lacked, the other, by the bounty of Providence, has been able to supply. My brother is hardy, I am not; he is very masculine, assertive, aggressive; I am much less so. I am subject to illness, he is never ill. I cannot abide medicines, and cannot take them, but he has no prejudice against them, and –'

'Why, goodness gracious,' interrupted the widow, 'when you are sick, does he take the medicine for you?'

'Always, madam.'

'Why, I never heard such a thing in my life! I think it's beautiful of you.'

'Oh, madam, it's nothing, don't mention it, it's really nothing at all.'

'But I say it's beautiful, and I stick to it!' cried the widow, with a speaking moisture in her eye. 'A well brother to take the medicine for his poor sick brother – I wish I had such a son,' and she glanced reproachfully at her boys. 'I declare I'll never rest till I've shook you by the hand,' and she scrambled out of her chair in a fever of generous enthusiasm, and made for the twins, blind with her tears, and began to shake. The boy Joe corrected her:

'You're shaking the wrong one, ma.'

This flurried her, but she made a swift change and went on shaking.

'Got the wrong one again, ma,' said the boy.

'Oh, shut up, can't you!' said the widow, embarrassed and irritated. 'Give me *all* your hands, I want to shake them all; for I know you are both just as good as you can be.'

It was a victorious thought, a master-stroke of diplomacy, though that never occurred to her and she cared nothing for diplomacy. She shook the four hands in turn cordially, and went back to her place in a state of high and fine exaltation that made her look young and handsome.

'Indeed I owe everything to Luigi,' said Angelo, affectionately. 'But for him I could not have survived our boyhood days, when we were friendless and poor – ah, so poor! We lived from hand to mouth – lived on the coarse fare of unwilling charity, and for weeks and weeks together not a morsel of food passed my lips, for its character revolted me and I could not eat it. But for Luigi I should have died. He ate for us both.'

'How noble!' sighed Rowena.

'Do you hear that?' said the widow, severely, to her boys. 'Let it be an example to you – I mean you, Joe.'

Joe gave his head a barely perceptible disparaging toss and said: 'Et for both. It ain't anything – I'd a done it.'

'Hush, if you haven't got any better manners than that. You don't see the point at all. It wasn't good food.'

'I don't care – it was food, and I'd a et it if it was rotten.'

'Shame! Such language! Can't you understand? They were starving – actually starving – and he ate for both, and –'

'Shucks! you gimme a chance and I'll –'

'There, now – close your head! and don't you open it again till you're asked.'

[Angelo goes on and tells how his parents the Count and Countess had to fly from Florence for political reasons, and died poor in Berlin bereft of their great property by confiscation; and how he and Luigi had to travel with a freak-show during two years and suffer semi-starvation.]

'That hateful black-bread! but I seldom ate anything during that time; that was poor Luigi's affair –'

'I'll never *Mister* him again!' cried the widow, with strong emotion, 'he's Luigi to me, from this out!'

'Thank you a thousand times, madam, a thousand times! though in truth I don't deserve it.'

'Ah, Luigi is always the fortunate one when honors are showering,' said Angelo, plaintively, 'now what have I done, Mrs Cooper, that you leave me out? Come, you must strain a point in my favor.'

'Call you Angelo? Why, certainly I will; what are you thinking of! In the case of twins, why –'

'But, ma, you're breaking up the story – do let him go on.'

'You keep still, Rowena Cooper, and he can go on all the better, I reckon. One interruption don't hurt, it's two that makes the trouble.'

'But you've added one, now, and that is three.'

'Rowena! I will not allow you to talk back at me when you have got nothing rational to say.'

CHAPTER 3

[After breakfast the whole village crowded in, and there was a grand reception in honor of the twins; and at the close of it the gifted 'freak' captured everybody's admiration by sitting down at the piano and knocking out a classic four-handed piece in great style. Then the Judge took it – or them – driving in his buggy and showed off his village.]

ALL along the streets the people crowded the windows and stared at the amazing twins. Troops of small boys flocked after the buggy, excited and yelling. At first the dogs showed no interest. They thought they merely saw three men in a buggy – a matter of no consequence; but when they found out the facts of the case, they altered their opinion pretty radically, and joined the boys, expressing their minds as they came. Other dogs got interested; indeed, all the dogs. It was a spirited sight to see them come leaping fences, tearing around corners, swarming out of every by-street and alley. The noise they made was something beyond belief – or praise. They did not seem to be moved by malice but only by prejudice, the common human prejudice against lack of conformity. If the twins turned their heads, they broke and fled in every direction, but stopped at a safe distance and faced about; and then formed and came on again as soon as the strangers showed them their back. Negroes and farmers' wives took to the woods when the buggy came upon them suddenly, and altogether the drive was pleasant and animated, and a refreshment all around.

[It was a long and lively drive. Angelo was a Methodist, Luigi was a Freethinker. The Judge was very proud of his Freethinkers' Society, which was flourishing along in a most prosperous way and already had two members – himself and the obscure and neglected Pudd'nhead Wilson. It was to meet that evening, and he invited Luigi to join; a thing which Luigi was glad to do, partly because it would please himself, and partly because it would gravel Angelo.]

They had now arrived at the widow's gate, and the excursion was ended. The twins politely expressed their obligations for the pleasant outing which had been afforded them; to which the Judge bowed his thanks, and then said he would now go and arrange for the Freethinkers' meeting, and would call for Count Luigi in the evening.

'For you also, dear sir,' he added hastily, turning to Angelo and bowing. 'In addressing myself particularly to your brother, I was not meaning to leave you out. It was an unintentional rudeness, I assure you, and due wholly to accident – accident and preoccupation. I beg you to forgive me.'

His quick eye had seen the sensitive blood mount into Angelo's face, betraying the wound that had been inflicted. The sting of the slight had gone deep, but the apology was so prompt, and so evidently sincere, that the hurt was almost immediately healed, and a forgiving smile testified to the kindly Judge that all was well again.

Concealed behind Angelo's modest and unassuming exterior, and unsuspected by any but his intimates, was a lofty pride, a pride of almost abnormal proportions, indeed, and this rendered him ever the prey of slights; and although they were almost always imaginary ones, they hurt none the less on that account. By ill fortune Judge Driscoll had happened to touch his sorest point, i.e., his conviction that his brother's presence was welcomer everywhere than his own; that he was often invited, out of mere courtesy, where only his brother was wanted, and that in a majority of cases he would not be included in an invitation if he could be left out without offense. A sensitive nature like this is necessarily subject to moods; moods which traverse the whole gamut of feeling; moods which know all the climes of emotion, from the sunny heights of joy to the black abysses of despair. At times, in his seasons of deepest depressions, Angelo almost wished that he and his brother might become segregated from each other and be separate individuals, like other men. But of course as soon as his mind cleared and these diseased imaginings passed away, he shuddered at the repulsive thought, and earnestly prayed that it might visit him no more. To be separate, and as other men are! How awkward it would seem; how unendurable. What would he do with his hands, his arms? How would his legs feel? How odd, and strange, and grotesque every action, attitude, movement, gesture would be. To sleep by himself, eat by himself, walk by himself — how lonely, how unspeakably lonely! No, no, any fate but that. In every way and from every point, the idea was revolting.

This was of course natural; to have felt otherwise would have been unnatural. He had known no life but a combined one; he had been familiar with it from his birth; he was not able to conceive of any other as being agreeable, or even bearable. To him, in the privacy of his secret thoughts, all other men were monsters, deformities: and during three-fourths of his life their aspect had filled him with what promised to be an unconquerable aversion. But at eighteen his eye began to take note of female beauty; and little by little, undefined longings grew up in his heart, under whose softening influences the old stubborn aversion gradually diminished, and finally disappeared. Men were still monstrosities to him, still deformities, and in his sober moments he had no desire to be like them, but their strange and unsocial and uncanny construction was no longer offensive to him.

This had been a hard day for him, physically and mentally. He had been called in the morning before he had quite slept off the effects of the liquor which Luigi had drunk; and so, for the first half hour had had the seedy feeling, and languor, the brooding depression, the cobwebby mouth and druggy taste that come of dissipation and are so ill a preparation for bodily or intellectual activities; the long violent strain of the reception had followed; and this had been followed, in turn, by the dreary sight-seeing, the Judge's wearying explanations and laudations of the sights, and the stupefying clamor of the dogs. As a congruous conclusion, a fitting end, his feelings had been hurt, a slight had been put upon him. He would have been glad to forego dinner and betake himself to rest and sleep, but he held his peace and said no word, for he knew his brother, Luigi, was fresh, unweary, full of life, spirit, energy; he would have scoffed at the idea of wasting valuable time on a bed or a sofa, and would have refused permission.

Chapter 4

Rowena was dining out, Joe and Harry were belated at play, there were but three chairs and four persons that noon at the home dinner-table – the twins, the widow, and her chum, Aunt Betsy Hale. The widow soon perceived that Angelo's spirits were as low as Luigi's were high, and also that he had a jaded look. Her motherly solicitude was aroused, and she tried to get him interested in the talk and win him to a happier frame of mind, but the cloud of sadness remained on his countenance. Luigi lent his help, too. He used a form and a phrase which he was always accustomed to employ in these circumstances. He gave his brother an affectionate slap on the shoulder and said, encouragingly:

'Cheer up, the worst is yet to come!'

But this did no good. It never did. If anything, it made the matter worse, as a rule, because it irritated Angelo. This made it a favorite with Luigi. By and by the widow said:

'Angelo, you are tired, you've overdone yourself; you go right to bed after dinner, and get a good nap and a rest, then you'll be all right.'

'Indeed, I would give anything if I could do that, madam.'

'And what's to hender, I'd like to know? Land, the room's yours to do what you please with! The idea that you can't do what you like with your own!'

'But, you see, there's one prime essential – an essential of the very first importance – which isn't my own.'

'What is that?'

'My body.'

The old ladies looked puzzled, and Aunt Betsy Hale said:

'Why bless your heart, how is that?'

'It's my brother's.'

'Your brother's! I don't quite understand. I supposed it belonged to both of you.'

'So it does. But not to both at the same time.'

'That is mighty curious; I don't see how it can be. I shouldn't think it could be managed that way.'

'Oh, it's a good enough arrangement, and goes very well; in fact, it wouldn't do to have it otherwise. I find that the teetotalers and the anti-teetotalers hire the use of the same hall for their meetings. Both parties don't use it at the same time, do they?'

'You bet they don't!' said both old ladies in a breath.

'And, moreover,' said Aunt Betsy, 'the Freethinkers and the Baptist Bible class use the same room over the Market house, but you can take my word for it they don't mush up together and use it at the same time.'

'Very well,' said Angelo, 'you understand it now. And it stands to reason that the arrangement couldn't be improved. I'll prove it to you. If our legs tried to obey two wills, how could we ever get anywhere? I would start one way, Luigi would start another, at the same moment – the result would be a standstill, wouldn't it?'

'As sure as you are born! Now ain't that wonderful! A body would never have thought of it.'

'We should always be arguing and fussing and disputing over the merest trifles. We should lose worlds of time, for we couldn't go down stairs or up, couldn't go to bed, couldn't rise, couldn't wash, couldn't dress, couldn't stand up, couldn't sit down, couldn't even cross our legs, without calling a meeting first and explaining the case and passing resolutions, and getting consent. It wouldn't ever do – now would it?'

'Do? Why, it would wear a person out in a week! Did you ever hear anything like it, Patsy Cooper?'

'Oh, you'll find there's more than one thing about them that ain't commonplace,' said the widow, with the complacent air of a person with a property-right in a novelty that is under admiring scrutiny.

'Well, now, how ever do you manage it? I don't mind saying I'm suffering to know.'

'He who made us,' said Angelo reverently, 'and with us this difficulty, also provided a way out of it. By a mysterious law of our being, each of us has utter and indisputable command of our body a week at a time, turn and turn about.'

'Well, I never! Now ain't that beautiful!'

'Yes, it is beautiful!'

'Yes, it is beautiful and infinitely wise and just. The week ends every Saturday at midnight to the minute, to the second, to the last shade of a fraction of a second, infallibly, unerringly, and in that instant the one brother's power over the body vanishes and the other brother takes possession, asleep or awake.'

'How marvelous are His ways, and past finding out!'

Luigi said: 'So exactly to the instant does the change come, that during our stay in many of the great cities of the world, the public clocks were regulated by it; and as hundreds of thousands of private clocks and watches were set and corrected in accordance with the public clocks, we really furnished the standard time for the entire city.'

'Don't tell me that He don't do miracles any more! Blowing down the walls of Jericho with rams' horns wa'n't as difficult, in my opinion.'

'And that is not all,' said Angelo. 'A thing that is even more marvelous, perhaps, is the fact that the change takes note of longitude and fits itself to the meridian we are on. Luigi is in command this week. Now, if on Saturday night at a moment before midnight we could fly in an instant to a point fifteen degrees west of here, he would hold possession of the power another hour, for the change observes *local* time and no other.'

Betsy Hale was deeply impressed, and said with solemnity:

'Patsy Cooper, for *de*tail it lays over the Passage of the Red Sea.'

'Now, I shouldn't go as far as that,' said Aunt Patsy, 'but if you've a mind to say Sodom and Gomorrah, I am with you, Betsy Hale.'

'I am agreeable, then, though I do think I was right, and I believe Parson Maltby would say the same. Well, now, there's another thing. Suppose one of you wants to borrow the legs a minute from the one that's got them, could he let him?'

'Yes, but we hardly ever do that. There were disagreeable results, several times, and so we very seldom ask or grant the privilege, nowadays, and we never even think of such a thing unless the case is extremely urgent. Besides, a week's possession at a time seems so little that we can't bear to spare a minute of it. People who have the use of their legs all the time never think of what a blessing it is, of course. It never occurs to them; it's just their natural ordinary condition, and so it does not excite them at all. But when I wake up, on Sunday morning, and it's my week and I feel the power all through me, oh, such a wave of exultation and thanksgiving goes surging over me, and I want to shout "I can walk! I can walk!" Madam, do you ever, at your uprising want to shout "I can walk! I can walk!"?'

'No, you poor unfortunate cretur', but I'll never get out of my bed again without *doing* it! Laws, to think I've had this unspeakable blessing all my long life and never had the grace to thank the good Lord that gave it to me!'

Tears stood in the eyes of both the old ladies and the widow said, softly:

'Betsy Hale, we have learned something, you and me.'

The conversation now drifted wide, but by and by floated back once more to that admired detail, the rigid and beautiful impartiality with which the possession of power had been distributed between the twins. Aunt Betsy saw in it a far finer justice than human law exhibits in related cases. She said:

'In my opinion it ain't right now, and never has been right, the way a twin born a quarter of a minute sooner than the other one gets all the land and grandeurs and nobilities in the old countries and his brother has to go bare and be a nobody. Which of you was born first?'

Angelo's head was resting against Luigi's; weariness had overcome him, and for the past five minutes he had been peacefully sleeping. The old ladies had dropped their voices to a lulling drone, to help him steal the rest his brother wouldn't take him up stairs to get. Luigi listened a moment to Angelo's regular breathing, then said in a voice barely audible:

'We were both born at the same time, but I am six months older than he is.'

'For the land's sake!'

''Sh! don't wake him up; he wouldn't like my telling this. It has always been kept secret till now.'

'But how in the world can it be? If you were both born at the same time, how can one of you be older than the other?'

'It is very simple, and I assure you it is true. I was born with a full crop of hair, he was as bald as an egg for six months. I could walk six months before he could make a step. I finished teething six months ahead of him. I began to take solids six months before he left the breast. I began to talk six months before he could say a word. Last, and absolutely unassailable proof, *the sutures in my skull closed six months ahead of his*. Always just that six months difference to a day. Was that accident? Nobody is going to claim that, I'm sure. It was ordained – it was law – it had its meaning, and we know what that meaning was. Now what does this overwhelming body of evidence establish? It establishes just one thing, and that thing it establishes beyond any peradventure whatever. Friends, we would not have it known for the world, and I must beg you to keep it strictly to yourselves, but the truth is, *we are no more twins than you are*.'

The two old ladies were stunned, paralyzed – petrified, one may almost say – and could only sit and gaze vacantly at each other for some moments; then Aunt Betsy Hale said impressively:

'There's no getting around proof like that. I do believe it's the most amazing thing I ever heard of.' She sat silent a moment or two and breathing hard with excitement, then she looked up and surveyed the strangers steadfastly a little while, and added: 'Well, it does beat me, but I would have took you for twins anywhere.'

'So would I, so would I,' said Aunt Patsy with the emphasis of a certainty that is not impaired by any shade of doubt.

'*Any*body would – anybody in the world, I don't care who he is,' said Aunt Betsy with decision.

'You won't tell,' said Luigi, appealingly.

'Oh, dear, no!' answered both ladies promptly, 'you can trust us, don't you be afraid.'

'That is good of you, and kind. Never let on; treat us always as if we were twins.'

'You can depend on us,' said Aunt Betsy, 'but it won't be easy, because now that I know you ain't you you don't *seem* so.'

Luigi muttered to himself with satisfaction: 'That swindle has gone through without change of cars.'

It was not very kind of him to load the poor things up with a secret like that, which would be always flying to their tongues' ends every time they heard any one speak of the strangers as twins, and would become harder and harder to hang on to with every recurrence of the temptation to tell it, while the torture of retaining it would increase with every new strain that was applied; but he never thought of that, and probably would not have worried much about it if he had.

A visitor was announced – some one to see the twins. They withdrew to the parlor, and the two old ladies began to discuss with interest the strange things which they had been listening to. When they had finished the matter to their satisfaction, and Aunt Betsy rose to go, she stopped to ask a question:

'How does things come on between Roweny and Tom Driscoll?'

'Well, about the same. He writes tolerable often, and she answers tolerable seldom.'

'Where is he?'

'In St Louis, I believe, though he's such a gadabout that a body can't be very certain of him, I reckon.'

'Don't Roweny know?'

'Oh, yes, like enough. I haven't asked her lately.'

'Do you know how him and the Judge are getting along now?'

'First-rate, I believe. Mrs Pratt says so; and being right in the house, and sister to the one and aunt to t'other, of course she ought to know. She says the Judge is real fond of him when he's away; but frets when he's around and is vexed with his ways, and not sorry to have him go again. He has been gone three weeks this time – a pleasant thing for both of them, I reckon.'

'Tom's ruther harum-scarum, but there ain't anything bad in him, I guess.'

'Oh, no, he's just young, that's all. Still, twenty-three is old, in one way. A young man ought to be earning his living by that time. If Tom were doing that, or was even trying to do it, the Judge would be a heap better satisfied with him. Tom's always going to begin, but somehow he can't seem to find just the opening he likes.'

'Well, now, it's partly the Judge's own fault. Promising the boy his property wasn't the way to set him to earning a fortune of his own. But what do you think – is Roweny beginning to lean any toward him, or ain't she?'

Aunt Patsy had a secret in her bosom; she wanted to keep it there, but nature was too strong for her. She drew Aunt Betsy aside, and said in her most confidential and mysterious manner:

'Don't you breathe a syllable to a soul – I'm going to tell you something. In my opinion Tom Driscoll's chances were considerable better yesterday than they are to-day.'

'Patsy Cooper, what *do* you mean?'

'It's so, as sure as you're born. I wish you could 'a' been at breakfast and seen for yourself.'

'You don't mean it!'

'Well, if I'm any judge, there's a leaning – there's a leaning, sure.'

'My land! Which one of 'em is it?'

'I can't say for certain, but I think it's the youngest one – Anjy.'

Then there were handshakings, and congratulations, and hopes, and so on, and the old ladies parted, perfectly happy – the one in knowing something which the rest of the town didn't, and the other in having been the sole person able to furnish that knowledge.

The visitor who had called to see the twins was the Rev. Mr Hotchkiss, pastor of the Baptist church. At the reception Angelo had told him he had lately experienced a change in his religious views, and was now desirous of becoming a Baptist, and would immediately join Mr Hotchkiss's church. There was no time to say more, and the brief talk ended at that point. The minister was much gratified, and had dropped in for a moment now, to invite the twins to attend his Bible class at eight that evening. Angelo accepted, and was expecting Luigi to decline, but he did not, because he knew that the Bible class and the Free-thinkers met in the same room, and he wanted to treat his brother to the embarrassment of being caught in free-thinking company.

CHAPTER 5

[A long and vigorous quarrel follows, between the twins. And there is plenty to quarrel about, for Angelo was always seeking truth, and this obliged him to change and improve his religion with frequency, which wearied Luigi, and annoyed him too; for he had to be present at each new enlistment – which placed him in the false position of seeming to endorse and approve his brother's fickleness; moreover, he had to go to Angelo's prohibition meetings, and he hated them. On the other hand, when it was his week to command the legs he gave Angelo just cause of complaint, for he took him to circuses and horse-races and fandangoes, exposing him to all sorts of censure and criticism; and he drank, too; and whatever he drank went to Angelo's head instead of his own and made him act disgracefully. When the evening was come, the two attended the Freethinkers' meeting, where Angelo was sad and silent; then came the Bible-class and looked upon him coldly, finding him in such company. Then they went to Wilson's house and Chapter II of 'Pudd'nhead Wilson' follows, which tells of the girl seen in Tom Driscoll's room; and closes with the kicking of Tom by Luigi at the anti-temperance mass meeting of the Sons of Liberty; with the addition of some account of Roxy's adventures as a chambermaid on a Mississippi boat. Her exchange of the children had been flippantly and farcically described in an earlier chapter.]

NEXT morning all the town was a-buzz with great news; Pudd'nhead Wilson had a law case! The public astonishment was so great and the public curiosity so intense, that when the justice of the peace opened his court, the place was packed with people, and even the windows were full. Everybody was flushed and perspiring; the summer heat was almost unendurable.

Tom Driscoll had brought a charge of assault and battery against the twins. Robert Allen was retained by Driscoll,

David Wilson by the defense. Tom, his native cheerfulness unannihilated by his back-breaking and bone-bruising passage across the massed heads of the Sons of Liberty the previous might, laughed his little customary laugh, and said to Wilson:

'I've kept my promise, you see; I'm throwing my business your way. Sooner than I was expecting, too.'

'It's very good of you – particularly if you mean to keep it up.'

'Well, I can't tell about that yet. But we'll see. If I find you deserve it I'll take you under my protection and make your fame and fortune for you.'

'I'll try to deserve it, Tom.'

A jury was sworn in; then Mr Allen said:

'We will detain your honor but a moment with this case. It is not one where any doubt of the fact of the assault can enter in. These gentlemen – the accused – kicked my client at the Market Hall last night; they kicked him with violence; with extraordinary violence; with even unprecedented violence, I may say; insomuch that he was lifted entirely off his feet and discharged into the midst of the audience. We can prove this by four hundred witnesses – we shall call but three. Mr Harkness will take the stand.'

Mr Harkness, being sworn, testified that he was chairman upon the occasion mentioned; that he was close at hand and saw the defendants in this action kick the plaintiff into the air and saw him descend among the audience.

'Take the witness,' said Allen.

'Mr Harkness,' said Wilson, 'you say you saw these gentlemen, my clients, kick the plaintiff. Are you sure – and please remember that you are on oath – are you perfectly sure that you saw *both* of them kick him, or only one? Now be careful.'

A bewildered look began to spread itself over the witness's face. He hesitated, stammered, but got out nothing. His eyes wandered to the twins and fixed themselves there with a vacant gaze.

'Please answer, Mr Harkness, you are keeping the court waiting. It is a very simple question.'

Counsel for the prosecution broke in with impatience:

'Your honor, the question is an irrelevant triviality. Necessarily, they both kicked him, for they have but the one pair of legs, and both are responsible for them.'

Wilson said, sarcastically:

'Will your honor permit this new witness to be sworn? He seems to possess knowledge which can be of the utmost value just at this moment – knowledge which would at once dispose of what every one must see is a very difficult question in this case. Brother Allen, will you take the stand?'

'Go on with your case!' said Allen, petulantly. The audience laughed, and got a warning from the court.

'Now, Mr Harkness,' said Wilson, insinuatingly, 'we shall have to insist upon an answer to that question.'

'I – er – well, of course, I do not absolutely *know*, but in my opinion –'

'Never mind your opinion, sir – answer the question.'

'I – why, I *can't* answer it.'

'That will do, Mr Harkness. Stand down.'

The audience tittered and the discomfited witness retired in a state of great embarrassment.

Mr Wakeman took the stand and swore that he saw the twins kick the plaintiff off the platform. The defense took the witness.

'Mr Wakeman, you have sworn that you saw these gentlemen kick the plaintiff. Do I understand you to swear that you saw them *both* do it?'

'Yes, sir,' – with decision.

'How do you know that both did it?'

'Because I *saw* them do it.'

The audience laughed, and got another warning from the court.

'But by what means do you know that both, and not one, did it?'

'Well, in the first place, the insult was given to both of them equally, for they were called a pair of scissors. Of course they would both want to resent it, and so –'

'Wait! You are theorizing now. Stick to facts – counsel will attend to the arguments. Go on.'

'Well, they both went over there – *that* I saw.'

'Very good. Go on.'

'And they both kicked him – I swear to it.'

'Mr Wakeman, was Count Luigi, here, willing to join the Sons of Liberty last night?'

'Yes, sir, he was. He did join, too, and drank a glass or two of whisky, like a man.'

'Was his brother willing to join?'

'No, sir, he wasn't. He is a teetotaler, and was elected through a mistake.'

'Was he given a glass of whisky?'

'Yes, sir, but of course that was another mistake, and not intentional. He wouldn't drink it. He set it down.' A slight pause, then he added, casually and quite simply: 'The plaintiff reached for it and hogged it.'

There was a fine outburst of laughter, but as the justice was caught out himself, his reprimand was not very vigorous.

Mr Allen jumped up and exclaimed: 'I protest against these foolish irrelevancies. What have they to do with the case?'

Wilson said: 'Calm yourself, brother, it was only an experiment. Now, Mr Wakeman, if one of these gentlemen chooses to join an association and the other doesn't; and if one of them enjoys whisky and the other doesn't, but sets it aside and leaves it unprotected' (titter from the audience), 'it seems to show that they have independent minds, and tastes, and preferences, and that one of them is able to approve of a thing at the very moment that the other is heartily disapproving of it. Doesn't it seem so to you?'

'Certainly it does. It's perfectly plain.'

'Now, then, it might be – I only say it might be – that one of these brothers wanted to kick the plaintiff last night, and that the other didn't want that humiliating punishment inflicted upon him in that public way and before all those people. Isn't that possible?'

'Of course it is. It's more than possible. I don't believe the blond one would kick anybody. It was the other one that –'

'Silence!' shouted the plaintiff's counsel, and went on with an angry sentence which was lost in the wave of laughter that swept the house.

'That will do, Mr Wakeman,' said Wilson, 'you may stand down.'

The third witness was called. He had seen the twins kick the plaintiff. Mr Wilson took the witness.

'Mr Rogers, you say you saw these accused gentlemen kick the plaintiff?'

'Yes, sir.'

'Both of them?'

'Yes, sir.'

'Which of them kicked him first?'

'Why – they – they both kicked him at the same time.'

'Are you perfectly sure of that?'

'Yes, sir.'

'What makes you sure of it?'

'Why, I stood right behind them, and *saw* them do it.'

'How many kicks were delivered?'

'Only one.'

'If two men kick, the result should be two kicks, shouldn't it?'

'Why – why– yes, as a rule.'

'Then what do you think went with the other kick?'

'I – well – the fact is, I wasn't thinking of two being necessary, this time.'

'What do you think now?'

'Well, I – I'm sure I don't quite know what to think, but I reckon that one of them did half of the kick and the other one did the other half.'

Somebody in the crowd sung out: 'It's the first sane thing that any of them has said.'

The audience applauded. The judge said: 'Silence! or I will clear the court.'

Mr Allen looked pleased, but Wilson did not seem disturbed. He said:

'Mr Rogers, you have favored us with what you think and what you reckon, but as thinking and reckoning are not evidence, I will now give you a chance to come out with something positive, one way or the other, and shall require you to produce it. I will ask the accused to stand up and repeat the phenomenal kick of last night.' The twins stood up. 'Now, Mr Rogers, please stand behind them.'

A Voice: 'No, stand in front!' (Laughter. Silenced by the court.) Another Voice: 'No, give Tommy another highst!' (Laughter. Sharply rebuked by the court.)

'Now, then, Mr Rogers, two kicks shall be delivered, one after the other, and I give you my word that at least one of the two shall be delivered by one of the twins alone, without the slightest assistance from his brother. Watch sharply, for you have got to render a decision without any if's and and's in it.' Rogers bent himself behind the twins with his palms just above his knees, in the modern attitude of the catcher at a base-ball match, and riveted his eyes on the pair of legs in front of him. 'Are you ready, Mr Rogers?'

'Ready, sir.'

'Kick!'

The kick was launched.

'Have you got that one classified, Mr Rogers?'

'Let me study a minute, sir.'

'Take as much time as you please. Let me know when you are ready.'

For as much as a minute Rogers pondered, with all eyes and a breathless interest fastened upon him. Then he gave the word: 'Ready, sir.'

'Kick!'

The kick that followed was an exact duplicate of the first one.

'Now, then, Mr Rogers, one of those kicks was an individual kick, not a mutual one. You will now state positively which was the mutual one.'

The witness said, with a crestfallen look:

'I've got to give it up. There ain't any man in the world that could tell t'other from which, sir.'

'Do you still assert that last night's kick was a mutual kick?'

'Indeed, I don't, sir.'

'That will do, Mr Rogers. If my brother Allen desires to address the court, your honor, very well; but as far as I am concerned I am ready to let the case be at once delivered into the hands of this intelligent jury without comment.'

Mr Justice Robinson had been in office only two months, and in that short time had not had many cases to try, of course. He had no knowledge of laws and courts except what he had picked up since he came into office. He was a sore trouble to the lawyers, for his rulings were pretty eccentric sometimes, and he stood by them with Roman simplicity and fortitude; but the people were well satisfied with him, for they saw that his intentions were always right, that he was entirely impartial, and that he usually made up in good sense what he lacked in technique, so to speak. He now perceived that there was likely to be a miscarriage of justice here, and he rose to the occasion.

'Wait a moment, gentlemen,' he said, 'it is plain that an assault has been committed – it is plain to anybody; but the way things are going, the guilty will certainly escape conviction. I cannot allow this. Now –'

'But, your honor!' said Wilson, interrupting him, earnestly but respectfully, 'you are deciding the case yourself, whereas the jury –'

'Never mind the jury, Mr Wilson; the jury will have a chance when there is a reasonable doubt for them to take hold of – which there isn't so far. There is no doubt whatever that an assault has been committed. The attempt to show that both of the accused committed it has failed. Are they both to escape justice on that account? Not in this court, if I can prevent it. It appears to have been a mistake to bring the charge against them as a corporation; each should have been charged in his capacity as an individual and –'

'But, your honor!' said Wilson, 'in fairness to my clients I must insist that inasmuch as the prosecution did not separate the –'

'No wrong will be done your clients, sir – they will be protected; also the public and the offended laws. Mr Allen, you will amend your pleadings, and put one of the accused on trial at a time.'

Wilson broke in: 'But, your honor! this is wholly unprecedented! To imperil an accused person by arbitrarily altering and widening the charge against him in order to compass his conviction when the charge as originally brought promises to fail to convict, is a thing unheard of before.'

'Unheard of *where*?'

'In the courts of this or any other State.'

The Judge said with dignity: 'I am not acquainted with the customs of other courts, and am not concerned to know what they are. I am responsible for this court, and I cannot conscientiously allow my judgment to be warped and my judicial liberty hampered by trying to conform to the caprices of other courts, be they –'

'But, your honor, the oldest and highest courts in Europe –'

'This court is not run on the European plan, Mr Wilson; it is not run on any plan but its own. It has a plan of its own; and that plan is, to find justice for both State and accused, no matter what happens to be practice and custom in Europe or anywhere else.' (Great applause.) 'Silence! It has not been the custom of this court to imitate other courts; it has not been the custom of this court to take shelter behind the decisions of other courts, and we will not begin now. We will do the best we can by the light that God has given us, and while this court continues to have His approval, it will remain indifferent to what other organizations may think of it.' (Applause.) 'Gentlemen, I *must* have order! – quiet yourselves! Mr Allen, you will now proceed against the prisoners one at a time. Go on with the case.'

Allen was not at his ease. However, after whispering a moment with his client and with one or two other people, he rose and said:

'Your honor, I find it to be reported and believed that the accused are able to act independently in many ways, but that this independence does not extend to their legs, authority over their legs being vested exclusively in the one brother during a specific term of days, and then passing to the other brother for a like term, and so on, by regular alternation. I could call witnesses who would prove that the accused had revealed to them the existence of this extraordinary fact, and had also made known which of them was in possession of the legs yesterday – and this would, of course, indicate where the guilt of the assault belongs – but as this would be mere hearsay evidence, these revelations not having been made under oath –'

'Never mind about that, Mr Allen. It may not all be hearsay. We shall see. It may at least help to put us on the right track. Call the witnesses.'

'Then I will call Mr John Buckstone, who is now present, and I beg that Mrs Patsy Cooper may be sent for. Take the stand, Mr. Buckstone.'

Buckstone took the oath and then testified that on the previous evening the Count Angelo Cappello had protested against going to the hall, and had called all present to witness that he was going by compulsion and would not go if he could help himself. Also, that the Count Luigi had replied sharply that he would *go*, just the same, and that he, Count Luigi, would see to that himself. Also, that upon Count Angelo's complaining about being kept on his legs so long, Count Luigi retorted with apparent surprise, 'Your legs! – I like your impudence!'

'*Now* we are getting at the kernel of the thing,' observed the Judge, with grave and earnest satisfaction. 'It looks as if the Count Luigi was in possession of the battery at the time of the assault.'

Nothing further was elicited from Mr Buckstone on direct examination. Mr Wilson took the witness.

'Mr Buckstone, about what time was it that that conversation took place?'

'Toward nine yesterday evening, sir.'

'Did you then proceed directly to the hall?'

'Yes, sir.'

'How long did it take you to go there?'

'Well, we walked; and as it was from the extreme edge of the town, and there was no hurry, I judge it took us about twenty minutes, maybe a trifle more.'

'About what hour was the kick delivered?'

'About thirteen minutes and a half to ten.'

'Admirable! You are a pattern witness, Mr Buckstone. How did you happen to look at your watch at that particular moment?'

'I always do it when I see an assault. It's likely I shall be called as a witness, and it's a good point to have.'

'It would be well if others were as thoughtful. Was anything said, between the conversation at my house and the assault, upon the detail which we are now examining into?'

'No, sir.'

'If power over the mutual legs was in the possession of one brother at nine, and passed into the possession of the other one during the next thirty or forty minutes, do you think you could have detected the change?'

'By no means!'

'That is all, Mr Buckstone.'

Mrs Patsy Cooper was called. The crowd made way for her, and she came smiling and bowing through the narrow human lane, with Betsy Hale, as escort and support, smiling and bowing in her wake, the audience breaking into welcoming cheers as the old favorites filed along. The Judge did not check this kindly demonstration of homage and affection, but let it run its course unrebuked.

The old ladies stopped and shook hands with the twins with effusion, then gave the Judge a friendly nod, and bustled into the seats provided for them. They immediately began to deliver a volley of eager questions at the friends around them: 'What is this thing for?' 'What is that thing for?' 'Who is that young man that's writing at the desk? Why, I declare, it's Jack Bunce! I thought he was sick.' 'Which is the jury? Why, is *that* the jury? Billy Price and Job Turner, and Jack Lounsbury, and – well, I never!' 'Now who would ever a' thought –'

But they were gently called to order at this point, and asked not to talk in court. Their tongues fell silent, but the radiant interest in their faces remained, and their gratitude for the blessing of a new sensation and a novel experience still beamed undimmed from their eyes. Aunt Patsy stood up and took the oath, and Mr Allen explained the point in issue, and asked her to go on now, in her own way, and throw as much light upon it as she could. She toyed with her reticule a moment or two, as if considering where to begin, then she said:

'Well, the way of it is this. They are Luigi's legs a week at a time, and then they are Angelo's, and he can do what ever he wants to with them.'

'You are making a mistake, Aunt Patsy Cooper,' said the Judge. 'You shouldn't state that as a *fact*, because you don't know it to *be* a fact.'

'What's the reason I don't?' said Aunt Patsy, bridling a little.

'What is the reason that you do know it?'

'The best in the world – because they told me.'

'That isn't a reason.'

'Well, for the land's sake! Betsy Hale, do you hear that?'

'*Hear* it? I should think so,' said Aunt Betsy, rising and facing the court. 'Why, Judge, I was there and heard it myself. Luigi says to Angelo – no, it was Angelo said it to –'

'Come, come, Mrs Hale, pray sit down, and –'

'Certainly, it's all right, I'm going to sit down presently, but not until I've –'

'But you *must* sit down!'

'*Must!* Well, upon my word if things ain't getting to a pretty pass when –'

The house broke into laughter, but was promptly brought to order, and meantime Mr Allen persuaded the old lady to take her seat. Aunt Patsy continued:

'Yes, they told me that, and I know it's true. They're Luigi's legs this week, but –'

'Ah, *they* told you that, did they?' said the Justice, with interest.

'Well, no, I don't know that *they* told me, but that's neither here nor there. I know, without that, that at dinner, yesterday, Angelo was tired as a dog, and yet Luigi wouldn't lend him the legs to go up stairs and take a nap with.'

'Did he ask for them?'

'Let me see – it seems to me somehow, that – that – Aunt Betsy, do you remember whether he –'

'Never mind about what Aunt Betsy remembers – she is not a witness; we only want to know what you remember yourself,' said the Judge.

'Well, it does seem to me that you are most cantankerously particular about a little thing, Sim Robinson. Why, when I can't remember a thing myself, I always –'

'Ah, *please* go on!'

'Now how *can* she when you keep fussing at her all the time?' said Aunt Betsy. 'Why, with a person pecking at *me* that way, I should get that fuzzled and fuddled that –'

She was on her feet again, but Allen coaxed her into her seat once more, while the court squelched the mirth of the house. Then the Judge said:

'Madam, do you know – do you absolutely *know*, independently of anything these gentlemen have told you – that the power over their legs passes from the one to the other regularly every week?'

'Regularly? Bless your heart, regularly ain't any name for the exactness of it! All the big cities in Europe used to set the clocks by it.' (Laughter, *suppressed by the court*.)

'How do you *know*? That is the question. Please answer it plainly and squarely.'

'Don't you talk to me like that, Sim Robinson – I won't have it. How do I know, indeed! How do *you* know what you know? Because somebody told you. You didn't invent it out of your own head, did you? Why, these twins are the truthfulest people in the world; and I don't think it becomes you to sit up there and throw slurs at them when they haven't been doing anything to you. And they are orphans besides – both of them. All –'

But Aunt Betsy was up again now, and both old ladies were talking at once and with all their might; but as the house was weltering in a storm of laughter, and the judge was hammering his desk with an iron paper weight, one could only see them talk, not hear them. At last, when quiet was restored, the court said:

'Let the ladies retire.'

'But, your honor, I have the right, in the interest of my clients, to cross-exam –'

'You'll not need to exercise it, Mr Wilson – the evidence is thrown out.'

'Thrown out!' said Aunt Patsy, ruffled; 'and what's it thrown out for, I'd like to know.'

'And so would I, Patsy Cooper. It seems to me that if we can save these poor persecuted strangers, it is our bounden duty to stand up here and talk for them till –'

'There, there, there, *do* sit down!'

It cost some trouble and a good deal of coaxing, but they

were got into their seats at last. The trial was soon ended now. The twins themselves became witnesses in their own defense. They established the fact, upon oath, that the leg-power passed from one to the other every Saturday night at twelve o'clock sharp. But on cross-examination their counsel would not allow them to tell whose week of power the current week was. The Judge insisted upon their answering, and proposed to compel them, but even the prosecution took fright and came to the rescue then, and helped stay the sturdy jurist's revolutionary hand. So the case had to go to the jury with that important point hanging in the air. They were out an hour and brought in this verdict:

'We the jury do find: 1, that an assault was committed, as charged; 2, that it was committed by one of the persons accused, he having been seen to do it by several credible witnesses; 3, but that his identity is so merged in his brother's that we have not been able to tell which was him. We cannot convict both, for only one is guilty. We cannot acquit both, for only one is innocent. Our verdict is that justice has been defeated by the dispensation of God, and ask to be discharged from further duty.'

This was read aloud in court and brought out a burst of hearty applause. The old ladies made a spring at the twins, to shake and congratulate, but were gently disengaged by Mr Wilson and softly crowded back into their places.

The Judge rose in his little tribune, laid aside his silver-bowed spectacles, roached his gray hair up with his fingers, and said, with dignity and solemnity, and even with a certain pathos:

'In all my experience on the bench, I have not seen justice bow her head in shame in this court until this day. You little realize what far-reaching harm has just been wrought here under the fickle forms of law. Imitation is the bane of courts – I thank God that this one is free from the contamin-

ation of that vice – and in no long time you will see the
fatal work of this hour seized upon by profligate so-called
guardians of justice in all the wide circumstance of this
planet and perpetuated in their pernicious decisions. I wash
my hands of this iniquity. I would have compelled these
culprits to expose their guilt, but support failed me where I
had most right to expect aid and encouragement. And I was
confronted by a law made in the interest of crime, which
protects the criminal from testifying against himself. Yet I
had precedents of my own whereby I had set aside that law
on two different occasions and thus succeeded in convicting
criminals to whose crimes there were no witnesses but themselves. What have you accomplished this day? Do you
realize it? You have set adrift, unadmonished, in this community, two men endowed with an awful and mysterious
gift, a hidden and grisly power for evil – a power by which
each in his turn may commit crime after crime of the most
heinous character, and no man be able to tell which is the
guilty or which the innocent party in any case of them all.
Look to your homes – look to your property – look to your
lives – for you have need!

'Prisoners at the bar, stand up. Through suppression of
evidence, a jury of your – our – countrymen have been
obliged to deliver a verdict concerning your case which
stinks to high heaven with the rankness of its injustice. By
its terms you, the guilty one, go free with the innocent.
Depart in peace, and come no more! The costs devolve
upon the outraged plaintiff – another iniquity. The court
stands dissolved.'

Almost everybody crowded forward to overwhelm the
twins and their counsel with congratulations; but presently
the two old aunties dug the duplicates out and bore them
away in triumph through the hurrahing crowd, while lots
of new friends carried Pudd'nhead Wilson off tavern-wards

to feast him and 'wet down' his great and victorious entry into the legal arena. To Wilson, so long familiar with neglect and depreciation, this strange new incense of popularity and admiration was as a fragrance blown from the fields of paradise. A happy man was Wilson.

CHAPTER 6

[A deputation came in the evening and conferred upon Wilson the welcome honor of a nomination for mayor; for the village has just been converted into a city by charter. Tom skulks out of challenging the twins. Judge Driscoll thereupon challenges Angelo (accused by Tom of doing the kicking); he declines, but Luigi accepts in his place against Angelo's timid protest.]

I T was late Saturday night – nearing eleven.

The Judge and his second found the rest of the war party at the further end of the vacant ground, near the haunted house. Pudd'nhead Wilson advanced to meet them, and said anxiously:

'I must say a word in behalf of my principal's proxy, Count Luigi, to whom you have kindly granted the privilege of fighting my principal's battle for him. It is growing late, and Count Luigi is in great trouble lest midnight shall strike before the finish.'

'It is another testimony,' said Howard, approvingly. 'That young man is fine all through. He wishes to save his brother the sorrow of fighting on the Sabbath, and he is right; it is the right and manly feeling and does him credit. We will make all possible haste.'

Wilson said:

'There is also another reason – a consideration, in fact, which deeply concerns Count Luigi himself. These twins have command of their mutual legs turn about. Count Luigi is in command now; but at midnight, possession will pass to my principal, Count Angelo, and – well, you can foresee what will happen. He will march straight off the field, and carry Luigi with him.'

'Why! sure enough!' cried the Judge, 'we have heard something about that extraordinary law of their being, already – nothing very definite, it is true, as regards dates and durations of power, but I see it is definite enough as regards to-night. Of course we must give Luigi every chance. Omit all the ceremonial possible, gentlemen, and place us in position.'

The seconds at once tossed up a coin; Howard won the choice. He placed the Judge sixty feet from the haunted house and facing it; Wilson placed the twins within fifteen feet of the house and facing the Judge – necessarily. The pistol-case was opened and the long slim tubes taken out; when the moonlight glinted from them a shiver went through Angelo. The doctor was a fool, but a thoroughly well-meaning one, with a kind heart and a sincere disposition to oblige, but along with it an absence of tact which often hurt its effectiveness. He brought his box of lint and bandages, and asked Angelo to feel and see how soft and comfortable they were. Angelo's head fell over against Luigi's in a faint, and precious time was lost in bringing him to; which provoked Luigi into expressing his mind to the doctor with a good deal of vigor and frankness. After Angelo came to he was still so weak that Luigi was obliged to drink a stiff horn of brandy to brace him up.

The seconds now stepped at once to their posts, half way between the combatants, one of them on each side of the line of fire. Wilson was to count, very deliberately, 'One – two – three – fire! – stop!' and the duellists could bang away at any time they chose during that recitation, but not after the last word. Angelo grew very nervous when he saw Wilson's hand rising slowly into the air as a sign to make ready, and he leaned his head against Luigi's and said:

'Oh, please take me away from here, I can't stay, I know I can't!'

'What in the world are you doing? Straighten up! What's the matter with you? – *you're* in no danger – nobody's going to shoot at you. Straighten up, I tell you!'

Angelo obeyed, just in time to hear:

'One –!'

'Bang!' Just one report, and a little tuft of white hair floated slowly to the Judge's feet in the moonlight. The Judge did not swerve; he still stood erect and motionless, like a statue, with his pistol-arm hanging straight down at his side. He was reserving his fire.

'Two –!'

'Three –!'

'Fire –!'

Up came the pistol-arm instantly – Angelo dodged with the report. He said 'Ouch!' and fainted again.

The doctor examined and bandaged the wound. It was of no consequence, he said – bullet through fleshy part of arm – no bones broken – the gentleman was still able to fight – let the duel proceed.

Next time Angelo jumped just as Luigi fired, which disordered his aim and caused him to cut a chip out of Howard's ear. The Judge took his time again, and when he fired Angelo jumped and got a knuckle skinned. The doctor inspected and dressed the wounds. Angelo now spoke out and said he was content with the satisfaction he had got, and if the Judge – but Luigi shut him roughly up, and asked him not to make an ass of himself; adding:

'And I want you to stop dodging. You take a great deal too prominent a part in this thing for a person who has got nothing to do with it. You should remember that you are here only by courtesy, and are without official recognition; officially you are not here at all; officially you do not even exist. To all intents and purposes you are absent from this place, and you ought for your own modesty's sake to reflect that it cannot become a person who is not present here to be taking this sort of public and indecent prominence in a matter in which he is not in the slightest degree concerned. Now, don't dodge again; the bullets are not for you, they are for me; if I want them dodged I will attend to it myself. I never saw a person act so.'

Angelo saw the reasonableness of what his brother had said, and he did try to reform, but it was of no use; both pistols went off at the same instant, and he jumped once more; he got a sharp scrape along his cheek from the Judge's bullet, and so deflected Luigi's aim that his ball went wide and chipped a flake of skin from Pudd'nhead Wilson's chin. The doctor attended to the wounded.

By the terms, the duel was over. But Luigi was entirely out of patience, and begged for one more exchange of shots, insisting that he had had no fair chance, on account of his brother's indelicate behavior. Howard was opposed to granting so unusual a privilege, but the Judge took Luigi's part, and added that indeed he himself might fairly be considered entitled to another trial, because although the proxy on the other side was in no way to blame for his (the Judge's) humiliatingly resultless work, the gentleman with whom he was fighting this duel was to blame for it, since if he had played no advantages and had held his head still, his proxy would have been disposed of early. He added:

'Count Luigi's request for another exchange is another proof that he is a brave and chivalrous gentleman, and I beg that the courtesy he asks may be accorded him.'

'I thank you most sincerely for this generosity, Judge Driscoll,' said Luigi, with a polite bow, and moving to his place. Then he added – to Angelo, 'Now hold your grip, hold your *grip*, I tell you, and I'll land him sure!'

The men stood erect, their pistol-arms at their sides, the two seconds stood at their official posts, the doctor stood

five paces in Wilson's rear with his instruments and bandages in his hands. The deep stillness, the peaceful moonlight, the motionless figures, made an impressive picture
and the impending fatal possibilities augmented this impressiveness to solemnity. Wilson's hand began to rise –
slowly – slowly – higher – still higher – in another moment:

'*Boom!*' – the first stroke of midnight swung up out of
the distance; Angelo was off like a deer!

'Oh, you unspeakable traitor!' wailed his brother, as they
went soaring over the fence.

The others stood astonished and gazing; and so stood,
watching that strange spectacle until distance dissolved it
and swept it from their view. Then they rubbed their eyes
like people waking out of a dream.

'Well, I've never seen anything like that before!' said the
Judge. 'Wilson, I am going to confess now, that I wasn't
quite able to believe in that leg-business, and had a suspicion
that it was a put-up convenience between those twins; and
when Count Angelo fainted I thought I saw the whole
scheme – thought it was pretext No. I, and would be followed by others till twelve o'clock should arrive, and Luigi
would get off with all the credit of seeming to want to fight
and yet not have to fight, after all. But I was mistaken. His
pluck proved it. He's a brave fellow and did want to fight.'

'There isn't any doubt about that,' said Howard, and
added, in a grieved tone, 'but what an unworthy sort of
Christian that Angelo is – I hope and believe there are not
many like him. It is not right to engage in a duel on the
Sabbath – I could not approve of that myself; but to finish
one that has been begun – that is a duty, let the day be what
it may.'

They strolled along, still wondering, still talking.

'It is a curious circumstance,' remarked the surgeon, halting Wilson a moment to paste some more court plaster on

his chin, which had gone to leaking blood again, 'that in this duel neither of the parties who handled the pistols lost blood, while nearly all the persons present in the mere capacity of guests got hit. I have not heard of such a thing before. Don't you think it unusual?'

'Yes,' said the Judge, 'it has struck me as peculiar. Peculiar and unfortunate. I was annoyed at it, all the time. In the case of Angelo it made no great difference, because he was in a measure concerned, though not officially; but it troubled me to see the seconds compromised, and yet I knew no way to mend the matter.'

'There was no way to mend it,' said Howard, whose ear was being readjusted now by the doctor; 'the code fixes our place, and it would not have been lawful to change it. If we could have stood at your side, or behind you, or in front of you, it – but it would not have been legitimate and the other parties would have had a just right to complain of our trying to protect ourselves from danger; infractions of the code are certainly not permissible in any case whatever.'

Wilson offered no remarks. It seemed to him that there was very little place here for so much solemnity, but he judged that if a duel where nobody was in danger or got crippled but the seconds and the outsiders had nothing ridiculous about it for these gentlemen, his pointing out that feature would probably not help them to see it.

He invited them in to take a nightcap, and Howard and the Judge accepted, but the doctor said he would have to go and see how Angelo's principal wound was getting on.

[It was now Sunday, and in the afternoon Angelo was to be received into the Baptist communion by immersion – a doubtful prospect, the doctor feared.]

CHAPTER 7

WHEN the doctor arrived at Aunt Patsy Cooper's house, he found the lights going and everybody up and dressed and in a great state of solicitude and excitement. The twins were stretched on a sofa in the sitting-room, Aunt Patsy was fussing at Angelo's arm, Nancy was flying around under her commands, the two young boys were trying to keep out of the way and always getting in it, in order to see and wonder, Rowena stood apart, helpless with apprehension and emotion, and Luigi was growling in unappeasable fury over Angelo's shameful flight.

As has been reported before, the doctor was a fool — a kindhearted and well-meaning one, but with no tact; and as he was by long odds the most learned physician in the town, and was quite well aware of it, and could talk his learning with ease and precision, and liked to show off when he had an audience, he was sometimes tempted into revealing more of a case than was good for the patient.

He examined Angelo's wound, and was really minded to say nothing for once; but Aunt Patsy was so anxious and so pressing that he allowed his caution to be overcome, and proceeded to empty himself as follows, with scientific relish:

'Without going too much into detail, madam — for you would probably not understand it, anyway — I concede that great care is going to be necessary here; otherwise exudation of the oesophagus is nearly sure to ensue, and this will be followed by ossification and extradition of the maxillaris superioris, which must decompose the granular surfaces of the great infusorial ganglionic system, thus obstructing the action òf the posterior varioloid arteries, and precipitating compound strangulated sorosis of the valvular tissues, and ending unavoidably in the dispersion and combustion of the marsupial fluxes and the consequent embrocation of the bicuspid populo redax referendum rotulorum.'

A miserable silence followed. Aunt Patsy's heart sank, the pallor of despair invaded her face, she was not able to speak; poor Rowena wrung her hands in privacy and silence, and said to herself in the bitterness of her young grief, 'There is no hope – it is plain there is no hope;' the good-hearted negro wench, Nancy, paled to chocolate, then to orange, then to amber, and thought to herself with yearning sympathy and sorrow, 'Po' thing, he ain' gwyne to las' throo de half o' dat;' small Henry choked up, and turned his head away to hide his rising tears, and his brother Joe said to himself, with a sense of loss, 'The baptizing's busted, that's sure.' Luigi was the only person who had any heart to speak. He said, a little bit sharply, to the doctor:

'Well, well, there's nothing to be gained by wasting precious time; give him a barrel of pills – I'll take them for him.'

'You?' asked the doctor.

'Yes. Did you suppose he was going to take them himself?'

'Why, of course.'

'Well, it's a mistake. He never took a dose of medicine in his life. He can't.'

'Well, upon my word, it's the most extraordinary thing I ever heard of!'

'Oh,' said Aunt Patsy, as pleased as a mother whose child is being admired and wondered at, 'you'll find that there's more about them that's wonderful than their just being made in the image of God like the rest of His creatures, now you can depend on that, *I* tell you,' and she wagged her complacent head like one who could reveal marvelous things if she chose.

The boy Joe began:

'Why, ma, they *ain't* made in the im—'

'You shut up, and wait till you're asked, Joe. I'll let you know when I want help. Are you looking for something, doctor?'

The doctor asked for a few sheets of paper and a pen, and said he would write a prescription; which he did. It was one of Galen's; in fact, it was Galen's favorite, and had been slaying people for sixteen thousand years. Galen used it for everything, applied it to everything, said it would remove everything, from warts all the way through to lungs – and it generally did. Galen was still the only medical authority recognized in Missouri; his practice was the only practice known to the Missouri doctors, and his prescriptions were the only ammunition they carried when they went out for game. By and by Dr Claypool laid down his pen and read the result of his labors aloud, carefully and deliberately, for this battery must be constructed on the premises by the family, and mistakes could occur; for he wrote a doctor's hand – the hand which from the beginning of time has been so disastrous to the apothecary and so profitable to the undertaker:

'Take of afarabocca, henbane, corpobalsamum, each two drams and a half: of cloves, opium, myrrh, cyperus, each two drams; of opobalsamum, Indian leaf, cinnamon, zedoary, ginger, coftus, coral, cassia, euphorbium, gum tragacanth, frankincense, styrax calamita, celtic, nard, spignel, hartwort, mustard, saxifrage, dill, anise, each one dram; of xylaloes, rheum ponticum, alipta, moschata, castor, spikenard, galangals, opoponax, anacardium, mastich, brimstone, peony, eringo, pulp of dates, red and white hermodactyls, roses, thyme, acorns, pennyroyal, gentian, the bark of the root of mandrake, germander, valerian, bishop's weed, bay-berries, long and white pepper, xylobalsamum, carnabadium, macedonian, parsely-seeds, lovage, the seeds of rue, and sinon, of each a dram and a half; of pure gold, pure silver, pearls not perforated, the blatta byzantina, the bone of the stag's heart, of each the quantity of fourteen grains of wheat; of sapphire, emerald and jasper stones, each one dram; of hazel-nut, two drams; of pellitory of Spain, shaving of ivory, calamus odoratus, each the quantity of twenty-nine grains of wheat; of honey or sugar a sufficient quantity. Boil down and skim off.'

'There,' he said, 'that will fix the patient; give his brother a dipperful every three-quarters of an hour—'

—'while he survives,' muttered Luigi—

—'and see that the room is kept wholesomely hot, and the doors and windows closed tight. Keep Count Angelo nicely covered up with six or seven blankets, and when he is thirsty – which will be frequently – moisten a rag in the vapor of the tea-kettle and let his brother suck it. When he is hungry – which will also be frequently – he must not be humored oftener than every seven or eight hours; then toast part of a cracker until it begins to brown, and give it to his brother.'

'That is all very well, as far as Angelo is concerned,' said Luigi, 'but what am I to eat?'

'I do not see that there is anything the matter with you,' the doctor answered, 'you may, of course, eat what you please.'

'And also drink what I please, I suppose?'

'Oh, certainly – at present. When the violent and continuous perspiring has reduced your strength, I shall have to reduce your diet, of course, and also bleed you, but there is no occasion for that yet awhile.' He turned to Aunt Patsy and said: 'He must be put to bed, and sat up with, and tended with the greatest care, and not allowed to stir for several days and nights.'

'For one, I'm sacredly thankful for that,' said Luigi, 'It postpones the funeral – I'm not to be drowned to-day anyhow.'

Angelo said quietly to the doctor:

'I will cheerfully submit to all your requirements, sir, up to two o'clock this afternoon, and will resume them after three, but cannot be confined to the house during that intermediate hour.'

'Why, may I ask?'

'Because I have entered the Baptist communion, and by appointment am to be baptized in the river at that hour.'

'Oh insanity! – it cannot be allowed!'

Angelo answered with placid firmness:

'Nothing shall prevent it, if I am alive.'

'Why, consider, my dear sir, in your condition it might prove fatal.'

A tender and ecstatic smile beamed from Angelo's eyes, and he broke forth in a tone of joyous fervency:

'Ah, how blessed it would be to die for such a cause – it would be martyrdom!'

'But your brother – consider your brother; you would be risking his life, too.'

'He risked mine an hour ago,' responded Angelo, gloomily; 'did he consider me?' A thought swept through his mind that made him shudder. 'If I had not run, I might have been killed in a duel on the Sabbath day, and my soul would have been lost – lost.'

'Oh, don't fret, it wasn't in any danger,' said Luigi, irritably; 'they wouldn't waste it for a little thing like that; there's a glass case all ready for it in the heavenly museum, and a pin to stick it up with.'

Aunt Patsy was shocked, and said:

'Looy, Looy! – don't talk so, dear!'

Rowena's soft heart was pierced by Luigi's unfeeling

words, and she murmured to herself, 'Oh, if I but had the dear privilege of protecting and defending him with my weak voice! – but alas! this sweet boon is denied me by the cruel conventions of social intercourse.'

'Get their bed ready,' said Aunt Patsy to Nancy, 'and shut up the windows and doors, and light their candles, and see that you drive all the mosquitoes out of their bar, and make up a good fire in their stove, and carry up some bags of hot ashes to lay to his feet—'

—'and a shovel of fire for his head, and a mustard plaster for his neck, and some gum shoes for his ears,' Luigi interrupted, with temper; and added, to himself, 'Damnation, I'm going to be roasted alive, I just know it!'

'Why, Looy! Do be quiet; I never saw such a fractious thing. A body would think you didn't care for your brother.'

'I don't – to *that* extent, Aunt Patsy. I was glad the drowning was postponed a minute ago, but I'm not now. No, that is all gone by; I want to be drowned.'

'You'll bring a judgment on yourself just as sure as you live, if you go on like that. Why, I never heard the beat of it. Now, there, – there! you've said enough. Not another word out of you, – I won't have it!'

'But, Aunt Patsy—'

'Luigi! Didn't you hear what I told you?'

'But, Aunt Patsy, I – why, I'm not going to set my heart and lungs afloat in that pail of sewage which this criminal here has been prescri—'

'Yes, you are, too. You are going to be good, and do everything I tell you, like a dear,' and she tapped his cheek affectionately with her finger. 'Rowena, take the prescription and go in the kitchen and hunt up the things and lay them out for me. I'll sit up with my patient the rest of the night, doctor; I can't trust Nancy, she couldn't make Luigi take the medicine. Of course, you'll drop in again during the day. Have you got any more directions?'

'No, I believe not, Aunt Patsy. If I don't get in earlier, I'll be along by early candlelight, anyway. Meantime, don't allow him to get out of his bed.'

Angelo said, with calm determination:

'I shall be baptized at two o'clock. Nothing but death shall prevent me.'

The doctor said nothing aloud, but to himself he said:

'Why, this chap's got a manly side, after all! Physically he's a coward, but morally he's a lion. I'll go and tell the others about this; it will raise him a good deal in their estimation – and the public will follow their lead, of course.'

Privately, Aunt Patsy applauded too, and was proud of Angelo's courage in the moral field as she was of Luigi's in the field of honor.

The boy Henry was troubled, but the boy Joe said, inaudibly, and gratefully, 'We're all hunky, after all; and no postponement on account of the weather.'

CHAPTER 8

BY nine o'clock the town was humming with the news of the midnight duel, and there were but two opinions about it: one, that Luigi's pluck in the field was most praiseworthy and Angelo's flight most scandalous; the other, that Angelo's courage in flying the field for conscience's sake was as fine and creditable as was Luigi's in holding the field in the face of the bullets. The one opinion was held by half of the town, the other one was maintained by the other half. The division was clean and exact, and it made two parties, an Angelo party and a Luigi party. The twins had suddenly become popular idols along with Pudd'nhead Wilson, and haloed with a glory as intense as his. The children talked the duel all the way to Sunday-school, their elders talked it all the way to church, the choir discussed it behind their red curtain, it usurped the place of pious thought in the 'nigger gallery'.

By noon the doctor had added the news, and spread it, that Count Angelo, in spite of his wound and all warnings and supplications, was resolute in his determination to be baptized at the hour appointed. This swept the town like wildfire, and mightily reinforced the enthusiasm of the Angelo faction, who said, 'If any doubted that it was moral courage that took him from the field, what have they to say now!'

Still the excitement grew. All the morning it was traveling countrywards, toward all points of the compass; so, whereas before only the farmers and their wives were intending to come and witness the remarkable baptism, a general holiday was now proclaimed and the children and negroes admitted to the privileges of the occasion. All the farms for ten miles around were vacated, all the converging roads emptied long processions of wagons, horses, and yeomanry into the town. The pack and cram of people vastly exceeded any that had ever been seen in that sleepy region before. The only thing that had ever even approached it, was the time long gone by, but never forgotten, nor even referred to without wonder and pride, when two circuses and a Fourth of July fell together. But the glory of that occasion was extinguished now for good. It was but a freshet to this deluge.

The great invasion massed itself on the river bank and waited hungrily for the immense event. Waited, and wondered if it would really happen, or if the twin who was not a 'professor' would stand out and prevent it.

But they were not to be disappointed. Angelo was as good as his word. He came attended by an escort of honor composed of several hundred of the best citizens, all of the Angelo party; and when the immersion was finished they escorted him back home: and would even have carried him on their shoulders, but that people might think they were carrying Luigi.

Far into the night the citizens continued to discuss and wonder over the strangely-mated pair of incidents that had distinguished and exalted the past twenty-four hours above any other twenty-four in the history of their town for picturesqueness and splendid interest; and long before the lights were out and burghers asleep it had been decided on all hands that in capturing these twins Dawson's Landing had drawn a prize in the great lottery of municipal fortune.

At midnight Angelo was sleeping peacefully. His immersion had not harmed him, it had merely made him wholesomely drowsy, and he had been dead asleep many hours now. It had made Luigi drowsy, too, but he had got only brief naps, on account of his having to take the medicine every three-quarters of an hour – and Aunt Betsy Hale was there to see that he did it. When he complained and resisted, she was quietly firm with him, and said in a low voice:

'No – no, that won't do; you mustn't talk, and you mustn't retch and gag that way, either – you'll wake up your poor brother.'

'Well, what of it, Aunt Betsy, he—'

''Sh-h! Don't make a noise dear. You mustn't forget that your poor brother is sick and—'

'Sick, is he? Well, I wish I—'

'Sh-h-h! Will you be quiet, Luigi! Here, now, take the rest of it – don't keep me holding the dipper all night. I declare if you haven't left a good fourth of it in the bottom! Come – that's a good boy.'

'Aunt Betsy, don't make me! I feel like I've swallowed a cemetery; I do, indeed. Do let me rest a little – just a little; I can't take any more of the devilish stuff now.'

'Luigi! Using such language here, and him just baptized! Do you want the roof to fall on you?'

'I wish to goodness it would!'

'Why, you dreadful thing! I've a good notion to – let that blanket alone; do you want your brother to catch his death?'

'Aunt Betsy, I've *got* to have it off, I'm being roasted alive; nobody could stand it – you couldn't yourself.'

'Now, then, you're sneezing again – I just expected it.'

'Because I've caught a cold in my head. I always do, when I go in the water with my clothes on. And it takes me weeks to get over it, too. I think it was a shame to serve me so.'

'Luigi, you are unreasonable; you know very well they couldn't baptize him dry. I should think you would be willing to undergo a little inconvenience for your brother's sake.'

'Inconvenience! Now how you talk, Aunt Betsy. I came as near as anything to getting drowned – you saw that yourself; and do you call this inconvenience? – the room shut up as tight as a drum, and so hot the mosquitoes are trying to get out; and a cold in the head, and dying for sleep and no chance to get any on account of this infamous medicine that assassin prescri—'

'There, you're sneezing again. I'm going down and mix some more of this truck for you, dear.'

CHAPTER 9

DURING Monday, Tuesday, and Wednesday the twins grew steadily worse; but then the doctor was summoned South to attend his mother's funeral, and they got well in forty-eight hours. They appeared on the street on Friday, and were welcomed with enthusiasm by the new-born parties, the Luigi and Angelo factions. The Luigi faction carried its strength into the Democratic party, the Angelo faction entered into a combination with the Whigs. The Democrats nominated Luigi for alderman under the new city government, and the Whigs put up Angelo against him. The Democrats nominated Pudd'nhead Wilson for mayor, and he was left alone in his glory, for the Whigs had no man who was willing to enter the lists against such a formidable opponent. No politician had scored such a compliment as this before in the history of the Mississippi Valley.

The political campaign in Dawson's Landing opened in a pretty warm fashion, and waxed hotter every week. Luigi's whole heart was in it, and even Angelo developed a surprising amount of interest – which was natural, because he was not merely representing Whigism, a matter of no consequence to him, but he was representing something immensely finer and greater – to wit, Reform. In him was centred the hopes of the whole reform element of the town; he was the chosen and admired champion of every clique that had a pet reform of any sort or kind at heart. He was president of the great Teetotalers' Union, its chiefest prophet and mouthpiece.

But as the canvass went on, troubles began to spring up all around – troubles for the twins, and through them for all the parties and segments and fractions of parties. Whenever Luigi had possession of the legs, he carried Angelo to balls, rum shops, Son's of Liberty parades, horse races, campaign riots, and everywhere else that could damage him with his party and the church; and when it was Angelo's week he carried Luigi diligently to all manner of moral and religious gatherings, doing his best to regain the ground he had lost before. As a result of these double performances, there was a storm blowing all the time, an ever rising storm, too – a storm of frantic criticism of the twins, and rage over their extravagant, incomprehensible conduct.

Luigi had the final chance. The legs were his for the closing week of the canvass. He led his brother a fearful dance.

But he saved his best card for the very eve of the election. There was to be a grand turnout of the Teetotalers' Union that day, and Angelo was to march at the head of the procession and deliver a great oration afterward. Luigi drank a couple of glasses of whisky – which steadied his nerves and clarified his mind, but made Angelo drunk. Everybody who saw the march, saw that the Champion of the Teetotalers was half seas over, and noted also that his brother, who made no hypocritical pretensions to extra temperance virtues, was dignified and sober. This eloquent fact could not be unfruitful at the end of a hot political canvass. At the mass meeting Angelo tried to make his great temperance oration, but was so discommoded by hiccoughs and thickness of tongue that he had to give it up; then drowsiness overtook him and his head drooped against Luigi's and he went to sleep. Luigi apologized for him, and was going on to improve his opportunity with an appeal for a moderation of what he called 'the prevailing teetotal madness,' but persons in the audience began to howl and throw things at him, and then the meeting rose in wrath and chased him home.

This episode was a crusher for Angelo in another way. It destroyed his chances with Rowena. Those chances had been growing, right along, for two months. Rowena had partly confessed that she loved him, but wanted time to consider. Now the tender dream was ended, and she told him so the moment he was sober enough to understand. She said she would never marry a man who drank.

'But I don't drink,' he pleaded.

'That is nothing to the point,' she said, coldly, 'you get drunk, and that is worse.'

[There was a long and sufficiently idiotic discussion here, which ended as reported in a previous note.]

CHAPTER 10

DAWSON'S LANDING had a week of repose, after the election, and it needed it, for the frantic and variegated nightmare which had tormented it all through the preceding week had left it limp, haggard, and exhausted at the end. It got the week of repose because Angelo had the legs, and was in too subdued a condition to want to go out and mingle with an irritated community that had come to distrust and detest him because there was such a lack of harmony between his morals, which were confessedly excellent, and his methods of illustrating them, which were distinctly damnable.

The new city officers were sworn in on the following Monday – at least all but Luigi. There was a complication in his case. His election was conceded, but he could not sit in the board of aldermen without his brother, and his brother could not sit there because he was not a member. There seemed to be no way out of the difficulty but to carry the matter into the courts, so this was resolved upon. The case was set for the Monday fortnight. In due course the time arrived. In the meantime the city government had been at a standstill, because without Luigi there was a tie in the board of aldermen, whereas with him the liquor interest – the richest in the political field – would have one majority. But the court decided that Angelo could not sit in the board with him, either in public or executive sessions, and at the same time forbade the board to deny admission to Luigi, a fairly and legally chosen alderman. The case was carried up and up from court to court, yet still the same old original decision was confirmed every time. As a result, the city government not only stood still, with its hands tied, but everything it was created to protect and care for went a steady gait toward rack and ruin. There was no way to levy a tax, so the minor officials had to resign or starve; therefore they resigned. There being no city money, the enormous legal expenses on both sides had to be defrayed by private subscription. But at last the people came to their senses, and said:

'Pudd'nhead was right at the start – we ought to have hired the official half of that human phillipene to resign; but it's too late now; some of us haven't got anything left to hire him with.'

'Yes, we have,' said another citizen, 'we've got this' – and he produced a halter.

Many shouted: 'That's the ticket.' But others said: 'No – Count Angelo is innocent; we mustn't hang him.'

'Who said anything about hanging him? We are only going to hang the other one.'

'Then that is all right – there is no objection to that.'

So they hanged Luigi. And so ends the history of 'Those Extraordinary Twins'.

FINAL REMARKS

As you see, it was an extravagant sort of a tale, and had no purpose but to exhibit that monstrous 'freak' in all sorts of grotesque lights. But when Roxy wandered into the tale she had to be furnished with something to do; so she changed the children in the cradle; this necessitated the invention of a reason for it; this, in turn, resulted in making the children prominent personages – nothing could prevent it, of course. Their career began to take a tragic aspect, and some one had to be brought in to help work the machinery; so Pudd'nhead Wilson was introduced and taken on trial. By this time the whole show was being run by the new people and in their interest, and the original show was become side-tracked and forgotten; the twin-monster, and the heroine, and the lads, and the old ladies had dwindled to inconsequentialities and were merely in the way. Their story was one story, the new people's story was another story, and there was no connection between them, no interdependence, no kinship. It is not practicable or rational to try to tell two stories at the same time; so I dug out the farce and left the tragedy.

The reader already knew how the expert works; he knows now how the other kind do it.

MARK TWAIN

PUDD'NHEAD WILSON'S
CALENDAR

Pudd'nhead
Wilson's
Calendar for
1894

☞ N. B. ☜

It should be remembered that
the *first day of* EACH MONTH is the
date on which The Century Magazine appears, containing Mark
Twain's interesting serial story,
Pudd'nhead Wilson.

which he can always be identified—and that without shade of doubt or question. These marks are his signature, his physiological autograph, so to speak, and this autograph cannot be counterfeited, nor can he disguise it or hide it away, nor can it become illegible by the wear and the mutations of time. This signature is not his face—age can change that beyond recognition; it is not his hair, for that can fall out; it is not his height, for duplicates of that exist also, wherever this signature is each man's very own—there is no duplicate of it among the swarming populations of the globe!"—

Pudd'nhead Wilson's Speech
In defense of the Twins ¶¶

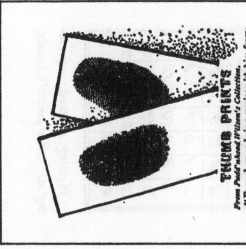

THUMB PRINTS

From Pudd'nhead Wilson's Collection.

"Every human being carries with him from his cradle to his grave certain physical marks which do not change their character, and by

FEBRUARY.

S	M	T	W	T	F	S
..	..	..	..	..	1	2	3

S	M	T	W	T	F	S
..	..	..	..	..	1	2
3	4	5	6	7	8	9
10	11	12	13	14	15	16
17	18	19	20	21	22	23
24	25	26	27	..	..	..

Behold the fool saith, "put not all thine eggs in the one basket," which is but a manner of saying, "scatter your money and your attention," but the wise man saith, put all tyne eggs in the one basket and—*watch that basket.*

4

JANUARY.

S	M	T	W	T	F	S
..	1	2	3	4	5	6
7	8	9	10	11	12	13
14	15	16	17	18	19	20
21	22	23	24	25	26	27
28	29	30	31	..	..	..

Nothing so needs reform-ing as · other people's habits.

3

April.

S	M	T	W	T	F	S
1	2	3	4	●	6	7
8	9	10	11	☽	13	14
15	16	17	18	⊕	20	21
22	23	24	25	26	€	28
29	30	.·.	.·.	.·.	.·.	.·.

April 1st: This is the day upon which we are reminded of what we are on the other three hundred and sixty-four.

MARCH.

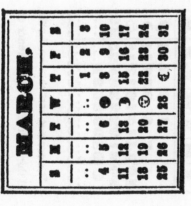

S	M	T	W	T	F	S
.·.	.·.	.·.	.·.	1	2	3
4	5	6	●	8	9	10
11	12	13	☽	15	16	17
18	19	20	⊕	22	23	24
25	26	27	28	€	30	31

When angry, count a hundred; when very angry, swear.

MAY.

S	M	T	W	T	F	S
..	..	..	1	2	3	4
...	6	7	8	9	10	11
13	14	15	16	17	18	...
20	21	22	23	24	25	26
28	29	30	31	...	...	...

It were not best that we should all think alike; it is difference of opinion that makes horse-races.

7

JUNE.

S	M	T	W	T	F	S
..	..	..	..	..	1	2
...	4	5	6	7	8	9
3	11	12	13	14	15	16
17	19	18	20	21	22	23
24	25	...	27	...	29	30

When I reflect upon the number of disagreeable people who I know have gone to a better world, I am moved to lead a different life.

8

JULY.

S	M	T	W	T	F	S
1	2	3	4	5	6	7
8	9	⊙10	11	12	13	14
15	16	⊙17	18	19	20	21
22	23	24	ℭ	26	27	28
29	30	31				

July 4th: Statistics show that we lose more fools on this day than in all the other days of the year put together. This proves, by the number left in stock, that one Fourth of July per year is now inadequate, the Country has grown so.

August.

S	M	T	W	T	F	S
			⊕	1	2	3	4
5	6	7	☽	⊙9	10	11
12	13	14	15	16	17	18
19	20	21	22	ℭ23	23	25
26	27	28	29	●30	31	

Why is it that we rejoice at a birth and grieve at a funeral? Is it because we are not the person involved?

September.

S	M	T	W	T	F	S
:	:	:	:	:	:	1
2	3	4	5	6	7	8
9	10	11	12	13	14	15
16	17	18	19	20	21	☾
23	24	25	26	27	28	●
30	:	:	:	:	:	:

If you pick up a starving dog and make him prosperous, he will not bite you. This is the principal difference between a dog and a man.

October.

S	M	T	W	T	F	S
:	1	2	3	4	5	6
7	8	9	10	11	12	13
☽	15	16	17	18	19	20
☾	22	23	24	25	26	27
●	29	30	31	:	:	:

October: This is one of the peculiarly dangerous months to speculate in stocks in. The others are July, January, September, April, November, May, March, June, December, August and February.

NOVEMBER.

S	M	T	W	T	F	S
..	..	..	..	1	2	3
4	5	6	7	8	9	10
11	12	13	14	15	16	17
18	19	20	21	22	23	24
25	26	27	28	29	30	..

Few things are harder to put up with than the annoyance of a good example.

13

DECEMBER.

S	M	T	W	T	F	S
..	..	..	..	..	..	1
2	3	4	5	6	7	8
9	10	11	12	13	14	15
16	17	18	19	20	21	22
23	24	25	26	27	28	29
30	31	..	..	..	..	..

Even the clearest and most perfect circumstantial evidence is likely to be at fault, after all, and therefore ought to be received with great caution.—Take the case of any pencil sharpened by any woman: if you have witnesses, you will find she did it with a knife; but if you take simply the aspect of the pencil, you will say she did it with her teeth.

14

Set up and Printed for
Mr. Wilson

by Henry Butt,
Dawson's Landing, Mo.

Fine Job Printing a
Specialty.

Portrait of **MARK TWAIN,**
From an amateur photograph by his friend
"Pudd'nhead Wilson."

NOTES

1. (p. 55) *below St Louis*: This places Dawson's Landing in a different geographical location on the river from St Petersburg, in *Huckleberry Finn*, and also from Hannibal, Missouri, the town to which the Clemens family moved when Samuel was four. Critics usually take Dawson's Landing as a recreation of Hannibal, as St Petersburg certainly is. There is some imaginative truth in this but, as my introduction notes, by moving the town farther south Clemens clearly has a deliberate purpose in mind, and seeks – as in the reference to 'the dim great world to the North' (St Louis) in Chapter 5 – to stress the southern-provincial, atmosphere of the town. The slaveholding economy and the dominance of the families who have moved in from Virginia can be much more stressed; and hence the town has a much more feudal and much less northern air. Hannibal and St Petersburg are a hundred miles or so north of St Louis; but Dawson's Landing, set 'half a day's journey, per steamboat' below it, must be between St Louis and Cairo – which in *Huckleberry Finn* is the point where 'real' slavery starts. From Cairo south, the states on both sides of the Mississippi (Missouri and Kentucky) are slave.

2. (p. 57) *a slaveholding town*: Missouri was a slave state. Part of the Louisiana Purchase of 1803, it was admitted to the Union in 1820 (ten years before the action of the novel begins). In order to keep some balance between 'free' and 'slave' states when these territories were admitted, the Missouri Compromise was worked out – slavery was accepted in Missouri but not in any other Purchase territory north of latitude 36° 30′N, so leaving Missouri surrounded on three sides by free territory. But Twain's comment that Dawson's Landing was backed by 'rich, slave-worked grain and pork country' suggests the differences between slavery in Missouri and farther south – where the crop was cotton and slavery was on a plantation or gang-labour basis.

3. (p. 57) *fifty years old*: In fact this seems historically improbable, though imaginatively necessary.

4. (p. 57) *old Virginian ancestry*: Virginia, the site of the first settlement in America, had by the beginning of the eighteenth century developed a markedly aristocratic style of life, on the landed-gentry pattern; the institutions of the English squirearchy were consciously transplanted. It is out of this consciously feudal pattern, with its patterns of intermarriage among the gentry, that the notion of the First Families of Virginia (the F.F.V.s) develops.

5. (p. 58) *another F.F.V.*: See above.

CHAPTER 2

1. (p. 62) *people's finger-marks*: Pudd'nhead's obsession was in fact prompted by a much later interest in such matters; Twain developed the idea after reading Francis Galton's *Finger Prints* (1892).

2. (p. 63) *I'd sell you down de river* . . .: The threat, here comic, later ominous, of being sold 'down the river' dominates the novel. Slavery down river was probably worse, on large, over-seered plantations; that is Roxy's experience in Chapter 18. Also the slaves here are household and familial slaves, obviously better off than they would be on the plantations. Laws about the freeing of slaves, etc., were also stricter in the southern states as opposed to a border state like Missouri. Above all, though, the terror refers to the ugly inter-state slave trade, which involved a large south-western migration of slaves to satisfy the rise of cotton. (Inter-state trading increased as the foreign slave trade ceased, and slaves rose in value and became a speculative investment.) Slavery in Dawson's Landing is obviously conceived more feudally and less commercially than in some states; it has more to do with the preservation of a way of life than with all-out profit.

3. (p. 64) . . . *as white as anybody*: Roxy is, of course, the product of miscegenation, and Twain uses this to give her marked distinction. Often such slaves were specially regarded, but of course they often found themselves in the socially paradoxical position that, in so many ways, Twain exploits for the making of his plot.

CHAPTER 4

1. (p. 77) *clabber*: Sour milk which has been thickened or curdled.

2. (p. 82) *On his death-bed Driscoll set Roxy free* . . .: The setting free of slaves (manumission), particularly on the death of the owner, was common. There were 319,000 free Negroes in the United States by 1830. But legislation began to make manumission more difficult as free Negroes seemed to be an increasing social problem; and some states required Negroes to leave the state on being freed. More, freedom was relative. Many states prohibited the entry of free Negroes; rights of assembly were often curtailed and rights of suffrage almost never granted; other prohibitive laws could make it virtually impossible for freed slaves to make a living.

CHAPTER 5

1. (p. 84) *'conditions'*: i.e. excused from taking certain courses.

2. (p. 89) *exact duplicates*: A remnant from the plot of 'Those Extraordinary Twins'.

CHAPTER 8

1. (p. 101) *fawn upon him, slave-like* ...: Twain's presentation of Roxy's powers of duplicity – and hence her assimilation of a double system of values – is imaginatively very satisfying and very probable. It is more convincing in many ways than more modern suggestions that the slaves in the south were 'infantilized' by their situation and their masters.

CHAPTER II

1. (p. 133) *There was a strong rum party and a strong anti-rum party*: Twain builds into his recreation of Missouri society here a significant passing reference to reform activity in the south. Temperance and eventually prohibition were growingly important matters in American progressivism, and such matters in some ways brought southerners and northerners closer together. Maine passed the first state-wide prohibition law in 1846, and by 1855 twelve states and the Minnesota Territory had followed suit.

2. (p. 134) *Sons of Liberty*: The title, and the rhetoric Twain uses, seem ironically conceived, since the original Sons of Liberty were secret organizations formed in the summer of 1765 to oppose the Stamp Act; they later led armed resistance against British soldiers, and in New York dumped tea into the harbour. But since some of the Southern temperance supporters were called Sons of Temperance, the title has an analogical significance.

3. (p. 135) *philopena*: A complicated joke to succeed in a town where irony 'was not for these people'? It means a nut with two kernels, and comes through into 'Philippine'. Bartlett (*Dict. Amer.*) comments: 'There is a custom common in the Northern States at dinner or evening parties when almonds or other nuts are eaten, to reserve such as are double or contain two kernels, which are called fillipeens. If found by a lady, she gives one of the kernels to a gentleman, when both eat their respective kernels. When the parties again meet, each strives to be the first to exclaim, Fillipeen! for by so doing he or she is entitled to a present from the other.'

CHAPTER 13

1. (p. 145) *calaboose*: Jail.

CHAPTER 14

1. (p. 157) *Cap'n John Smith*: Smith was an English explorer who joined the Virginia colony in 1607 and was elected president of it. During one of his explorations in Virginia he was captured by the Indians, and his *General History of Virginia* (1624) tells the famous story of how the Indian princess Pocahontas interceded to save him from death. Later, converted to Christianity, she married John Rolfe and came to England. The accuracy of Smith's romantic tale is usually questioned by historians, though Bradford Smith's *John Smith: His Life and Legend* (1953) reinstates it in part.

NOTES

CHAPTER 16

1. (p. 175) *this treachery*: The treachery clearly lies in Tom's selling
Roxy down the river and so to a cotton plantation, rather than to an up-
country farm – and hence, as has been said, into a different and more
rigorous kind of slavery.

CHAPTER 18

1. (p. 187) *$100 REWARD*: As a runaway slave, Roxy is, under The
Fugitive Slave Act of 1850, liable to be arrested and returned to her master
in any State or Territory of the Union. Tom is now trapped, therefore,
between the illegal act of selling Roxy, who is free, and his legal obligation
to assist in her recovery by her master.

CHRONOLOGY

1835 *30 November:* Samuel Langhorne Clemens born in Florida, Missouri, where his family had recently moved from Tennessee; the fifth surviving child of John Marshall Clemens and Jane Lampton Clemens.

1839 Family move to Hannibal, Missouri (on the Mississippi River).

1847 *24 March:* Death of father.

1848 Apprenticed to Joseph Ament, Hannibal printer.

1851 Publishes first extant sketch, 'A Gallant Fireman', in his elder brother Orion's newspaper, the *Western Union*.

1853-7 Works as printer and journalist in St Louis, New York, Philadelphia, Keokuk (Iowa) and Cincinnati.

1857-60 Works as steamboat pilot on the Mississippi, training under Horace Bixby. Gets job on the steamboat *Pennsylvania* for his brother Henry, who later (1858) is fatally injured in a boiler explosion. Licensed as pilot 9 April 1859. Publishes a few humorous newspaper sketches.

1861-4 Civil War begins 1861 (will end 1865). Clemens has two-week military career with a volunteer Confederate group, the Marion Rangers (an experience later fictionalized in 'The Private History of a Campaign That Failed', 1885). Travels to Nevada with Orion, where he briefly and unsuccessfully prospects for silver. From August 1862, works as a reporter for the *Territorial Enterprise* (of Virginia City, Nevada), writing many humorous sketches. On 3 February 1863, publishes for the first time under the pseudonym 'Mark Twain'. His taste for journalistic hoaxes and scandals finally forces him out of Nevada.

1864–6 While living in San Francisco, works as reporter. Early contacts with Bret Harte (then editor of the *Californian*, in which he publishes).

18 November 1865: Publishes 'Jim Smiley and His Jumping Frog', in the *Saturday Press*; this sketch makes him nationally known. Visits Hawaii, and writes 24 letters on his journey for the *Sacramento Union*. Follow-up lecture tour is a great success.

1867–8 Publishes his first book, *The Celebrated Jumping Frog of Calaveras County, and Other Sketches*. Visits Europe and the Middle East. Lectures and writes. Courts Olivia ('Livy') Langdon.

1869–70 Engagement to Livy Langdon, whose father lends him money to purchase an interest in the *Buffalo Express* (New York). Publishes *The Innocents Abroad* (describing European trip). Early contacts with William Dean Howells, who becomes a lifetime friend. 2 February 1870, marries Livy. Langdon Clemens born prematurely 7 November.

1871 Family move to Hartford, Connecticut.

1872 Publishes *Roughing It*. Susan Olivia ('Susy') Clemens born in March. Langdon dies in June.

August to November: tours England and is received as celebrity.

1873 Publishes his first novel, *The Gilded Age* (written in collaboration with Charles Dudley Warner).

1874 Clara Langdon Clemens born in June.

1875 *Atlantic Monthly* serializes 'Old Times on the Mississippi'. Publishes *Sketches New & Old*.

1876 Publishes *The Adventures of Tom Sawyer*. Begins writing *Huckleberry Finn*.

1877 Quarrel with Bret Harte; end of their friendship.

1878–9 Family travel in Europe. In Paris, Clemens meets Turgenev; in the Lake District, Charles Darwin.

Accompanied by Joseph Twichell, takes walking tour through the Black Forest and the Swiss Alps. Further work on *Huckleberry Finn*.

1880 Publishes *A Tramp Abroad* (based on tour with Twichell). Jane Lampton ('Jean') Clemens born in July. Early investments in Paige typesetting machine.

1881 Publishes *The Prince and the Pauper*.

1883 Publishes *Life on the Mississippi*. Further work on *Huckleberry Finn*.

1884 *19 December: The Adventures of Huckleberry Finn* published in England and Canada.

1885 *16 February: The Adventures of Huckleberry Finn* published in the United States. Webster & Co., Clemens' firm, buys and publishes Ulysses Grant's *Memoirs*. Invests in many inventions, especially the Paige machine. Pays board for a black student at Yale Law School.

1888 Receives honorary M.A. from Yale University.

1889 Publishes *A Connecticut Yankee in King Arthur's Court*.

1890 Death of his mother.

1891 Losing money at a great rate, from publishing and technological ventures. Family give up their Hartford home, and take trip to Europe for Livy's health.

1892 Publishes *The American Claimant*.

1893–4 Heavy investments in Paige typesetting machine, compounded by panic of 1893, compel Clemens to declare the bankruptcy of Webster & Co. (April 1894). Publishes *The Tragedy of Pudd'nhead Wilson* and *Tom Sawyer Abroad*.

1895–6 Beginning in August 1895, takes world lecture tour, as a way of paying back debts. Death of Susan. Publishes *Personal Recollections of Joan of Arc* and *Tom Sawyer, Detective and Other Stories*. Two collected editions of Twain's work underway.

1897 Publishes *Following the Equator*. Death of Orion.

1898 Finally works his way out of bankruptcy.

1899 Publishes 'The Man That Corrupted Hadleyburg' in *Harper's Magazine*.

1900 Portrait painted by James McNeil Whistler.

1901 Honorary doctorate from Yale.

1904 Death of Livy.

1906 Publishes *What Is Man?* in private, anonymous edition. Begins publishing instalments of autobiography in *North American Review*.

1907 Honorary Litt.D. from Oxford University. Publishes 'Extract from Captain Stormfield's Visit to Heaven' in *Harper's Magazine*.

1908 Moves to house Clemens names 'Stormfield', in Redding, Connecticut.

1909 Death of Jane. Clara Clemens marries the pianist Ossip Gabrilowitsch.

1910 *21 April:* Death of Samuel Langhorne Clemens.

1916 Publication of *The Mysterious Stranger* (edited – drastically – by Albert Bigelow Paine, his literary executor).

Richard Maxwell

PENGUIN ✎ CLASSICS

The Classics Publisher

'Penguin Classics, one of the world's greatest series' JOHN KEEGAN

'I have never been disappointed with the Penguin Classics. All I have read is a model of academic seriousness and provides the essential information to fully enjoy the master works that appear in its catalogue' MARIO VARGAS LLOSA

'Penguin and Classics are words that go together like horse and carriage or Mercedes and Benz. When I was a university teacher I always prescribed Penguin editions of classic novels for my courses: they have the best introductions, the most reliable notes, and the most carefully edited texts' DAVID LODGE

'Growing up in Bombay, expensive hardback books were beyond my means, but I could indulge my passion for reading at the roadside bookstalls that were well stocked with all the Penguin paperbacks ... Sometimes I would choose a book just because I was attracted by the cover, but so reliable was the Penguin imprimatur that I was never once disappointed by the contents.

Such access certainly broadened the scope of my reading, and perhaps it's no coincidence that so many Merchant Ivory films have been adapted from great novels, or that those novels are published by Penguin' ISMAIL MERCHANT

'You can't write, read, or live fully in the present without knowing the literature of the past. Penguin Classics opens the door to a treasure house of pure pleasure, books that have never been bettered, which are read again and again with increased delight' JOHN MORTIMER

CLICK ON A CLASSIC

www.penguinclassics.com

The world's greatest literature at your fingertips

Constantly updated information on over 1600 titles, from Icelandic sagas to ancient Indian epics, Russian drama to Italian romance, American greats to African masterpieces

•

The latest news on recent additions to the list, updated editions and specially commissioned translations

•

Original scholarly essays by leading writers: Elaine Showalter on Zola, Laurie R. King on Arthur Conan Doyle, Frank Kermode on Shakespeare, Lisa Appignanesi on Tolstoy

•

A wealth of background material, including biographies of every classic author from Aristotle to Zamyatin, plot synopses, readers' and teachers' guides, useful web links

•

Online desk and examination copy assistance for academics

•

Trivia quizzes, competitions, giveaways, news on forthcoming screen adaptations

•

eBooks available to download

READ MORE IN PENGUIN

In every corner of the world, on every subject under the sun, Penguin represents quality and variety – the very best in publishing today.

For complete information about books available from Penguin – including Puffins and Penguin Classics – and how to order them, write to us at the appropriate address below. Please note that for copyright reasons the selection of books varies from country to country.

In the United Kingdom: *Please write to* Dept EP, Penguin Books Ltd, Bath Road, Harmondsworth, West Drayton, Middlesex UB7 0DA

In the United States: *Please write to* Consumer Services, Penguin Putnam Inc., 405 Murray Hill Parkway, East Rutherford, New Jersey 07073-2136. *VISA and MasterCard holders call 1-800-631-8571 to order Penguin titles*

In Canada: *Please write to* Penguin Books Canada Ltd, 10 Alcorn Avenue, Suite 300, Toronto, Ontario M4V 3B2

In Australia: *Please write to* Penguin Books Australia Ltd, 487 Maroondah Highway, Ringwood, Victoria 3134

In New Zealand: *Please write to* Penguin Books (NZ) Ltd, Private Bag 102902, North Shore Mail Centre, Auckland 10

In India: *Please write to* Penguin Books India Pvt Ltd, 11, Community Centre, Panchsheel Park, New Delhi 110017

In the Netherlands: *Please write to* Penguin Books Netherlands bv, Postbus 3507, NL-1001 AH Amsterdam

In Germany: *Please write to* Penguin Books Deutschland GmbH, Metzlerstrasse 26, 60594 Frankfurt am Main

In Spain: *Please write to* Penguin Books S. A., Bravo Murillo 19, 1°B, 28015 Madrid

In Italy: *Please write to* Penguin Italia s.r.l., Via Vittoria Emanuele 451a, 20094 Corsico, Milano

In France: *Please write to* Penguin France, 12, Rue Prosper Ferradou, 31700 Blagnac

In Japan: *Please write to* Penguin Books Japan Ltd, Iidabashi KM-Bldg, 2-23-9 Koraku, Bunkyo-Ku, Tokyo 112-0004

In South Africa: *Please write to* Penguin Books South Africa (Pty) Ltd, P.O. Box 751093, Gardenview, 2047 Johannesburg

TOCQUEVILLE

Democracy in America
and Two Essays on America

*'A new political science is needed for a totally
new world'*

In 1831 Alexis de Tocqueville made a nine-month journey
through eastern America. The result was *Democracy in
America*, a monumental study of the strengths and weaknesses
of the nation's evolving politics and institutions. Tocqueville
looked to the flourishing democratic system in America as a
possible model for post-revolutionary France, believing that the
egalitarian ideals it enshrined reflected the spirit of the age –
even that they were the will of God. His insightful work has
become one of the most influential political texts ever written on
America and an indispensable authority for anyone interested in
the future of democracy. This volume includes the rarely translated 'Two Weeks in the Wilderness', an evocative account of
Tocqueville's travels in Michigan among the Iroquois and
Chippeway, and 'Excursion to Lake Oneida'.

This is the only edition that contains all Tocqueville's writings
on America, and it includes a chronology, further reading and
explanatory notes. Isaac Kramnick's introduction discusses
Tocqueville's life and times, and the enduring significance of
Democracy in America.

Translated by GERALD BEVAN
With an introduction and notes by ISAAC KRAMNICK

MADISON, HAMILTON
AND JAY

The Federalist Papers

'The establishment of a Constitution, in a time of profound peace, by the voluntary consent of a whole people, is a PRODIGY'

Written at a time when furious arguments were raging about the best way to govern America, *The Federalist Papers* had the immediate practical aim of persuading New Yorkers to accept the newly drafted constitution in 1787. In this they were supremely successful, but their influence also transcended contemporary debate to win them a lasting place in discussions of American political theory. Acclaimed by Thomas Jefferson as 'the best commentary on the principles of government which ever was written', *The Federalist Papers* make a powerful case for power-sharing between state and federal authorities and for a constitution that has endured largely unchanged for more than two hundred years.

In his brilliantly detailed introduction, Isaac Kramnick sets the *Papers* in their historical and political context. This edition also contains the American constitution as an appendix.

'The introduction is an outstanding piece of work ... I am strongly recommending its reading' WARREN BURGER, former Chief Justice, Supreme Court of the United States

Edited with an introduction by ISAAC KRAMNICK

E. W. HORNUNG

Raffles: the Amateur Cracksman

*'Old Raffles may or may not have been an
exceptional criminal, but as a cricketer I dare
swear he was unique'*

Gentleman thief Raffles is daring, debonair, devilishly handsome – and a first-class cricketer. In these eight stories the
master burglar indulges his passion for cricket and crime:
thieving jewels from a country house, outwitting the law, stealing from the nouveau riche and, of course, bowling like a demon
– all with the assistance of his plucky sidekick Bunny.
Encouraged by a suggestion from his brother-in-law Arthur
Conan Doyle to write a series about a public-school villain, and
influenced by his own days at Uppingham, Ernest Hornung
created a unique form of crime story, where, in stealing as in
sport, it is playing the game that counts, and there is always
honour among thieves.

This edition of Raffles stories is new to Penguin Classics. It
contains a fascinating introduction discussing contemporary
events that inspired the plots, placing the stories in their literary
context and exploring the connection with Sherlock Holmes.

**'One of the most remarkable triumphs of the late nineteenth-
century Romantic imagination' C. P. SNOW**

Edited with an introduction and notes by
RICHARD LANCELYN GREEN

OSCAR WILDE

The Picture of Dorian Gray

*'The horror, whatever it was, had not yet entirely
spoiled that marvellous beauty'*

Enthralled by his own exquisite portrait, Dorian Gray
exchanges his soul for eternal youth and beauty. Influenced by
his friend Lord Henry Wotton, he is drawn into a corrupt
double life, indulging his desires in secret while remaining a
gentleman in the eyes of polite society. Only his portrait bears
the traces of his decadence. *The Picture of Dorian Gray* was a
succès de scandale. Early readers were shocked by its hints at
unspeakable sins, and the book was later used as evidence
against Wilde at his trial at the Old Bailey in 1895.

This definitive edition includes a selection of contemporary
reviews condemning the novel's immorality, and the introduction to the first Penguin Classics edition by Peter Ackroyd.

Edited with an introduction and notes by ROBERT MIGHALL

A Tale of Two Cities

*'Liberty, equality, fraternity, or death; – the last,
much the easiest to bestow, O Guillotine!'*

After eighteen years as a political prisoner in the Bastille, the ageing Doctor Manette is finally released and reunited with his daughter in England. There the lives of two very different men, Charles Darnay, an exiled French aristocrat, and Sydney Carton, a disreputable but brilliant English lawyer, become enmeshed through their love for Lucie Manette. From the tranquil roads of London, they are drawn against their will to the vengeful, bloodstained streets of Paris at the height of the Reign of Terror, and they soon fall under the lethal shadow of La Guillotine.

This edition uses the text as it appeared in its first serial publication in 1859 to convey the full scope of Dickens's vision, and includes the original illustrations by H. K. Browne ('Phiz'). Richard Maxwell's introduction discusses the intricate interweaving of epic drama with personal tragedy.

Edited with an introduction and notes by
RICHARD MAXWELL

THOMAS DE QUINCEY

Confessions of an English Opium-Eater

*'Thou hast the keys of Paradise, oh just, subtle,
and mighty opium!'*

Confessions is a remarkable account of the pleasures and pains of worshipping at the 'Church of Opium'. Thomas De Quincey consumed daily large quantities of laudanum (at the time a legal painkiller), and this autobiography of addiction hauntingly describes his surreal visions and hallucinatory nocturnal wanderings though London, along with the nightmares, despair and paranoia to which he became prey. The result is a work in which the effects of drugs and the nature of dreams, memory and imagination are seamlessly interwoven. *Confessions* forged a link between artistic self-expression and addiction, paving the way for later generations of literary drug-users from Baudelaire to Burroughs, and anticipating psychoanalysis with its insights into the subconscious.

This edition is based on the original serial version of 1821, and reproduces the two 'sequels', 'Suspiria De Profundis' (1845) and 'The English Mail-Coach' (1849). It also includes a critical introduction discussing the romantic figure of the addict and the tradition of confessional literature, and an appendix on opium in the nineteenth century.

Edited with an introduction by BARRY MILLIGAN

DUMAS

The Count of Monte Cristo

'On what slender threads do life and fortune hang'

Thrown in prison for a crime he has not committed, Edmond Dantes is confined to the grim fortress of If. There he learns of a great hoard of treasure hidden on the Isle of Monte Cristo and he becomes determined not only to escape, but also to unearth the treasure and use it to plot the destruction of the three men responsible for his incarceration. Dumas's epic tale of suffering and retribution, inspired by a real-life case of wrongful imprisonment, was a huge popular success when it was first serialized in the 1840s.

Robin Buss's lively English translation remains faithful to the style of Dumas's original. This edition includes an introduction, explanatory notes and suggestions for further reading.

'Robin Buss broke new ground with a fresh version of *Monte Cristo* for Penguin' *Oxford Guide to Literature in English Translation*

Translated with an introduction by ROBIN BUSS